# CAROUSEL

## BY
# ELIZABETH
# YOUNG

### ✳✳✳

## A sequel to HELTER-SKELTER

# CHAPTER ONE - 1952 - THAMBAY

Albie drove his pony cart full of children through the familiar streets of Thambay and turned along the seafront. After a winter spent inland he was hungry for a sight of the sea – registering the kids for another few months of schooling could wait a few more minutes.

"Dad, can we go on the pier?" Joey asked – it would be Joey, who couldn't sit still for a minute. Then Ben and Davy joined in with a chorus of, "Go on, Dad, let us!" and their cousin Nico added his plea, "Just a few minutes, Uncle Albie!"

Albie clicked his tongue at Blossom, who moved on obediently. "Depends how good you are at school, then we'll see."

"We'll see always means no," wailed Ben.

"No it don't," Nico said. "It just means you'd better behave!"

The infant and junior schools were housed in the old yellow-brick boys' school which Albie had attended. When he drew into the playground and saw the look of apprehension on Davy's face, he recalled his own first day there and ruffled his son's curls. "It's nicer inside, Davy – you'll make lots of new friends."

"I don't need any more friends – I've got Ben to play with."

Albie laughed and jumped down to tie Blossom's reins to the railings. The entire family trooped indoors, breathing in the smell of chalk, linoleum and children that meant education, and went up the stairs, holding the banister polished by hundreds of small hands.

In the headmaster's office Mr Crossman greeted them with genuine warmth. "Back again, Smith?"

"Like a bad penny, sir!" Albie replied cheerfully, shaking the hand that had wielded a cane more than once on his own young backside. "See you've got one of them prefabs in the old playground."

"We need the extra classrooms for all the children that have been born since the war," the headmaster told him. "Have you brought me a new one?"

Albie pushed Davy forward. "This is Davy, our youngest."

Mr Crossman looked across his desk at the child, thinking he was big for five, but then Albert Smith was a big man. The Smith children always looked healthier than the others in his school, no doubt due to the abundance of fresh air in their lives. "So you want to come to my school do you, Davy?"

"Dad says I've got to, but I can read already so I don't see why," said Davy.

The headmaster clamped his teeth round his pipe-stem to smother a smile as Joey, with all the wisdom of his fifteen years, told Davy sternly, "There's more to learning than reading Mama's magazines, and you say 'sir' when you talk to the headmaster."

"You don't!" responded Davy, rubbing his ear. "You call him Old Crosspatch."

Mr Crossman's pipe nearly snapped in two in his effort to suppress a chuckle as Joey blushed bright scarlet, just like his father used to, and the two older girls tried to pretend they were somewhere else. Hastily he pulled a large ledger from a shelf and dropped it on his blotter. "Well now, let me see. Ben must be eight now so I'll put him in First Juniors, and Mrs Middleton in Infants will take care of David." He added with a smile, "Mr Daly's little girl Rita started in Mrs Middleton's class this term."

"There you are, Davy," said Albie. "You like Rita, don't you? Uncle Bert's girl."

"I s'pose she'll do," said Davy. "Though I'd sooner be with Ben."

Albie quickly held out his hand. "Thanks, sir, all settled then. Seeing as it's nearly the Easter holidays we'll see you next term."

He was halfway to the door when Ben tugged at his coat

and muttered, "You forgot the sack."

Albie patted his son's head. "Good job you remembered." He lifted a heavy sack from the floor as if it weighed nothing and dumped it on a chair. "Maria sent this, sir. There's a stone of spuds and a bit of bacon, and she put in a bottle of her elderberry wine. You'd better leave that to settle for a day or two – it's been a bit shook up in the cart."

While the family clattered noisily down the stairs, Mr Crossman smiled to himself – despite the logistical problems caused by this annual influx of gypsies, he liked the blast of fresh air they blew through the school. He also enjoyed the food parcels that were such a welcome supplement to the meagre rations that were all one could get in the shops. He peered inside the sack – the 'bit of bacon' must weigh at least four pounds – then he concealed it beneath his desk and went to inform the relevant teachers that the Smith family was back.

Albie's next stop was the Secondary Modern on the other side of the railway, where the headmistress, Miss Briggs, re-registered her four extra pupils resignedly.

"Joseph can rejoin his friends in Four B," she said. "Clara and Nicolas in Two A." She looked at Fleur, wondering yet again who had seeded this slender lily of a girl among the robust cottage-garden plants of the Smith family. "Fleur – you will go into One C."

"Can't I be with Clara?" Fleur pleaded. "They let us be together in the winter school. I'm only nine months younger."

Miss Briggs raised her eyebrows and stared until Fleur shifted uneasily. "This is not a gypsy school, child, and I am not accustomed to having my decisions questioned. You will go into One C. Good day to you, Mr Smith."

Relieved that was over, Albie drove to the pier, where the gateman waved them through, saying, "You can stand me a pint later – the rides don't start till Easter."

The boys ran off, their boots echoing down the boardwalk, but Clara and Fleur simply sat at opposite ends of the nearest bench, watching the waves.

Albie leaned on the rail to light a cigarette, sheltering the match flame from the wind with his lapel, and gazed across the mouth of the Swale estuary at the cold North Sea. The pewter waves rolled in through the pier girders to die, foaming, on the beach and pull back in a clatter of shingle. Albie took deep breaths of the spray-laden air, interspersed with drags on his cigarette, and felt the tension drain away. It had taken two days to drive four wagons and the cart from Ruxley, with impatient motor traffic repeatedly spooking the horses, often deliberately. He flicked the butt away and turned to look at the space where his helter-skelter used to stand.

He'd been nearly twelve when George Smith, the proprietor of the helter-skelter, took pity on the half-starved urchin and adopted him. For ten years he'd helped George to run the ride – ten years before the big storm of 1935 ripped it from its moorings. He fancied he could hear again the buzz and bustle of those days, the blare of loudspeakers pumping out music. If he closed his eyes he could even see the colourful pre-war clothes, and the carefree faces of children rushing down the curved slide of his helter-skelter.

He opened his eyes and shook himself. Those days were long gone, along with the ride. He should have left this visit till Easter, when the pier's shabbiness would be hidden by the crowds. Today every blister on the paint showed because, apart from a few fishermen and a middle-aged couple dowdy in washed-out clothes, he and his kids were the only customers. The boys were down the far end, involved in some mysterious game of their own, but Clara and Fleur were leaning on the rusty rail gazing at the sea, not even talking, which was odd. Then he remembered Maria saying that Clara had become a woman at the winter camp, which probably explained her moodiness.

Clara could feel the ebb and flow of the sea through her own body as the hypnotic whoosh and tug of the waves was echoed by the blood in her veins. She was uncomfortably aware of Fleur's heavy silence, but she couldn't cope with her sister's sulks while last night's dream was still so vivid in her mind. It still frightened her now just to think about it.

She had dreamed she was picking mushrooms in the dim early morning of a wood when the trees around her began to breathe, their trunks swelling to suck in air, then creaking as they expelled great gusts of green breath. The tendrils of mist had reached for her like claws, but when she ran, her feet sank into the ground and she fell helplessly through into an earthy cave where weird lights flitted amongst the gnarled roots. She tried to climb out, but each time she stood on a root the tree above yielded to her weight. Inexorably the massive trees settled lower and lower, trapping her inside the shrinking cave, but when she opened her mouth to scream, the green mist of tree-breath rushed into her lungs.

When she woke, gasping for breath, Fleur had asked what was wrong, but Clara had just said, "Only a dream, go back to sleep."

Fleur had been sulking ever since, and Clara didn't know why she hadn't told her. She shuddered. They had always shared their dreams up till now, but this dark feeling of dread was impossible to describe. Still – Fleur *had* asked if they could be in the same class, so she couldn't be too upset. She dragged her eyes from the waves and slid her hand into Fleur's elbow. "Come on, let's go, we're having dinner at Grandad's."

Albie took the hint, rounded up the others, and they piled into the cart for the short ride to George's home.

The old man's face lit up at their arrival. "You're early this year, son!" he said happily, gripping Albie's hand in both his own.

"The last farmer on our way here didn't need us," Albie said. "He'd taken on an ex-soldier as odd-job man."

While George hugged his grandchildren, Albie studied him surreptitiously – in the past few months the years had caught up with his father. Also noticeable was the increased shabbiness of the kitchen – the only living room in this small house. Since Mum died Dad had kept it clean enough, but it missed her touch. The curtains at the window onto the street were limp from lack of starch, the range was dull where Mum would have black-leaded it to a shine, and the rag rug that she had shaken every day lay flat and lifeless before the hearth. He looked back at George, who had Clara and Fleur clasped to his sides with their arms round him – even Dad's middle had shrunk.

"How's old Wilf doing?" Albie asked. "You two still cooking together?"

"Upped and died on me, the old bugger – just when we were getting the hang of making a decent stew between us."

"Oh Dad – what a damn shame – 'specially as pooling your rations made them go so much further. Who's living next door now?"

"Nobody – it's stood empty all winter. But never mind that now – I'll open a bottle of beer while you cut into that bacon."

So Albie cut thick slices of bacon and shared a bottle of beer with George, while Clara and Fleur peeled potatoes to boil in the big black pot that had sat on the range for as long as Albie could remember. Half an hour was long enough to relate the details of the tribe's previous few months: their autumn round of potato-picking and hedge-trimming; a winter spent in the shelter of a disused chalk-pit with several other tribes, then odd-jobbing and planting their way back to Pinetree Farm on the outskirts of Thambay. By the time Albie had finished describing the bonfire wedding held at the Ruxley chalk-pit, the potatoes were cooked, the bacon was sizzling in the frying pan, and half-a-dozen eager children were at the table demanding their share of Grandad's attention.

Albie and George were drinking a second cup of tea before Albie asked, "So, Dad, what's the news in town?"

George put his cup down onto its saucer with a clatter.

"Town Council wants to build prefabs on the rec. Where will the football teams play if they do that? It's the only area big enough."

Albie sucked a breath in through his teeth. "And what about the Town Fair?"

"I suppose they'll have to use the Common," George said doubtfully.

"There's trees all over the bloody place there – definitely no room for the travelling fair – them rides are huge."

The two men, so alike that no-one would guess they were not related by blood, looked at each other in dismay. Albie had met Maria when her tribe was helping to set up those rides, and the July fortnight in Thambay was an enduring fixture in all their lives. The seafront recreation ground had been left to the town, but apart from the fair and the occasional football match, the bare patch of sandy, salt-scorched grass was little used. It would be all too easy for the Town Council to erect rows of the prefabricated homes that were being thrown up everywhere in these post-war years.

"Is anyone putting up a fight?" Albie asked.

"Your mate Bert, for one. Councillor Price died so Bert's standing for the Council – as a Labour man of course. He'll get my vote if he can stop 'em building on the rec."

"Who's standing against him?" asked Albie. "Anyone I know?"

"Oh, you'll know him all right!" said George bitterly. "Gerald Smythe – him as owns half this street. He's all for the prefabs so his tenants will move into them – he wants to knock these terraces down and build blocks of flats."

"But you've lived here all your life!" Albie was appalled.

"So I have, son, and I'll leave feet first or not at all!" George sat back with his arms folded and such a look of stubborn determination on his face that Albie smiled, until George added, "Got a feeling that won't be long in coming now."

"Dad, don't say that!" Albie's hand flew to his chest to

clutch the leather talisman he'd worn for twenty years. "Come on, Dad. Maria's expecting us for tea, and I've left Blossom standing outside for long enough."

So George pulled on the boots he hadn't worn since he went for his ration of bread three days earlier, and thought that perhaps life wasn't so bad after all.

Blossom was an old pony now, and would have struggled with George's extra weight on the uphill road out of town, so the children walked. As they had learned to do since infancy, they scoured the hedgerows systematically as they went along – wood to burn, metal to sell for scrap and food for the pot. Before they reached home the younger ones had found tender new dandelion and wood sorrel for a salad, Joey and Nico had armfuls of scrap, and Fleur had picked her mother a posy of primroses. Only Clara was empty-handed, and as soon as they entered the camp she rushed past Maria to duck inside the wagon, shutting the door almost in Fleur's face.

Maria looked up in surprise – if Clara was going to throw one of her moods she would have to talk to her again. She sighed – her daughter's body had matured early but her mind was still a child's, and that was not an easy combination for her or the family.

George looked around with a satisfied expression – it was good to be back. The wagons and tents were set in a square with a fire in the centre, as they were arranged every summer on this patch of land that Farmer Finch had set aside for the gypsies at the start of the war. Mind you, George thought, the man had had his reasons – the tribe had worked his land all through the war while other farmers struggled to cope with diminished workforces. George headed straight for Mateo's vardo – the only traditionally painted wagon the tribe owned – where the patriarch was sitting on the little rear platform enjoying the afternoon sun. Mateo stood to shake his hand. "Good to see you again, George."

"You too, Mateo – the place ain't the same when you're

gone." George sat on the other side of the steps and offered his tobacco pouch for Mateo to fill his little clay pipe, while Maria's father Josef and the other men drew up stools to join the conversation.

"We like being on the move, you know that," said Mateo. "Though how much longer we will be able to is hard to say. Half the old stopping-places have gone – bombed or built on or fenced off."

"It's not as safe on the road as it was before the war, either," Josef added. "We've been robbed twice this spring."

"Robbed? You couldn't fight them off?"

Mateo shifted uncomfortably. "They came when the younger men were off laying hedges. There were four of them and it was only me and the women here."

"They took the cauldron of stew from right under my nose," his wife Lydia said from the doorway. "I hit one with the ladle and Mateo chased them, but their legs were younger and they got away."

George experienced a pang of sympathy for his friend – getting old was bad enough without the shame of being unable to protect your family. "I expect they were just hungry."

Lydia snorted indignantly. "So were we that day thanks to them."

"There are a lot of homeless ex-soldiers on the roads," Albie added. "You'd think the government would do something. Still, I did find the cauldron in a field later that night."

"Just as well you did," said Lydia. "They've used all the iron for guns and I'd never have got another one as good."

Meanwhile Maria had mounted the steps to her own wagon, where she found Clara lying on the bed, staring at the curved wooden ceiling. Maria sat on the side of the high bed and patted Clara's knee. "What is it, dear? Have you squabbled with Fleur?"

"No! Yes – well, not squabbled exactly, but I had a bad

dream and didn't tell her about it, so she's upset."

"I'm not surprised."

"But Mama! She'd say it was just a dream, and it wasn't." Clara's voice rose to a wail. "It felt like a warning."

Maria moved to the bottom of the bed and leaned back against the wooden wall, regarding Clara's woebegone face. She had suspected for some time that the child had inherited her gift of foresight. "I think you'd better tell me your dream," she said, and her matter-of-fact tone steadied Clara enough to describe her nightmare of holes opening up in forest floors and suffocating green tree-breath.

## CHAPTER TWO – LUKE

Meanwhile Fleur had crossed the lane to skirt another pine wood and climb the stile into the yard of Pinetree Farm. She knocked perfunctorily on an open kitchen door and walked in to be swept into a welcoming hug by Daisy, one of Farmer Finch's three daughters-in-law.

"Fleur! How lovely to see you again. Isn't Clara with you?"

"She's in a mood."

"Never mind, dear, she'll get over it. You'll find Linda in her room – she got back from school ten minutes ago," said Daisy, returning to her baking as Fleur darted through to the flagged passage and up the stairs.

Fleur and Linda were first cousins once removed. When George and Dot Smith adopted Albie they already had a grown-up son Eric, whose daughter Daisy had married Adam Finch's son Luke. Linda was their only child – at eleven years old she was considerably younger than Luke's brothers' children, and she loved the months when her gypsy cousins camped on Pinetree Farm.

When Fleur burst into her bedroom to fling herself face down on the eiderdown exclaiming, "God, I hate her!" Linda was so thrilled that she dropped her hairbrush on the chintz-trimmed dressing-table. Leaving her hair still tangled from her bike-ride home, she sat on the bed, patted Fleur's shoulder and demanded, "Who do you hate? Tell me all!"

"Clara, of course!" Fleur said, sitting up now that she'd found a suitably attentive listener. "She thinks she's so grown-up since she's started her monthlies."

"Gosh!" Linda breathed. "She's not thirteen till July."

"Mama started at the same age."

The two girls stared at each other, shocked by this reminder that childhood couldn't last forever. Linda was the first to recover – Fleur had come to her for sympathy and it was her duty to provide it. "Has she been awful? My cousin Val is bad-tempered for days, but Mum says I have to be kind to her. I don't think that's fair, do you?"

"Mama says the same to me," said Fleur. "She says I'll get them myself soon and then I'll understand, but Clara's got no right to be horrid." She bit her lip and Linda fished in her pocket for a rather grubby hankie into which Fleur blew her nose loudly.

"What's she said to upset you?" Linda settled comfortably against a pillow – a good gossip with Fleur would give her lots to talk about in the playground tomorrow.

"She hasn't said anything. That's the trouble. She had a bad dream last night – she woke up screaming – and she wouldn't tell me what it was."

"Screaming? What, really loud?" Linda was entranced – this was better than any programme on the wireless.

"Well, she only screamed once," Fleur admitted. "But she was gasping for breath and white as a sheet." She clutched her own throat and acted out the scene, hamming it up shamelessly and then, warming to her theme, she added, "And this morning when we were on the pier I thought she was going to throw herself in the sea!"

"Golly! What did you do?"

"I grabbed her arm and pulled her off the railing," Fleur improvised. "'You're too young to die,' I told her, and I held her tight so she couldn't jump."

"Do you think she had a warning, like your mum gets?" Linda was half-whispering with excitement.

Fleur threw her a disgusted look. "Not you as well! I get enough of that gypsy stuff at winter school without you starting. 'Tell us our fortune, Fleur.' Or 'Don't upset her or she'll put a curse on you.' I'm sick to death of it all!"

Linda could have kicked herself for forgetting how sensitive Fleur was about this. "Can't you tell them you've got different blood?"

"It's none of their business – not that they'd believe me

anyway – they're all horrible."

"Haven't you got any friends at all at winter school?"

"Only Clara, and now even she's not talking to me!" Fleur punched the pillow.

"Well, now you're here you've got me, so you don't need Clara. We can be best friends, just you and me." Recalling a story she'd recently finished reading, Linda added, "Hey, I've just thought of something – maybe they stole you and you're really a princess!"

Fleur glared at the younger girl. "My dad rescued me from a burning farmhouse – how dare you suggest he's a kidnapper?"

Linda hastened to cover up yet another serious mistake. "I didn't mean your dad, silly, I meant the woman who died – perhaps she wasn't your real mother either."

As Fleur's expression changed from anger to speculation, Daisy called from the kitchen, "I'm just taking some biscuits out of the oven – anyone hungry?" and the danger of the girls falling out completely was averted.

Later, walking home through the dusk carrying a basket of bread and ham for her mother, Fleur wondered if there might be some truth in what Linda said. As soon as she was old enough, Dad had told her how he'd found her beside her dead mother in a burning farmhouse in France, and hidden her inside his uniform when he escaped from Dunkirk. She had been too tiny then to remember any mother apart from Maria, who had breast-fed her alongside Clara and registered her as her own baby – but she could be anyone, even royalty! When she got back to the camp Clara tried to make amends, but Fleur brushed her aside with haughty disdain – her foster-sister was only a common gypsy whereas she, Fleur, might have royal blood in her veins.

Maria noticed their continuing coolness but decided not to comment, hoping the girls would talk it through at bedtime in their shared tent, but she did ask Fleur, "Did you see Linda's dad?"

"No – Auntie Daisy took him a tray. Linda says he hardly ever comes downstairs now."

Maria glanced at Albie. "I'll run over and see Daisy when the children are asleep."

"I think it'd be better if we went together tomorrow," Albie said. "Now – is supper nearly ready? I've got to take Dad home after."

"Don't you worry about me," George called from Mateo's wagon steps. "I'll stop here the night if Josef's still got my mattress under his bed."

Albie grinned at his father – the years had dropped off him like an old coat with Mateo to talk to and his grandchildren running around. George had spent many a night on that mattress in Josef's small wagon when Albie was away fighting Germans.

"All right – Blossom will be asleep in her field by now anyway," he said, and opened a bottle of cowslip wine to celebrate the tribe's return to Pinetree Farm.

By the time supper was ready, Joey and Nico had come back from seeing their friend Frank at Coppin Farm, but Maria had to shout twice before her two youngest appeared, covered in dirt and cobwebs.

"Where have you two been?" Albie demanded, marching them to the side of his wagon to scrub their hands and faces in a bucket of water.

"The bomb shelter, Dad," Ben told him. "It's super in there – loads of spiders."

"We were playing cavemen," Davy added.

"You've come out as dirty as cavemen," Albie said.

"It's too dark in there to see where the dirt is," Davy explained solemnly.

Joey laughed. "You've got an answer for everything! We had torches and brazier fires during the war."

"It was still dark and damp," Maria said, shuddering at the

memory of sleeping in the shelter Albie had dug before going away. "I only used it because I'd promised your dad."

"I'll demolish it this summer," Albie said. "All that timber we shored it up with shouldn't be going to waste."

"You've been saying that for years and never done it," Maria grumbled.

"I mean it this time – though the wood's probably all rotten by now."

When Albie and Maria had bought their own wagon, the tent that had been George and Dot's wedding present became Clara and Fleur's. After seventeen years of use it was weather-worn but still sound, and its tough canvas sides exuded the perfume of herbs and lavender that Maria used to keep their clothes sweet. The sisters shared a mattress, which invited shared secrets, and as soon as they'd blown out their candle Clara said, "I'm sorry about last night – I didn't mean to be horrid to you."

"Well you were," Fleur snapped, "Why wouldn't you tell me your dream?"

"Because it felt peculiar – more like a warning of danger than just a nightmare."

"Oh God!" Fleur exclaimed. "More gypsy stuff!" and in one angry movement she turned her back and feigned sleep.

*** 

The next morning Albie and Maria walked through to Pinetree Farm together. The farmhouse had originally been just one block, but as each of his three sons married, Adam Finch had added more wings, and now it sprawled round three sides of the big concreted yard. Two mud-spattered tractors and other bits of farm machinery stood in front of the outbuildings that completed the square, and several horses poked their heads over the half-doors of their stables, curious to see who was visiting. Albie went to greet the animals, giving Maria a little shove in the direction of Daisy's door. "You keep Daisy busy. Luke shouldn't shut himself away in his room and I'm going to have a serious word with him."

Maria found Daisy in her kitchen, sitting by the big range listening to the wireless. Her friend jumped up to hug her, protesting, "You didn't have to bring that basket back today."

"It's really just an excuse to see you," said Maria. "And to say thank you for the food – we haven't had any work for three days so my cupboards were nearly empty."

"Well, there's plenty to do here," Daisy assured her, spooning tea into the brown pot from a big square caddy. "I suppose Albie's in the stables?"

"Where else would he be?" Maria laughed. "He's known those horses from foals. Now tell me, Daisy – what's this Fleur tells us about Luke – I thought he was getting better?"

"Oh Maria! I thought he was too, but somehow this winter pulled him back down." Daisy set the teapot on the range to brew and sat down heavily, twisting her apron between her hands. "Brian got married again at Christmas and Luke refused to go – said he'd only ruin the occasion."

"But that's dreadful – not going to his own brother's wedding!"

"Brian tried his best to persuade him but it was no good. Poppy was one of the land girls who came down from London to work on Coppin Farm. Her folks are quite rich so it was a fancy do, especially as they must have thought she'd never get married at her age. Anyway, Luke said everyone would stare at him and flatly refused to go."

"So you missed it too?"

"I went without him." Daisy looked somewhat shamefaced but continued defiantly. "Everyone else was going and Linda would never have forgiven Luke if she'd missed it. She hardly speaks to him as it is, he's so snappy around everyone."

"Oh Daisy – and after he was doing so well! What set him back, do you know?"

"I can guess," Daisy replied, concentrating on pouring tea so that she wouldn't have to meet Maria's eyes. "He saw Brian and Poppy kissing in the stables and came in shaking, saying that it was disgusting at their age. When I pointed out that Brian was only forty and it was perfectly natural, Luke just exploded."

"What's wrong with them kissing? Albie and me do it all the time." Then Maria saw the tears in Daisy's eyes and the penny dropped. "But you and Luke don't?"

Daisy shook her head miserably and her tears spilled over. "He says if he can't bear to look in the mirror he's not about to inflict himself on anyone else. I've tried everything I can think of – I even sewed lace on my nightie – but it's no good, he won't touch me!"

"What – not ever?" Maria was appalled. Luke and Daisy were only thirty-two – no wonder they only had Linda.

"Not once since his plane crashed," Daisy wailed. "I could understand when his skin was so sore, but even after that had healed he said his hands were as ugly as his face and not fit to touch anyone else. I said I wasn't just anyone else, I was his wife and I loved him, but he told me I should never have married him and I'd be better off if he'd died."

"And Brian getting married just rubbed salt in the wound, I suppose."

"I really thought I might be getting somewhere before that happened. He was coming down for his meals and even put his arm round me once or twice, but that's all stopped now." Daisy stared down at her clasped hands. "He keeps telling me I should find someone else, and I must confess that sometimes I'm tempted."

Albie had heard some of this on his way upstairs and barged into Luke's room without bothering to knock. It was bad enough that the man slept alone without shutting himself away all day as well. Albie wasn't going to let politeness keep him from speaking his mind.

When Luke didn't even look up at his abrupt entrance, Albie's anger evaporated to be replaced by something like dread. He had become used to the shiny tight skin that covered Luke's face and neck – he looked fairly normal, though he'd never be handsome again. What blew a chill into Albie's soul was Luke's aura of barely contained tension coupled with a dead-pan stare. Albie had seen that look before in the hospital where he was recuperating from a damaged shoulder after Dunkirk. Some of the soldiers rescued from the beaches would wake screaming and dive under their beds, thinking that bombs were still falling. One man in the bed next to Albie's only had a few broken ribs but became convinced he had an incurable disease – he had climbed onto the roof and jumped to his death before the porters could reach him. After that episode the worst of the shell-shocked patients had been moved to a separate ward, but Albie had never forgotten that man's face.

Now, seeing the same blank expression on Luke's, he sat down opposite him and said quietly, "Good to see you again, lad." Luke flicked a glance at Albie and back to a spot on the wall, saying nothing, so Albie tried again. "We only got here yesterday. I've not talked to your dad yet – what's to do on the farm?"

An infinitesimal shrug was Luke's only response so Albie chattered on, trying to fill the heavy silence with his own news, taking in the dismal aspect of the room as he did so. The thick curtains were drawn, the fire unlit, and the only lamp was as far away from Luke's chair as it could possibly be, casting his ravaged face into deep shadow. He pulled a cigarette from his pocket and struck a match and Luke croaked, "Put that out!"

Albie was startled enough to obey. "Don't like the smoke in your bedroom? Fair enough, but it's freezing in here – shall I light the fire?"

"No!" This time it was the closest Luke's burned throat could manage to a shout and he jumped up, actually backing away from the cold hearth and holding his hands out as if to fend off Albie and his box of matches. "Not the fire – I can't stand fire!"

So that was it. Luke had been shot down in flames during the Battle of Britain, and borne stoically numerous operations in the famous East Grinstead hospital, only to succumb years later to delayed shock. As Luke stood trembling violently in the corner, Albie was reminded of a nervous horse he had seen once on a farm. The farmer had been about to shoot it for meat when Albie bought it, and it had taken him months of patient coaxing to turn it from a nervous wreck into an animal he could sell on with a good conscience.

He returned the matches to his pocket, aware that Luke was watching his every move, then stood up and approached him slowly, murmuring in the same tone he had used with the horse. "Come on, son – I ain't going to hurt you. It's me – Albie – I pulled you out of the sea when you was a nipper, remember? I'll pull you out of this too if you'll let me." When Luke could back no further into the wall, Albie drew him gently into his chest and after a brief struggle Luke allowed his body to relax against Albie's comforting bulk. He was as tall as Albie but heart-wrenchingly thin, and Albie had a fleeting impulse to carry him downstairs like a child. Instead he said, "Maria's in the kitchen asking for you," and steered him firmly to the door.

Maria wished that Daisy had confided in her before things had got this bad – there were more effective ways than lace on a nightdress to tempt a man's appetite, and she had the very herbs in her storage chest. She was about to say so when she sensed the change of atmosphere from upstairs. Taking a cloth from the airer, she passed it to Daisy saying, "Wipe your face and top up the teapot – they'll be down any minute."

"Luke won't come in here with the fire lit," Daisy replied, but then she heard the bedroom hinges squeak and hastened to do as she was told.

"Don't make a fuss of him," Maria warned. "Act as if it was

normal for him to be here," and when Albie pushed Luke ahead of him into the warmth of the kitchen and sat him down at the table, Daisy poured them both a cup of tea with a hand that only shook a little.

"Luke was going to tell me what needs doing tomorrow," Albie said, winking at Daisy behind Luke's back.

She picked up her cue. "Pete was saying he'd have to get the wheat seed in before Easter."

Luke merely grunted, so Maria said brightly, "Joey and Nico can help with that this year if Luke will show them what to do."

"They'll need watching," Albie said. "But I can't do it – I always help Brian with the pruning this time of year."

Luke still said nothing, so Albie leaned across the table and clicked his fingers under Luke's nose. "Flying Officer Finch – pay attention!" Luke's chin jerked up, and Albie said, "That's more like it! We'll be here at eight tomorrow and I'll expect you to be ready – is that clear?" When Luke nodded dumbly, Albie continued, "Good. You'll be in charge of Joey and Nico, so make sure they work hard. Now Maria and me must be going. Daisy, thanks for the tea, and Finch…"

"Sir?"

"Eat a good breakfast tomorrow and wrap up warm – it'll be frosty first thing."

"Do you think it will work?" asked Maria when she and Albie were crossing the yard.

"Worth a try, ain't it?" said Albie. "Thought he might snap out of it if I used my Corporal Smith voice."

"You even made me jump, you sounded so masterful!"

"Masterful, am I?" Albie grinned wickedly and pulled her towards the barn door. "I'll show you masterful! What do you say we nip into the barn for a quickie?"

"Albie Smith! At our age?" Maria ducked out of his embrace and ran off laughing, but he caught her easily and wrapped her small body in his big embrace.

"I'm only thirty-nine, I'm not past it yet."

"What if someone comes?" Maria protested, but Albie knew she was weakening.

"They're all out in the fields. Come on – it'll be like our first time," Albie said, nuzzling her hair and pushing her into the darkness of the barn, and Maria, thinking of poor Daisy who hadn't made love with her husband in years, melted into his arms. Albie needed no further invitation and scooped her up, kicked the big barn door shut, and flung her in a heap of flying skirts onto the hay.

"You're right – this *is* like our first time," Maria giggled as he fumbled with his flies.

"Different barn," Albie murmured against her mouth. "Different frock too," and he lifted her cotton skirt to make love to his wife with much more abandon than they had been able to when, having slipped away from their own wedding party, they had had to be careful not to tear the heirloom lace dress.

# CHAPTER THREE – SQUABBLES

When Albie arrived at Pinetree Farm the following morning he was accompanied by Josef, Joey and Nico, but he left them outside while he went in search of Luke. He found him standing in the kitchen, with Daisy wrapping him in a long scarf like a mother dressing her child for school. She grimaced at Albie, clearly telegraphing, 'I'm not sure this is going to work,' but Albie asked briskly, "You ready, Flying Officer Finch?"

Luke's back straightened. The overcoat he was wearing drooped on his thin frame, but with his hands encased in gloves and his face obscured by cap and muffler, he could have been any other man dressed ready for work on a cold day.

"Come on, then," said Albie, taking his elbow. "Joey and Nico are waiting for orders."

As they went outside together, Daisy felt round blindly for a chair and sank into it with her heart pounding. It had taken her half an hour to persuade Luke out of his room and into the kitchen, and he'd only eaten half of his porridge, but at least he'd gone with Albie without protest. When Linda came into the kitchen later, she found her mother sitting at the table over a cold cup of tea, staring into space.

Outside in the yard, Luke's older brothers Pete and Brian glanced at him anxiously, but Josef had prepared them and they said, "Morning, Luke," as if his appearance was an everyday occurrence. Brian went to start up one of the tractors while Pete led the way to the barn. Albie looked round hurriedly to make sure there were no clues to the previous day's tryst, but the place where he and Maria had made love was now occupied by a couple of hens.

"I'd like the wheat planted today," Pete said, looking doubtfully at Luke, but Josef said cheerfully, "We did it last year, and with Mr Luke in charge we'll have no problem."

For the first time Luke met his brother's eyes. "I have done it before, you know."

"I'll leave you to it, then," Pete said. "If you run into any problems I'll be in the top potato field with Brian," and he walked away with a jaunty stride. He would check the work later, but if the responsibility of getting the seed in brought Luke back to life, it was worth risking a few sacks of grain.

Luke looked at Albie, clearly expecting him to take over – his face was too stiff with scar tissue to convey much emotion but his eyes signalled panic. Albie didn't rise to the bait – in his army days he had come across many nervous young officers who had arrived in the regiment senior in rank but totally lacking in experience. "I'll get the horse," he said, moving towards the door. "Officer Finch – you're in charge of the seeder," and he walked off to the stables without a backward glance. Luke took a deep, shuddering breath and, helped by a few hints from Josef, organised his troops into manoeuvring the awkward metal contraption into the yard to hitch it behind the patient carthorse.

An hour later Adam Finch tramped over his farm to the wheat field to see how things were going. Not normally an emotional man, he had to clench his jaw to hold back tears at the sight that met him. Luke, who yesterday had been fading away in the darkness of his room, was standing beside the far hedge, waving his arms and shouting, "Keep the line straight!" while Joey led the horse-drawn seeder towards him.

Albie spotted Adam by the gate and went to join him. "He's doing great, Mr Finch. I'm off now to take Dad home but I'll be back this afternoon."

Adam gripped Albie's big brown hand between both his own. "I can't thank you enough, Albie – this is the second time you've saved Luke's life. And how many more times must I ask you to call me Adam?"

"I couldn't change the habit now, Mr Finch, and besides, it wouldn't do in front of the boys – got to learn 'em respect by example."

On his way back to the camp Albie met Fleur and Clara trudging along in silence. "Going to see Linda?" he asked cheerfully, wondering what had caused the cloud that hovered between his daughters – he'd never fathom out what went on in female minds. He took a chin in each hand to tilt their heads up and ask, "You two all right?"

Fleur shrugged him off but Clara threw herself at him, wrapping her arms round his waist and declaring passionately, "I love you, Dad."

He held her close and asked, "What's the matter, lovey?" and only just heard her answer, "I had a bad dream – a warning."

Fleur gave an audible sniff and Albie's heart sank. Dreams were Maria's department – all the tribe's women had the Sight to some extent – so he just stroked Clara's hair and moved her gently away saying, "You want to talk to your mama about that." He watched the girls walk away and shook his head with concern – they'd obviously fallen out over something and it needed sorting out fast. When he got back from town he'd have a word with Maria – there was no room in their small tribe for long-drawn-out squabbles.

Fleur and Clara found Linda helping her mother to make bread, and for a while the three girls worked together, knocking back the dough that had risen beside the range and kneading it into loaves and rolls, while Daisy made gingerbread with clarified dripping from the Sunday roast. Once the bread had been covered with damp cloths and put aside to rise again, Daisy made a pot of tea and they sat round the big kitchen table, dunking yesterday's biscuits in strong tea sweetened with honey from their own bees. After they had put the bread in the oven Daisy shooed them away saying, "Go and play," and all three clattered upstairs.

Linda shut the door of her room with an air of anticipation, bounced down onto her bed and said to Clara, "Fleur says you've started your monthlies – tell me all!"

Clara glared at Fleur. "You'd no right to tell her – that's private stuff!" She was horribly embarrassed that she'd started so young – as far as she knew she was the first in her class. She had managed to conceal her budding breasts under loose blouses, and the dreaded games lessons, for which girls stripped down to their vests and navy-blue knickers, had been mercifully few in the winter months. So far no-one had even suspected when she wore the horrid pink sanitary belt, but now that Fleur had let the cat out of the bag to chatterbox Linda, everyone would know. "What did you have to go and tell her for?" she cried, the too-ready tears springing to her eyes. "That was supposed to be a secret."

Fleur had the grace to look guilty – it was true that Clara had sworn her to silence.

"We've never had secrets before," Linda protested, "We tell each other everything."

"That's what you think," Clara said. "We only tell you things we don't care if everyone knows."

Linda leapt off the bed and pummelled Clara's tender chest with sharp fists, shoving her face within inches of Clara's as she spat, "You beast – that's not fair! I never told about that time you stole a cake off the market stall."

"Only because you ate half of it," Clara retorted, pushing Linda away so roughly that she fell to the floor.

"That's it!" Linda yelled. "Get out of my room and don't come back!"

"I wouldn't come back if you paid me!" Clara shouted back and yanked the door open. "You coming, Fleur?"

But Fleur was kneeling on the rug, patting Linda's shoulders sympathetically. Linda was her only friend here and this farmhouse her only escape from the gypsy camp. She wasn't prepared to lose either for a foster-sister who'd gone all moody and distant on her. Stamping on the feeling that she might be making a mistake, she shot a look of disgust at Clara and spat, "You can push off, Clara Smith – go and pick on someone your own age."

Clara stormed out, took the stairs two at a time and ran across the yard sobbing, only stopping after she had climbed the stile that separated the farmyard from the pinewood. She longed to run home and howl into her mother's bosom like a baby, but Mama had said she was a woman now so she probably wouldn't let her. She didn't want to grow up yet, Clara thought hopelessly, pressing her tiny breasts as if she could will them back into her chest.

For a while she sat on the stile, relishing the pain as a distraction from her other miseries, but then she thought she'd better get home before Fleur came along and found her sitting there moping. She stepped down from the stile onto the damp earth of the wood and her shoe filled instantly with water – it had rained overnight and soaked into the deep leaf mulch. Holding onto the fence, she removed the shoe to empty it and her other foot slipped under a loop of tree-root. Falling heavily, she landed in a puddle. Now she was soaked through to her knickers, her dress which had been clean on that morning was muddy, and her ankle hurt. At least now she'd have a good excuse for one of Mama's cuddles, she thought, trying to stand, but her ankle slid further under the root and she was held fast.

Clara tugged at the root in an attempt to break it – she braced her arms and tried to wriggle out backwards – she scraped at the mud with a stick, but to no avail. Try as she might, she couldn't get free, and when she dropped her face into her hands for a good howl they were covered with slimy moss juice. Gazing at them in horror, she realised that her dream was coming true – the trees had reached out deliberately to trip her up, and now they wouldn't let go until she was completely contaminated by their green slime. She could hear them breathing all around – a swishing sound that she should have heard on the way to the farm – which she *would* have heard if Fleur hadn't rushed her along to see her precious Linda. She could see their trunks moving and their heads coming closer together, whispering and plotting her death – any minute now the ground would open up to swallow her and she'd be gone forever. They would search, of course, but they wouldn't find her, and no-one would miss her because they all hated her. She opened her mouth to howl out her anguish but then she remembered the mist of green tree-breath in her dream, covered her mouth with the cleanest bit of skirt she could find, and rocked backwards and forwards in utter, delirious despair.

\*\*\*

George unlocked his front door and shivered as he and Albie stepped into the kitchen. "Cold as the grave in here."

"I'll light the range for you, Dad," Albie offered.

"I ain't past lighting my own range yet, son – you get yourself round to see Bert. He tells me he's thinking of running for the Council."

"Well, if you're sure – I'll fetch you again on Sunday in time for dinner." As George bent to rake out the ashes, Albie left him and drove round to the butcher's shop just off Market Square.

Bert and Albie had been best friends since their schooldays and had fought the Germans together. Bert had worked his way up from delivery boy to assistant butcher before the war, and when Mr Wallace retired the shop had become Bert's. There was the usual queue of housewives, all wearing the pinched expressions of women who had weathered the war years buoyed up by the belief that things would be better soon, only to find that now there was even less food. The ration books everyone had hoped to see the last of were even more necessary in peacetime. One or two women scowled when Albie bypassed the queue, but to many of them his was a familiar face, and when he kissed a few cheeks he caused a flutter of feminine excitement.

"Could you come every day?" Bert asked, wiping his hand to shake Albie's. "There's nothing like a good-looking bloke to cheer 'em up!"

"Get away with you!" Albie retorted, blushing hotly. "It's you they come for – I've seen 'em giving you the glad eye more'n once."

"Only 'cause they're hoping for an extra sausage." Bert winked at the woman by the counter. "Ain't that right, missus?"

"I'll have a sausage off you any time," she replied, winking back.

"Told you so!" Albie laughed. He leaned against the scrubbed wooden block to watch Bert serve his customers, noting with approval how he gave more than her allowance to a pale girl with a pair of scrawny toddlers, while a snooty woman who called Bert 'my man' had her meat weighed out meticulously to the ounce.

Bert locked the door at one o'clock with a sigh. "No point in opening this afternoon – it's all sold."

Albie followed him upstairs to the flat where Alice shared a pan of soup between the three of them. Her thin face broadened into a smile when Albie enquired after her children.

"Our Susie's doing really well at grammar school," she said. "The headmaster says she might even get into a London nursing college."

Albie shook his head in wonder. "One of our kids going to college, Bert – it don't seem possible!"

"It'll cost us a fair bit, what with uniforms and such," said Bert. "But it's what she wants so we'll pull our belts in and manage." His pride in his eldest was almost painful to see but then he laughed and continued, "No danger of Ted following her, that's for sure – he's already doing the deliveries and says he'll come in with me when school's finished with."

"And Rita wants to get married and have babies," Alice

added fondly. "A real little mother, that one – dollies everywhere, and she tidies her doll's house every day."

"Talking of doll's houses," said Albie. "What's this about prefabs being built on the rec?"

"Over my dead body!" Bert snarled. "That land belongs to everyone in the town, not just them with money. Gerald Smythe's not getting his sticky paws on the rec. Our Ted's team plays football every week on that land, then there's the Town Fair – and on top of everything else, them prefabs would be an eyesore. The Council should be looking at fixing up the pier and buying new deckchairs for the tourists. They can stick their prefabs on the old airfield and leave our rec alone!"

"Dad said you're standing for the Council. You've got your election speech worked out already," said Albie.

Bert grinned sheepishly. "Sorry, mate – got a bit carried away, but it makes me so mad!"

"Me too," said Albie. "I'll help you all I can, but I don't know how."

"You can stir up your fellow-owners, for a start," said Alice suddenly. "If those flats lose their view of the sea they'll only be worth half as much."

"Which reminds me I ain't looked at it yet." Albie reached for his jacket. "Thanks for the soup, Alice – I'll go round there now before I go home."

Driving the cart across Market Square to the seafront, Albie left Blossom outside Seaview and let himself into the flat his godmother had left to him in her will. Shutting the door, he leaned against it and took a deep breath, but even his sensitive nose could detect no lingering trace of Norah's lavender scent. He told himself it wasn't surprising – it had been let out for twelve years, and now he was thinking of selling it. He crossed the living-room in a few strides to open the balcony door, lean on the rail and take in the view of the bay.

There were a couple of boats heading back to the small

harbour with fishermen scurrying about on deck, preparing to sell their morning's catch on the quay; further out he could see bigger craft making for the London docks that were only just beginning to recover from the air raids. The pier was off to his left with the harbour beyond it, and a low headland to the right protected the long sweep of beach. It had been covered with barbed wire and mines during the war but was now clear again, and in a few days' time the trains and charabancs would bring the crowds for the first holiday weekend of the season. Those sands, where today seagulls strutted undisturbed, would be covered in people, some brave children would strip off despite the breeze to splash in the sea, and fathers and sons would kick footballs on the recreation ground. Bert was right – any plans to spoil this view in which he and his fellow owners had a vested interest must be nipped in the bud.

There were seven other flats in Seaview apart from Albie's, and within an hour he had spoken to most of his neighbours. He drove home confident that each of them would cast his vote for Bert in the Council elections. All were keen to save their view, of course, but there was also the fact that Albert Daly, Family Butcher, had earned their respect. Everyone knew him to be an honest businessman at a time when many other shopkeepers were lining their pockets by under-the-counter trade.

When Albie got home, Ben and Davy were sitting on the paddock gate, obviously bursting with news.

"Clara's dream came true," Ben yelled when Albie was still fifty yards away, and he jumped down to open the gate with Davy riding the top bar. Albie unhitched the cart and began rubbing Blossom down with an old towel before he asked, "Do you mean to say the forest swallowed her?"

"No, silly," Ben giggled. "She only got her ankle caught under a root."

"She was really scared, though," Davy said. "Mama knew

something was wrong and she went looking for her."

"Clara'd only been there a little while but she was all muddy," Ben reported gleefully. "Grandpapa cut the root and got her out but her ankle was all sore."

"I'll bet it was," said Albie. "I hope you've been nice to her to make her feel better."

"Course we have!" said Davy indignantly. "Everyone has except for Fleur. She says Clara's making a big fuss over nothing and she's fed up with her dreams."

"Mama told her off," said Ben with a satisfied smirk. "She said having the Sight was a blessing."

Albie lifted Davy onto his shoulders to cross the lane. "It *is* a blessing – it saved my skin many times during the war."

"You, Dad? I thought it was only for girls," said Ben, but Davy whispered in Albie's ear, "I wish I had the Sight," and as Albie swung him to the ground he whispered back, "I hope you never need it like I did."

## CHAPTER FOUR – BOMB SHELTER

When Joey and Nico arrived to collect George on Easter Sunday, he was waiting for them by the front door. "Where's your dad?" he asked immediately. "I want to ask if I can stop with you for a day or two. I've let the range go out."

"You know you're always welcome, Grandad," Joey said. "One of Mr Finch's horses is foaling and Dad wouldn't leave her."

"Your dad always did have a thing about horses," George said, but he seemed reluctant to get into the cart.

"You can trust my driving, you know," Joey said. "I'm fifteen now."

"Well, as long as you don't go too fast, lad." George picked up Dot's old shopping basket from the table. "I've got a few bottles of beer wrapped up in my pyjamas."

The minute they arrived at the campsite, Davy and Ben were tugging at George's hands. "You've got to come and see the foal, Grandad – Dad wouldn't take us with him."

George had never been comfortable around horses, especially the big Welsh Shires that Adam Finch favoured, but with two pairs of dark eyes pleading he couldn't refuse.

Ben and Davy climbed nimbly over the stile and hopped about impatiently while George followed more sedately. "Come on, Grandad, if you don't hurry up we'll miss all the fun!"

George fervently hoped they would, but when they reached the stables it was clear from the sounds of distress from one stall that the foal hadn't been born yet, and when Davy raised his arms demanding, "Lift me up, Grandad," George could do nothing but acquiesce.

An oil lamp hanging from a beam illuminated an almost biblical scene, and George was thankful that the business end was hidden from view by Adam Finch. Albie was kneeling in the straw with the mare's head in his lap, murmuring encouragement into her ear and stroking the sweat-soaked black neck. Then Adam backed away hauling on a rope, and George caught a glimpse of two tiny hooves attached to the other end. Dear God – Adam was dragging the foal out by its feet and here he was holding a five-year-old up to watch! He tried to lower Davy to the cobbles but the little boy had a surprisingly strong grip on the stable door. A moment later the mare screamed – a sound George hoped never to hear again – and the foal slithered out onto the straw, where it lay limp and apparently lifeless.

Adam rubbed the newborn vigorously with a handful of straw urging, "Breathe, little fellow, breathe," while Albie continued to stroke the mare's head, talking soft nonsense.

Before George could take his grandsons away, Albie said, "Let his mum have a go," and as the mare's big tongue began to lick her baby George held his breath. Then suddenly it happened – the foal's legs kicked, its chest heaved and it gasped its way into life. Ben said, "Hooray," softly and Davy said, "Look, Grandad, it's all right! But why are you crying?"

"These are happy tears, Davy."

"That's silly," Davy said, but then he saw that Mr Finch was wiping his eyes, and even Dad's cheeks were wet. Davy was happy too but he didn't want to cry – he had this huge fizzy feeling in his tummy and there was only one way to get rid of that. Wriggling out of Grandad's hold, he spread his arms out like a fighter plane and zoomed off, Ben joined him, and they both raced round the yard making engine noises.

Upstairs in the farmhouse Luke Finch pulled aside his curtain to watch them, his mind flashing back twenty-five years. He'd done exactly the same when he was a boy obsessed with aeroplanes, but look where that obsession had landed him – so disfigured that his own daughter wouldn't look at him. He had dressed as usual this morning and gone into the kitchen, but when Daisy said, "It's Sunday, Luke – Albie's not coming," he'd gone straight back to his room.

Seeing Albie walk out of the yard with George and the boys, Luke's feeling of abandonment was so acute that he slid down into the darkest corner, where the black cloud that had begun to lift out in the fields descended once more to engulf him.

*** 

Wherever they'd been working during the week, the whole tribe gathered each Sunday for the midday meal. Mateo and Lydia, Maria's grandparents, headed their branch of the family, while Mateo's widowed sister-in-law Rosanna was the matriarch of another branch. Her son Ricardo, with his wife Olivia and their sons Pedro and Nico, brought the total number tucking into today's stew to sixteen. People sat on wagon steps, stools, or on the ground, and George loved the informal atmosphere. The stew was tasty as ever, though that might be down to the open air and the company – eating alone at home wasn't nearly so much fun.

After dinner most of the adults huddled round the campfire with their coats on. They were sheltered from the afternoon breeze by the hedge but it was still cold, and Mateo and George used the privilege of age to claim the extra shelter of the rear platform of Mateo's vardo. Maria wrapped her shawl tightly round her shoulders and went off to Pinetree Farm to spend an hour in Daisy's warm kitchen, taking Fleur with her to find Linda. Only Clara remained beside George, leaning so hard against his legs that he pulled her onto his lap and wrapped her in his jacket. Resting her face against his broad chest, she closed her eyes and breathed in carbolic and tobacco, feeling safe for the first time in a week.

She had only been trapped by that root for ten minutes before Mama came to rescue her – Mama always knew when she was needed – but what scared Clara the most was that she'd dreamed it before it happened, which meant she had the Sight. She didn't want to have the Sight. She wanted to be normal like her brothers, who bounced through life without a care, or like Fleur who didn't have gypsy blood to make her different. Mama said that she'd learn to understand her dreams, but now that the tree dream had come true, Clara didn't know why she had dreamed it a second time last night.

She snuggled closer into Grandad's comfortable body and tugged his watch and chain out of his waistcoat pocket. Holding the warm metal against her ear, she listened to the tick-tock that had fascinated her since babyhood and, with Grandad's chest rising and falling beneath her cheek, she dropped off to sleep.

It was fully half an hour before she jumped awake with a cry of alarm and looked wildly round asking, "Where are the boys?"

"Where they usually are, I expect," said Albie idly. "Playing in the bomb shelter," then he saw the alarm on Clara's face. "Why – what's wrong?"

"They've got to get out of there!" Clara cried. "I've had that dream again." She tumbled off George's lap and ran towards the shelter.

At the start of the war, Albie and the other men of the tribe had excavated a wide tunnel beneath the pine wood, lining it with timber and building bunks to create an air-raid shelter. At one time it has housed up to a dozen people, but only the youngsters used it now.

Ben and Davy had been playing at pirates when their 'ship' was invaded by Joey and Nico, so they had retreated to the deepest corner of the shelter, where their hoard of treasure was hidden behind a loose board in one of the double bunks. Some long roots had penetrated the plank wall and Ben opened his pocket knife to prise one loose. It was as thick as his thumb and he dug busily for some time, climbing onto the top bunk to follow its course upwards. When Davy scrambled up to watch, Ben wound the root round his hand and leaned back like a rock-climber, yelling, "Joey – look at me!"

Joey looked up just as Ben's weight pulled down a rotten plank from the roof. There was an instant of inertia followed by a cascade of earth, and with a dreadful creaking, tearing sound the entire roof shuddered violently and collapsed inwards. The older boys shot out of the short entrance tunnel in a cloud of dirt, straight into the arms of the men running the other way.

When Maria arrived five minutes later, breathless from having run all the way from the farm, Clara ran to her sobbing, "I'm sorry, Mama – I didn't see it in time!"

"Hush, child," Maria said, "I need to find them," and she shut her eyes to concentrate.

Albie and Josef had already dug away some of the loose earth that filled the entrance, and were heaving at a plank that had become wedged across the tunnel. The space they were working in was barely big enough for them both, and when the plank came free they shovelled the dirt behind them like dogs after a rabbit. Behind them Ricardo and Joey scraped the loose spoil further away, while George and Mateo hovered in the background, desperate to help but unable to get close enough. Then there was a stream of curses followed by another cloud of dirt, and Albie and Josef were buried by a fresh fall. George and Mateo hauled them out by their feet.

"Shore it up as you go or you'll all be dead," George said brutally.

Mateo backed George up. "He's right. Maria says they're alive, but if you go at it like mad bulls you'll kill them."

The little pause calmed Albie and Josef down and they returned more cautiously to their digging. Joey and Nico ran to get help from Pinetree Farm and returned accompanied by Adam and Luke, bringing spades, timber and a large sheet of corrugated iron.

As the work continued to a steady rhythm of dig, clear and shore up, Maria stared into the campfire, the flames of which usually enhanced her Sight, willing her little sons to live long enough to be rescued. She could sense they were in a tiny space, though to her dismay she couldn't see them. She could feel the weight of earth and trees pressing closer and closer, and she concentrated all her efforts on calming them so they wouldn't use up the precious air before Albie could reach them.

Clara was convinced it was her fault. Her dream could have averted this disaster if only she had realised the danger was to Ben and Davy, not to herself. Unable to watch the painfully slow progress of the rescue effort, she trailed miserably away into the plantation. The trees muffled the sounds of digging, and she sank down into a hollow full of pine needles, castigating herself for her stupidity. Her own accident had blinded her to the real warning in her dream, and in an agony of self-loathing she cried, "Ben, Davy, I'm so sorry!"

And then she heard them calling, "Clara – we're here!"

She looked around fearfully – what if they were dead and those were their ghosts? – but then she heard them again, crying faintly, "Help – we can't breathe!" and the sound was coming from right underneath her.

She drummed her feet on the ground shouting, "Ben, Davy!" and heard them answer. Yelling, "Mama – over here!" she jumped bodily down into the hollow. The ground began to give way in a horrible reminder of her dream, but she gritted her teeth and jumped again. This time there was a rush of foul air, and she fell straight down into the earth through a tangle of roots.

Immediately two pairs of arms clung round her neck and her little brothers wailed in terror. Cuddling them tight, Clara looked around their prison and saw, by the dim green light filtering into the hole, that she had landed in her dream. There were even flashes of light, just as in her dream, but it was only the collection of shiny objects that comprised her brothers' pirate treasure. A moment later Maria appeared above them.

"Get us out, Mama!" all three children pleaded, but the ground was too fragile to enlarge the hole without burying them again. So Maria lay flat above them, calling down comfort while the men continued digging. Eventually Albie reached his children, passing them one at a time up to Maria's waiting arms, and they were saved. The moment they were free, the men demolished the shelter, and soon there was nothing but a bank of earth to show where it had been.

When all the drama was over, Luke disappeared back to the farm as silently as a shadow. Adam Finch watched him go with sad eyes. "It'll take more than a week of farming to get him back to normal," he said to George. "But Albie's got him started – I thought we were going to lose him last month."

"Shell shock's a dreadful thing," George replied. "I lost a brother that way in the first war." The two elderly men exchanged agonized looks, afraid to put their fears into words, but then Ruth Finch appeared, insisting that the muddy adventurers come back to Pinetree Farm to use the bath, and they dropped the well-worn subject of Luke.

The last vestiges of Ben and Davy's fright dissolved at the sight of the huge bath that stood on lion feet in the centre of what had once been a bedroom. They splashed happily for ages in the hot water, but when it was Clara's turn she hung back, refusing to remove her petticoat until they had gone. Once Maria had wrapped Ben and Davy in some threadbare pre-war towels and sent them downstairs to dry off in front of the range, Clara slid her aching body into the luxury of an all-over bath for the first time in her life. Maria poured jugs of clean water to wash the dirt out of her daughter's hair, noting her budding breasts, and wondered whether Clara's emerging Sight explained why her own had weakened. Was it possible that she had passed on the gift of Sight to her daughter and lost her own?

"Did you really hear Ben and Davy calling?" she asked quietly.

With her mother's sensitive fingers working shampoo into her scalp, Clara felt the stress draining away and was able to think back to that moment in the hollow without trembling.

"Not their voices exactly. It was more like a feeling than a sound."

"That's what I thought. You do have the Sight." Maria felt the tension return to Clara's body but continued her gentle massage. "You mustn't fight it, my love. I know it can be a burden sometimes, but it's a gift you can't refuse."

"It scares me, Mama. What if I see something I can't stop?"

"You can only do your best. I'll teach you what I can. Grandmama and Olivia will help too – the Sight runs in the family and you can't escape it."

"But I don't want to be different – the other girls make fun of me."

"That's only because they don't understand," said Maria, thinking that when she was Clara's age she hadn't had to contend with a class-full of gadjos.

"Fleur should understand," Clara said bitterly, stepping out of the bath. "Even if she's not a gypsy she's lived with us all her life." Just then Fleur burst into the room, and Clara grabbed a towel, crying, "Haven't you ever heard of knocking?"

"What's got into you?" Fleur demanded. "I've seen you bare before and I want a bath too."

"Why should you? You didn't get dirty," Clara said, her voice muffled as she pulled her petticoat on over her damp skin.

"I'd have saved them if I'd got there first, so there's no need to be snooty about it," said Fleur. "And I can have a bath if I want, can't I, Mama?"

"You can jump in here if you're quick," said Maria, looking from one angry face to the other. "Clara, go and tell Dad I'll be running clean water for him in five minutes."

Throwing a satisfied smirk at her sister, Clara ran downstairs, leaving Fleur to jump into the cooling bath of brown water and pretend she was enjoying it.

By the time everyone had bathed, the farm women had

assembled a feast. Ruth had unhooked from her chimney an entire ham, given it a cursory wipe with a damp cloth and put it in the centre of her table. Her daughters-in-law had raided their own larders to produce bread and rich yellow butter, cheese and jars of pickles, sweet wrinkled apples and jugs of lemonade. With a huge pot of soup and a barrel of home-brewed cider, the impromptu party continued until the children were too tired to stay awake. Even then, while their mothers took them to bed, the men remained chatting by the fire.

"Are you going to stay around here for a while?" Adam asked George. "I think Daisy would appreciate having her grandad nearer."

"I'll pop over and have a proper talk with Daisy tomorrow," George promised. "I don't have to be back till rent day."

Adam sat up straighter in his cushioned wooden armchair. "Your house is only rented?"

"Where would I get the money to buy a house? Anyhow, what difference does it make?"

"The difference..." said Adam, leaning forward to pour some more cider into George's pewter mug. "The difference is that you could pack up and leave at any time."

"And why would I want to do that?" asked George, wondering what had got into his old friend all of a sudden.

Adam grinned and answered, "Because most of your family is here, and I've got an empty cottage not five minutes away."

"You mean those ones next to the paddock? I thought your farmhands lived in them."

Adam shook his head. "Only three came back here after the war. I've got two lads who cycle in each day but they prefer living in town. That end cottage has been empty for too long. So what do you say?"

George lit a cigarette with hands that shook slightly,

mulling over this startling proposition. His house in Church Street wasn't the same without Dot, and since Wilf died it had felt even emptier. He'd have fought to the bitter end Gerald Smythe's plans to oust him, but the idea of leaving voluntarily didn't seem too dreadful. The thought of Albie and his kids running in to see him every day was very appealing, and he'd have Mateo just over the road as well. Even when the tribe went away in the winter there'd still be Adam, who was a mere slip of a lad at only seventy but still a good friend, and he could keep an eye on Daisy and young Linda much more easily from next door. "How much rent are we talking about?" he asked at last.

"I don't want any rent," Adam said. "Standing empty isn't doing the place any good."

"You'll take rent or I ain't coming," snapped George. "I'm no charity case."

"For God's sake, man, that's not what I meant – you'd be doing me a favour."

"I'll give you the same rent as I'm paying now and no arguments," George said stubbornly. "I'll have to look at it first, mind." His eyes twinkled with more humour than they'd held for a long time and Adam took a deep pull on his drink to conceal a smile. He'd found a convivial tenant for the cottage and rescued a friend from a lonely old age, and while the little argument over rent had livened them both up, George's fierce pride remained intact.

***

The party atmosphere in the Finches' kitchen had done much to ease the tension between Clara and Fleur, and the next morning's announcement that Grandad would soon be moving in across the lane drove away their last vestiges of coolness. The spooky cottage with its overgrown garden became instantly a potential haven of peace, cuddles and cups of tea.

George had hoped for a quiet look round with Adam, but

the whole family insisted on accompanying him – and a surprise addition to the party was Luke, whom Adam had persuaded to act as site inspector. The spring sunshine revealed the cottage at its best: daffodils waved their yellow heads through the tangle of weeds that bordered the gravel path, a cherry tree that had grown from a stray pip was in blossom, and the box hedge twittered with birds. Adam pushed open the gate with a scrape of gravel and said to Luke, "You'd better start that list of repairs, son – this gate needs lifting." Luke dutifully made a note, and as they inspected the outside the list grew. Several of the Kent peg tiles had slipped, a drain was blocked, and a creeper effectively sealed the side gate, but the row of four cottages had been solidly built and these were minor problems.

"A week's work and fresh paint on the woodwork will have the outside good as new," Adam said as he unlocked the front door and stood aside for George to enter.

In the hallway George sniffed. "I smell mice – they'll eat through anything, mice will, including electric wires."

"One of the barn cats has kittens," Luke volunteered. "She comes from a long line of good mousers."

"How do you know that?" Adam asked, hope rising like fermenting cider – Luke showing an interest in anything was a miracle.

Luke almost smiled. "I've known every cat on the farm since I was a little boy."

When George opened the door to the front room, Fleur skipped into the middle and did a slow twirl, her face thoughtful. "This room needs more light. Creamy wallpaper and primrose yellow curtains."

George tugged her blonde pigtail. "Who made you the expert?"

She jerked her hair out of his hand and pouted. "Don't laugh at me. I can see it – this room won't get the sun till evening and it needs yellow."

"All right, child, I was only teasing – what d'you think I should do in the other rooms?"

Fleur shot off immediately to explore and the men followed, leaving Maria and Clara standing in the bare room.

"That was unexpected," Maria remarked.

"Fleur's good with colours," Clara said. "She always gets top marks in Art. She's right, too – this room does need cheering up – there's a feeling of sadness."

"I don't think it was used much," said Maria. "I expect the kitchen's brighter."

As the group toured of the rest of the cottage, which comprised the kitchen and scullery and two upstairs bedrooms – Luke made meticulous notes. There was no shortage of input from the Smith family – if George was going to live here it had to be right. Albie shook the banisters and dug a penknife into the doorframes. Fleur stood in the centre of each room trying to visualise it with curtains and furniture. Maria and Clara opened cupboards and decided a few mouse-traps would give the promised kitten a fighting chance. George peered up the chimneys to check for birds' nests and said he'd move in as soon as the cottage was ready. Then he unbolted the back door, saw the long walled back garden and grabbed Adam's hand to shake it heartily. "I should be paying you more, Adam – I'll be selling veg at market from a garden this size. It must be what – fifty or sixty feet long?"

"Eighty," said Luke.

Adam stared at him. "How can you be so certain?"

"You can't fly a plane without learning to judge distance," Luke said, and another brick fell out of the wall that had surrounded him for so long.

Adam told himself not to expect his son to run before he could walk, but he began to envisage Luke taking over the maintenance of all the farm buildings.

Into the little pool of silence George said, "It'll take me weeks just to dig it over."

"The boys can help," said Albie. "They don't start school for two weeks."

"They can help," said George, "though they can't be trusted to get all the roots out – just look at 'em now!" His three grandsons were racing down one brick wall and up the other, swiping at nettles with sticks. "I'd spend all my time watching those young hooligans."

"I can't do it, Dad – I've got to work," Albie said. "The fair's going to Ashford for Easter and me and Ricardo are going down on the train to set it up – we need the cash."

"I'll supervise them," said Luke, startling everybody yet again. "We'll start tomorrow. It needs clearing straight away or you'll be too late getting your seeds in."

"Good man," said George. "There's not many as would take that lot on."

Luke's back straightened, his head lifted, and the morning sun shone full on his ruined face as he said, "We had chaps in my squadron who behaved like children – I can handle them. Joey!" he called. "Bring your gang back here – we've got work to do."

"What about us?" Fleur asked, and Clara added, "Yes – we want to help too."

George hugged them both. "Let's find out how good you are with a paintbrush, shall we?"

## CHAPTER FIVE – PADDY

Albie was lifting a horse onto the carousel in Ashford when a sledgehammer blow hit his back and a rich Irish brogue yelled in his ear, "Corp! Sweet Mother of God – after all these years! How's it going?"

Albie gripped a hand as calloused as his own and beamed happily into the other man's face. "Paddy O'Brien – I never thought I'd see you again! What are you doing here?"

"Same as you, Corp, by the look of it," said Paddy, his face splitting into the broad grin that brought Albie's memories of France flooding back. "I got took on as a driver and rigger for the season – I was lucky the army taught me the driving." He patted the horse's dappled rump. "Didn't you get enough of these in France?"

"This one's hardly likely to explode, is it?" Albie said, wincing as the memory leapt afresh to his mind. It was twelve years since he had been injured when he stopped to admire an abandoned carousel in France, and a stray German bomb hit them both: twelve years since he and Paddy O'Brien were rescued from the beach at Dunkirk. Albie had been shipped straight off to hospital and the two soldiers had never seen each other again.

"How's the shoulder now?" Paddy asked, but the boss shouted, "Are you two planning to stand there jawing all day?" so Albie and Paddy returned to their work, dropping straight back into the instinctive anticipation of each other's moves that had bound their wartime squad into such a tight unit. When the carousel was finished they broke off for a cup of tea, and Albie studied the man who had been the only soldier bigger than he was in basic training.

Noting that Paddy's skin was as weather-beaten as his own, he said, "I guess we both went back to casual labouring after the war." He offered Paddy a cigarette and lit them, extinguishing the match immediately afterwards.

"Good job there's only two of us," Paddy said.

Albie knew exactly what he meant. "Funny, ain't it, how we still blow it out after two lights? Even in the middle of the desert we'd never risk a sniper getting a bead on us."

"So that's where you got to," said Paddy. "I fetched up in Italy, and what an arsehole of a place that was. Too hot, thousands of flies, and the girls had moustaches bigger than mine."

"At least you had girls to look at – we just got sand and flies."

The two men gazed into the distance for a moment, each remembering those years and the friends they had lost, then Paddy shook himself and said, "But forget all that – at least we came back. Tell me what happened to that babby."

"Fleur?" said Albie with a fond smile. "The minute you handed Fleur over, Maria hid her inside her shawl. She was still feeding Clara and she had enough for two, so she made out Fleur was one of ours and no-one knew any different – gypsies move around too much for anyone to keep proper tabs on us. Fleur's twelve now." He gave a reminiscent chuckle. "Did the MPs take that little goat off you?"

"I made fecking sure they didn't find it," said Paddy, pinching out his cigarette carefully and putting the stub in his pocket. "After feeding the babby for days it deserved better than to be having its throat cut, even if it did shit all over me jacket on that boat!"

"So what did you do with it?"

"Sold it to an auld farmer for his orphan lambs." Paddy shrugged. "He most likely ate it later but I did me best. I'd've kept it if I could but I had to go back and fight."

They split up after their tea-break – Albie to help Ricardo fix a faulty generator and Paddy to build another ride – but that evening Albie and Ricardo shared their supper with Paddy. From the state of his clothes it looked as if he was only just surviving, and he hadn't brought any food with him. As they tucked hungrily into farm-cured ham sandwiched between thick slices of bread Paddy said, "I've not had grub like this since I was a cub. Our mammy used to keep a ham up the chimney. A slice of ham on top of tatties and cabbage was our regular Sunday dinner."

"Why didn't you go back home after the war?" Ricardo asked.

"I've no family left and there's no work across the water," Paddy said briefly. "What about you, Ric – what did you do in the war?"

In the immediate post-war years Ricardo had learned to answer that question with a joke. "I grew tatties for you. I never had a birth certificate so I didn't get called up."

"You didn't miss much," said Paddy through his last mouthful. "The best grub we ever got in the army was Albie's rabbit stew."

They unrolled their blankets in an empty trailer and settled down for the night with the ease of men accustomed to sleeping where they could, but before he fell asleep Albie asked Paddy, "Do you know if the rest of our squad made it through the war?"

"Every man jack of us," said Paddy with a touch of pride. "We made sure we stuck together. Except for Titch, of course – he caught his Blighty one in 1940."

"I remember that," said Albie. "Same day as Bert's brother Eddie died."

"We all thought your gypsy luck had run out that day," said Paddy. "But it must've rubbed off on Bert 'cause it got us through the rest of the war. Even when Joan got in the way of a great lump of shrapnel, Auntie managed to save his leg."

"Who are Joan and Auntie?" asked Ricardo. "Were there girls in your army?"

"God love you, no!" laughed Paddy. "Auntie was our medic – and the closest we had to a girl!"

"And Joan's real name was Darby," Albie said. "You know

– like in Darby and Joan?"

"You gadjos are very strange," said Ricardo, shaking his head, but Albie just grinned at the insult that had lost its sting over the years, closed his eyes and drifted off.

The fair stayed in Ashford for a week, the three men working side by side on trucks and generators for which there was still a shortage of spare parts. On the final day, when they'd loaded the rides back onto the trailers ready for a move further south, Albie shook Paddy's hand in farewell and said, "Don't forget you're stopping with us in July – the fair always stays two weeks in our town."

"Sure and haven't I promised already?" replied Paddy. "It'll be a grand holiday, staying in a gypsy camp."

Watching the cumbersome fair rides thread their way through the narrow streets, Albie thought that if the Council built their prefabs there would be no recreation ground in Thambay for the fair to use. As the train chugged through hop-fields where workers were tying up the vines, he resolved to ask Mateo if he could take time off from the usual agricultural work so he could help Bert get elected to the Council.

*** 

Looking forward to seeing Maria at the railway station, Albie was disconcerted to be met by Josef, and asked at once, "Where's Maria – is something wrong?"

"She's having a rest," Josef said. "She's been working hard in George's cottage."

"But I've been away a whole week – Maria always meets me."

Josef simply clicked his tongue at Blossom and flipped the reins to drive them home, but when Albie found Maria lying on their bed in the wagon his heart flipped painfully. "Are you ill or summat?" he asked, feeling her forehead for fever.

Maria just smiled a slow, contented smile. "Not ill, Albie – I'm having another baby."

Albie sat down with a thump. Maria was thirty-three – old to be having a baby – and he'd thought Davy would be their last. "How did that happen?"

"You should know. It must have been in Luke's barn – or don't you remember?"

"Course I remember!" Albie protested. "It must've been being in the barn that did it." He peered at Maria's face in the dim light that filtered through the net curtain and frowned. "You're a bit pasty, though. You've never gone to bed in the day before."

"I'm just being lazy," Maria said, swinging her legs off the bed and reaching for her shawl. "We've had a busy week getting the cottage ready – come and see."

Albie tucked Maria's arm protectively in his elbow as they walked slowly down the lane past the paddock, where Blossom poked her head over the five-bar gate to say hello.

"She was a bit slow on the drive in from the station," Albie remarked.

"She's getting old," said Maria. "She must be at least sixteen."

Albie stroked the soft nose of the pony that Josef had given them as a wedding present and she blew gently down her nostrils in response. "She ain't ill, is she?"

"Just tired," Maria assured him. "Like me."

There was a patch of uncultivated land, thick with brambles, between the paddock and the cottage, but on George's side of the hedge it was evident that Luke had kept his team of boys hard at work. Albie pushed open the gate, noting with approval that it no longer scraped the path, the flower beds had been cleared of the larger weeds and the little patch of lawn was roughly cut.

"Luke did that with a scythe," Maria told him. "He wouldn't let the boys use it."

"I should bloody well hope not!" said Albie, shuddering at the thought of his sons being let loose with a scythe. "They've not got all the weeds out, neither."

"Your dad told them not to," said Maria. "He said he wanted to see what plants he'd got before they pulled them all up. They've done a better job out the back."

They went along the path at the side of the cottage to be confronted by a scene of frenzied activity – Joey was at the far end, hacking down the last few square yards of brambles for Ben and Davy to drag onto a towering pile, while Luke and Nico were methodically digging out roots and clumps of nettles and couch grass. The two younger boys shrieked "Dad!" and ran to cover him with muddy hugs, but Joey merely waved his brushing-hook yelling, "Wotcher, Dad!" and attacked the brambles with renewed vigour.

Luke wiped his hand on the seat of his trousers and shook Albie's hand. "We should just get this finished before they start school – what do you think of it?"

"I think you've done a great job," said Albie. "Did the kids behave themselves?"

A sudden tension in the air informed Albie that not all had gone smoothly, but Luke forbore to mention the mud-fights he had broken up, or the cigarettes he'd confiscated from Joey and Nico. "More or less," he replied with a wink that only Albie could see. "They've been quite a good squad, all things considered."

"A crew's only as good as the officer in charge," said Albie.

Luke's face, shiny with Maria's herbal salve beneath his broad-brimmed sun-hat, flushed with pride.

"Is Mr Luke an officer?" asked Davy.

"Yes he is, and you're his crew. Now get back to work while I look inside."

Fleur and Clara shot out of the back door to pull him in. "We'll show you round – we did most of the painting. Grandpapa Josef did the ceilings but we did the rest," they said proudly.

They hadn't done a perfect job, but the kitchen and scullery were clean and fresh. The smell of paint had replaced that of mice, and a week of slow fires in the range had warmed and aired the cottage. Albie had to admire the clothes-airer on the scullery ceiling with its new rope and pulley – "Mr Luke did that" – the draining board that the girls had scrubbed back to the wood and polished, and the range that Maria had black-leaded.

Then Fleur pushed her father along the hallway to the front room. "I did this room all by myself – Clara wouldn't stay in here."

"Why not?" Albie asked.

"No special reason – I was painting Grandad's bedroom."

"She says it feels wrong in here," Fleur said, scorn dripping from every syllable. "There's nothing wrong with this room – it's all in her imagination."

"Now Fleur – I've told you about that before," Maria scolded. "Don't make fun of things you don't understand."

"You were right about the yellow," Albie said hastily, "those curtains are pretty."

"Ruth Finch helped me make them on her Singer," Maria said. "We couldn't believe the material in the shops – all without coupons, too!"

"No wonder you're tired out, doing all this in a week," Albie said, hugging her. "When's Dad moving in?"

"On Saturday. John Daly's fetching him in his van."

"Only two days! I'd better get over to Dad's and help him pack up."

"He's not expecting you till tomorrow," said Maria firmly, sliding her arms round his waist. "The children are still busy here and until tea-time you're mine."

They slipped away from the activity like schoolchildren playing hookey, through the side gate and up the lane to the campsite. Albie drew an ecstatic breath – the air tasted of spring, of fresh leaves and yellow flowers. "Ah, that's better! I've been smelling engine grease and candyfloss all week."

The camp was deserted as Albie and Maria went up the steps of their wagon and closed the door to let the cosy warmth of their own home envelop them. Maria removed the dikla from her hair and moved towards the bed, but Albie caught her from behind and lifted a long twist of her hair to his face to inhale her scent. "You don't smell any different – are you sure you're expecting?"

She caught his wrist, placed his hand on her belly and asked, "Can't you feel it?"

Albie shifted his hands to her breasts. "This is a better way to tell," he said, and Maria twisted her head round for his kiss. A moment later they were in the bed with the curtain closed around them, making up for a week away from the comfort of each other's bodies.

When supper was over, Maria told everyone about the baby. The adults made appropriate noises of pleased surprise, although they had all guessed already. Joey said, "Oh, not another one!" in a resigned voice, and Ben and Davy said in unison, "Hope it's a boy," but Fleur cried, "How could you? Joey's fifteen – you're too old!"

"I'm only thirty-five, love – some women have babies when they're forty."

"Not normal women – Linda's mum only had her."

Maria flushed, and Albie slapped his hands on his knees. "That's enough, Fleur! I won't have you talking to your mama like that." He so rarely raised his voice that Fleur burst into tears, but Clara moved closer to her mother and put a hand on her knee.

"A baby will be lovely, Mama," she said, but a second later she snatched her hand away. Her great-grandmother Lydia caught her eye and shook her head, so Clara clamped her lips together, but suddenly she was deathly afraid. This baby girl was bringing danger in her tiny hands – and Mama didn't seem aware of it.

***

The following morning Albie was banging on his father's door in town for a full two minutes before it opened. George stood there covered in cobwebs. "Didn't hear you at first, son – I was in the shed. Come on through – I could use a hand."

"Why was the door bolted, Dad? You never locked it in daytime before."

"Can't trust people like you could in the war. Folk used to look out for each other then, but I don't even know half my neighbours now. I won't be sorry to go."

In the scullery Albie stared aghast at the boxes full of rusty tools, an odd assortment of flower pots and even an old bicycle wheel.

"You're not taking all this rubbish, are you?" he asked, but George was already in the yard, digging a crown of rhubarb from beside his compost heap. Albie opened his mouth to protest, but when he saw the glow on George's face he merely said, "Shall I start upstairs?"

"All done, lad, all done – except for me bed, and I'll need that tonight. You can pack the china if you want."

So Albie lifted his mum's treasured willow pattern tea service down from the dresser and wrapped it tenderly in newspaper, packed it into the strongest box he could find, and put it on the table out of harm's way. George came in wiping his hands on a rag, and put the kettle on the hob while Albie cleared the mantelpiece.

"Careful with that clock," George warned. "That was a wedding present from Dot's Mum and Dad." As Albie put the clock down on the table with exaggerated care it tinkled softly as if adding its own warning. George gave it an affectionate pat. "Stood up there for fifty-nine years, that clock has, and always kept good time." He blew dust from its ornate mouldings and added in a conspiratorial whisper, "Your mum, God rest her soul, loved this clock – never could bring meself to tell her I loathed the bloody thing!"

Albie laughed at the gleam of mischief in his dad's eyes.

"Why are you whispering – afraid she'll hear you?"

George tapped the side of his nose with one finger. "You never know, do you? Best not take any chances." Father and son sat to drink their tea with the offending object between them, and George said, "You've got to admit it looks more like a mausoleum than a clock with them pillars."

"What's a mausoleum when it's at home?" Albie spluttered. "One of them long words from Norah's books?"

"I've read right through them encyclopaedias four times since I got 'em," said George with justifiable pride. "I used her dictionary when they explained one long word with a dozen more. Norah didn't just leave me her books, she left me an education. Talking of Norah, have you decided what to do about her flat?"

Albie hit his forehead with the heel of his hand. "I knew there were summat else I meant to do! I've got to see Bert about this election – if Smythe gets in he'll ruin the view from the flats."

"Bert could use some help," George said. "That Gerald Smythe needs to learn he can't have it all his own way."

"I'll call in on my way home," Albie said, and carried the boxes of china out to the cart.

George handed him the clock wrapped in an old blanket. "Put it on the mantelpiece in the front room. At least there I won't have to look at it when I'm eating." Then even more carefully he handed over a damp newspaper-wrapped bundle. "That's me rhubarb. I'll dig it in meself tomorrow, so make sure you save me some horse-shit."

***

Back at George's cottage Luke was facing a crisis. Joey and Nico had cut down most of the brambles and the obvious next step was a bonfire, but he couldn't do it. Daisy always shut the range fire-door when he was in the kitchen, and his brothers had learned to warn him before they lit a cigarette. He knew his fear was irrational and he'd have to confront it sometime, but not today – not so soon after Albie had hauled him by the scruff of his neck out of that awful black depression.

"Ben!" he called. "Go and tell Mr Adam there's a bonfire to light."

"Right-ho, Chief!" Ben yelled cheerfully, climbing over the wall at the far end of the garden to run along the track to the farmhouse. The gate had rusted shut behind the brambles they hadn't had time to clear, but preparing the ground for George's planting had taken precedence over these minor jobs on Luke's list.

Clara and Fleur were in the back bedroom of the cottage with Linda Finch, sweeping up scraps of wallpaper, when Clara suddenly screamed, "Davy's on fire!" and dashed to the window. She sagged with relief when she saw Davy was unharmed and Linda said scornfully, "He looks fine to me."

"You're at it again, aren't you?" Fleur said, but then they heard Joey say, "What do you need Mr Adam for? We can do it ourselves," and saw him take a box of matches from his pocket and strike one. The tinder-dry brambles caught instantly and, fanned by the breeze, flames shot through the heap with a whoosh. The clumps of damp couch-grass and nettles made a dark patchwork against the red glow of flames, and Joey and Nico began poking them into the bonfire with sticks. Davy scampered round the garden gathering up the last of the weeds, darting between the bonfire and the wall to throw them into the flames.

As the fire crackled in the spring sunshine, Luke shrank back against the scullery wall eighty feet away, desperate to flee but unwilling to abandon his crew. Fleur and Linda leaned out of the bedroom window to watch the bonfire, but Clara knew with an awful certainty that Davy was in danger, and ran downstairs with her heart hammering. She was halfway across the kitchen when Nico poked too vigorously and the unsteady pile collapsed, setting light to the un-cleared patch of ancient bramble that covered the gate – and Davy was trapped between the fire and the wall.

Clara catapulted out of the scullery door as Davy tried to climb the wall, but his arms were too short to reach the top. As he screamed in terror, Clara beat on Luke's chest with her fists shrieking, "Help him!" and her voice finally penetrated Luke's paralysis. Davy was only a child – one of his crew – and his safety was the responsibility of the officer in charge.

Stamping on his fear, Luke raced the length of the garden, leapt over the wall to the lane, and ran to the corner where Davy was trapped with the flames starting to lick at his clothes. Ignoring the heat searing his damaged skin, Luke said, "Davy – give me your hands!" His calm voice stopped Davy's screams and he lifted his arms for Luke to yank him over the wall to safety.

Maria burst onto the scene just as Adam Finch and Ben came pounding down the track from the farm, and Luke put Davy into his mother's arms. As she took him into the cottage to splash his singed hair and face with cold water, Adam asked Luke, "Are you all right, son?"

Luke was trembling but triumphant. "I was in a blue funk for a while but I couldn't let Davy burn, could I?"

"You did a brave thing there, my boy, and I'm proud of you."

"I'm not that proud of myself," Luke said with a shaky laugh. "I stood by while those kids played with fire and was too scared to stop them."

"I know, Luke, I know," said Adam, gripping Luke's arm hard. "At the end of the day you saved Davy and that's what counts." He glanced at the old gate that was now burning merrily and added with a grin, "You'd better add a new gate to your list."

Maria bundled Davy back home to change out of his smoke-saturated clothes, leaving the girls to put the finishing touches to the cottage. While Fleur toured the rooms, scraping off a paint-spot here, twitching a curtain straight there, Clara banked down the range. She was drawing out the ash-tray when she felt Linda's eyes on her back and asked without turning round, "What do you want now?"

"Did you really know Davy was in danger?"

"Yes."

"So what's it like – this Sight? Do you see things like at the pictures?"

Clara was so astonished that the younger girl was interested that she answered without thinking, "No – not pictures – it's more like I'm being told things."

"So you hear voices as well, do you? You're as crazy as my dad," Linda laughed and ran off, leaving Clara kneeling in front of the range with tears running down her cheeks.

A moment later there was a rush of air as Fleur hurtled through from the scullery and out of the front door. She caught up with Linda in the lane and swung her round by her cardigan to hiss in her face, "You've no right to tell my sister she's crazy."

"But you said she gets these weird dreams – I thought *you* thought she was off her head."

"Well, maybe, sometimes – but she was right about Davy, wasn't she? And besides, she's my sister – you leave her alone."

"Last week you were saying you weren't even related – I wish you'd make up your mind." Linda tore herself free and ran off up the lane, yelling over her shoulder, "You're all the same, you gypsies – you're all mad!"

## CHAPTER SIX – THE MOVE

John Daly's three-ton van with the legend 'Daly Deliveries' emblazoned on its sides pulled up at the cottage in the middle of Saturday morning. George was perched in the cab clutching his aspidistra in its Chinese-style pot, which he passed to Joey with a terse, "Drop that and you're dead!" before climbing out of the cab to be presented ceremoniously with his keys by Adam Finch. Immediately he opened his wallet and handed over three ten-shilling notes. "That's me first month's rent, Adam, and I hope it's enough – a week's pension for a month's rent seems fair to me."

"Very fair," said Adam, shaking George's hand and pocketing the cash. "I'll mark it in your rent book."

Honour satisfied, George turned to his family. "Right – let's get on with it. John can only spare the van for a couple of hours and we're running late as it is – dismantling the bed took longer than we thought."

Turning the key in the cheerful red front door, he stepped inside his cottage and said at once, "I smell cake."

Clara and Fleur, swathed in large aprons, took his hands to drag him into the kitchen, where a fruit cake sat in splendid isolation on the table.

"My word, you have been busy," George exclaimed, looking round. "Albie told me you painted it but I never expected it to be so nice."

"We've got the kettle on too," Clara said.

"We'll have a cuppa when the furniture's unloaded – we'll need one by then."

By the time Albie arrived with the small cart, the van had been unloaded and John Daly was on his way to his next job. Half of George's furniture was still on the front lawn, and sounds of hammering came from upstairs where Josef and Ricardo were reassembling George's bed-frame. George called from the front door, "Come in, son, but wipe your feet –

Adam put a carpet runner in the hall and I ain't had a chance to roll it up out of the way."

Joey came in carrying a rocking chair. "Where do you want this, Grandad?"

"In the front room," said George promptly. "That was Dot's chair and it belongs with her clock. Albie – put Norah's books in there too – I'm going to sit by that window to read 'em."

Once Albie had arranged the heavy set of Encyclopaedia Britannica in the bookcase, he sat in Dot's chair and listened to the contented ticking of her black marble clock. He chuckled at the thought that it obviously liked it here – clocks could refuse to work if they weren't content. He pushed off with one foot to set the chair moving, and the combination of creaking rocker and ticking clock brought his mum vividly to mind. He felt his hair move as if she was running her hand through it, and then she was gone, leaving behind a hint of coal tar soap.

Upstairs in the back bedroom, where the wall radiated warmth from the range chimney, Clara stopped halfway through tucking in a blanket to see her nan standing in the corner. It was eight years since Dot died but Clara still remembered that apron – an all-over floral garment like a sleeveless dress – and the feather duster with which she used to dust her horrible clock. Nan flicked a speck of dust from Grandad's chest of drawers before she faded away into the curtains that exactly matched her apron. Clara wondered whether Fleur had chosen that material on purpose, but before she could ask her, Maria called, "Soup's ready!" and they clattered down the stairs just as Albie came out of the front room.

Clara leaned over the banister to whisper in his ear, "Nan likes this house – I saw her in the bedroom."

Albie laughed and swung her off the stairs. "Your nan must've done the grand tour, then, 'cause I seen her in the front room."

After lunch George carefully placed his big wooden

wireless on the dresser. As it crackled into life he asked Albie, "How am I going to take the accumulator for recharging?"

"Maria and me thought you could use the cart. You can prop the accumulator up in a box of newspapers and take it in when you go for your pension."

"Me drive a cart? I can't learn to drive one at my age."

"Dad – Blossom knows the way into town – you'll only need to sit and hold the reins. We'll leave her and the cart with you – it will give you some independence, 'specially when we're not here."

"I'd forgotten you wouldn't be here all the time," George said, his face falling briefly, but then Adam and Luke arrived bearing a pair of old armchairs.

"They've been in the barn and they're rather shabby," Adam said, "I want to be comfy when I come visiting," and George cheered up.

Bert Daly arrived in his butcher's van that evening and found a group of men in the kitchen – Albie, Josef and Mateo, plus Adam and Luke, all crowded round the table in a comfortable fug of beer fumes and cigarette smoke.

"Thrown all the women out, have you?" Bert joked as he shook George's hand. "I've brought a pound of sausages and a couple of chops as a house-warming present."

"That's kind of you, Bert. The women have gone home and left us in peace. Squeeze in on that bench and grab a beer – Adam brought a whole crate."

"Don't mind if I do," Bert replied, as Albie moved up to make room for him.

"I hear you're running for the Council against Smythe," Adam said to Bert.

"He's got posters plastered all over town," Bert said. "I don't reckon he's got as many supporters as he thinks. James Evans – him as owns the biscuit factory – is standing as an independent. Evans grew up in the streets Smythe calls slums, and he says he'll fight any planning application that involves demolishing them. He's got quite a following among the working-class voters."

"So what's left for you to say?" Albie asked. "You're against Smythe building prefabs too."

"What prefabs?" Adam asked. "I've heard nothing about any prefabs."

"You don't get into town often enough," said George, pushing another log onto the fire. "The Council want to build some on the rec and Smythe's after the contract."

"That ground can't be built on!" Adam exclaimed. "Old Gilchrist's grandfather gave that to the whole town."

"Well, if Smythe gets onto the Council you can bet your boots he'll persuade 'em," George said. "And he wants to knock down the old houses and build flats."

"Well, we'd better make sure he doesn't get the opportunity," said Adam, raising his glass to Bert. "If you think you can stop him you've got my vote, young Daly."

"I'll give it my best shot, but I don't reckon much to my chances of winning."

"None of that talk!" said Albie. "In my book you've got a better chance than the others. Folks know that Smythe is only out for himself, and Evans is a good bloke but he's getting on a bit. You're the right age and you're a local man – they'll vote for you, just you see."

"But there'll be speeches to make," Bert said. "And I don't talk right – I never could get the hang of posh talk."

"Listen to me, Bert." Albie gripped Bert's wrist across the table. "Posh talk ain't what matters when you've got summat important to say."

"And if you want someone to run your election office, I can do that," Luke said. "We've got a telephone and my desk is standing unused – what do you think?"

"And when the Bowls Club hears what Gerald Smythe is up to," Adam said, "I'll bet you even get a few Tory votes." He beamed mischievously at Luke. "You've got no call to look so astonished, son – it's a free country and a man can change his mind."

"If this country is free," said Mateo, who had listened in silence to the talk of elections, "why do the police make us move all the time? The common land is for everyone, no? But they dig ditches to keep us out, or they come at dawn with dogs that frighten the children. Sometimes we can't even light a fire for fear of being discovered."

"What about caravan sites?" Luke asked. "There's one on the Whitstable Road."

"We tried there once," Josef said. "The owner said it was full even though we could see it was half empty. The only time we can camp in town is when the fair comes."

"It sounds as if I'd better register your campsite on my farm, doesn't it?" said Adam thoughtfully. "I'll slip an application through before my friends on the Council discover Luke and I have changed sides!"

Bert sat in a daze – this unexpected support from Adam and Luke had stiffened his resolve. Gerald Smythe might have been to public school, and James Evans was counting on his factory workers to vote for him, but he, Albert Daly, was as qualified as either of them to be on Thambay Town Council. He'd give it his best shot, dropped aitches and all.

***

On the first day of the summer term, Linda came down to breakfast to find her mother still wearing her dressing gown. "Mum, you're not ready! We can't be late on the first day!"

Daisy ladled porridge into three bowls and poured milk over them while Linda plunged her spoon into the honey jar. "Your dad's driving you in today."

"Dad? But he can't! You always take us." Linda waved her spoon wildly, spilling honey on the oil-cloth.

Daisy wiped it up with an angry swipe of a dish-cloth and snapped, "I've got enough to do here, my girl, and you're lucky not to be cycling in. Now eat your porridge."

"But Mum – the others will stare at him!"

When Linda had come downstairs eight years earlier to be confronted by a hairless, red-faced stranger, she had screamed and hidden her face in her mother's apron, refusing to accept that this was her dad. Her dad was a handsome, smiling man with a moustache and a blue uniform, who came to visit sometimes bringing treats in his pockets – not this ugly silent monster. A few weeks later her mother had unthinkingly opened the fire door on the range, and Luke had run screaming from the kitchen. Linda had been so scared that she was relieved when he stayed in his room from then on, and over the years her habit of ignoring him had become set. The new Luke who had begun to emerge in the last two weeks was no longer frightening, but he was an almost total stranger, and Linda was horribly afraid he would embarrass her in front of her friends.

For his part, Luke had found the isolation of Pinetree Farm a mixed blessing. The staff at the hospital had treated him and his fellow burn victims like any other patients, even when they resembled alien creatures with tubes of skin snaking from one part of their bodies to another. Doctor McIndoe and his team had even organised a social life for their long-term patients, and East Grinstead had been known as the town that never stared. The contrast when Luke got off the train in Thambay and mothers hurried their children away had been a dreadful shock, and he had sunk into a depression which had seldom lifted until now.

He was outside the door when Linda's words struck another blow, but he pinned a brave smile on his face before he came into the kitchen and sat down in front of his bowl of porridge. "You let me worry about people staring, Linda." He looked across the table until Linda was forced to meet his eyes. "I can't do anything about my face, so everyone will just have to get used to it."

Linda scowled and ate her porridge in sullen silence. Daisy

opened her mouth to admonish her, but Luke shook his head and she turned away biting her lip. After eight years of letting her shield him from the world, Luke was coming out of his depression, and she must stand aside and let him fight his own battles.

Fifteen minutes later eight children squeezed onto the worn leather seats of the Finch's big pre-war Rover. Clara, Fleur and Linda claimed the front seat while Joey, Nico, Ben, Davy and Frank Coppin from the neighbouring farm jostled for space in the back until Luke said, "Settle down, crew, unless you want to walk."

"Sorry, sir," Joey said.

Linda swivelled round to stare at him. "Why d'you call him sir?"

"Because we're his crew, like he said, and he's in charge," Joey said. "I wouldn't expect a mere girl to understand that."

"My dad was a Pilot Officer, not just an ordinary airman," said Linda haughtily.

"We know that, stupid!" said Joey. "That's how he got shot down and his face all burned. But he's our officer now, and he saved Davy's life, so he's a hero twice over."

"Oh," Linda said in a small voice. She'd never thought of Dad as a hero before, but if Joey Smith said he was one, perhaps Dad's burned face wasn't that embarrassing after all. She looked at him properly for the first time in years – the moustache that used to tickle her cheeks with butterfly kisses had gone, but the eyes in his shiny face were the same ones she remembered. She tried a smile on for size and said, "We'd better get going or we'll be late."

"Righty-ho!" Luke said breezily, and swung the starter handle.

*** 

Davy had flatly refused to allow his parents to take him to school for his first day. "I know all about it from Ben," he'd said. "And I won't be treated like a baby." Even so, he walked very close to Clara as she took him through the crowded playground. Ben vanished to catch up with his old friends while Clara marched Davy straight inside.

The classroom with its low tables and small chairs was a strange new experience, and Davy's nostrils flared to take in the unfamiliar smells. The walls under the high windows were hung with bright pictures, and he was looking at those when a thin lady with glasses bustled in and said, "Hello, Clara – how are you getting on at secondary school?"

"Fine thanks, Mrs Middleton. This is my little brother Davy who's starting today, but I've got to run or I'll cop it for being late."

Mrs Middleton shook Davy's hand solemnly. "I'm pleased to meet you, David."

Clara gave the teacher Davy's dinner money and dropped a quick kiss on his head. "I've got to go now, the others are waiting. Mr Luke will be back this afternoon to get you, so be sure and behave yourself," and she was gone.

Panic flashed across Davy's face, but Mrs Middleton was well-used to dealing with children and she said briskly, "Well now, David, let's get you settled in. Mr Crossman tells me you know Rita Daly, so I've put you next to her." Two minutes later a bell clanged and twenty-four other children streamed into the room – Davy's first day at school had begun.

Luke dropped his other passengers off at the gates of the secondary school just as the bell rang. Joey and Frank ran off to the seniors' entrance, leaving Clara, Fleur and Nico to tag onto the end of their line. Fleur turned reluctantly into Form 1C's room, then Nico and Clara pushed the door of 2A open. Spotting two empty desks, they aimed for them with their heads down, but the shrill voice of Sally Biggins yelled, "Look out – the pikeys are back!" and they were drowned in a sea of cat-calls. Nico slid into the chair nearest to the door, Clara bagging the desk behind him – their instincts for marking escape routes had been well-honed. The few friendships they had made last year appeared to have faded in their absence, and 2A's collective antagonism washed over them in a dirty tide of spiteful remarks.

The second bell rang, a wave of silence spread out from the door and the teacher barked, "Settle down, 2A!" After a minute's scramble for places and the scrape of thirty chairs, the form-room was quiet enough for him to call the register, slotting Nicolas Perez and Clara Smith in without comment, and they noted with sinking hearts that the familiar litany contained exactly the same names as last year's Form 1A.

No-one in Fleur's new form knew who she was, but her blonde beauty earned their attention the moment she entered the room. Last year's most popular girl decided in a heartbeat that taking her under her wing was preferable to rivalry, and beckoned Fleur over. "You're new here, aren't you? I'm Julie – what's your name?"

Fleur switched on a beaming smile and answered simply, "Fleur."

"That's French for flower – are you French?"

Fleur picked up her cue like a professional. "I was born in France, but my mother was killed by the Germans."

Several girls gasped and Julie cried, "Oh you poor thing!"

When the second bell rang and the class spread out to claim their desks for the year, Julie took the favoured one by the radiator, ousting another girl to make room for Fleur beside her – this blonde newcomer with the romantically tragic history must be kept close.

When the classes spilled outside for the morning break, Nico abandoned Clara as soon as he spotted Ted Daly, so she scuttled to a bare space by the wall and looked round for Fleur. When she saw her coming down the steps she waved, but Fleur affected not to see her and Clara's arm dropped limply to her side. There was nobody else to talk to, and the aura of distress that surrounded her acted as a barrier in this place where everyone knew somebody. She was glad when the short break ended and she could hide her despair in her books.

At dinner-time the story was much the same. When Clara saw Fleur chatting animatedly to her new friends, the carrot pie and over-cooked cabbage turned to sawdust in her mouth, and she couldn't even look at her semolina pudding. A smaller girl beside her asked, "Ain't you going to eat that?" and swapped plates swiftly – this was the only meal she got all day and she wasn't going to miss any opportunity for seconds.

Outside after dinner Sally Biggins stirred up trouble again. The feud between the Smith and Biggins families had lasted ever since Albie beat Wally Biggins in a playground fight thirty years earlier, and although Wally had died in France he came from a large family. Skipping up to Clara, Sally pulled her plait and scampered back into a giggle of girls. "Come on then, pikey girl," she taunted. "Put a curse on me."

When Clara said nothing, Sally nudged another girl forward saying, "Go on – you're not afraid of gypsies, are you?" Another tug on her plait, harder this time, and Clara lashed out, catching the second girl a glancing blow on her chest.

"Did you see that? She bashed my bosom!" the girl howled, clutching herself dramatically, and the gang pounced. They pushed Clara from one pair of arms to another, never giving her time to catch her balance between shoves, pinching and scratching her and spitting in her face and hair while she sobbed uncontrollably, helpless against so many.

Then she heard Joey roar, "What the hell's going on here?" The girls scattered, but he caught the ringleader. "Sally Biggins – I might have guessed. You leave my sister alone or there'll be real trouble."

"You take your dirty pikey hands off me, Joey Smith, or I'll tell my dad."

"Next visiting day, I suppose?"

Sally turned pink and flung her arm out of Joey's grip –she didn't think anyone knew her dad was in jail – and then she saw Fleur standing a few yards away with Julie. "Don't know what you're staring at, Fleur Smith – you're another of 'em," she spat and flounced off.

Julie's eyes narrowed with suspicion. "Fleur? What did Sally mean? You're not a gypsy, are you?"

"No, of course not," Fleur said but then Joey called, "Fleur – take your sister to the cloakroom to get clean," and her lie was in tatters. In a desperate effort to save something from the wreck, Fleur said, "I'm only adopted," but the damage was done.

She washed the spit from Clara's hair in a furious silence that for Clara was far worse than Sally's jibes, and when Fleur returned to 1C's form-room she found her satchel had been moved to the least favourite desk, right in front of the teacher's podium.

***

Luke had spent the morning sorting out an unexplained but suspicious oversight at the Town Hall that had resulted in Bert's name not being listed as a candidate. He had taken shameless advantage of the Clerk's shocked reaction when confronted by his ravaged face, and when he went round to Bert's at dinnertime to discuss the campaign he said, "I reckon this face of mine is an asset we should make the most of. Many people will be too embarrassed to refuse when I ask them to put up a poster."

"And if they've got my name in their windows they'll most likely vote for me," said Bert.

"Exactly. I'm not saying your manifesto isn't a good one, because it is, but if we can just sway a few floating voters I reckon we've got a fighting chance."

"I ain't looking forward to Wednesday's meeting," Bert confessed, glancing at his wife. "The thought of standing up in the Church Hall making a speech gives me the willies."

"You'll be fine, love," said Alice loyally. "Your brother Billy's going to mind the hall with Albie."

Bert brightened a little at this reminder. "It's handy having a policeman in the family, and Dad'll be there too – it's just the speechifying that bothers me."

"Keep it short and to the point," Luke advised. "Ten minutes at the outside, then answer questions – I'll ask a couple to get the ball rolling. Have you planned your speech yet?"

"Can't seem to get it right in me head, and writing was never me strong point – would you take a gander at it?"

Luke perused the scrappy child's notebook in silence while Bert watched him anxiously.

"It's rubbish, ain't it?" said the would-be Councillor.

Luke put the notebook down on the table and smoothed it with his hands, well aware that Bert relied on him to tell the truth. "Your opening remarks are good but the rest is a mess – you've covered your major points several times over. Have you got any postcards?" Alice rummaged in a drawer and produced a packet of them. "Right," said Luke, taking out his fountain pen. "You don't write every word down – you'll only stand there and read them which won't keep their attention. Just make notes, like this," and he wrote on the top cards in big capitals: NO PREFABS ON REC – GILCHRIST'S GIFT TO TOWN – FOOTBALL CLUB – TOWN FAIR. He held them up. "See? They're just reminders for yourself. Make one card for each subject, then all you have to do is talk."

"And that's all? You make it sound easy."

"You're an eloquent man, Bert – I've heard you holding forth to your customers. Just talk to the man at the back of the hall as if he was in your shop."

Leaving a much happier Bert to write out more cue cards, Luke took his courage by the scruff of the neck and spent a couple of hours knocking on doors to distribute leaflets. After stammering his way along the first street he found his confidence growing, and by the time he collected the children from school he had covered all the streets around the Market Square. Albie had promised to help the next day, but Luke had managed this first foray alone.

During the following two days Luke and Albie visited the rest of the town delivering leaflets. While Albie braved the sprawling council estate, Luke's obvious war service gained him entrance to the old fishing cottages by the harbour and to the big houses on Cliff Road alike.

On the Wednesday evening Luke drove into town with his father and brothers and George in the Rover, while Albie borrowed the farm truck to take the entire male population of the gypsy camp to support Bert's launch into politics. The Church Hall was packed, but Albie and Luke went down the side alley, where they found Bert smoking furiously.

"I'm a bag of nerves," he said. "I don't reckon I can do this."

"Yes you can," Albie said, and Luke added, "What you need is a bit of Dutch courage."

"Have you got some?" Bert asked eagerly, so Luke checked there were no press photographers lurking and allowed him one swig from a hip-flask. It seemed to do the trick, because when the church clock struck eight, Bert squared his shoulders and walked onto the platform to face his public with remarkable aplomb.

The cue cards enabled him to speak from the heart and his audience listened attentively, their murmurs of approval and the occasional 'hear! hear!' giving him encouragement. Mindful of Luke's instructions he restricted his speech to ten minutes before answering a few questions briefly and honestly.

Albie, who had chosen to prop up a wall halfway down one side, was just thinking how well Bert was doing when a voice from a few rows in front of him shouted, "Never mind the bloody football club – we want prefabs!" and then a dozen men were on their feet chanting, "We want prefabs!" When Albie and Ricardo closed in on the obvious ringleader, another group nearer the back unfurled a banner exhorting, "VOTE FOR SMYTHE" in bold blue letters, and the chanting increased in volume. Bert and Luke, trying their best to restore order, couldn't make themselves heard over the uproar.

Bert's younger brother Constable William Daly, who had been standing in the porch, flung the swing doors open and blew his whistle. In the confined space of the hall it was deafening, and in the moment of silence that ensued the troublemakers were overcome. Albie's forearm closed painfully round the ringleader's windpipe, Josef and Ricardo captured another man each, and Pete and Brian Finch lifted two more from the rear seats. John Daly confiscated the banner and gave it to his younger son. "Gerald Smythe's at the back of this, Billy."

"A banner's not proof of that, sir," replied Constable Daly solemnly, but then one of Bert's supporters caught a man trying to sneak out of a side door and shouted, "This bloke works for Smythe!"

"They all do," said another man and within minutes all the troublemakers had been removed to the lobby. A reporter licked his pencil and asked, "What you going to do with them, Constable?"

Constable Daly looked slowly along the line. "I could arrest them all for disturbing the peace," he said with ponderous deliberation, and the men shrank visibly – they had come for the sake of their jobs and the promise of a pint after the meeting, not to get arrested. Only the ringleader said belligerently, "It's a public meeting – we've got a right to be 'ere if we want."

Constable Daly looked at him. "A right to come and listen, yes, same as everyone else, but not to incite a riot." In the silence that followed, Billy heard Bert getting back into his stride, and the reporter slipped back into the hall to complete his write-up. Billy decided to go easy on these miscreants for Bert's sake. "All right, you lot – I'll let you off with a caution this time." As the first man edged towards the outer doors, Constable Daly added a warning. "I've made a note of your names. If there's any more trouble you'll all be spending the night in the cells."

***

Gerald Smythe was livid when he saw the headline on the front page of Friday's Courier: 'NEAR RIOT AT LABOUR MEETING' and read the article that followed, coupling his name with the unruly behaviour and singing the praises of his opponent. He threw the paper down in a fury, cursing the plan that had gone so horribly wrong and which had, without doubt, dealt his campaign a mortal blow.

## CHAPTER SEVEN – BULLIES

"I've got a tummy-ache," Clara complained the next day, clutching her stomach.

"Me too," Fleur said, but they should have known that they couldn't get a lie past their mother, who simply asked, "What happened at school yesterday?"

"Nothing much," Clara said. "Just the usual gypsy stuff – we didn't get it at our winter school."

"Half that school's Roma in the winter months," Albie said. "You're the only ones in Thambay. Want me to have a word with Miss Briggs?"

"No!" Both girls spoke at once, falling over themselves to avert that ultimate humiliation. "We'll be all right."

The mere presence of Joey, who was built like his father, was enough to prevent another playground attack on the Smith girls, but in their classrooms it was a different matter. Nico did his best to shield Clara but he was a target too, and for the remainder of that week they both endured numerous sly kicks from passing shoes, or nudges that jarred their elbows and sent their pens skittering across previously neat pages, the whole campaign orchestrated by Sally Biggins, and the undercurrent of seething prejudice made every day a trial.

Fleur fared slightly better because the boys in her Form 1C were mesmerised by her silky white-blonde hair and startling bluebell eyes. A troop of adoring boys acted as a bodyguard by default – any other girl who wanted to attract their attention couldn't afford to be overtly hostile to Fleur. But boys weren't allowed in the girls' cloakroom, and that was where Sally and Julie took their revenge.

All week Clara and Fleur had hidden among the coats in the cloakroom rather than risk confronting the crowds at break times, but on Friday the greasy fried fish dinner sent them dashing to the toilets. As they sat in adjoining cubicles they could hear other girls coming and going in the cloakroom beyond, and stayed put until the sounds ceased. Clara was about to open her door when she felt as if ice had been poured down her back and knew instinctively Sally was out there. "Wait," she whispered to Fleur, but Sally said loudly, "Cor – what a stink!" Her face appeared over Clara's door. "What a surprise! It's the Smith girls – have you been eating hedgehog again, Clara?"

Clara flung her door open so fast that Sally fell off, and Fleur exploded out of her own door at the same moment – they each got one good kick into their tormentors before they were overwhelmed by a dozen girls.

"The bitch kicked me!" Sally screamed, and spat in Clara's face, smearing it in with her hand, so Clara bit her. Fleur scratched Julie's arm so Julie punched her in the stomach, causing her to throw up all over Julie's new skirt. The other girls darted in with mean little twisted pinches and Chinese burns, then Sally looked at the tooth-marks on the ball of her thumb and pronounced sentence. "Hang them."

In that awful moment Clara was sure they were going to die. "Joey!" she screamed at the top of her voice.

"He's miles away," Sally sneered. "He won't hear you."

"You mustn't kill us!" Fleur cried.

Julie said, "Sally – we can't murder them."

"I didn't mean kill them – just hang them up by their stupid plaits."

Relieved that they weren't expected actually to kill their captives, Sally and Julie's gang embraced the lesser crime with enthusiasm. They dragged Clara and Fleur out to the cloakroom, tied each pair of plaits into a loop with their ribbons, and suspended the sisters from coat-hooks.

The pain was instant and unbelievable. Clara's mind clouded briefly, but then she found the strength to scream again, distracting her tormentors while she grabbed the wooden framework and took the weight off her hair. Through swimming eyes she saw Fleur do the same, and felt her sister's pain recede along with her own as they got their feet onto the bench. Clara had almost un-hooked her hair when Sally kicked her feet and jerked her off the bench again. Across the aisle Julie was pushing Fleur from side to side like a pendulum, and all the time there was that awful chant – "Pikey girls – pikey girls!"

Then Joey burst through the door with Frank and Nico behind him. The two senior boys threw girls aside to lift Clara and Fleur down, and Sally and her friends headed for the door, only to be confronted by Nico holding them closed.

Sally snarled, "Move aside, titch," grabbing a fistful of his jumper while Julie tugged his arms, but a big hand yanked each of them back by their hair.

"Mind my perm!" Sally shrieked.

Joey's answering laugh would haunt her nightmares for weeks. "Your perm is the least of your worries. I told you to leave my sisters alone or there'd be big trouble. You've not heard the last of this. Let them out now, Nico."

Sally and Julie and their cronies scuttled out to the playground, grateful to have suffered no worse consequences than two ruined hairdos, but one girl said, "You've really gone and done it now, Sally Biggins – you've brought a gypsy curse on us all."

Each form met in its own room for the last period of the week, and although 1C was very quiet, nothing out of the ordinary happened. In 2A the teacher congratulated himself on a trouble-free first week, although she noticed a distinct aura of danger around the two gypsy children, as if some threat lurked beneath their calm exteriors.

Luke noticed a similar suppressed atmosphere in the car on the way home, reminding him of the air in the briefing room before a bombing raid. When the Rover halted at Pinetree Farm, the children spilled out quickly and headed home, leaving Linda alone with Luke.

"They never even said goodbye," she said, sounding so

forlorn that Luke put an arm round her. To his delight she reciprocated by sliding her arm round his middle.

Luke swallowed a lump in his throat and said, "Let's see what Mum's made for us – she was baking when I left."

Seeing her daughter and husband enter the kitchen together brought a lump to Daisy's throat too, but she refrained from comment. Linda swiped a jam tart and ran upstairs to get changed while her parents shared a pot of tea. Pouring two cups with an unsteady hand, Daisy plucked up the courage to say, "I've stripped your bed for the wash, Luke – shall I make it up again or…?" She left the question hanging in the pastry-perfumed air.

Luke picked up his cue. "Don't worry about it, Daisy – I'll come in with you." His hand slid across the oil-cloth to cover hers. "Don't expect too much, love – those flames came right up to the top of my legs."

Daisy's smile remained in place though her heart ached for the suffering he had endured. "I just want a cuddle – anything else is up to you."

Luke's eyes softened in a smile his mouth couldn't match, and he stroked her hair. "We'll see how it goes, shall we? One step at a time."

***

Nico and the girls were only halfway through the pine woods when Maria met them and swept both her daughters into her arms. "I was washing the dishes with Olivia when we saw you – those horrible girls!"

"Oh Mama, it was awful!" Fleur wailed. "If Joey and Frank hadn't rescued us they could have killed us."

Maria's hands flew to her stomach and Clara hissed, "Shut up, Fleur."

"Well, they could have."

"You mustn't say things like that in front of the baby."

"Oh God – more superstitious rubbish! We only got bullied because you're a gypsy and I'm fed up with it – I'm going back to Linda's."

As she ran off, Nico said, "I rescued you too."

"Yes you did. Was it you heard us scream?" replied Clara.

"No – Joey did, but I don't know how – he was way over in the science building."

Maria tousled Nico's hair and said, "Of course he heard – they're his sisters – but you were a hero just the same. Now you can do something else to help. Go and cut a handful of thin stems from that willow behind Grandad George's cottage – I have an idea."

At Pinetree Farm, Fleur barely stopped to say hello to Luke and Daisy before running up the stairs and bursting unannounced into Linda's bedroom. Once again she found her young friend sitting at the dressing-table, and once again Linda was the delighted audience for Fleur's anger at the world in general and her sister in particular.

"Sit here and I'll brush your hair," Linda offered. "It'll calm you down." As she brushed Fleur's silk-straight hair with long, soothing strokes she said, "I think you should go in for the May Queen contest – you're much prettier than Wendy Jones who won last year."

Fleur preened in the triple mirror of the kidney-shaped dressing-table – Linda's open adoration was balm to her soul after being ostracised and then attacked by every other girl she knew. "We've never been here in May before. D'you really think I could win?"

Linda gathered the fall of blonde hair, twisted it and held it on the top of Fleur's head. "Of course you could. You'd look lovely in a crown of flowers, and I bet your mum could make you a frock – or you could wear one of her long skirts."

Fleur scowled into the mirror. "Not flipping likely! I will *not* dress up as a gypsy."

\*\*\*

That evening it rained – only a typical April shower, but it was enough to break up the fireside group early. The men trooped across the lane for a comfortable smoke in George's kitchen, Joey went to Coppin Farm to do his homework with Frank, and Maria lay on the bed in her wagon while Clara and Fleur did theirs at the little table.

"What are the names of those girls?" Maria asked with a nonchalance that didn't fool Clara. "You're not going to the school. Mama – you'll only make it worse."

"I know – that headmistress doesn't like us – but do you know who they all are?"

"Oh yes – we know."

Maria swung her legs off the bed. "Leave your homework for now and get that bunch of willow that Nico cut."

Mystified, the girls fetched the slender willow stalks, still damp from the rain, and under Maria's watchful eyes twisted them into eleven bracelets, each one woven with a specific bully in mind. It was Fleur who dared to ask, "Are we weaving a curse?"

"Not a curse, Fleur, though they might think so. What you're doing is taking away their power to harm you."

"With these bracelets? That's stupid – they won't work," Fleur said, but Clara could feel the hatred seeping from the tips of her fingers as she worked. "It won't hurt to try. Just think about what they did to us and twist it into the willow."

\*\*\*

On Monday morning Luke was surprised at the alacrity with which Clara and Fleur jumped out of the car. Linda had heard about the cloakroom drama from Fleur and recounted it in gruesome detail over Sunday dinner, and he drove away feeling pleased that their traumatic experience had had no lasting effect.

With Joey standing guard outside and Nico in the corridor, the girls placed a bracelet in the centre of each relevant desk, slipping outside again just before the bell to join the queue. In Form 1C Fleur walked into a ring of hostile faces.

"What's this?" Julie demanded, shoving her bracelet under

Fleur's nose. "Trying to worm your way back in?"

Fleur had rehearsed a contrite expression with Linda and now she switched it on like a born actress. "I just wanted to say sorry for fibbing to you all about being a gypsy."

Julie peered at her suspiciously, but she was a bit ashamed of the way they had let the situation get out of control on Friday. She looked at the bracelet again – it was quite pretty in a countrified kind of way – so she slipped the willow knot onto her wrist. "All right – we'll forget all about it." The other girls immediately put their own bracelets on, the form-mistress entered the room, and Fleur slid into her front desk hiding a triumphant smile.

When Sally Biggins saw the bracelet on her desk she took an involuntary step back, her expression as horrified as if a snake was coiled there rather than a twist of willow. "Where did that come from?" She pointed an accusatory finger at Clara. "If this is another of your pikey tricks you'll pay for it."

"Well, I'm not scared of her gypsy magic," said Wendy Jones, putting one on her own wrist. Sally reacted predictably. "I never said I was scared," she claimed, and slipped her bracelet on. When the day's lessons began, all the willow bracelets that had spent the night outside in the rain were drying out on their new owners' wrists.

By the mid-morning break every first- and second-year knew what had happened to Clara and Fleur. The majority believed the Smith girls were trying to buy themselves back into favour with the bracelets, but by lunchtime the grapevine was heavy with a different theory.

Form 2A was the first to report something disturbing. They had all handed in their Maths homework, which the teacher marked while the class worked on a problem he had chalked on the blackboard. After a while he tapped a ruler on his desk for attention. "Six of you have got your homework completely wrong. This in itself is not unusual, but what strikes me as suspicious is that all six have given identical answers." He wrote Sally Biggins' and Wendy Jones' names on the board together with four others. "These pupils will remain after school to redo the exercise under supervision." Despite their protestations of innocence, Sally and her gang had been given detention.

In Geography, none of Julie's group could remember a single item from the list of American exports they had memorised over the weekend, and they too had to stay behind after school to copy the list a hundred times each.

In the Science lab Wendy Jones' Bunsen burner wouldn't light, her bench partner dropped a Petri dish, and Sally's entire experiment went up in flames, singeing her eyebrows and carefully waved fringe, while at the same time Julie's netball team was losing by seven goals.

As soon as the morning's lessons were over the recipients of the Smith girls' bracelets tried to remove them, and that set the rumour-mill seething like a cauldron. The prettily-entwined knots of willow wouldn't come off. The girls tugged and twisted until their skin was red and sore, but the innocent-seeming little gifts had shrunk as they dried and were now too tight. Sally was the first to voice the thought in each girl's mind. "You put a curse on 'em, didn't you?" She grabbed Clara's single plait but dropped it again with a shriek and said, with genuine fear in her voice, "And now my hand's bleeding." Julie and the other girls crowded round to gawp at the spots of blood.

"It's only a few drops – this time," Clara said sweetly, then she looped her arm through her sister's and strolled over to join the boys.

"That worked like a dream," Nico said, and Joey tapped his fist on their shoulders in delight at the success of their plan, but Frank looked genuinely worried. "Did you really curse them?" he muttered to Clara.

"What makes you think I can?"

"That blood was real enough."

Clara laughed with genuine amusement for the first time in a week. Glancing round to make sure they couldn't be overheard, she confided, "I've got typical Roma hair, Frank – so thick and curly you can plait a bramble into it without it showing."

***

There wasn't a bracelet in sight the next day – every one of them had been cut off the instant the wearer reached home – but doubts lingered about the power of gypsy curses and the other girls gave Clara and Fleur a wide berth. When they climbed into the car beside Linda that afternoon, she asked immediately, "How did it go today?"

"Julie practically curtsied when I came through the door," Fleur said.

"Oh come off it!" Clara scoffed. "You told me she ignored you."

"You weren't there – she was definitely respectful."

"What – as if you were a princess?" Linda began, but Fleur shot her a warning glance and for once Linda interpreted it correctly. "Well, I believe you – come round later and tell me."

## CHAPTER EIGHT – MAY QUEEN

On Wednesday Fleur and Linda sneaked out of their respective schools at dinner-time and met in Market Square.

"Did you eat your dinner?" Fleur asked. "I was too excited."

"I had to eat mine or Miss would've noticed," Linda said, taking Fleur's hand as they tiptoed into the imposing entrance of the Town Hall.

"Where do we go?" Fleur whispered, awed by the faded grandeur of the lobby.

"Town Clerk," Linda whispered back. "Mum told me."

"You didn't tell your mum?"

"Of course not! But she wouldn't have listened anyway – she's gone all soppy over Dad."

"Ssh! Tell me later – this is the door."

The Town Clerk only just heard their timid knock and barked, "Come in!" He had been about to take his lunch-break and wasn't too pleased to see a pair of children poke their noses round the doorframe. "Yes?"

"Please sir, are you the Town Clerk?" asked Linda, holding Fleur's arm tightly to stop her running away.

"That's what it says on the door, child, so I must be, mustn't I? What do you want?"

"We want to put Fleur's name on the list."

"What list?"

"The May Queen list, of course!"

"Brought your mums, have you?"

"Didn't know we had to," said Linda cheekily. "Does it say so in the rules?"

The Clerk wasn't sure what it said in the rules about mothers, and besides that he was hungry. "I don't suppose it matters, seeing as your mums will make your costumes – what are your names?"

"It's only Fleur who's doing it," said Linda sadly. "I'm not old enough."

Fleur's name went on the register, but before they parted in Market Square she said, "I've just thought – no-one will vote for me anyway – not for a gypsy."

"But you're not one, are you? You don't even look like one – they'll vote for you."

That afternoon Linda told all her friends that Fleur's dad had found her in France and she wasn't a real gypsy. Those girls told their big sisters, and by Thursday half the schoolchildren in Thambay believed that the gypsies had stolen Fleur from her real parents. The daring move of registering her on the May Queen list without permission only added to her mystique.

At morning break on Friday, Fleur was surrounded by a crowd of fans, and when Clara demanded to know what was going on, Fleur told her but swore her to secrecy. "I want to tell Mama myself."

Fleur really believed she meant to, but Maria was always busy – helping Davy learn his letters, teaching Grandad to drive the cart – and Fleur couldn't seem to find the right moment to tell her. What was more important was deciding what she should wear for the voting on Saturday morning. The other girls would be wearing their best Sunday frocks, but Fleur only had her gingham school dress or the clothes she wore on the farm – a plain blouse and a pair of Joey's cut-down trousers. All she could hope was that her waist-length satiny hair would outshine the other girls. With this in mind she went to Pinetree Farm after school on Friday for Linda to wash it with Daisy's perfumed shampoo. While it dried they searched Linda's wardrobe, but everything was too short until Linda delved in the back of the wardrobe and brought out an old frock of her mother's.

"I knew it was here somewhere! This is the same colour as your eyes," she said, holding it against Fleur, and after they had pinched in the waist with a little white apron it was a perfect ankle-length on her tall figure.

As she admired her reflection in Linda's mirror Fleur said, "I can't go to market in this."

But Linda, who was revelling in the intrigue, had the answer to that as well. "I'll hide it in my basket and you can change in the tea shop cloakroom."

Meanwhile Clara was sitting in George's kitchen with a cup of tea, picking through the tin of broken biscuits for her favourites. George watched a soft shower watering his seeds and let Clara settle before he asked, "Summat's bothering you, pet – want to tell your old grandad?"

"Fleur's going in for the May Queen contest tomorrow."

"That's nice, lovey – why aren't you doing it too?"

"I'm not as pretty as Fleur – and besides, it feels dangerous, but I don't know why." She pulled the tin closer and concentrated on finding two matching biscuit halves. George waited patiently, thinking that Clara looked exactly like her dad had at that age, struggling to find words to explain something he didn't understand. Albie had wanted to know why his first mum had rejected him, but nothing in Clara's life could be that awful – even so she looked as if she was carrying a hundredweight of spuds on her narrow shoulders. He took the tin away and held her hands, unconsciously echoing the words he'd used to Albie all those years ago, "Come on, lass, spit it out."

Just as Albie had done, Clara stared at the tattoo on George's wrist, and suddenly she *was* Albie, sitting with George in the tearoom on the pier, shivering in a thin shirt and ragged trousers, ribs bruised from a beating inflicted by Mum's latest boyfriend. "Mum says he don't want no kid old enough to earn a living."

George's grip tightened on Clara's arm almost painfully – those had been Albie's words, spoken in Albie's voice. "What did you say?" he asked sharply.

Clara snapped back to the present. "Fleur shouldn't do it,

Grandad, something bad will happen. Not only that – I'm worried about Mama too. I keep dreaming she's fading away a bit at a time until all that's left is the baby."

Fear clutched at George's heart – if Clara had inherited the gypsy sight this sounded serious – but he forced a smile. "I expect she's just tired. I'll speak to your dad about making her rest more, but you don't want to let a few dreams worry you." He heaved his elderly body upright. "Look, the rain's stopped – I've got summat to show you."

In a far corner of the garden, near where he had planted his rhubarb, George had unearthed the foundations of two flint walls, which linked the garden walls to form a ten-foot square. "This is a perfect place for a compost heap," he said. "Look at that." He pointed to some blackened flints. "I'll lay odds I'll find a hearthstone when I dig further down. Someone must have lived here once – not very big for a cottage, was it?"

Clara picked up a shard of pottery and knew at once Grandad was right – a whole family had lived here. As she rubbed the dirt off the brown glazed scrap it became an entire teapot in her mind's eye, and she felt the sorrow of the woman who had dropped it. She began totting up how many months she would have to save to buy another, and the intensity of the despair she felt frightened her so much that she dropped the shard and grabbed George's hand. "Come on, Grandad – Mama says there's enough supper for everyone," and for the remainder of the evening she refused to worry about Mama or about Fleur, telling herself that her dreams were just dreams, not supernatural warnings.

\*\*\*

Early on Saturday morning Maria, Lydia and Olivia loaded a cart with a trestle table and boxes filled with their papier-mâché trays, wooden toys and willow baskets, and drove into Thambay. In Market Square they set up their stall next to the Pinetree Farm stall from which Ruth Finch and her three daughters-in-law sold spring greens and cottage cheese, salad and cakes, fruit pies and bottles of cloudy cider. Other farmers were there too, and the fishermen whose boats filled the small harbour came to sell freshly-caught fish.

Professional market traders had also come down from London on the early train. They set up their awnings with lightning speed and attached washing-lines from which they suspended cheap clothes and fabrics. Others sold soap by the ounce which they cut from large blocks, gaudy factory-produced sweets, and a variety of black-market goods when Constable William Daly was looking elsewhere.

All the stalls were doing a brisk trade when Luke drove the Rover into town with Albie and the children. While Luke and Albie wandered among the crowds, talking to the stallholders and shoppers about the Council election, the older boys went to spend their pocket-money on the pier. Ben and Davy had to be satisfied with Albie's promise to take them later, because he would never forget the day when Luke Finch, then only eight years old, had nearly drowned off that pier, and he didn't trust his two small sons to be any more sensible.

By midday a group of men had set up a stage by the back steps of the Town Hall, and the stallholders hurried to fold their trestles and put away their unsold goods before the twelfth stroke of the church clock died away. Then a fanfare blared out from speakers and the Mayor himself, wearing a dark suit and his Chain of Office, emerged from the Town Hall and tapped the microphone. "Ladies and gentlemen, boys and girls, your attention please!"

The buzz of chatter died down to an excited murmur as everyone crowded round the platform, and late-comers hurried from the adjoining streets to swell the throng. The Mayor held up a sheet of paper. "These girls have been entered for the May Queen Competition – will they please come onstage as their names are called. Doris Peters!" Doris, a bubbly blonde girl, marched confidently up the steps and waved gaily while her large family cheered and whistled.

"Cynthia Barco!" Cynthia was thin and dark with olive skin inherited from a Portuguese sailor ancestor, and her supporters clapped more sedately as she took her place next to Doris. Cynthia had a sweet smile and Maria decided that Cynthia would get her vote. "Mandy and Sadie Holroyd!" The twin daughters of a Brigadier mounted the platform together and stood side-by-side wearing extremely frilly party frocks. They looked like two overblown pink peonies. "Heaven knows how we're supposed to choose between these two!" the Mayor remarked, waiting for the ripple of laughter to die down before announcing, "We have one more entry who only signed up this week – Fleur Smith, where are you?"

Fleur stood at the back of the crowd with pounding heart and sweating palms, wishing she was anywhere but here. When the clock had started striking midday she had nipped into the café cloakroom with Linda and pulled the blue dress on over her shorts and blouse in a panicky rush. There had only been time for Linda to drag a comb through her hair and tie the apron-string in a limp bow. Sure she looked a mess, Fleur started to back away but Linda gave her a shove and shouted, "She's over here – we can't get through!" On a great gale of laughter the crowd parted to create a passageway through which Fleur had to walk right across the square.

Albie met her at the stage to help her up the steps saying, "You're a sly one, ain't you?"

Joey, Nico and Frank whistled and cheered as loudly as Doris's family had done, while Ben and Davy yelled from the wagon, but Maria was shocked. "Did you know about this?" she asked Clara.

"She promised she'd tell you."

"Well, she didn't." Maria said, forcing her hands together to applaud the daughter who had betrayed her sister's trust.

Voting was by popular acclaim – not the most reliable way of judging because there were politics involved even in this minor election, and those people with the strongest views often had the loudest voices. Nevertheless, something about the gentle smile of little Cynthia Barco touched more hearts than Maria's and she was elected May Queen of Thambay.

"I promised Ben and Davy I'd take them on the pier," Albie said to Maria.

"I'll come too," Clara said, and Fleur tugged her apron strings into a knot in her haste to go with them.

"Help me get this undone, Mama," she begged.

"You'll wear it till bedtime, my girl, to remind you how badly you've behaved."

"What've I done wrong?" Fleur cried, tightening the knot further as she struggled. "There's no reason I couldn't have been May Queen!"

"No reason at all, Fleur, and if you'd asked me I'd have helped you, but you went behind my back even though you promised your sister you'd tell me."

Fleur finally managed to undo the knot, dragged the blue dress off and flung it into the cart, yelling defiantly, "Clara's not my sister and you're not my real mother. I'm not a gypsy – I'm not even English!" and she hared off down a side street.

Maria slumped against the cart looking stricken. "Did you hear what she said to me, Grandmama?"

"You've never kept it secret that she's adopted," Lydia said. "She's at a difficult age and she's probably upset by this new baby – she'll be back when she's calmed down."

"But she too young to be running off alone – she's only twelve."

"In my day, Roma girls were married at her age." Lydia patted Maria's shoulder. "We know everyone in Thambay – what harm can she come to?"

But when Albie came back to the square half an hour later, Fleur was still missing. While Maria sat in the cart in case she returned, Albie and Joey quartered the streets around the Market Square, Clara and Nico searched on every ride on the pier, and Frank ran along the promenade from the recreation ground to the harbour, but there was no sign of the missing child. Finally they called at the Police Station, where Constable Daly did his best to calm the agitated family. He licked his pencil and listed all the places they'd already searched. "She can't have gone far – have you asked all her friends?"

"That's it!" Albie exclaimed. "She'll be at Linda's." But a telephone call revealed that Fleur hadn't gone home in Luke's car and, as Clara pointed out, Fleur didn't have any other friends.

"What, none at all?" the constable asked incredulously.

"None with parents who'd welcome a gypsy in their house," Albie said with certainty.

Ten minutes later Luke arrived at the Police Station bringing his brothers and George, who rounded up friends and neighbours to conduct a systematic hunt. The churchyard, the grounds of the brewery, the timber yard adjoining the furniture factory, even the old public air-raid shelter beneath the promenade – all were thoroughly searched and turned up nothing.

Then the police sergeant enquired at the railway station, and discovered that a girl answering Fleur's description had been seen boarding a London train at one o'clock.

"One o'clock!" Albie roared. "One o'clock! That were two hours ago – she could be anywhere by now!"

The sergeant immediately telephoned London, but one girl at a London terminus would have passed unnoticed in the crowd – the sergeant could do nothing more than report Fleur as missing.

"Dad, will you take Maria and the kids home?" Albie asked.

"Bring her back safe, son," George said, handing over all the money he had in his pocket.

"I'm coming with you," said Joey.

Albie grunted assent, gave Maria a quick hug, saying,

"Look out for her," and they ran to catch the next London train.

# CHAPTER NINE – LONDON

Fleur had fled the Market Square blindly, but instinct had taken her to the seafront, where the Bank Holiday crowds were enjoying the late spring sunshine. For a few minutes she had stomped along the beach, kicking the sand into angry little spurts, but then she thought if she was quick she might persuade Dad to take her on the pier after all. She ran to the entrance but when she got there Dad and the others were already halfway down the boardwalk. Briefly she considered returning to Market Square, but the echo of what she'd said to Mama still rang in her ears and she couldn't force her feet to take her there.

Walking aimlessly, she was caught up in the stream of market traders heading for the station. A fat woman with a pile of boxes was struggling to push her trolley up the slope and when the top box slipped sideways, Fleur caught it.

"Ta, dearie," the woman panted. "This slope's a bugger, and me own kids are never around when I need 'em." She moved on, leaving Fleur with no option but to follow. On the up platform the woman took the box from her with a brief smile and climbed on board.

Fleur stood back and watched with fascination as the crowd ebbed and flowed, searching for empty seats and rounding up stray children. There was an air of urgency and purpose about this milling crowd that surged into Fleur's blood and tingled along her veins like a drug. When doors started slamming and the engine spat out a hiss of steam she turned away with a dragging sense of being abandoned, but a porter held a door open saying, "Come on, girlie, you'll get left behind," and before she knew it she was on the train.

The same woman shifted sideways saying, "Room 'ere for a little'un," and Fleur was wedged into a corner by a window. She regretted her impulse as soon as the carriage door slammed shut, but she was pinned in her seat by one fat thigh, and before she could wriggle free the guard had blown his whistle. The jerk as the train started threw her back into her seat, and it was too late.

Fleur had never been on a train before and, once the initial shock had receded, the smell of dusty upholstery, smoke and soot was intoxicating. She looked at all the framed pictures screwed to the carriage walls, admired the little fringed lampshades and mirrors, wondered how those insubstantial-looking racks could support the weight of bundles they held, and all the while the train was picking up speed. Not even Linda's Dad's car goes this fast, she thought, as fences whizzed past in a blur, fields of cows or sheep and crops approached and vanished in orderly sequence, and glimpses of the sea appeared between hills.

She jumped guiltily when the fat woman asked, "Lose yer Mum, did yer?" She was saved from the necessity of answering when the woman continued, "Lose me own kids every time in that scramble but they always turn up again, more's the pity!" Her vast bosom rippled with a chuckle and she delved into the basket perched on her lap. "Don't s'pose yer fancy a sarnie, do yer?" she said and unfolded some greaseproof paper to reveal a pile of sandwiches.

Fleur had been too nervous to eat breakfast and her stomach rumbled at the sight of food. "Are you sure?" she asked even as her hand reached in to take one.

"Bless 'er 'eart!" her benefactress said to the carriage at large. "Proper little lady, this one."

Stale sandwiches made of sliced shop bread, margarine and fish paste were not Fleur's usual fare but she was too hungry to care – she had wolfed down a whole round before the enormity of what she had done dried her mouth. She had run away – Dad and Mama had no idea where she was – and the food turned to stone in her stomach as the train click-clacked inexorably onward into the unknown.

The stations came and went – Sittingbourne, Rainham,

Rochester – people got on and off, and still Fleur sat frozen with fear. None of the place-names meant anything to her, and if she got off the train she'd lose the sandwich woman who was her only link with home. The fields gave way to houses with back gardens strewn with toys and bikes, or strung with lines of washing. After that came pokey backyards stacked with rusting scrap, the occasional brave little tower of runner beans, and even a garden pond surrounded by windmills and gnomes. The train thumped into a tunnel so suddenly that Fleur whimpered in fright, clutching her friend's hand tightly in the soot-smelly darkness. Then they burst out again into daylight, but the landscape had changed. The buildings were taller, the colours merged into a uniform grey, and the railway tracks criss-crossed bewilderingly like a game of spillikins.

Soon after that, as if there had been an announcement that Fleur hadn't heard, people began gathering their belongings and the carriage suddenly seemed crammed. Fleur's outdoor soul cringed at the wall of backs and bellies, and when someone trod on her toes she tucked her feet up, rubbing the backs of her legs where the upholstery had made her itchy.

"That's right, dearie – you stay put till the rush is over," said the fat woman. When the train slowed and slid into the station, Fleur's protector jumped up with surprising agility to commandeer the doorway and drop the window. A spatter of smuts rushed into Fleur's eyes and while she was wiping them away, the woman flung the door open and jumped onto the platform. With a swift backwards glance and a "Bye, dearie," she hurried off to retrieve her goods and, presumably, her children. Fleur was left alone to watch everyone bustle away, each person obviously knowing exactly where they were going.

Fleur craned her neck through the open window and saw that the station building stretched right across the track. That was a relief – the train was obviously going no further. She hoped it would simply turn round and take her home, so she folded herself into a tight ball in the corner of the seat to wait. Worn out by sheer fright, she was half-asleep when a woman carrying a broom jumped into the carriage and snapped, "What yer doin' 'ere? Out yer get – I've only got ten minutes to clean this train," and she stood with arms akimbo until Fleur stepped nervously over the gap onto the platform.

This was nothing like the bright, friendly station at Thambay, where the station-master took great pride in his flower beds. Vast pillars supported a distant roof that was obscured by smoke and echoed with a hundred hollow sounds – steam hissed, voices shouted, doors slammed, whistles blew, and feet hurried along a dozen or more platforms. Porters pushed trolleys piled high with luggage, pigeons strutted and flapped, people scurried to and fro with set expressions, and for one lost little girl there wasn't a friendly face among them.

Another train pulled in on the opposite platform, so Fleur joined the stream of alighting passengers, thinking it must be from Thambay and searching for a familiar face. Without realising it she was swept through the barrier onto the bewildering concourse beyond.

She drifted with the crowds towards the exit and emerged into daylight, but the noise was just as bad as inside. Big black taxis panted at the kerb while their drivers hurled suitcases into the space where, in a normal car, a front-seat passenger would sit – huge red buses shuddered and belched dragon-breath into Fleur's face, and there were more people rushing about than she had ever imagined could exist. A porter yelled, "Mind yer backs – comin' froo!" But she wasn't quick enough – the corner of his trolley caught her painfully on the calf as it went by and she stumbled.

A hand on her elbow lifted her up and a voice asked, "You OK, me pretty?" Fleur brushed the grit from her hands and one grazed knee and raised swimming eyes to her rescuer, but she didn't trust his gap-toothed leer and jerked free, spun round and ducked back inside the station.

Everywhere she stood she seemed to be in somebody's way, and gradually she was swept by the tide into a backwater beside a café. She saw people sitting by the steamed-up windows drinking cups of strong brown tea, and wished she could have some to dissolve the lump of undigested sandwich, but she didn't possess the courage to go inside and ask whether her unspent pocket-money was enough. The café doors swung open and a waft of heat enveloped her, but when they shut again a draught blew cold round her bare arms and legs. For the first time she noticed the cardigans and jackets other people were wearing – she was horribly conspicuous in her shorts and little blouse.

Edna Green had watched the girl for some time but hesitated to approach her. The girl was a good two or three years younger than the usual pieces of flotsam that washed up on the shores of London, and she lacked that unmistakable air that spoke of abuse. In fact she looked clean and cared-for – her fair skin in those skimpy clothes was undeniably healthy and that sweep of gleaming blonde hair was incredible. There was an innocence in this girl-child that she was reluctant to besmirch. *"Don't be so soft,"* Edna told herself as she sipped her tea. *"If you don't take her someone else will."* But there was another thing that made her uneasy. Although the girl was alone and obviously frightened out of her wits, Edna couldn't shake off the impression that a protective wall of figures surrounded her – dark, tough-looking men and women in old-fashioned clothes. As she gazed at that glorious hair, a ripple passed over it like the stroke of a shadow hand. The girl seemed unaware of her guardians, but Edna was a firm believer in ghosts – she'd be well-advised to let this one go. On the other hand, she wasn't the only one haunting the station on the lookout for likely strays. She saw the girl shiver and rub her arms – she must be cold in those summer clothes

– and seemingly of its own volition Edna's hand lifted to tap on the window.

Fleur jumped and turned frightened-rabbit eyes to see Edna smile and beckon. Edna raised her cup and mouthed, "Want one?" and Fleur nodded. The door was heavy, but once inside she relaxed a little in the warmth and sat down opposite Edna. She wasn't supposed to speak to strangers, let alone accept anything from them, but surely a cup of tea couldn't hurt – and everyone was a stranger here. Edna glanced through the window and spotted Ivy walking back to her usual place beside the newspaper-seller. Edna knew if she'd left it a minute longer this child would have been on her way to the docks, her innocence gone before nightfall and her bruised but still valuable body shipped across the Channel on the next tide.

"*Is what you've got in mind any better?*" asked an unwelcome voice in her head but she answered it angrily. "*At least Fred will ease 'er into it slowly.*" Even so, she took a risk by handing over some coins and saying, "Get two more cups and a plate of chips," watching with an almost detached interest as Fleur edged up to the counter, wondering if the girl would do a runner.

But Fleur wasn't running anywhere, having nowhere else to go, and the sharp, vinegary smell of chips made her mouth water. She balanced the tray carefully back to her new friend and sipped the scalding tea from its thick cup. The lump in her stomach melted enough for her to smother the chips in tomato ketchup, and she devoured the lot with a concentration that gave Edna the chance to take a proper look at her latest acquisition.

Now that the pinched expression had faded from the girl's features, Edna blessed the luck that had sent her to the café from her usual bench on the far side of the station, because the girl was a real find – Fred would've been livid if she'd let Ivy snatch this prize. Flawless skin, long eyelashes that would look even longer with a coat of mascara, a wide mouth that would soon learn what was expected of it, but the crowning glory was that hair. Edna thought of the bonus she'd get for bringing her in, and then Fleur looked up and smiled. The blue eyes held nothing but gratitude for a kindness given and Edna's long-dormant maternal instincts did a flip, but the idea of letting her go was ridiculous.

"You got a name, dearie?" she asked, in an accent the same as the fat woman on the train.

Fleur relaxed – not all strangers were to be feared. "Fleur," she said. "Fleur Smith."

"Well, Fleur Smith – what's a little girl like you doin' on 'er own in the Smoke?"

"I'm not little!" Fleur protested hotly. "I was nearly May Queen today!"

"Someone beat yer to it, did they?"

"Cynthia – and I'm much prettier than her!"

"Got a 'igh opinion of yerself, ain't yer?"

"Linda says I'm prettier."

"Oo's Linda – yer sister?"

"My friend – the only one I've got now – she voted for me."

"I bet yer mum voted for yer an' all, didn't she?" Edna was fishing for information, still wondering whether to yield to this inexplicable urge to send the girl home.

Fleur missed her chance – all the resentment of the past few weeks boiled up and spewed out in one angry outburst. "My mum's dead. I was stolen by gypsies but I've escaped – I haven't got anyone."

Edna's eyes narrowed. "Don't give me none of yer fairy tales, girl, or we won't be pals no longer. Stolen by gypsies my arse!"

"But it's true! My mum was killed and the gypsies took me," said Fleur and, determined not to lose this source of chips and security, recounted enough details of her gypsy life to persuade Edna her story was true.

Sure now that nobody would come looking for Fleur, Edna made up her mind. "We'd better get yer into some warmer gear," she said, so Fleur slipped her hand trustingly into Edna's and they left the station.

*\*\*\**

As Edna led Fleur out of the steamy warmth of the café, in the cart leaving Thambay market, Clara shivered.

"We'll be home soon, love," Lydia said, wrapping the end of her shawl round Clara's back. Clara snuggled into the old woman's side. "Thank you – but it's not that – I can feel Fleur is cold. Cold and scared in a big noisy place with a cloudy roof."

Maria and Lydia exchanged a nod – Clara's Sight was growing fast – but Maria only said, "She didn't have a jumper – of course she's cold. Olivia – can't we go any faster?" and as Olivia flicked the reins to encourage a little more speed out of her trotting pony, Clara, Maria, Lydia and the boys held hands in a circle, imagining Fleur protected in their midst.

*\*\*\**

Martin Darby was mopping the front steps of his hotel when Edna Green went past with Fleur. He called a greeting but Edna waved a hand in a "can't stop now" gesture and hurried round the corner to the market. They were only just in time, for the stallholders were packing up to go home before the rain started, and ragged children were scavenging through the piles of rubbish for cabbage leaves and bruised fruit. Fleur stared as two boys fought over possession of an orange – gypsy life was hand-to-mouth but it was never this bad.

Edna pulled her round roughly. "Make yer mind up quick – blue or green?" she asked, holding up two cardigans. Neither of them looked very clean and they both had buttons missing, but Fleur was cold in the chilly breeze and pointed to the blue one. She slipped it on gratefully while Edna picked out a skirt and made her put that on too, then paid the man and hurried Fleur back past the hotel and down a side-street.

***

The gypsy campsite was grey when the women and children arrived home with the news that Fleur had got on a train to London. Ben ran to get George, but when Josef threw half the woodpile on the fire and Mateo called his tribe into a ring around it, George hung back to let the circle form without him.

"Fleur's warmer now," Olivia said after a moment. "A woman gave her some clothes."

"So she's found someone kind," Maria sighed with relief.

"No," Clara said. "Those clothes are dirty and the woman is planning something bad."

"Oh God!" Maria cried and began rocking back and forth, keening her distress.

"Maria!" Mateo snapped. "We will speak to Devla properly – now be quiet while I pray."

George sat on the steps of Mateo's vardo watching the circle around the fire and, for the first time since Albie had married into the tribe, he felt excluded. There was nothing in the group that George hadn't seen a hundred times before – the women in their shawls and the men in flat caps and collarless shirts – yet today even his own grandchildren seemed distant and alien. In the shadows cast by the tall pines the grey of the afternoon was deepened by the contrast of leaping flames. The silhouetted figures seemed like one entity rather than separate people, and George was struck by the notion that a mouse couldn't have squeezed through the wall they formed with their clasped hands. Clara stood between Olivia and Josef as Mateo prayed aloud for Fleur's safe return.

Mateo's words were more of a command to God than a prayer, and Mateo's Spanish roots showed when he spoke to the God that Roma people called Devla. "One of our children is lost, Señor, and we ask You to watch over her. Fleur is not of our blood but she was raised on Roma milk – protect her and give her back to us unharmed."

Maria's sight was clouded by the introspection of pregnancy, but when she recalled the sensation of stroking Fleur's silken hair as she lay on her breast, she saw her pass Martin Darby in the London street. "I know that man!" she cried. "He was on the boat at Ramsgate with Albie."

*\*\**

Martin leaned on his mop and frowned as Edna scurried past – that girl looked far too young to be part of Fred's stable. Strange though – for a second he thought there were other people with them, but when he blinked they had vanished. As Edna disappeared round the corner he lit a cigarette and wondered why he was even considering calling the police. Edna was bound to guess it was him who'd grassed her up, and he didn't fancy a visit from Fred. This hotel was barely making a profit as it was – if he got beaten up, Thelma's job wouldn't bring in enough to pay for help while he was in hospital. His best bet was to pretend he hadn't seen Edna or the girl. He stubbed out his cigarette and got back to work, but while he mopped his way back along the passage to the kitchen he couldn't get that blonde child out of his mind. She couldn't be much older than his Angela, and it was rotten luck to have fallen into Fred and Edna's clutches. Sometimes luck was all it took for a flipped coin to fall one way or the other.

Martin Darby, a hotel page-boy-cum-boot-cleaner before the war, had survived the first months in France by sheer luck – a luck that his entire squad had attributed to Private Albert Smith. Martin hadn't seen him since Dunkirk, but the remnants of the squad had stuck together afterwards in the belief that Smith's gypsy luck would still protect them. In a way it had, Martin thought now as he limped to tip the dirty water down the sink – when the shrapnel hit his leg he would have bled to death if Auntie Jones hadn't patched him up and got him to a field hospital. *The paintwork in this kitchen is the same colour as that ward*, he thought suddenly – *fancy me remembering the war after all this time!*

As the tribe circled the fire slowly, moving their feet in unison, George wished he'd gone on that train with Albie and Joey instead of sitting here like a useless old man. He half stood, intending to go and see Adam with some vague idea of making a phone call to London, when Mateo started speaking again. This was the language the tribe used sometimes among themselves, but as the whole tribe began chanting, "Meery dearie Dad," George recognised the rhythm and his lips moved in the words he'd learned at school. The tribe was saying the Lord's Prayer and, when George joined in, one more strong man who loved Fleur was drawn into the collective consciousness of the tribe.

***

Martin put his mop and bucket away and mixed up a batch of dumplings to accompany the evening stew – potatoes were still difficult to get – keeping an eye on the clock as he worked. Angela and Dick would be back from their nan's soon, and with Thelma working till six he had to go to the station to meet them off the bus. When the dumplings were rolled and sitting on the pastry-board dusted with flour, he just had time for another smoke before he had to go, so he locked the door behind him and sat on the step to roll a cigarette. *I can do it without even looking,* he thought suddenly – *I even managed to roll one in the back of that rattle-trap of a van on the way to Dunkirk with a baby yelling in my ear.* He shook his head in puzzlement – *why am I remembering the war after all these years? Maybe the memory of that baby is telling me to save the little blonde girl from Edna and Fred. But that's nonsense – I've already decided not to get involved.*

His hotel – known as Joan's Hotel – was only a step up from a boarding-house, and catered mainly for commercial travellers and railway workers stuck for the night at the wrong end of the line. The weekends were always too quiet, and occasionally Martin would rent the rooms by the hour, which was how he'd come to know Edna. It was years since she'd entertained a client, but Fred's other girls knew they'd be safe with Martin around, and although Thelma didn't like it much, this tenuous connection with Fred gave Martin added insurance in the volatile tapestry of villages that was London.

He finished his cigarette and pulled himself up by the iron railing, wondering again why they hadn't been melted down for guns. The feel of the metal reminded him of the handles on the Bofors anti-aircraft gun – *bloody heavy thing that had been to move, especially after the lorry broke its axle in France until Smith found a horse to haul it for us.* At that moment a horse clopped past, and Martin spun round so fast on his gammy leg that he nearly fell over, half-expecting to see it hitched to a gun instead of a cart. He shook his head, trying to clear the peculiar thoughts that were popping into it uninvited. *Maybe I'm suffering from that delayed shell-shock you read about in the paper,* he thought, but as he started walking he decided it wouldn't hurt to have a word with the coppers about that girl. He could ask them to keep his name out of it, but at least his conscience would be clear.

***

Thinking about it afterwards, Albie reckoned he'd have gone mad on that journey to London if Joey hadn't been with him. At every stop along the line Joey held the door open while Albie leapt off the train to ask the ticket-collector if he'd seen a girl in shorts with long blonde hair.

Between stations Albie talked non-stop, telling Joey about that other frantic journey – the one through France in an old ice-cream van with his squad and the baby girl they'd rescued. Joey had been just old enough to remember the hordes of returning troops, and the moment when he'd witnessed the surreptitious transfer of that baby from an Irish soldier's uniform to Mama's shawl, but Albie hadn't said much about his fellow soldiers before today. As the fields and houses and factories sped by the window, Albie told Joey about Paddy O'Brien, who had caught the small goat whose milk had fed Fleur – about Auntie Jones the medic who had dressed his shattered shoulder – Tommy Thompson and Joan Darby who had kept the van going all the way to Dunkirk, and even about Ratty Green the spiv, who'd jumped the queue for the rescue boats and drowned right in front of them.

"I didn't bring Fleur all that way for her to end up like my mother," Albie growled.

"Like Nan? What's wrong with that?" asked Joey.

Albie was too distracted to be discreet. "My first mother were a tart, and if we don't find your sister that's what'll happen to her."

"She's only twelve," Joey protested, but the genuine fear on his father's face gave him a horrifying glimpse into another world and he lapsed into a stunned silence.

When they reached the terminus Albie raced along the platform to collar a startled ticket-collector. "You seen a little girl about this high with long blonde hair?"

"Not me, mate."

"Couple of hours back it would've been."

"I only come on at three – lost her, have yer?" but Albie was already on the concourse pushing through the crowds, frantically searching.

Joey caught up and stood in his path, holding Albie back with his hands on his chest. He could feel the tension screaming through every nerve in Albie's body, the heart pounding like a hammer. "Dad, calm down. We'll never find her rushing about like this – we're two hours behind."

Albie knew he was right – the thought of what could have happened in those two hours was tormenting him – but he took a deep breath. "OK, Joey, you're right – let's think, where would she go?"

At that moment the café doors opened and the smell of chips drew a rumble of hunger from Joey's stomach. "Food," he said. "She'd've been hungry."

The woman behind the counter recalled the blonde girl who had sat for such a long time by the window with a scruffy woman.

A tramp begging by the entrance, his memory jogged by a
florin, remembered seeing her with Edna. "The rozzer moved
me on before I seen what road they took." Then Joey spotted a
policeman talking to a man with two children and they
hurried across.

"My daughter's missing," Albie began breathlessly and, as
Constable Rees turned to deal with this all-too-familiar
problem, a voice from the past exclaimed, "Corp! By all that's
holy – Gyppo Smith!"

"Joan! Fancy meeting you!" For a second Albie was
distracted enough to tell Joey, "This is Joan Darby – I was
telling you about 'im on the train."

It only took seconds for Albie and Martin to realise that
Fate had meant them to meet, and Martin offered to take them
to Fred's house.

"No call for you to get involved, sir," the constable said. "I
know the place."

"I can't let the Corp down," Martin protested.

"I understand that, sir – I was a soldier too – but it's not a
place to take your kids."

"Take 'em home, Joan," Albie said. "I've got Joey to 'elp
me," and he pulled the policeman along the road at a run,
leaving Martin with a renewed belief in gypsy magic.

***

Fleur's grand adventure had turned sour as soon as the train
left Thambay, but now she was really frightened. Edna's
friend Fred had smiled a welcome but his eyes were cold, and
if Edna hadn't been right behind her, she would have turned
tail at the door and run. Instead she was taken along a dark
corridor to a back kitchen that smelled of grease, cigarettes
and cats, and listened in silence as Edna repeated her story
about Dad stealing her. Edna made it sound as if Dad had
murdered her mother and, although Fleur was ashamed of
making all that stuff up, she was too scared to contradict Edna

and put it right. After a while Fred lit a cigarette, tilted his chair back and peered at Fleur through the smoke – really stared as if he was trying to decide whether to buy something in a shop window – and Fleur shuddered. Then the chair dropped down with a bang that made her jump and Fred's hand closed around her wrist.

"Poor little Fleur – what a terrible story. It's lucky Edna found yer or Gawd knows what could've 'appened to yer." He rubbed his dirty thumb over her skin and muttered, "Soft as a baby's," half under his breath. Fleur snatched her arm away – his touch was bad enough, but the way he looked at her made her skin crawl. Even the air in this stinking house felt dirty.

"Please can I go in the garden?" she asked in her politest voice.

Fred let out a guffaw and Edna stood up saying, "It's raining, dearie – I'll brew some tea."

But it wasn't raining and Fleur tried again. "I just want to look – I can't breathe in here."

"We ain't good enough for our little gypsy, Edna," Fred sneered. "Turning yer pretty little nose up at our 'ouse, yer 'ighness?"

"No!" Fleur cried desperately. "I just want to go outside in the garden!"

"Shit, Edna, how come yer didn't get scratched when yer picked up this wild-cat?" Fred laughed. He twisted Fleur's hair into a rope and pulled her head back, bringing his face within inches of hers. "Well, me lady, we ain't got no garden, only a backyard with a lavvy."

Fleur wrinkled her nose at his sour breath and said, "Well, I need to go to the toilet."

"Toilet, is it? 'oity-toity! Edna, escort our guest to the toilet, if yer please."

"I can go on my own."

"And slip out the back alley? Nice try, girlie, but I weren't born yesterday." Fred gave her hair one final tug and released it slowly, his blood running faster as he pictured it spread over his belly, though he'd have to tame her first or she'd bite him where it hurt most.

"I don't have to stay here if I don't want to," Fleur said in uncertain tones, trying to catch Edna's eye, but Edna busied herself with kettle and teacups and wouldn't look at her.

"You got another place to go?" Fred asked with a smirk.

Fleur's chin wobbled. "I want to go home," she wailed miserably. "I want my dad."

"'Ear that, Edna? She wants 'er dad. Would that be the dad what murdered yer mum, gypsy brat?"

Edna spun round from the stove and snapped, "Don't call 'er that, Fred – it's bad luck."

"Don't talk rot, Edna, we makes our own luck."

"I ain't so sure, Fred," said Edna, who usually didn't argue with him when he was in this mood. "This one's got protection – I seen it – I shouldn't never have brung 'er."

"Well, it's done now, Edna," said Fred, thinking of the imagined delights to come. "She wants a dad so I'll be 'er dad." He pulled Fleur out of her chair and onto his lap, holding her head against his waistcoat. "Yer'll be OK with Uncle Fred. Such pretty 'air yer've got."

For a brief moment Fleur felt comforted enough to close her eyes, and in that moment Fred jerked his head at Edna to get out. As the door closed softly behind her, Fred tightened his grip on Fleur's head and moved his other hand down to settle her more comfortably on his lap, but Fleur had breathed in more than enough of his malodorous person and wriggled to escape.

"Oh no yer don't," Fred snarled, pinning her in place over his throbbing groin, and in one swift movement his free hand shot up her skirt. When his probing fingers encountered tough worsted shorts instead of the expected flimsy knickers he growled in frustration and fumbled with the buttons, smothering Fleur's scream of shocked indignation with his mouth.

The sound of the scream sent Edna hobbling faster along the corridor – when Fred was 'training' a girl it was best to be somewhere else – but she was surrounded by looming shadows that hissed and shoved her from wall to wall. She felt the chill of their ghostly hands probing through her clothes, and she almost stumbled in her haste to escape.

As she scuttled down the passageway there was a pounding on the front door and a voice commanded, "Open up – open up now!" Whimpering with terror she fumbled to turn the key as Fleur screamed again, then the lock clicked, the door crashed open and the blue serge arm of a policeman knocked her aside.

Albie and Joey had gone down the alley to the back gate and reacted instantly to Fleur's screams. The back gate disintegrated into a thousand splinters, the same thing happened to the kitchen door, and when Constable Rees barged through from the corridor he was just in time to see Fred with his hand up the child's skirt before Albie's arm closed round Fred's neck and Joey snatched his sister away.

The girl was safe, clinging like a limpet to her tall brother, but her father was in imminent danger of being had up for murder. Fred dangled from Albie's arm like a Smithfield carcass, his face turning from bright red to an engorged shade of puce. Constable Rees, who had never been able to pin a charge on the scum-bag before, was half-inclined to let the enraged father finish him off, but duty was duty. "Mr Smith – ease off or you'll kill him."

"That's the idea," said Albie, gripping Fred's chin and pulling it back.

Constable Rees recognised the move from basic training – if he wasn't quick Fred's neck would be broken and he'd be arresting Mr Smith instead. "Mr Smith – we caught him in the act and he'll be going to jail – you don't want to be going with him. In fact," he added, struck by happy inspiration, "the fate that awaits him there is far worse than a broken neck. They don't like rapists in jail, especially those that go after little girls."

"Dad, please!" Joey added his voice to the policeman's entreaties.

Albie reluctantly lowered Fred into his chair, holding him there by a hand twisted in his hair. "You sure he'll go to jail?"

"No doubt about it, sir – saw the crime myself with my own eyes. His hand was up her skirt and the little lass was screaming – no way Fred Baker's squirming out of this one. Lift him up now and I'll put the cuffs on him."

"Well, if you're sure you can handle him, we'll get the next train home." Albie hauled Fred up again to be handcuffed, before taking Fleur from Joey.

"I'll need a statement, sir. If you like you can wait at Mr Darby's hotel and I'll pop round as soon as I've dealt with this." Constable Rees pointed out the way to Joan's Hotel when they reached the corner. "I'll be as quick as I can, sir. It's a crying shame this happened to your little girl, but I must say I'm glad to have this piece of rubbish off the streets."

Half an hour later Constable Rees opened the door of Joan's Hotel and went straight through to the kitchen, where he found Martin Darby, his children and the Smiths sitting round the table with cups of tea and a tin of biscuits. A big pan of stew simmered on the gas stove, filling the atmosphere with fragrant steam, and the policeman thought with distaste of the spam, bread and scrape that would doubtless constitute his tea back at his own digs. Removing his helmet and taking out his notebook, he sat down, and Martin put a cup of tea in front of him, together with a full sugar-bowl. Constable Rees raised an eyebrow but refrained from asking where the sugar had come from, helping himself to two heaped spoonfuls as payment for keeping his mouth shut.

"Now, Mr Smith," he began, "I've a few questions to put to

you. Mr Baker and Mrs Green have been singing like canaries. They claim this child isn't your daughter at all – in fact they say they rescued her. Apparently she told them you murdered her mother and kidnapped her. Is there any truth in these allegations?" The fact that Fleur was snuggled as close as she could get to Albie without actually climbing inside his waistcoat was really answer enough, but the Sergeant had told him to follow it up. The silence that his question induced sharpened his instincts and he caught the glance that shot between Smith and Darby – maybe there was some mystery here after all.

Albie cleared his throat to speak but Fleur took her thumb out of her mouth and said, "I'm sorry, Mr Policeman – I just made up a story to get the lady to buy me some chips."

"That was no lady," said Constable Rees, glad to have his own interpretation of events confirmed. "You're a very silly little girl and you've had a lucky escape. If Mr Darby here hadn't seen you we wouldn't have found you in time. Do you know what was about to happen?"

"No she don't!" said Albie forcefully. "And I'll thank you not to tell her."

Spoken like a true father, thought Constable Rees. Speaking more gently, he proceeded to draw from Fleur precisely what Fred Baker had done, which fortunately was no more than he'd witnessed, but enough to prove his intentions and ensure a long sentence. "Right, I think that's all for now," he said, standing up to leave. "I'll telephone Thambay police to let them know Fleur is safe – I expect you've called your family already?"

"Corp – I never thought!" exclaimed Martin. "You can use my phone."

"We ain't got a phone in our wagon," said Albie with a smile. "I s'pose I could call Luke and ask him to meet the train, but Maria will know already that she's safe."

"I should have known," Martin said. "Gypsy magic, like in

France?"

"They'll have circled the fire to protect her – that's how we found her before too much harm were done." Albie stood up still holding Fleur. "Joan – can you lend us a jumper to take her home in? I'll make sure you get it back – this other stuff can go on the fire."

While Angela ran to fetch a jumper, Albie made his telephone call and then, after promising to return soon for a proper reunion, Albie, Joey and a very chastened Fleur walked with Constable Rees back to the railway station. Constable Rees waited until they had bought Fleur a ticket before asking, "So that bit was true – about you being gypsies?"

"Gypsies and proud of it," Albie said and, having had time to think on the walk to the station, added, "And Fleur's mine, birth certificate an' all – we're not all dark-haired."

The other passengers on the train, most of them going home laden with bags after a day's shopping, must have wondered at the trio who sat so silently in a corner – the rough-looking man, the boy who was obviously his son, and the pale, subdued girl who wouldn't let go of their hands.

When they alighted at Thambay they were met by Constable Daly, who told Albie, "They phoned from London to say that pervert will be up in court on Tuesday. He's already got a black eye, so a Constable Rees told me – must have fallen down the steps to the cells. I told that Rees chap you're a friend of my brother's, and not to bother you to go back as a witness unless you had to."

"Ta, Billy, I 'preciate it, but I wouldn't mind helping put him away."

Luke was there to collect them and at dusk they were home, where George and the tribe welcomed Fleur back into the fold with love and tenderness and no hint that she had brought her awful experience on herself. When she and Clara crawled into their bed that night, Fleur said, "I wish they'd shout at me or something."

"We're just pleased you're safe."

"Why? I've been horrible to you."

"Yes, you have," said Clara, doubting that this new, chastened Fleur would last more than the weekend. "But you're my sister and I was really scared when that awful man got you."

"Oh my God! You saw it? When he tried to kiss me and put his hand up my skirt? It was disgusting! You have to promise you won't tell anyone!"

"Not even Linda?" Clara asked wickedly.

"Especially not Linda – she'd tell the whole town."

## <u>CHAPTER TEN – MAY DAY</u>

Unfortunately, keeping secrets from Linda was impossible – she seemed to sniff them out like a master spy. She bounced into the campsite the next morning while the tribe were still eating their breakfast. "Oh Fleur – I'm *so* glad you're safe!" she gushed, dropping onto the rug beside her. "Tell me all. Were you kidnapped?"

Fleur crammed a piece of bread into her mouth and turned pleading eyes on her sister, who was the acknowledged expert at telling stories. Clara didn't even pause before she launched into a half-truth. "It was all a mistake. Fleur was helping one of the market women put her boxes on the train and it left before she could get off."

"But she was gone *hours*!"

"They wouldn't let her get a train back home without a ticket."

Fleur picked up the story, playing for sympathy. "I begged and begged but they wouldn't even lend me fourpence for the telephone."

"Why didn't you ask a policeman?"

Fleur caught her mother's eye and decided she'd be wise to quit while she was ahead. "I was just looking for one when Dad and Joey found me."

"I was afraid you'd been kidnapped or murdered. I am *so* happy you weren't!" Linda rubbed her face on Fleur's sleeve like an affectionate puppy and put a hand up to stroke her hair, but Fleur jerked away, crying, "Don't touch me!" and turned to Maria. "Oh Mama, *please* cut my hair."

"But Fleur – you have beautiful hair!"

"That's what *he* said." Fleur's voice rose to a wail. "I'll do it myself if you won't."

Linda's mouth had dropped open at Fleur's outburst, and Clara said the first thing she could think of. "Those girls at school hung us up by our hair, Mama – I want mine cut too."

There was a clamour of protests from the women but Albie overruled them. "Lots of girls have short hair now – let them have it cut."

***

On Bank Holiday Monday morning the entire Smith family climbed into the tribe's big cart for the ride into Thambay. As the family left the campsite Lydia muttered to her sister-in-law, "Maria should never have cut the girls' hair – it wouldn't have been allowed in our day."

"Mateo should have forbidden it," Rosanna said, adding slyly. "He was always too soft."

Lydia bridled, as Rosanna knew she would. "Mateo never interferes unless it's absolutely necessary, and at least the girls are friends again – that's one less worry for Maria."

"Friends, yes, but they hardly look like girls in those boys' clothes."

Olivia listened with a wry smile to the two old women enjoying their daily sparring match. "It won't last," she said. "I wish I'd had the same freedom when I was growing up."

"Ricardo would never have married you if you'd looked like that," Rosanna said. "I raised him with decent standards."

Olivia bit her lip, which left Lydia to have the final word. "They'll see boys differently in a year or two and then we'll have other problems – I can't imagine either of them letting us choose their husbands."

***

The May Day parade was typical of thousands of similar events taking place all over the country. First the Town Band marched along, enthusiasm and an outsized drum making up for the wrong notes. The band was followed by the Mayor and Mayoress, waving regally from the back of an ancient landau driven by the local postman, who was the only available man with a suitable hat to be a chauffeur. Then came a procession of bicycles and tricycles large and small, lavishly decorated, and finally the brewers' dray horse, polished to a glossy conker brown and tossing its head proudly under a plume of feathers, hauled a decorated cart in which the May Queen and her attendants were enthroned on a dais of hay bales.

Clara and Fleur rode with Maria and Daisy as they drove the cart to the east end of the promenade to leave the horse in the quiet garden behind Norah's flat. In the little first floor flat, Maria opened the French windows to let the sea air freshen the rooms, Clara wiped down the two cast iron balcony chairs while Fleur found cushions, then Daisy shooed them away saying, "Go down now or you'll miss the maypole dancing."

"We can watch from here, and I want to stay with Mama," Clara said.

"I'll look after your mum," Daisy said, unpacking the makings of a cup of tea from her capacious basket, and Fleur dragged Clara to the door. "Let's go – there'll be bobbing for apples and we haven't got long hair to get in the way now."

Clara cast one more look at her mother and said, "Norah will look after you here," before she followed her sister down the stairs.

Maria leaned over the balcony to watch them cross the road, and Daisy asked, "What did she mean about Norah – do you think she's still here?"

"Only our memory of her. I haven't sensed her since Albie came back from the war."

Maria's matter-of-fact relationship with spirits had taken Daisy a while to get used to, but she said now, "Well, if she's gone, why not sell the place?"

"Albie used to say we'd only fritter the money away, but he's thinking about it now."

"I'm sure Luke could recommend an agent."

"We're leaving it till after this baby is born. Now – tell me about you and Luke."

"Nothing gets past you, does it?" Daisy flushed like a teenager. "Luke moved back into our bedroom a week ago."

"And?"

"He's got horrible scars down there, but that cream you gave me helps."

"I'll give you some herbs to make a bedtime drink as well – just don't let Linda get hold of it." Maria laughed softly. "And make sure your door is locked. Oh look! The maypole's starting!"

From their vantage point they could see everything – they cheered Ben and Davy in the children's races, laughed at the Morris Dancers, and watched Luke and Albie shaking the hands of potential voters. The afternoon sped by, and after the Mayor had carved the ceremonial first slice off the hog roast, Albie brought the cart round, got the children on board, and helped Maria and Daisy into the back.

"Did you see me, Mama?" Davy cried. "I won a race!"

"Didn't you hear me cheering? I watched everything."

"So you know I got an apple in the bobbing," Ben said.

"You cheated," said Fleur.

"Didn't!"

"Did – I saw your hand in the water."

"At least nobody tried to drown him," Clara said. "I had to bad-wish Julie Webb when Fleur was having her turn."

"Clara – that's not allowed," Maria scolded half-heartedly.

Clara tossed her head. "She only got the sneezes, Mama, and I had to keep Fleur safe."

When they stopped in Market Square to collect George, Clara put a gentle hand on Maria's lap. "Mama – what is it? Something's hurting you."

"It's nothing, Clara – just the movement of the cart jarring my back." Maria pushed the heels of her hands into her belly. "Not only that – this baby thinks she's going to be a footballer like her big brother."

Clara sat back, not wanting to contradict Mama, but she knew there was more to it.

"Ooh, I nearly forgot," said Joey. "I've got a match after

school tomorrow. Can I borrow your bike, Dad? I'll have to walk home else."

"I'll come and fetch you," George said. "I reckon I can handle Blossom now."

"Only if you promise not to have a beer on the way, Grandad."

"Cheeky young bugger – oops! Sorry, Maria."

***

The football match was the last of the season, and there was quite a crowd on the touchline to cheer the home side, including George and Luke and all the children. The supporters for the visitors stood on the opposite side of the pitch, and Clara noticed one man whose attention was focussed almost exclusively on Joey. He was watching her brother with a kind of hunger and, with Fleur's experience fresh in her mind, Clara felt distinctly uneasy. Later, after Joey had scored twice and the home team had won by five goals to three, again Clara felt the stranger's keen interest. "Hurry up, Joey!" she called.

Joey was about to climb into the cart when the man approached and asked George, "Are you Joe Smith's father?"

"His grandfather – what's it to you?"

The man smiled and gave George his card. "I represent Margate Football Club. I would like your permission to talk to Joe about trying out for the team."

Joey had frozen with one foot on the step, but when the scout's words sank in he gasped, "A try-out for The Gate! Oh my God, yes!"

"You'll have to talk to his dad," George said, pocketing the business card. "But I reckon you've got your answer already."

***

When Clara and Nico walked into 2A's form-room on Tuesday morning, the silence thudded down like a rock, and Clara sensed a disquiet that bordered on fear. She whispered to Nico, "Have you seen Sally anywhere?" Nico shook his head.

When the teacher called the register, Wendy Jones answered for Sally. "She's absent, Sir – she fell off her bike on Sunday and broke her wrist." The class flicked glances at Clara and Nico and quickly away again – their belief in the gypsy curse obvious.

At the morning break Fleur ran up as soon as Clara and Nico emerged into the playground. "Julie's got a massive spot on her chin and she says it's my fault."

"What do her mates say?" Clara asked with a grin of delight.

"They're not talking to me but I don't care. Christine even said she likes my hair short."

Nico raised his eyebrows at Clara, who shook her head to deny responsibility. She didn't need to curse anyone – the power of rumour was enough.

Sally's wrist and Julie's acne were two-day wonders – by the end of the week all the school could talk about was Joey Smith's coming trial for Margate Football Club. When Albie arrived on Friday afternoon in Luke's Rover to drive Joey to the Hartsdown Park stadium, Joey walked out of school through a double line of well-wishers. Even the Headmistress was standing at the top of the steps to see him off – an unprecedented honour.

As they drove away, everyone could see Bert's posters in the back window – posters over which Luke had pasted strips triumphantly announcing, "Elected to Thambay Town Council!" Bert had won the election by a respectable margin, and the recreation ground on which Joe Smith, future England player, had kicked a football would remain undisturbed.

## CHAPTER ELEVEN – PADDY & MAY

On the first Tuesday in August the travelling fair arrived in Thambay, and waiting on the recreation ground to help erect it were Albie and Ricardo. When they drove the cart home that evening they took Paddy O'Brien with them for his long-awaited holiday.

Despite Paddy declaring that he'd be 'sound' sleeping under a wagon with the boys, he was installed in the spare room of George's cottage, but he spent his days working in the fields with Albie and the others.

"You're supposed to be on holiday," Albie said, but Paddy insisted he was loving it. "This is a grand craic – it puts me in mind of the old country."

The local workers came out from Thambay in a bus that Pinetree and Coppin Farms hired between them, and the fields and orchards of both farms seethed with activity. Maria rested at home, exhausted by the heat, while the other women and children picked strawberries and raspberries, black and red currants, beans and peas. The men turned potatoes out of the ground by the ton, pulled onions and carrots, and cut cabbages.

By Friday the fifteenth, when Clara turned thirteen, the entire tribe was nut-brown from working in the fields, and in the soft summer dusk they threw a party. All their friends and fellow workers were invited, and everyone had brought something. There was bread and cheese and ham cut into chunks for easy eating, beer and wine for the adults and freshly squeezed apple juice for the children, a variety of cakes, and a huge basket of strawberries set beside a net-covered bowl of cream. May Coppin, mother of Joey's pal Frank, had brought the cream, her plump figure proving that she ate her fair share at home.

Paddy couldn't take his eyes off her. "Your woman over there talking to Maria," he said to Albie. "She's got a tidy little body on her. She'll be married, will she?"

"That's May, Bert Daly's sister."

"Her that was married to Ken Coppin from our squad? And is she a widow-lady still?"

"She is." Albie winked. "And she still lives on Coppin Farm."

Over the next ten minutes Paddy worked his way round the campsite with a ponderous nonchalance that fooled nobody, and when he finally reached his goal, Maria handed him a pile of bowls saying, "Paddy – help May dish out the strawberries, will you?"

Paddy was uncharacteristically tongue-tied with May, and after handing round the strawberries he went to talk to George, but when the party was over and May collected the fruit bowls together, Paddy approached her. "Will I be helping you with that, then?"

"You can bring these to the house if you like," she replied, handing him the bowls. By the time they had washed them up and shared a pot of tea in her kitchen, Paddy had found the courage to ask May if she would go with him to the dance-hall on the pier the next night.

"It's only a local band, but some of the lads went last week and they said it were a grand craic." He grinned at her puzzled expression. "You English would say 'good fun'."

"I haven't danced for years," May demurred. "And won't they all be youngsters?"

"Sure and aren't we still youngsters ourselves? Will I fetch you at six o'clock? There's a bus back at ten so you won't be late home."

May gazed into his battered but oddly boyish face, smiled a broad smile that flipped Paddy's heart clean over and said, "Yes, I'd love to go dancing." When Paddy left her to return to his bed in George's cottage, she ran up the stairs like a girl to rummage through her wardrobe and agonize over what to wear for her first date in fifteen years.

Promptly at six o'clock the next day Paddy was on May's doorstep. George had heated water in his copper boiler so that the Irishman could bathe in the tin bath in the scullery, and Olivia had cut his hair – his greying but still exuberant curls shone with Brylcreem. He shyly presented May with a fistful of wild flowers, which she arranged in a jug as carefully as if they were a florist's bouquet before they walked up to the main road to catch the bus.

"That's a pretty frock," Paddy said as they waited at the bus stop.

May blushed and hitched her cardigan more securely round her shoulders. "This old thing? I made it during the war out of some curtains – I've not had a reason to get anything new."

"Me neither," said Paddy. "This suit is George's, but you look as pretty as a picture. I'll be fighting the fellers off, so I will."

May drew her eyebrows together in an attempt to look stern. "There'll be no fighting while you're with me, Paddy O'Brien."

Paddy sketched a salute and helped her onto the bus as if she were a queen, thinking he had just this one night to make a good impression before the fair moved on, so he'd better not blow it.

Over a beer for Paddy and a port and lemon for May while the band took a refreshment break, they swapped life stories. The gaps in May's account of her brief marriage were enough to tell Paddy it hadn't been a happy one, and May sensed that Paddy's tales of life on the road, which he related as a grand adventure, masked a deep loneliness. When, footsore from dancing almost every dance, they caught the ten o'clock bus, they each knew that the other could become special and, as they walked down Farm Lane in the warm starlight, Paddy outlined for May his itinerary for the coming months.

"We leave on Tuesday and the fair's going east along the

coast next – Whitstable then Herne Bay and Ramsgate and down south from there. I could get a train back sometimes to take you to the dancing, but it wouldn't be regular." He peered at her face, trying to gauge her reaction. "A grand woman like yourself deserves a steadier feller than me."

May tucked her arm through his, and Paddy thrilled to the touch of her soft breast against his elbow as she said, "Any time you can make it over here you'll be welcome, Paddy – that's regular enough for me."

That was the closest they got to an understanding that night, and May wouldn't let him in the house again for fear of waking Frank, but they kissed in the shadows of the porch before they parted, and both of them went to bed smiling.

*** 

Monday was Paddy's last day in the fields and he was up and about early, lifting potatoes with Albie and Luke in a field on Pinetree Farm. The women and children were across the lane at Coppin Farm, picking the second crop of strawberries.

Halfway through the afternoon, Frank brought a horse and cart along the lane to collect the filled baskets, with May sitting on the back to hand out cups of lemonade. Without warning, the horse collapsed between the shafts, and Frank ran back to the farm to fetch help.

The first Clara and Fleur knew of the approaching drama was the sound of a tractor shattering the peace. She clutched Fleur's wrist and asked, "Who's that driving the tractor?"

Fleur shaded her eyes to peer across the field. "It looks like Frank's uncle Tim."

"He's going to do something awful!" Clara cried and they raced to the lane. They were only yards away when Frank's adolescent voice yelled, "No!" and Clara and Fleur watched aghast as Tim calmly put a rifle to the horse's forehead and fired. The shot echoed across the lane, accompanied by horrified screams and the sobbing of terrified children, and May hid her face in her apron.

Albie and Paddy's army surplus boots flew over the potato field to rescue their family, and Albie was almost knocked off his feet as all four of his children threw themselves at him. Paddy headed unerringly for May who, without a care for who might be watching, buried her face in his chest. Paddy held it there with one hand and said to Tim Coppin, "Your horse might have been knackered, but only an ignorant gobshite would shoot it in front of women and children."

Tim took a breath to tell the Irishman where he could stick his opinion, but when he saw his size and clenched fist he thought better of it. "You keep your nose out of it – and you're fired. Frank – give me a hand here."

After a helpless glance at his mother, Frank began roping the animal's legs for Tim to attach it to the tractor, but May had got over her fright – now she was simply angry. She marched up to her brother-in-law and, with an arm strengthened by years of churning butter, dealt him a slap that resounded almost as loudly as the rifle shot. "You're an insensitive lout, Tim Coppin. That horse deserved a decent death in its stable, not to be dragged through the dirt behind a tractor."

"You shouldn't have married a farmer if you can't handle country ways."

"I shouldn't have married your brother at all – he was a nasty piece of work too."

"Well, you got rid of him good and proper, didn't you? If you hadn't opened your fat mouth about a few slaps he wouldn't have gone off and got himself killed."

"Don't you dare speak to my mother like that!" Frank shouted.

Tim rounded on him. "You can keep your opinions to yourself, young Frank."

The townswomen of Thambay had come out for a nice day in the sun earning a few bob picking fruit, not to see a horse shot in front of their eyes, but they had got over their shock by now and were thoroughly enjoying this glimpse of the Coppin family's skeletons. They liked May, and were delighted when her Irish man friend put the icing on the cake by walking up to Tim and growling right in his face, "And you, you thick gobshite, should watch your mouth in front of the ladies."

Clara held her breath – for a brief moment she was certain that Mr Tim was about to shoot Paddy – but Albie had obviously had the same thought and took a threatening step forward. Tim looked at the pair of them and affected disdain, hooked the gun over his arm and stalked off, but his dramatic exit was spoiled by Frank shouting, "You can't leave this poor animal just lying in the dirt."

So Tim had to turn back, hitch the carcass to his tractor and haul it away in front of an audience he should have had the sense not to offend. Every worker demanded her money there and then, and sat down by the hedge to wait for the bus ride home – Coppin Farm was forced to offer higher wages to persuade them to return the next day.

"I'm not going back to Coppin Farm however much they pay," Clara said at supper. "Mr Tim is dangerous."

"He's just a thick eejit," said Paddy. "Though he did look nasty with that gun in his hand."

"It's not the gun – it's him we should stay away from. He's going to do something else – something much worse."

"Well, I won't be there tomorrow – I'm off with the fair again." Paddy stood up, shifting on the spot like a bashful child. "Albie and Ric are taking me at the crack of sparrows, so I'll be off to me bed now, and I thank ye all kindly. It's been a grand holiday, so it has."

He walked round the fire, solemnly shaking hands with everyone from Mateo down to little Davy, and then walked into the lane with George.

The tribe waited until his footfalls had died away before bursting into laughter. George had gone straight home, but Paddy's boots hadn't turned towards the cottage at all – he'd walked up the lane towards Coppin Farm, going to visit May.

# CHAPTER TWELVE – ANNIE

The sun lay on the horizon with the promise of a scorching day when Maria awoke with her first contraction. She eased her body carefully off the bed, trying not to disturb Albie, and descended the wagon steps to sit on the bottom one. This baby was her biggest yet and her small frame hurt abominably. Her back ached, the sling of muscle that cradled her baby tightened painfully, and it felt as though she was being torn in half. Even so, she stroked her belly affectionately and whispered, "Good morning, baby – we'll meet before tonight."

Clara emerged sleepily from her tent to sit beside her mother. "It's today, isn't it?"

Maria ruffled Clara's short curls. "It's today – by the time you get back from the fields you'll have another sister."

"I'm not going to the fields," Clara said. "I have to be here – you will need me."

Maria hadn't the strength to argue, and then Olivia appeared in her own doorway. "This is women's business, Clara – you should not be here."

"I'm a woman now," Clara argued. "And I make the best raspberry tea."

"That's true, she does," said Maria, "And she has the Sight – if she thinks she should stay, let her stay."

Light-footed with relief, Clara ran through the dawn to pick fresh raspberry leaves for the tea that would ease labour. When she returned, smoke from the small summer fire was rising in a thin column to a sky of palest yellow, and Olivia had brought a pot of water to the boil. While Maria sipped the tea and forced down a few spoonfuls of porridge, Clara got dressed. As she pulled on a skirt for the first time in weeks – Joey's old shorts seemed wrong for such a female matter – Fleur watched through half-open eyes. "You can't pick fruit in that skirt."

"I'm not going picking – Mama's baby's coming today."

Fleur shuddered theatrically – she didn't want anything to do with babies, or with the messy business of having them. "What about me? I don't want to go picking on my own."

"You've got Linda."

"But she keeps asking what happened in London."

"Oh for heaven's sake, Fleur! Make up a story or tell her to shut up. I can't be bothered with your little dramas today," Clara snapped, and ducked out of the tent wishing it had a door she could slam.

The camp was astir now, and Albie roused Maria from a self-absorbed trance by stroking her neck. "Is the baby coming? Will I stay?"

Maria turned her head to kiss his palm. "No, love, you go to work."

"We'll be all day packing up the fair."

"This is women's business – you can meet your daughter when you get home."

So Albie left with Ricardo and Paddy to dismantle the fair and May, who had come to see them off, offered to take the younger boys home with her. After two soft kisses and, "See you later, Mama," finally Maria could allow her face to mirror the pain. She was in agony already – this was worse than any of her other births and she was afraid.

When the next contraction had faded, Rosanna said, "Ten minutes."

"Is it really that long since the last one?" Despite the pain searing through her groin, Maria stood up to hurry things along. "Walk with me, Clara."

Clara was there in an instant, offering her shoulder as a prop for a slow progress from one wagon to the next – stop – tense – breathe. Walk to the gate – stop – tense – breathe. Maria gripped the wooden gate, gaining comfort from the many hands that had smoothed it to a grey sheen. Clara rubbed the small of her back, and some of the pain receded under her sensitive fingers. As the sun rose over the cottage roofs the lane filled with light – golden light that flooded over the paddock and washed the backs of the grazing horses with wisps of morning mist. But today Clara didn't see the beauty – those tendrils of mist were writhing and weaving into figures of menace, and she was frightened for her mother.

"I should go to the birthing tent," Maria said, turning round, but then she froze. Where there should have been tents and wagons she could see only a dense, swirling fog. "Not here," she cried, shrinking back against Clara. Seeing the fear on her face, Clara opened the gate and Rosanna called for Lydia, who bustled out carrying a sheet – if Maria was going to give birth under a hedge, she should at least have something clean to lie on.

"Where are we going?" Lydia asked. "The paddock?"

Maria couldn't answer – she only knew it mustn't be in the campsite – but Clara said, "Grandad's" with such conviction that no-one argued. Leaning on Rosanna and Lydia, Maria staggered down the lane while Clara ran ahead to the cottage.

George rose magnificently to the occasion. Taking one look at Maria he said, "No way she'll make it upstairs," and dragged the spare bed mattress into the front room, where Lydia threw her sheet over it and eased Maria down. George retreated to the scullery, pumped water into the big copper boiler, and lit a fire under it in the certain knowledge that childbirth always needed hot water.

Maria looked round the front room without comprehension – books on a shelf, and a clock that ticked away the minutes. *I know that sound – ah yes, Albie's mother's clock.* The books exuded a faint perfume which her nose wrinkled to identify – *lavender.* A cup touched her lips and she sipped in reflex – *tea, of course, Norah always makes tea. I must be at Norah's. But where's Clara?* "Clara?"

"I'm here, Mama."

The day dragged on to afternoon but there was no sign of

the baby. George made pot after pot of tea and a plate of sandwiches, and still Maria laboured without result. Then the sound of her cries changed and Rosanna examined her. She turned a serious face to Lydia. "I see a foot – the baby's coming the wrong way. Clara, hold Mama's hands tight."

Clara was crying so much she couldn't see, but she held her mother's hands, not even letting go when Maria bit down hard on her arm. As Rosanna pushed the foot back and turned the baby, Maria screamed, then a minute later she felt the baby move downwards. The pain came again, but this time she welcomed it, knowing she was near the end. She took a deep breath, and as the wave reached its height she pushed her daughter out into the world.

Rosanna wiped the baby's face and gave her to Maria, but the pain that should have gone once her baby lay on her breast refused to stop. Maria sobbed with the agony of it. Her new daughter gazed at her with unfocussed eyes and she tried to concentrate – these precious first moments were when she must connect with the new soul behind those dark blue eyes – but instead she felt her own soul slipping away. As her arms began to weaken, Rosanna passed the baby to Clara saying, "Hold your sister for a minute," and delivered the afterbirth, but after that there was a great gush of blood and all became panic and confusion.

While the women battled to stop the bleeding, Clara sat in the rocking chair by the window, concentrating fiercely on the baby to shield her from the death she could feel in the room. The baby wailed, and through the haze in her mind Maria struggled to sit up. Lydia commanded, "Lie still" but the thin cry of her newborn daughter was more insistent. Battling against her body's weakness, Maria turned her head to see both her daughters silhouetted against the light, but between her and them stood another figure – a young Roma woman holding out her arms and calling, "Maria".

Lydia felt the chill in the air and recognised the figure as

Josef's young wife who had died giving birth to Maria. While her hands worked to save her granddaughter, Lydia pleaded with the pale ghost, "Maria's baby needs her," but the answer came back, "I never even held mine." Lydia spoke aloud in her agitation. "At least wait till the child is weaned."

Olivia gripped her wrist and said, "You can't argue with Death," but Lydia shook her off and raised her voice, offering a bargain. "Take me instead."

Clara's eyes were wide and terrified. If she looked at her mother she saw only blood, but if she looked away she saw that pale ghost, and she could do nothing but sit helplessly. When Lydia raised her voice, the baby in Clara's arms whimpered and the ghost turned, its face twisted with the pain of a mother who had died too soon. Drifting nearer, it brushed its phantom fingers over the baby's face. Suddenly Clara forgot to be afraid – now she was angry. "Get away from her!" She jumped out of the chair to crouch beside her mother and put the baby's starfish hand on Maria's mouth. "There!" she said defiantly to the ghost. "A living bond is stronger than your dead one."

Maria was shivering violently, but the tiny fingers exploring her mouth were warm and her lips pursed to kiss them. Clara gently laid the swaddled baby across Maria's chest.

Rosanna nodded approvingly. "Well done, child, but we must warm Maria up."

Olivia hurried to the kitchen, where she found George sitting and smoking furiously. Desperate for something to do, he had draped the boiler with towels from the previous day's wash – they were dry and warm, and Olivia took them gratefully to pack round Maria.

Maria's soul yearned for the mother she had never known, but every time she shifted her gaze to the ghost, Clara moved deliberately between them, denying the link with every ounce of her strength. Rosanna and Lydia worked to stem the flow of blood, and gradually the warmth of George's towels seeped into Maria's body. Each time she thought of dying, Clara bent close to her ear and urged, "Mama, we need you – Mama, don't leave us." She held the baby's hand on her mother's face, repeating over and over again, "Mama – don't go!"

At last the ghost faded, yielding to the needs of Maria's living daughters. The chill lifted from the room, leaving nothing but the warmth of an August afternoon, and the bleeding slowed to a trickle.

When the doctor arrived, having been dragged from his full surgery and driven to Farm Cottages at break-neck speed by Daisy Finch, Maria was deathly pale and obviously in pain but alive, propped up on a mattress on the floor with a baby at her breast.

"Why isn't she in bed?" the doctor demanded.

"She couldn't climb the stairs," said Rosanna. "She's hardly been able to walk for weeks."

On checking the baby, the doctor said more calmly, "I'm not surprised – this infant must be a nine-pounder." He crouched to examine Maria, but each time he touched her she screamed, and his expression became grave. "I've only seen this once before, but it looks as if the birth has broken her pelvis – she'll have to go to hospital."

"No!" Maria cried with surprising vigour. "I would die there."

"By the look of you, you nearly died here," the doctor replied severely. "You need total rest and proper care, which you won't get here with a baby to feed."

But Maria was adamant. "There is no-one else to feed my baby. Grandmama and Rosanna will look after me – they stopped the bleeding."

"What bleeding? There's no more blood than I'd expect on this sheet."

"I'll show you blood," said Lydia grimly, and dragged him out to the scullery. At the sight of the sheets soaking in the tin bath, the doctor thought privately that gypsy magic must be more than superstition if the new mother had survived that amount of blood loss, but he only repeated, "Your granddaughter needs professional nursing care."

Lydia was implacable. "You give us the medicine and we will do whatever Maria needs – she stays with us."

Conceding defeat, the doctor said, "She'll need a proper bed – a firm one."

"She'll get one."

"If her pelvis is to mend, she mustn't move."

"She won't have to."

"She might never walk again, you realise?"

"We'll face that trouble when we have to."

"A healthy diet is essential – liver, green vegetables, milk and eggs – can you provide that?"

"We can," said Daisy, carrying in a tray of tea. "Maria will get the best we have."

"Very well," said the doctor. "I'll leave her in your hands for now." He wrote a prescription for iron tablets before Daisy took him back to town, leaving him at his surgery to deal with those of his patients who hadn't given up and gone home.

*\*\**

Instinct had sent Albie racing home, and when he found the campsite almost deserted he had a moment of panic until Mateo told him they were at George's. Albie ran down the lane and burst into the kitchen. Seeing Clara's cheeks still patchy from crying, he was afraid he had come too late, but Clara smiled reassuringly and said, "Mama's all right."

"And the baby?"

This time Clara's smile spread to her eyes. "She's lovely – they're in the front room."

Albie's first thought was that Maria had shrunk more than was usual after giving birth, but he kissed her quickly and took his new daughter to the window. He had been carrying the traditional red cord in his pocket for the past week, and he

unwrapped the swaddling to tie it round the baby's neck
before inspecting the rest of her. Only then did he ask Maria,
"Why are you here – what's wrong with the tent I set up?"

"Death was waiting there," said Lydia. "It almost found her
here."

Albie fumbled behind him for the chair and sat down.
"What happened? You never had problems before."
Rosanna's brief explanation left him gasping. "How long's
that going to take to mend?"

Maria's eyes filled with tears as Rosanna told him, "We
don't know yet, but she needs a proper bed."

"I'll carry her to the wagon," Albie said at once. "I can doss
in with Josef."

"The doctor said she mustn't be moved from this room."

So Albie and Ricardo brought downstairs the single bed
that had been Albie's before his marriage, and set it up in
George's front room, winding the mechanism until the springs
were as tight as they would go. When May brought Fleur, Ben
and Davy to meet their new sister, Maria was already installed
in the bed beside the window – her view for the foreseeable
future would be restricted to the front lane and the hedge
around the campsite. Fleur and the boys peered at Maria and
the baby over the iron rail at the foot of the bed – there was a
frailty about their mama that made them afraid to go any
closer – but their reluctance was barely noticeable because
Lydia only allowed them a minute before shooing them away.

When they were in bed that night, Fleur asked Clara, "Why
were you crying at Grandad's? Your face was all blotchy."

"Mama nearly died – I saw a ghost waiting for her." Clara
shuddered again at the memory and Fleur, who since the
London episode had been less scornful of Clara's ghost
stories, asked, "How do you know it was after Mama?"

"Because Olivia said it was Mama's mother who died when
she was born."

"My mother died just after I was born – do you think she's

waiting for me?" Fleur sounded so plaintive that Clara hugged her.

"I expect so – but she'll have a jolly long wait, because we're going to live to be a hundred."

Later that night, Mateo peered at Albie through the smoke of a cigarette and said, "Lydia told me we nearly lost Maria today. We must baptise the baby quickly– have you chosen a name?"

"Maria wants to call her Annie like the little princess."

"Annie is a good name."

Albie's smile was strained. "She can call her what she likes – I'm just thankful Maria made it through."

In the small hours, when all strength is at its lowest, Clara woke with a start. Fleur was breathing evenly beside her and she was about to lie down again when she felt the touch of a cold hand – it was that sensation which had woken her. "What do you want?" she whispered.

"*To warn you.*"

Clara shivered. "Warn me about what?"

"*That man on the farm – the dangerous one.*"

Recalling the shadowy fog she had seen yesterday, Clara snuggled into the solid warmth of Fleur's back before she asked, "The danger is still here on the campsite?"

"*Here – there – everywhere. If you want to save your mother, guard her well – I will wait for her.*"

Clara dared to ask, "For how long?" but there was no answer – only a murmur of spirit voices repeating, "*We will wait,*" and she shrank deeper into the mattress as the chill faded.

***

With Maria confined to bed, Mateo and Albie took baby Annie and baptised her in the running water of the stream behind George's cottage the next afternoon. The baptismal feast also served as a farewell party for Joey, who was off to Margate to start his football career.

"One child working, four growing and another at the breast – I wish my stock was that fertile," Adam joked.

Albie's smile was forced. "Joey'll be earning a tenner a week – that's double my wages."

"I pay the going rate," Adam said stiffly.

"Sorry, Mr Finch," Albie said. "Didn't mean it like that. It just seems wrong Joey getting all that money for playing a game. I ain't complaining – I've got rent money from the flat on top of my wages."

"How are your new tenants working out?" asked George, appearing with a jug of ale to top up their tankards.

"Pay on the nail, which is more'n the last lot did, and they love it there – even asked me if I were looking to sell the place."

"So why don't you?" said George. "You've talked about it often enough."

"'Cause I'd only spend the money – having it tied up in that flat keeps it safe."

"How about having it tied up in a cottage instead?" Adam suggested.

"Where would I find one of those?" Albie asked.

But George had seen the glint in Adam's eyes. "Right here, son. Adam's already offered to sell it to me but I ain't got the money. If you bought it I could pay you what I give Adam now, and it'll be yours when I go."

"You serious, Mr Finch?" Albie asked.

Adam nodded. "I've been talking to Luke about it. The sale of this cottage would cover the cost of installing electricity at Pinetree – there's not as much money in farming as there used to be."

"You should do it, Albie," George said. "With the work the Council's doing on the prom and the pier you'll get a good price for that flat."

"I'd have to talk to Maria about it," Albie said cautiously, but Adam knew he was hooked.

Indicating the patch of rough ground beyond George's side wall he said, "Luke suggested we add that bit of land to the deeds as well. It's all stones and brambles but you could clear it."

"You could stick your wagons on there," George said, grinning broadly, and when Mateo and Josef offered to buy the patch of land for the tribe, the deal was struck on a handshake.

While the men were discussing business, the women were dishing out sandwiches and tea and taking it in turns to sit with Maria. Her first visitor was Daisy, who had taken shameless advantage of being Albie's niece to claim the privilege. Looking at the way she held little Annie, Maria smiled and said, "You're expecting, aren't you? That tea I gave you must have worked."

Daisy blushed. "And the lotion. One night I was putting it on Luke and it just happened." She faltered and reached for Maria's hand. "Did this awful thing happen to you because of your age? I'm over thirty as well."

"Of course not – the doctor said I was just unlucky."

"But you will get better?"

"Oh yes – I'll get better," Maria declared, crossing her fingers beneath the covers. She was convinced evil still hovered close by – there was a chill wafting over from the old campsite that couldn't all be explained away by the approach of autumn.

The news that their camp was going to move across the lane made little difference to the boys, who were used to change, but Clara was ecstatic, pleading, "Can we move today?"

"Them brambles are chest high, love," Albie said. "They'll take more'n a couple of hours to clear and I've got to work for me living."

"We'll do it," Clara said. "Me and Fleur and the boys."

"Yes – do let us, Dad!" Ben begged. "Mr Luke can be our

officer again."

"Me and my big mouth!" Luke said, laughing. "I'll take you on again on one condition – no unsupervised bonfires."

***

With Maria in the cottage, George became accustomed to coming down in the mornings to find one of the women there and a kettle already boiling, but one day he was up earlier than usual and discovered Clara asleep in his armchair by the range. George shifted the kettle over the hob and she jumped awake, so rumpled that it was obvious she had spent the night there.

"You all right, lovey?" George asked, spooning tea into the big brown pot.

"Just dropped off for a minute, Grandad."

"Hmph! Worn yourself out chopping brambles, I suppose."

"We've nearly finished – Dad says he'll move our tents and wagon this weekend."

Clara's joy was transparent as glass and George tousled her curls. "If you want to sleep here till then, bring a bedroll and use the spare bedroom." He laughed aloud at the expression on Clara's face. "You think I hadn't guessed you're scared of that campsite? The memory of that bomb shelter is enough to give anyone nightmares."

Clara buried her face in his dressing gown and didn't tell him she'd forgotten about the bomb shelter in the face of the new, unspecified danger.

At the weekend, as promised, Albie moved his children's two tents to the other side of George's garden wall before fetching his horse from the paddock to move the wagons.

"I'll be happier when we're on the new site," Lydia said to Rosanna. "This one hasn't felt right since the shelter collapsed."

"You're right – and have you noticed how George's kittens won't come near the place?"

"They're only just starting to leave his garden," Mateo said.

"Give them time."

Both the women remained uneasy even after the move. They hung charms in the hedge, tended the fire with extra care, and prayed nothing else bad would happen.

# CHAPTER THIRTEEN

Over the next few weeks Maria gradually improved, and by the hop-picking season she could be lifted from bed to commode without wincing. Lydia, Rosanna and Olivia were in and out all the time, bathing her and baby Annie, even cooking in George's kitchen, and for the months of September and October the cottage was the social centre of the tribe.

At least once a day one of the women would take the shawl-wrapped baby and walk her along lanes and across fields, introducing her to the sights, sounds and scents of the open-air life that was her birthright. Sometimes Clara took Annie and sat with her in the girls' tent for a few minutes – "Just to get her used to it, Mama," – but Maria forbade anyone to take her to the old campsite.

When the first frosts prompted Mateo to take his tribe to the winter meeting-grounds at Ruxley, Maria could only shuffle along with the aid of a walking-frame. The tribe had already shrunk when Mateo's second son Theo took his family to sit out the war on his in-laws' farm, and Mateo was loath to lose more, but for Maria to live in a wagon would be impossible. Josef was heartbroken to leave Maria and his grandchildren behind, but he knew his ageing parents needed him more.

The day before they left, Joey arrived home unannounced – he always knew when there was a party in the offing. The tribe's numbers were doubled by their party guests – all of the Finches, May Coppin and Frank, and Paddy O'Brien who, when the travelling fair season ended, had found work at a garage in Thambay and now rented a room in town.

They lit a bonfire beside Albie's wagon on the new campsite and passed over the wall a constant supply of food and drink from George's kitchen. When the afternoon warmed up, George lifted an armchair over as well, and Albie carried Maria round to cocoon her in a blanket with baby

Annie in the lee of the wagon. For the first time since Annie's birth Maria felt part of the tribe and, with a glass of wine in her hand, some colour returned to her cheeks.

Luke said to George, "Maria could get here much more easily if there was a gate through the wall from your garden – I'll organise that tomorrow."

"Seems a shame to cut through a perfectly good wall for just a few wagons in a field."

"It's got to be a proper registered campsite these days, George, or it'll be closed down. We're calling it Perez Field after Mateo. The Town Hall says we've got to lay on a water supply too before they'll give it a licence."

"They've been using my backyard pump."

"Not good enough these days, especially as they're gypsies – you know what the Town Hall are like. Luckily they're bringing mains water out here next spring – Bert has certainly livened things up at the Council."

Early the following morning Mateo drove his vardo out of the campsite, with Lydia and Rosanna perched on the seat beside him. Josef followed in his own small wagon, with Ricardo and Olivia bringing up the rear. They drove down Farm Lane so that Maria could see them go past her window, but by mutual agreement they didn't stop – all their farewells had been said the night before, and it would bring bad luck to begin this journey with tears. Albie stood by the gate with the boys, Maria held Annie up to see them pass by, and George stood in the doorway, still wearing his dressing gown.

"Where are Clara and Fleur?" Mateo asked. "Can't they be bothered to wave goodbye?" Then the upstairs window was flung open and the two girls in their warm winter nightdresses blew kisses and called, "See you next year!"

Mateo waved his whip, and within moments the small convoy had vanished into the mist. George went indoors to liven up the fire, shivering and thinking that winter couldn't be far away. Joey, Ben and Davy followed him in the hope of an early breakfast, and Clara and Fleur dived back into their still-warm bedrolls. Only Albie at the gate and Maria at her window remained, listening to the fading clip-clop of hooves and watching the mist swirl in to refill the empty lane.

***

Number One Farm Cottages seemed very quiet when Mateo's group had gone, but after a day or two those left behind established new patterns to fill the void. The highlights of Maria's day were the homecomings. Ben and Davy would erupt into the cottage after school like a whirlwind to tell her about their day and to smother Annie's placid little face with kisses. Then would come Clara and Fleur to drop their satchels of homework with promises to do it before bedtime, and last of all came Albie, always ready to relate some small detail of his work on the farm.

Fleur's kisses for Annie were perfunctory – the overpowering baby atmosphere of Maria's room disturbed her – but Clara had discarded her shorts and gone back to being a girl. She was content playing mother to her baby sister, fetching and carrying for Maria and taking Annie along the lane in a big-wheeled pram. She loved this private time with Mama and Annie, although whatever the weather she always opened the window for a while to dispel the taint of sickness before Albie came home.

In November, when Wilson's factory sold off their wartime utility stock, Albie bought a double bed. He had slept alone in the wagon for long enough, in his opinion – if he couldn't make love to his wife, at least they could share a cuddle. To make more space he moved the bookcase to the kitchen, but when he wanted to move Dot's clock, Maria refused to allow it. "It's company – when you're at work and the children are at school it fills the silence." What she didn't tell him was that Dot's presence was at times more real than Annie's. Whenever George came in to tend the fire, Dot watched him carefully, tutting if a spark escaped onto the rug, and when he dusted the mouldings on her treasured clock – a duty he would allow no-one else to perform – Dot's shadow-hand made sure the duster went into every crevice.

"You could listen to the wireless with Dad," Albie suggested. "You got yourself and Annie to the kitchen once with that walking frame."

"She's getting too heavy to be carried in a shawl," Maria said, but the truth was that she was afraid she would wet herself in George's chair while she waited for Albie to come home and carry them back. By shuffling on her frame she could reach the commode or the chair by the window – and when she was tired she could lie on the bed and save her energy for her family. No-one knew, for she managed to hide it even from Clara, about the pain that gnawed at her womb, or about the darkness she was holding at bay by an effort that tested her will-power to its limits.

Around the deserted campsite the hedges grew taller in a final spurt of growth, then winter set in with gales that dispersed the ashes of the fire-pit and drifted a layer of pine needles into the deep ruts where the wagons had stood. The buried logs of the bomb shelter that had almost killed two children were eaten away by rot, the earth above settled lower, and the hinges of the gate succumbed to rust. The corner plot that had sheltered the tribe for fifteen years exuded an air of abandonment that repelled even Ben and Davy when they ventured there in search of a hideout, and they found instead a deserted outhouse on Pinetree Farm. Fleur spent her free time in the baby-free haven of Linda's bedroom, and Clara took care never to go near the old site, for she couldn't shift the memory of the fog she had seen on the day Annie was born. Even the wild country creatures gave the little patch of ground a wide berth, for it had been denied several deaths and they sensed the debt had yet to be paid.

And Maria, sitting at her window to watch the cows go to milking or a tractor chug up the lane trailing a clatter of machinery, noticed the unkempt hedge move when there was no wind, saw the mist that filled the space stretch trailing fingers towards the cottage, and cuddled Annie closer – if Death still hunted her it would have to wait, because her first duty was here.

***

On Christmas Day May cooked a turkey which Paddy carried, still sizzling and fragrant, down to the cottage. Maria, from the comfort of George's kitchen chair, had supervised the preparation of huge pans of vegetables, all grown by George. Joey and Frank brought down an extra table, and the crowded kitchen rang with unrestrained laughter for the first time in months. After dinner they opened their presents, and while the other children played a game of Chinese Chequers, Joey and Frank fiddled about tuning in the small battery wireless Albie had bought for Maria.

After the Queen's speech the men went outside for a smoke and a chat. George nudged Paddy in the ribs. "You and May look as if you're getting on alright."

"Aye, she's a grand woman altogether, but we'd be getting on better if Frank'd let us alone," muttered Paddy. "You'd think he was her auld feller the way he hangs around."

"Queering your pitch, is he?" George grinned. "Want me to have a word?"

"Best not – he'll get used to it in the end – but we have to sneak around like a couple of kids." Paddy matched George's grin as he added, "Mind you, it adds a bit of spice!"

"I could do with a bit of spice myself," said Albie, the alcohol he'd drunk making him drop his guard.

"Maria must've mended by now, surely?" George said. "Four months is a long time."

"There's summat in her face tells me she's not right. She don't wince when she stands up now, but I'm still afraid of breaking her."

"She's just thinking too much, spending all her time in that room," was George's opinion. "We'll have to get a wheelchair if she's not going to get any better than this."

"She told me not to, but I'm on the lookout for one anyway."

Two days later – a Saturday – Albie and Paddy went to Margate with Joey to watch him play in a friendly game against another trainee team from their arch rivals, Ramsgate. After celebrating Margate's win in the nearest pub, they left Joey at his digs and, slightly tipsy, were on their way to the station when they stumbled upon a second-hand shop. The poor man stood no chance against Albie and Paddy's combined bargaining powers, and when they boarded the train to go home, Albie was carrying a wheelchair small enough to fit through the narrow doorways in the cottage. An hour later he marched proudly through the back door with the folded wheelchair tucked under his arm.

Maria was in the kitchen with a kitten on her lap when Albie came in. Clara had propped Annie up on the hearthrug with cushions – the baby looked up and squealed with joy to see her father, Clara automatically drew the kettle onto the hob, and Maria asked, "What have you got there?"

Albie opened the wheelchair and snapped the braces to hold it firm. "What do you think?"

"Very nice," Maria said with a marked lack of enthusiasm. "Except I've got nowhere to go in it."

"You don't sound too thrilled – I carried this all the way from Margate."

"Then you'll be needing a cuppa," George said briskly. "Sit yourself down."

Albie sat obediently to drink his tea, and by the time he'd told them about Joey and the game, Maria had gathered her scattered wits. The wheelchair was an unwelcome reminder that she was an invalid, but Albie had gone to a lot of trouble, so when he had finished his tea she said, "Can I try the wheelchair now?"

Albie jumped up with a pleased smile to help her into it and push her along the hallway. "We'll be able to wheel you up the back lane to see Daisy in this," he said. "We can put Annie on your lap."

"Maybe when it's a bit warmer," Maria said.

Clara laughed. "You are funny, Mama. We've lived outside all our lives and you've never worried about the cold before. We'll wrap you both up in a blanket."

"And before you ask where the money's coming from," Albie added, "we *can* afford it – Luke told me when he picked us up from the station. A mate of his valued the flat for me this afternoon."

"What did the man say?" George asked.

"You'd hardly credit it, Dad – not sure as I believe it meself – fourteen hundred quid!"

George spluttered on a mouthful of tea. "I know prices've shot up lately but it sounds an awful lot – Norah told Dot she paid five hundred. Mind you, wages've doubled since the war. Everything's gone up except me pension – I'd be in a right pickle if it weren't for the garden."

"It looks like I'll have some cash to spare," said Albie as the enormous amount spun into a storm of ideas. "I could get a van to take your stuff to market, Dad. Maria could go too in her wheelchair and help you on the stall."

"You haven't sold it yet," Maria warned. "And we don't know what Mr Finch is asking for the cottage."

"Well, if we can't afford to buy it we'll live next door in Perez Field – we own that already – and I'll have enough money to buy you the fanciest caravan in the showrooms."

But Adam Finch only wanted nine hundred for the cottage, saying it was just one of a terrace in the middle of nowhere, not a seafront flat in a bustling town with shops round every corner. When the couple who were renting the flat paid the asking-price without a murmur, Albie paid Adam for the cottage and bought a second-hand Jowett Bradford van for forty pounds.

The day he brought the van home he carried Maria out to install her in the front seat with Annie on her lap, put the wheelchair in the back, and drove into town. Maria looked around like a tourist. "It's been so long since I left Pinetree I'd forgotten half of this," she said. "Can we go along the seafront?"

"We've got summat to do first," Albie said mysteriously, and drove along beside the railway to park in Market Square. As he lifted Maria and Annie out again she demanded to be told where they were going, but he just shook his head and wheeled her straight into the Midland Bank. The cashier looked down his nose and said, "May I help you?" in icy tones.

"You can stop being snooty, for a start," Albie said. "And call the manager – I want to open an account here." When the man didn't move, Albie rummaged in the pockets of his thorn-snagged coat and slapped four bundles of notes on the counter. "There's four hundred pounds there – d'you want it or shall I go to the Post Office?"

"We would be happy to open an account for you, sir," came the treacly voice of the manager, and after Albie had given Luke Finch's name as a reference, he was soon the proud possessor of a deposit account and a little navy-blue book to prove it. As the bank's doors shut behind them Albie looked up at the Town Hall clock and said, "We've got time for a cuppa," so they spent another few shillings on tea and cakes in the little tea shop before they collected Ben and Davy from school.

"It's a bit hard taking all this in, Albie," Maria said as they drove home. "We own a cottage and a van and now a bank account."

"We'll go by the farm to tell Luke I put him down for a reference, and you can tell Daisy – that'll make it real."

They were sitting at the big kitchen table at the farm,

enjoying a comfortable gossip, when the telephone shrilled and Luke picked it up. A moment later he laughed. "You must have known he was here – Albie, it's your father-in-law."

Maria and Daisy stopped talking to listen when Albie took the receiver. "I'll have to think about it, Josef … well, I could ask her … and I've just bought a van, it might be big enough … right, we'll talk again on Sunday." He put the phone down and pulled a face, but it was obvious he was excited. "Dan's youngest is getting wed and Josef wants me to take the girls – says at their age they should be meeting some nice Roma boys."

"He's right – they should," Maria said. "But I can't take them."

"Lydia and Rosanna will chaperone them, he says, and we could ask May to look after you and the little ones while we're gone."

"It's at Ruxley, I suppose? You'd be gone for a week – I don't like the sound of that."

Albie reached across the table to clasp Maria's hands. "We can be there and back in three days now I've got the van. And it's not at Ruxley – it's on Canvey Island."

***

A couple of days before they left, a man from the Water Board called at Pinetree Farm to ask Adam if he could spare a bit of land for several trailer-loads of pipes and equipment, and Adam offered him the former gypsy site in exchange for installing extra pipes to the new site on Perez Field. The rumble of trucks jerked Maria awake the next morning and she looked out of the window in horror. "They shouldn't go in there – it's dangerous."

Albie put his arm round her shaking shoulders. "It's just a bit of ground now, love – we ain't living there no more."

While he brewed a pot of tea he thought for the thousandth time that these baby blues should have gone by now – she'd had them after Ben was born, but then she'd got over them inside a month. The old Maria had been replaced by a nervy woman who was nothing like the joyful girl he'd married. She looked after Annie and the other children well enough, even cooking meals and washing their clothes with a bit of help from George, but Albie couldn't remember the last time he'd heard her laugh. He'd even spoken to May and Daisy about it, but May and Paddy were too dewy-eyed to notice anything, and Daisy was soppy with pregnancy. Besides, this fear of the old site wasn't normal. When Lydia returned in the spring he'd ask her if she knew what to do.

## CHAPTER FOURTEEN – CANVEY ISLAND

Lydia almost refused to go to Canvey Island. "I saw a shooting star last night," she said to Mateo. "That means a death."

"We all saw it – are we all to die?" Mateo scoffed. "We must be there – our people are scattered enough as it is and we haven't seen some of them for a year."

Mateo was king of the tribe, so they went.

Other families opted to stay behind at Ruxley, and the day before she left, Lydia carried a bundle over to her cousin Pilar's wagon and put it on the bed. "Look after this for me – Clara and Fleur will need it one day."

Pilar opened a corner of the linen bundle to reveal some exquisite lace. "This is your family wedding dress!" She grasped Lydia's wrist. "Please don't go."

"I must," Lydia replied. "Mateo insists, and we can't escape our fate."

Pilar gazed deep into Lydia's eyes and saw the calm acceptance that lay there. Without another word she opened the cupboard beneath her bed and laid the precious dress inside.

***

Wrapped up against the bitter January wind that threatened to freeze their hands to the bridles, Josef, Ricardo and Pedro led their horses on the long trek to Canvey Island, and on the afternoon of the fourth day parked their wagons in the large back garden of the bride and groom's bungalow.

Mark and Sonia were a modern couple who had given up the travelling life, but their gypsy roots remained strong – there were twenty-odd wagons in their secluded garden.

Albie, having driven his van over from Pinetree with Clara and Fleur, was already there talking to Nate, the gypsy who had unwittingly fathered him forty years earlier. As she did every winter, Lydia looked at them together and knew there could never be any doubt about Albie's true paternity. She was relieved to see Clara and Fleur were wearing the long skirts and warm shawls of Roma girls, rather than the boys' clothes they often wore on the farm, but their short hair raised some eyebrows among Lydia's friends.

"We must move with the times," she told one woman. "That gadjo school they go to had a plague of nits," she told another, and when the girls tied scarves over their heads to keep out the cold, the subject was dropped in favour of more interesting topics.

After everyone who was expected had arrived, Albie moved his van to block the driveway, so that anyone going past would see only its unremarkable brown bonnet – the tall hedges hid all the caravans. Those very hedges made Clara uneasy – with their untrimmed branches silhouetted against the winter sky they reminded her of the abandoned campsite back home, and the cold wind whispered through them in the same ghostly way. Clutching Fleur's arm, she begged her, "Don't go too far away," then Olivia called them to help prepare the food, and in the bustle as a dozen meals were cooked and shared in the crowded garden she forgot her fears.

When the tribe gathered around a huge driftwood fire later that night, catching up on news and gossip under the cold light of an almost full moon, Lydia was glad after all that they had come. If the death she had seen was hers or Mateo's, at least they had had this night among their family and friends first. She held out her glass more often than usual to be refilled, dulling her unease with alcohol, and when they finally went to bed Mateo's snores drowned out any ghostly whispers.

***

Mark and Sonia were married the next morning at the Catholic Church like any regular couple, but the party afterwards was pure Romany. Ignoring the miserable weather, they danced to the wild music of gypsy fiddles, cooked masses of food over open fires, and drank vast quantities of home-made wine.

The celebrations and the alcohol drove any premonitions of danger into the background, and it wasn't until Mateo, who had overdone his drinking the night before, took himself off to bed early, that Lydia began to heed them again. What first caught her attention was the far-off sound of a choir, which she took for angels singing until she heard applause and remembered seeing a poster for a concert at the War Memorial Hall.

She checked that their old horse was well-blanketed against the bitter wind, and before she retreated into the warm vardo she paused on the top step to check on her family. Light spilled from Olivia's wagon next to hers, Josef and Albie were among a huddle of men a few wagons away, and she could see Clara and Fleur settling into their bed in the back of Albie's van.

She saw salty green flames flickering uneasily in the central fire, briefly resembling a burning wagon, but when she looked again it was only a fire. Her old heart skipped painfully when she heard the cry of an owl and she shut the door quickly, determined that, whether Mateo liked it or not, they'd be leaving this sodden, sea-girt place first thing in the morning.

Clara and Fleur had seen Lydia at her vardo door, and waited until she shut it before drawing the van's curtains. Giggling, they slipped out of their skirts and petticoats and pulled on the trousers and jumpers they had concealed in their pillowcases. Clambering over the seats, they crept out of the passenger door to hear Nico hiss, "Over here!" Running across a patch of moonlight, they joined him behind the hedge.

"I hope no-one saw you," Nico said. "Girls aren't supposed to do things like this."

"Oh stop fussing," Fleur said. "We just want a look round before we go home tomorrow."

"All right – but we're not staying out long – what if your dad finds out?"

"He's too busy drinking," Fleur said, grabbing Clara's hand. "Come on – I want to see the houseboats."

Somewhat unsteadily, for they had all sampled the wine, they made their way through the deserted streets and climbed the sea wall. The wind on the exposed height threatened to bowl the three adventurers over, and when water splashed her feet Clara felt a surge of fear. "This is a bad idea," she said, but Nico sneered, "Chicken!" and Fleur pleaded, "Just five minutes to look, Clara." So they put their heads down against the wind and carried on past the moored houseboats.

"Sort of like floating wagons, aren't they?" Nico said, rather too loudly, and a man came out onto his tiny deck.

"You kids are out late," he said, tugging his mooring-rope. His attention sharpened. "My gangplank's under water – I don't like the look of this!"

"What's wrong with that?" Clara asked.

"It's clear you're not local," he said. "It's another hour to high tide, but look at that sea."

Wind-blown waves were slapping the top of the sea wall, and the three youngsters recalled Mark saying that Canvey Island was reclaimed land, below sea-level.

Clara quivered at the swollen menace of the grey waves. "Let's go back – I don't like the look of it either."

Leaving the houseboat owner splashing across his gangplank with a spare mooring rope, they hurried past more houseboats and dinghies to slither back down the sea wall, but even there they didn't feel safe – the earth was spongy, not like solid ground at all. Clara looked at the height of the wall, visualising the millions of gallons of water it must be holding back, and the thought made her sag at the knees.

"I do believe you're drunk, Clara Smith," Nico laughed.

"No I'm not! It's all that water. Something dreadful's going to happen, I can feel it. Let's get away from here."

"They build those walls bloody strong," Nico said, to reassure himself as much as her, but Fleur said, "She's right – we shouldn't be here," and they broke into a run.

***

A sudden fierce gust of wind rocked the vardo and Lydia snapped awake from the edge of sleep. Reflections from the bonfire filtered through her dark curtain and washed over the curved ceiling in waves. She sat up, fighting for breath like a drowning woman, and pulled on her skirt and a thick shawl. When she opened her half-door she saw Olivia and the other women leaning out of theirs – unease had disturbed them all.

Clara and Fleur were just heading for the van, hoping to get into it unseen, when Clara saw a silver circle gleaming at her feet. As she bent to pick it up the outline shattered – she had tried to catch the moon's reflection! She almost laughed, until she noticed they were standing in water, and their shoes were surrounded by worms – thin drowned worms gleaming ghostly pale in the moonlight. Grabbing Fleur's wrist she ran towards the bonfire, looking for her father and yelling, "We're sinking!"

Then a shout echoed from the distance, "The sea wall has collapsed!" and there was instant pandemonium.

As each man tried to save his own wagon, Albie sent the girls to Josef and ran to his van, fumbling for his keys as he went – no-one else could escape the garden with his van in the way. Fortunately the engine started at the first attempt, so he put his foot down and raced up the road, certain he remembered seeing a hill. It was only a slight rise, but he drove up the grassy slope, hoping that the tree roots were firm enough to hold the earth in place, and left the van there before wading back through the rapidly rising flood.

In the few minutes he had been gone, the rush to get the wagons out of the garden had descended into chaos. Mateo's horse refused to be backed into the shafts, and Josef had the same trouble with his horse. "They know what's coming," he said. "They'll drown if they're harnessed."

They were about to set them free to fend for themselves when Nico said, "We'll look after them," and, collecting all the reins in their fists, he and his brother Pedro set off through the flood to find higher ground.

Fleur wailed, "We might never see them again."

"They'll be all right," Clara said. "Horses can swim."

"We can't," Fleur said, and the sisters looked at each other with wide, horrified eyes.

Then the bridegroom Mark appeared at his back door and yelled, "The loft's boarded over! You'll be safe up there!" and he hauled himself up through the hatch to drop the ladder.

"Women and children into the loft!" Mateo bellowed. "Once you're out of the way we can save the wagons."

A line immediately began to form at the back door. Only Lydia argued, but Mateo was adamant and finally she allowed herself to be led away. Glancing back from the door for a last sight of her husband, she climbed the ladder with almost fatalistic calm, and found a space as close to the hatch as she could. Looking around, she counted heads. Rosanna was there with her family, Olivia with hers, Sofia was leaning against a pile of suitcases, but she couldn't see Clara and Fleur.

"Where are Maria's daughters?" she shouted.

Albie found them inside Josef's wagon, dragging everything out of the under-bed cupboard and piling it on top of the mattress to keep it out of the rising flood.

"Didn't you hear Great-grandpapa? Women and children should be in the loft – now!" The water was already sizzling into the pot-bellied stove, and Josef's home was beginning to rock. Albie looked at his bedraggled girls, wondering briefly why they were dressed like boys again, and said more gently, "I know you're trying to help but you've gotta leave it now."

"It should go down soon – the man said high tide was midnight," Fleur blurted out.

"What man?"

"In a houseboat by the sea wall."

"We'll talk later about why you were there," Albie said sternly. "It must be midnight by now and it's still getting deeper – you're going into the loft and no more arguments." Scooping them both up as if they weighed nothing, he carried them to the house and pushed them up the ladder, where they joined the other frightened women and children sitting on the bare boards of the loft space. The moonlight, chopped into flashes by scudding clouds, shone fitfully through the slanting window onto the dozens of shivering bodies, and Clara and Fleur clung to each other. The loft was packed – the only remaining space was a corner by the window, as far from the hatch as it was possible to be, and the sensation of being trapped was intensified when a toddler started crying. In seconds the confined space was flooded with sound as every other small child began to wail.

"I can't stand this!" Clara yelled in Fleur's ear.

"Neither can I," Fleur answered. "I've got to open this window."

The latch was sticky with corrosion, but eventually it yielded and they pushed the sloping window outwards. The shock as icy air rushed into the room instantly quietened the howlers, and Fleur stuck her head through the gap. "There's room for us all out here. There's a flat roof."

The panic subsided when the women realised they had an escape route, and when Olivia said, "Now all we have to worry about is freezing to death," one woman actually laughed.

Leaving the window open a crack, Clara and Fleur wrapped their arms round each other for warmth, listening to the sounds carried on the frigid air – unidentifiable crashes and bangs, barking dogs, and the voices of people screaming for help – people like themselves, caught unawares by the catastrophe.

Meanwhile Mateo, along with the other men of the tribe, was up to his chest in the freezing salt water, fighting to prevent the ton weight of his home from floating away. Josef had to abandon him briefly – his own wagon had already lifted free of the mud and was drifting towards the bungalow with Albie clinging to its shafts. Nate's wagon was between theirs and the building, where the force of the tide held it wedged in a corner by the back porch, and Josef spotted an opportunity. "Over here!" he yelled, and with one last desperate effort they managed to jam the shafts through one of Nate's wheels. The jolt sent Josef flying but he was up in a second, grinning widely – they had saved it.

But they had no time to gloat – Mateo's vardo was now afloat too, and all three men leaned their weight against it in an attempt to repeat the manoeuvre. What they hadn't seen was one of the modern caravans bobbing along like a bath toy and bearing down on them. Nate yelled a warning and Albie and Josef jumped aside in the nick of time, but Mateo was slower – the caravan swung ponderously round and crushed him against the side of his own vardo. Josef just managed to grab him before he slid beneath the water, but the caravan carried on inexorably, pushing Mateo's home along the drive and out into the street.

Up in the loft, Lydia shrieked once and dropped through the hatch before anyone could stop her. Several feet of water cushioned her fall, and with a strength born of desperation she forced her way through the flooded bungalow to reach the back door just as Albie and Josef heaved Mateo onto the platform of Josef's wagon. As Lydia emerged from the doorway the current swept her off her feet, but Josef caught her and lifted her up beside Mateo, where she pulled his head into her lap and stroked his brow with frozen fingers. "I knew we shouldn't have come," she murmured. "Stubborn old fool."

At the sound of her voice Mateo opened his eyes and forced

his flooded lungs to take another breath. "*Adios, mi corazón*," he whispered and Lydia kissed him. A moment later he exhaled a bubble of blood and died. Lydia threw back her head and howled – a dreadful keening sound that reached Clara and Fleur in the loft.

"Mother, you're soaked through – go back indoors," Josef begged, but she flatly refused to leave Mateo. All Josef and Albie could do to protect her from the freezing temperature was to wrap her in some of the dry blankets the girls had rescued, and then they had to leave her. The tide had turned, and those wagons that had been corralled in the garden by the overgrown hedge were on the move again in a different direction.

***

Miraculously, the next morning Mateo's vardo drifted back on the receding tide to end up, virtually intact, opposite the front door. Josef found it at first light, and asleep on the bed was Mateo's mongrel. Josef smiled at the picture it made, thinking the dog would be a comfort to his mother. Splashing through the muddy water to tell her the news, he found Lydia sitting with Mateo's head in her lap, Clara and Fleur asleep beside her, all of them cocooned in blankets. Josef gently touched the girls' shoulders. "Wake up, little ones – I must tell Mama I've found her vardo."

"We're not asleep, Grandpapa, but you can't wake her – she died soon after we got here."

"Not Mama too!" Josef cried, clasping his mother's hands, but they were cold and stiff. He had lost both parents in the one disastrous night, and he would be the one needing the comfort of his father's dog.

At dawn a large, shallow-draughted cockle-boat with a motor and furled brown sails chugged along the main road looking for survivors. To avoid being rounded up, the gypsies retreated behind the hedge and hid their newly-lit fires.

At low tide an hour or so later the water level had dropped

enough for the army to drive by with loudhailers, telling everyone to wait at their gates to be picked up and evacuated. The distorted voice said that only one change of clothing was permitted, and the reason became obvious when they saw survivors packed like sardines into the army lorries – there was no room for suitcases. One of Rosanna's grandsons nipped out to talk to a soldier, who told him they were to be driven to Benfleet Station and thence to evacuation centres. The boy barely escaped being loaded into the lorry. The wedding party remained hidden behind the bungalow until there were no further sounds from the road – they preferred to deal with their own troubles in their own way.

The first sign of cheer that morning was the return of the horses, though how Pedro and Nico had slipped them past the army remained a mystery. Mateo's old horse would no longer be needed to pull the vardo, but Pedro gave it a good rub down while Josef tackled the sad task of preparing his parents' home for their funeral. With help from Clara and Fleur he cleaned the vardo from top to bottom, removing only his personal possessions and his savings from their niche behind a picture on the wall.

Olivia came in to remake the bed, but when she opened the sliding panel beneath the high bed to find the linen, she asked Josef, "Was this cupboard open when the flood came?"

Josef raised an eyebrow. "No, it's never open – why do you ask?"

"Because the wedding dress has gone." Olivia pulled everything out onto the floor, wrinkling her nose at the smell. Then her brow cleared. "Of course! I saw her carry something over to Pilar before we left Ruxley."

Josef leaned against the cold stove and stared at the linen. "So Mama saw it coming – I should have guessed."

Out of respect for the dead, only the children had been given breakfast – eggs that Nico had found inside a china chicken on someone's kitchen table. No-one else would eat, or even begin repairs, until tradition had been observed.

While the women put Mateo and Lydia in their bed for the last time, the men scoured the neighbourhood for any dry timber – a daunting task in which the spirits of Mateo and Lydia must have helped, for by mid-afternoon they had found enough. They built the pyre actually inside the vardo because the ground beneath it was still covered by sea water, then Josef doused the timber with a can of petrol and tossed a flaming rag into the open door. The fire burned fiercely, pouring a sheet of red over the flooded ground, and to the people perched on the wagons or in the beds of trucks, Josef and Albie appeared to be standing in a sea of blood.

When the flames finally burned through the axles and dropped the remains of the vardo into the sea of red, the mourners raised their voices in a howl of lament that sent Mateo and Lydia straight to heaven. The sound wafted across the devastation that was Canvey Island, sending superstitious shivers along the spines of those people who still remained in their sodden homes.

The tide was rising again, the wind was bitter, and no-one had eaten all day. They had shown Josef's parents as much respect as they could in the circumstances, but now it was time to address the practicalities of their situation. Taking torches along the deserted streets, they emptied abandoned kitchen cupboards of their contents, rescuing disintegrating packets of macaroni and rice, tins already showing signs of salt-water corrosion, sacks of potatoes, and bottles of everything from orange squash to fine Napoleon brandy. They found enough dry fuel to relight the stoves in the remaining wagons, and Mateo and Lydia were sped on their journey by the strangest of funeral feasts – a stew of corned beef, tinned vegetables and macaroni washed down by very expensive brandy.

***

First thing on Monday morning the gypsies got on with

patching their lives back together. Albie found his van stranded high and miraculously dry on its private hill. A few men briefly joined a salvage team and returned with a cartload of sandbags with which, bulked out by ruined mattresses, they barricaded off an area behind the bungalow to keep the sewage-tainted water at bay. The women spread blankets on the flat roof to dry out in the weak sunlight, wagons were mended, vans and lorries dried out and persuaded to start. Pedro and Nico even found a sack of horse-nuts – the only other animal feed available was brine-soaked grass. And still no-one except Mark and Sonia knew they were on the island. Any neighbours who might have heard their party on Saturday night had been evacuated, drowned, or died of exposure on their own roofs.

That night, when the army had retired to its temporary barracks, a procession of wagons and caravans slipped quietly away to the mainland, the usual clip-clop of horses' hooves muffled by a thick layer of mud. Only Nate's wagon remained at the bungalow, with one corner propped up on a concrete block until he could replace the shattered wheel, and there were some vehicles whose owners were still working on their engines. Apart from these few, the scores of wedding guests melted into the night as if they had never existed.

# CHAPTER FIFTEEN – THAMBAY

On the morning of Sunday 1st February, in his cottage on Pinetree Farm, George turned on the wireless and listened to the news in stunned silence. Reports were just coming in about a tidal wave that had swept down the east coast on gale-force winds. A car ferry – the *Princess Victoria* – had sunk between Stranraer and Larne with a loss of over a hundred souls, and a wall of water had barrelled down the North Sea, devastating the coast from Scotland to Kent, where the bottleneck of the English Channel had forced it over sea-defences. Hundreds of lives had been lost, the newsreader told them, though no figures were yet available. In a place called Wells-Next-the-Sea a 160-ton vessel was stranded high and dry on the quay – in the East End of London the surge had inundated gasworks and electricity stations, leaving thousands of homes without power – but the worst news for the Smith family was that Canvey Island was flooded so badly that it might have to be abandoned completely.

Looking at Maria, George asked uncertainly, "You would know, wouldn't you?"

"I know someone died last night," she answered slowly. "It wasn't Albie or my babies." She stroked Annie's soft cheek and smiled across the table at Ben and Davy. "Dad and your sisters will come home soon," she said, so confidently that they believed her.

But it was late on Monday night before the wanderers returned. Ben and Davy were woken by the sound of the engine when Albie parked next to their wagon, and they threw themselves at him before he was even out of his seat.

"Steady on, boys," he protested, fending them off. "I'm too tired to carry you right now – go and help your sisters unload the back."

George had kept the cottage boiler going, and after hot baths and a night's sleep, Albie, Clara and Fleur told their story of the flood, the funeral, and their nightmare journey home. The flooding had forced them inland almost as far as Slough before they could cross the Thames and turn back east along the devastated coast.

"We didn't go into Thambay," Albie said. "Have you heard anything from there?"

"May got a phone call to say Bert's shop was flooded," George told him, and Albie snatched up his jacket. Ten minutes later, with George beside him and the children sitting in the back with George's garden tools, Albie sped through the country lanes to discover what had befallen his friends.

Thambay was built round a shallow, north-facing bay bounded by low chalk cliffs. The promenade sloped gradually down from the recreation ground at its eastern end, levelled out from the pier to the quay that enclosed the harbour, and then the old fishermen's quarter rose sharply to Cliff Road in the west. At its lowest point the sea wall was a mere six feet above the beach. Every winter, waves battered this wall to rear up and lacerate the promenade buildings with stinging spray, but never since the hurricane of 1935 that had destroyed their helter-skelter on the pier had George and Albie seen such damage.

The massive tidal surge had washed over the sea wall with contemptuous ease, smashed through the windows and doors of every house and shop between the recreation ground and the harbour, then swept inland as far as the railway embankment. The water had snarled back at this obstruction to drain north again into the bay, but successive waves had held it on land for long enough to wreak havoc on the church, the Town Hall, and every building around them. Some water had even poured through the North Street bridge beneath the railway to spread brine over the secondary school playing fields, Wilson's timber yard, and a broad swathe of the council estate.

Albie's main concern was for Bert, whose shop was just off

Market Square, but there was still too much debris to get the van through so he stopped near the pier. George was getting his tools out of the back when a familiar figure stepped carefully over a broken shop front and hailed them. Constable William Daly's normally immaculate uniform was mud-smeared and his face grey with fatigue. "Albie – I heard you'd been away. Bert's OK but the shop took a bit of a battering – good job they live upstairs. Some weren't so lucky – we've four dead so far."

They walked with Billy through the filthy streets, leaving him at the Police Station while they went on to Market Square. Everywhere, weary people were shoveling debris onto the pavement and throwing sodden belongings from their homes. Through every open door they could see living-rooms full of ruined furniture, grey tide-marks halfway up every wall, peeling wallpaper and mud-soaked carpets. Seaweed and dead fish lay in stinking piles on the cobbles of Market Square, and the King's Head – George's local – reeked of salt water mixed with beer. George stopped there to help Clive the landlord and some other regulars empty the flooded cellar with a chain of buckets, while Albie crossed the square to find Bert.

The road outside the butcher's shop was a nightmare of broken glass, and there was more inside. Bert was hosing down the filthy walls when Albie walked in. Without lifting his head, Bert gestured at the counter where joints of meat were laid out. "Help yourself, mate – if you cook it today it should be alright."

"Bert – it's me – Albie. I've come to help."

Bert's face was grey behind his freckles and his red hair was spiky with mud. "God, Albie, am I glad to see you! What a fucking mess this is, eh? Alice is going round the neighbours telling 'em to come and get the meat before it goes off – the fridge room shorted out."

"You're insured, ain't you?"

"Course I am, but that ain't the point." Bert's slumped shoulders said it all – the shop that was his pride and joy would take more than an insurance cheque to put right.

Within an hour every joint of meat and all the chops and sausages had gone to grateful customers. Albie and Bert, together with Ben and Davy, used George's tools to shift the broken window-glass onto the growing pile in the centre of Market Square, while Clara and Fleur helped Alice to scrub the interior of the big fridge with disinfectant.

At the end of the morning Bert stood at the doorway surveying his kingdom and said, "It don't look so bad now it's clean, does it?"

Looking at his old friend's woebegone face, Albie patted him awkwardly on the shoulder. "Cheer up, mate – it might never happen."

"Oh sod off, Albie – it already has," Bert snapped, then his expression cracked into a grin. "We lived through worse in the war though, didn't we?" He put his arm round Alice and added, "We're grateful for your help, but we can manage the upstairs on our own now."

"Come on, kids – let's see how Grandad's getting on," Albie said, so they returned to the King's Head, to discover George on the cellar ladder struggling to lift up a barrel.

Albie took it from him and helped George up the ladder, Clive followed with a bottle of beer for each of them, and they knocked the tops off on the edge of the counter. Clive gestured gloomily at the wooden barrels. "They've all got to go – it'll take a good while to sort this lot out. Still, the fishermen came off much worse – I was down by the harbour last night and it's a right old mess. You're lucky you live inland."

"We were on Canvey Island when it happened," Albie said, and told his story briefly before going in search of anyone else who was in need of their help.

That day Albie lost count of the number of carpets he tore

up and saturated armchairs he carried to the dump, while the Smith children's offers of help were welcomed with relief by many old, bewildered people. During the afternoon the Town Council installed washing machines and two of the new tumble dryers in the brickworks canteen, and the girls made several trips there with sea-stained sheets and towels. On one trip through the littered streets, Clara spotted a piece of driftwood, beautifully sculpted by the sea.

"Frank would love this," she said without thinking.

Fleur's antennae shot up. "Frank?"

Clara blushed. "It's his birthday party next week, remember? This would make a lovely present."

When Albie drove them all home that evening, electricity had been restored to some of the houses, but many of the lights that shone from upstairs rooms were dim and flickering – the hardware store had sold out of candles and lamp oil.

*** 

There was already quite a crowd in May's kitchen when the Smiths arrived for Frank's birthday party. As soon as Maria's wheelchair had been settled at the table, Frank said, "Joey rang up – he sends everyone his love and says he'll score a goal today to celebrate my birthday."

"He'll score three!" Davy cried. "When can we go and see him play, Dad?"

"Soon as he's in the team proper, son. Now give Frank his birthday present."

When Frank had opened his presents and blown out all his sixteen candles with one breath, the adults sat round the table with cups of tea, leaving the youngsters to spread out around May's wing of the sprawling farmhouse. There were puppies to be cuddled in the scullery, a train set laid out on the dining room table, and a wireless in Frank's bedroom.

Clara hadn't wanted to give Frank his present in front of everyone, and when she found him on the half-landing she said shyly, "I brought you a present just from me." She had been clutching the piece of driftwood for so long that it was warm when she gave it to him.

Turning the piece of wood over in his hands, he murmured, "It's beautiful."

Clara let her breath out in a relieved sigh. "I found it after the storm – I thought it looked like a horse."

"It does – a horse from the sea – a sea-horse," Frank said, impulsively leaning forward to kiss her mouth. The shock zipped right down to their toes and their eyes locked in surprised recognition. Clara covered her lips to stop the kiss from flying away while Frank wound one of her curls round his finger. "Beautiful," he said again, and Clara wasn't sure whether he meant her or the sea-horse.

The moment stretched and stretched until Paddy's shout broke the spell. "Any of youse up there wanting some hot chocolate?"

A thunder of feet passed the wonder-struck pair, heading for the kitchen. When the last one had disappeared through the door, Clara took a deep breath for courage, stood on tiptoe and brushed Frank's lips with a butterfly kiss. "You have the softest mouth," she said, and as his arms moved to hold her she slipped away and ran down to join the others.

Paddy had come in from town with Bert and would stay the night, sharing George's room, so when all the guests had gone and Frank was in his room starting on a new Airfix model, May washed the dishes while Paddy dried. After everything was tidied away he wrapped her in a hug and kissed her soundly, stroking her from shoulder to bottom with his big, warm hands. May pressed her body against his, half-inclined to drag him upstairs despite Frank's presence in the house, but Paddy held her away from him and smiled at her tenderly. "Lovely cake that was – will you be baking one like that every week when we're married?"

"Is that a proposal, Paddy O'Brien, or are you taking me for granted?"

"I'd never do that, me darlin', but you will, won't you?"

"Of course I will! Now kiss me again quickly before Frank comes down." Five minutes later, she pushed Paddy away reluctantly. "You'd better go before I get carried away," she said and ran upstairs.

Paddy put his jacket on and was about to open the back door when Frank barged into the kitchen. "I saw you kissing my mum – it's disgusting at your age."

"No it ain't – you don't have to be sixteen to enjoy kissing."

"Have you been spying on me?"

"No more than you have on us, Frankie boy – there's no closed doors at a party. Besides, Joey's mam's the same age as May and she's even got a babby."

"She's married – that's different." Frank's voice broke slightly.

"So if your mam and me was married it'd be all right?"

"You're not getting married, are you?" Frank dashed his hand across his face, mortified to find his cheeks were wet.

Paddy knew better than to notice and waited a moment before he said, "Frank, you listen to me. Your da's been gone many years, God love 'im, and your mam's been a widow-lady all that time – is she not entitled to a bit of happiness?"

"She was happy before you came along," Frank said, sulky as a child.

"Sure and why wouldn't she be, with a fine big cub like yourself? But now we're after getting wed and then she'll be even happier." Paddy waited. He sensed a change in the atmosphere but he knew Frank could still jump either way. He kept his gaze fixed determinedly on a pile of cow-muck in the yard as the silence lengthened, then Frank leaned on the draining board beside him and stared at the same pile of muck.

"I'm not calling you Dad."

"Wouldn't expect it from a great cub like yourself – Paddy'll do well enough."

"I don't want to leave the farm."

"Your mam don't want to neither, but it's up to your uncles."

"I could talk to them if you like," Frank offered tentatively.

Paddy's big hand descended on his shoulder. "Good man! You and me'll get along fine. Will we be telling your mam now?"

But May, who had been standing in the corridor, biting her knuckles and listening to every word, rushed in to hug them both. "Let's go and talk to Raymond now," she said, linking arms with them both to cross the yard to the main house, where they found Raymond with his brother Tim and their wives, the men discussing work for the next day.

Paddy muttered to May, "This is grand – we'll get it over in one hit." He remained standing to say his piece. "Mr Coppin, sir – seeing as you're the head of the family like, I've come to ask for May's hand in marriage."

"We wondered when you'd get round to it," Raymond replied, shaking Paddy's hand and then Frank's while the women kissed May.

Only Tim remained seated and scowling. After a pause he raised his voice over the congratulations. "What makes you think you're good enough to marry into this family?"

The room fell silent as Paddy turned to face Tim with slow deliberation. "'Cause I'm a bog-ignorant Irishman, you mean?"

"If you want to put it like that, yes."

May put her hand on Paddy's arm where the muscles were bunched iron-hard. "No fighting, please."

"I wouldn't soil me fists," Paddy answered and then added for everyone to hear, "At least I'm free to be a'courting, which is more'n can be said for your man sitting there. May ain't the only one he's been sniffing round."

Tim exploded out of his chair shouting, "What the hell do you mean by that, you – you – common labourer?" and launched himself at Paddy. Paddy side-stepped neatly, pushing May behind him, but Tim's ill-judged charge knocked Frank flying and his head hit the door-jamb with an audible crack.

Paddy grabbed Tim's collar. "I'm common, am I, you miserable gobshite? Not as common as the whores I seen you with in town."

Even Raymond was having difficulty restraining a grin by this time, but May, wiping a trickle of blood from Frank's forehead, said quietly, "That's enough, Paddy."

"Right you are, me darlin'," Paddy said, releasing Tim so suddenly that he staggered. "But if he touches you or Frank one more time he's a dead man."

Muttering vows to get even, Tim took his injured pride outside, slamming the door. A minute later they heard the roar of his sports car followed by a squeal of tyres as it skidded across the cobbles.

"That'll be that pile of cow-shit," Frank said with a grin.

Paddy cuffed the back of his head. "Which pile of shit would that be, boy? And mind your language in front of your mam."

## CHAPTER SIXTEEN – BIRTH & DEATH

Although the war had been over for eight years, rationing was still biting hard, but for the families living on Pinetree Farm there was plenty to eat. One Sunday in early March, Albie was carving a leg of pork when the sound of a car sent the boys running to the front window. They were just in time to see Josef, at the wheel of an Austin estate car, tow a small caravan into Perez Field and stop beside Albie's wagon.

"Rosanna has my wagon now," Josef told them, accepting a plate of food. "With the tribe so scattered, it makes sense for me to have a car."

"Of course, you're our King now," Maria said.

Davy's eyes widened. "Does that mean I'm a prince?"

Josef laughed and pinched his cheek. "A fat one, which is not surprising on good food like this. Are these your vegetables, George?"

"All me own 'cept the spuds," George said with pride. "Spuds ain't worth the bother when there's fields of 'em next door – and there's bottled plums for afters."

"I might have to move in with you," Josef said with a smile.

"You're more'n welcome, Josef – you know that," George said, thinking that the man looked as if he could do with a spell of home comforts – Josef's long face was grey beneath its tan and his still-black hair had lost its usual healthy sheen.

Josef shook his head. "No, I go to the hop-training next week. I will just take the car to sleep in and leave the caravan here for you to keep an eye on."

Josef put his pot-mending skills to good use that week, patching holes in a variety of pans the thrifty housewives of Thambay had rescued from their flood-damaged homes. Every day he ate with the family, but he refused George's offer to share his bedroom. "I could not sleep in a house," he said. "I am used to the wind rocking my home."

*\*\*\**

A week after Josef departed for the hop fields, Perez Field began to fill up. Ricardo and Olivia parked their wagon next to Albie's, and beside them was Josef's old wagon, now occupied by his aunt Rosanna. There was also a trio of modern caravans belonging to distant cousins who had nowhere else to go – the restrictions on where gypsies could camp were becoming tighter every year. While the younger ones drove off to local farms to look for work, the old men took scythes to Perez Field. On fine days Maria was able to leave the confines of George's cottage walls and sit within a circle of wagons and tents around a bonfire, her cheeks acquiring a healthy tan.

As if she had been waiting for the gypsies' arrival, Daisy went into labour in the first week of April. Luke telephoned the midwife, who bustled in a couple of hours later to find her patient sitting up, calmly sipping at a steaming cup while Rosanna and Olivia sat in the bedside chairs chatting away as if it were a normal day. The midwife sniffed, taking in the herbal smell of the brew and managing at the same time to convey her disapproval. "You should be lying down, Mrs Finch," she said severely. "Having a baby at your age is a risky business – and what's that you're drinking?"

"Raspberry tea," Olivia answered, taking the cup from Daisy when she sensed another contraction building up. "It's good for childbirth – and Daisy's more comfortable sitting up."

"Hmph!" the midwife snorted. "I'll be the judge of that!" She lifted the sheet to examine Daisy. "You've a while to go yet. I'll just pop down to the cottages to take a look at Mrs Jones – I'll be back in an hour."

"You'd better be quicker than that or you'll be too late," Rosanna said. "This baby's going to be here soon."

"Nonsense!" the midwife snapped and, gathering her professional reputation around her with her gabardine coat, she stomped out of the room.

"You've hurt her feelings," Daisy giggled, but a few minutes later she gasped and her tea slopped into the saucer. Olivia moved it to the table while Rosanna knotted an old towel to the bedpost saying, "Hang on to that, love – not long now," and wrung out a flannel to wipe Daisy's brow. When the pain had passed, Daisy raised anxious eyes to her friends. "I am a bit long in the tooth to be having a baby, aren't I?"

"Take no notice of that woman," Olivia said firmly. "You're only thirty-one and you're going to have a fine healthy boy – now let's get him born."

An hour later, when the midwife returned, Daisy was once again sitting up in bed drinking tea. Beside her, beaming all over his scarred face, sat her husband, cradling his new son in his arms. The midwife snatched the baby and unwrapped him on the bed to inspect every inch, then shooed Luke out of the room while she checked Daisy, whom she had to admit was remarkably undamaged after such a rapid delivery.

"Well," she said, closing her black bag with an infuriated snap, "you seem to have managed all right in my absence." She glanced with disdain at Rosanna and Olivia in their long skirts and shawls. "I suppose you have your babies in one of those primitive wagons?"

"Gosh, no," Olivia said, smiling wickedly. "We squat under a hedge to give birth and then go straight back to work."

*\*\**

The news of Daisy's safe delivery lifted Maria's spirits briefly – she had been afraid for her friend, for she sensed death everywhere.

That evening, cooking over the fire in Perez Field, Rosanna said to Olivia, "I must admit I prefer this new site. The old one turned bad last year, and it's still affecting Maria."

"It isn't just the site," Olivia said. "It's as if Maria's only tethered to this world by a slender thread – the one that connects her to Annie."

"She loves all her children," Rosanna protested.

"Of course she does, but the others don't need her like Annie does, and even she seems to be trying to grow up faster than normal."

Olivia was right – Annie was growing up quickly. Once the baby could sit unaided she had perfected a bottom-shuffle that got her along at amazing speed, and Maria could no longer keep up with her. Annie was a stolid, unflappable baby who took to a solid diet as if she had been waiting for the variety of tastes all her short life, and it wouldn't be long before Maria stopped breast-feeding her. Rosemary was afraid that even her centuries-old remedies of rosemary and lavender wouldn't anchor Maria's soul once her baby no longer needed her.

*** 

At the beginning of May, Patrick O'Brien and May Coppin née Daly were married in the church in Thambay. With the Coppin, Daly, Perez and Smith families plus assorted friends, the church was packed, and there were the usual onlookers leaning on the churchyard wall and gravestones to witness the marriage of a member of one of the area's most influential farming families with an Irish garage mechanic.

Albie, as Best Man, stood up beside Paddy when the rousing first notes of the Bridal March filled the church and Frank proudly escorted his mother down the aisle. May wore a low-cut three-quarter-length dress in a pale blue that set off her buxom figure to perfection, and on her head a froth of white lace was held in place by a circlet of forget-me-nots and maiden's breath.

"Is she not the loveliest woman you've ever set eyes on?" Paddy whispered.

Albie nodded absently but he wasn't looking at May – he was remembering the dark beauty in antique lace he had married. The contrast between that memory and the pale shadow sitting now beside George hit him like a fist, and he could scarcely breathe for the fear that surged up in a great

wave. As May walked towards the altar on Frank's arm, all
Albie saw was his own family seated in a line – Ben and Davy,
whom he'd scrubbed ruthlessly an hour ago, being pinned in
place by Joey, Fleur's blonde figure pretty in a dress for once,
Clara the little mother with Annie bouncing on her lap, and
George as solid and indestructible as an oak – but Maria
seemed hardly there at all. She was like a wraith – so
insubstantial that Albie fancied he could see through her to
the pew behind. When Olivia leaned forward to touch Maria's
shoulder he was surprised her hand didn't go right through.

A waft of flowery scent from May and a sharp nudge from
Paddy recalled him to his duties, but he performed them
absent-mindedly. The wedding group was outside being
photographed in the sunshine before he could shake the cloud
from his mind.

Josef had taken charge of Maria's wheelchair for the day,
and when Albie looked round for them, Maria was holding
Annie and looking animated and happy. Persuading himself
that his fear was merely a fancy brought on by being in the
church where he'd married Maria, Albie shook off his
preoccupation and escorted Paddy and May to the car. Mr and
Mrs Patrick O'Brien sat like royalty in the rear seat of the
polished black saloon bedecked with ribbons, and Martin
Darby, who had driven it down from London to be with his
old army comrades, took them back to Coppin Farm.

In the rarely-used dining-room of May's home, Albie
stammered through his Best Man's speech, Paddy and May
cut their cake, and the crowd spilled out into the sunshine of
the yard. Raymond Coppin had hosed the cobbles down for
the occasion and people crossed back and forth all afternoon,
forming groups, breaking up and re-forming. Martin Darby
talked soldiering with Raymond's son who had just returned
from National Service in Malaya; Josef and Albie shared a joke
with a couple of Paddy's friends from the fairground; George
flirted with Mabel Coppin, to their mutual enjoyment, and

Bert discussed town politics with Luke.

Clara, with Annie astride her hip, couldn't shake a niggling feeling that something was wrong, but she could see her mama in the middle of the yard, her aura shining brightly for once as she chatted with Daisy – if there were any ghosts here today they had been pushed into the shadows. The only bad vibrations came from Mr Tim, and as he was always in a bad mood Clara paid them scant heed. Blowing her mother a kiss, she pointed to Annie's bottom, and went upstairs to change her nappy.

Tim Coppin slouched against a wall by the beer barrel, drinking in morose solitude and watching May, the sister-in-law who had been his mother's kitchen maid till she married his late brother. He seethed with resentment at her for rejecting his advances, at Paddy for the instant acceptance he'd received from Raymond, and at everyone in general for enjoying the occasion – even his own wife and children were ignoring him. Muttering, "Time they all buggered off, it's damn nearly milking time," he collected a herdsman's thumb-stick and slipped away from the party.

Clara had just pinned a clean nappy on her baby sister when a dreadful premonition clutched at her heart. She grabbed Annie and raced downstairs, reaching the kitchen door just as Tim drove thirty cows into the yard. The animals were unaccustomed to being herded so roughly along with full udders, and were confused by the crowd between them and the milking parlour. The lead cow paused, her bell clanging as she swung her head from side to side, but Tim was still there behind them, beating the rumps of the tail-enders with his stick, and the herd pushed through the gate to mill about the yard in a bellowing panic.

The wedding guests scattered, scooping up children and running for doorways, and Josef grabbed the handles of Maria's wheelchair to haul her out of danger. They nearly made it, too, but one cow stepped on an abandoned plate, lost her balance and stumbled into them, knocking Josef off his feet and tipping Maria's wheelchair onto its side. As Maria fell, Josef threw himself on top of her, but it wasn't enough to protect her from the frightened cows. In the mayhem of mooing and shouting, the herd trampled their prone bodies and reduced the wheelchair to a battered wreck.

To Albie, who had just managed to snatch Davy from beneath a swaying udder, the whole episode passed in dreadful slow-motion. He recalled it later frame by frame – the milling herd, the snap of the plate shattering, the cow lurching into Josef, then Maria's arms and skirts flying wide as she tumbled among dozens of angular brown legs and sharp hooves. He tossed Davy onto a hay bale and dodged through the herd to lift Josef off Maria.

"I think my ribs are broken," Josef groaned. Albie handed him over to George and knelt beside Maria, afraid to move her, but when he put his hand on the ground it landed in a pool of blood. He stared at it aghast – *so much blood* – and laid his ear to Maria's breast, searching for a heartbeat. As Raymond and others steered the panicked animals into the milking parlour, Olivia knelt beside Albie, but after a few seconds she closed Maria's eyes. "She's gone, Albie – she knew it would be soon."

When Albie slid his arms beneath his wife's limp body and stood up, there were still some who thought she was merely injured, but Clara knew that death had finally won. She held Annie's head against her neck to shield her from the horror and Fleur, who had witnessed the entire catastrophe from Linda's bedroom window, ran downstairs. Their brothers formed a protective ring around them and then, to make the nightmare complete, their father – their big strong dad whose arms could lift tree-trunks – threw back his head and howled.

Tim Coppin, who had been leaning over the gate gloating at the chaos he'd caused, felt the hairs crawl on the back of his neck. Suddenly sober, he saw the blood on Maria's body and knew with an awful certainty that his prank had gone disastrously wrong. He tried to slip away without being noticed but he was too late. In a voice that the Coppin family rarely heard, Raymond bellowed, "Tim Coppin – what the bloody hell were you thinking?"

Tim might have got away with it even then if he'd shown some remorse, but instead he ran. Still holding the stick with which he'd goaded the cows along the track, he fled away down the lane. Albie laid Maria's body down on a bed of hay beside her children with the terse command, "Stay put," and set off in pursuit roaring, "I'll fucking kill him!"

"Stop him, Bert!" George pleaded and, with Paddy at his shoulder, Bert ran to save his friend from committing murder.

At the junction with Farm Lane Tim hesitated, glanced behind him, and saw three furious men on his tail. He turned and ran on, ducking into the old gypsy campsite where the Water Board's machinery slept the weekend away. As Albie and the others stormed through the gateway, Tim dodged into the cover of the stack of huge terracotta pipes.

"He went behind them pipes!" Albie shouted. "We'll flush him out like the rat he is."

"It's a bit dodgy back there," Paddy said. "We should wait him out."

"Let the Law deal with 'im," Ber added. "Our Billy seen what 'appened."

But Albie's need for vengeance was stronger than any sage advice and he raised his voice to a scream. "Come out and fight like a man or I'm coming in to get you!"

At the sound of Albie's rage Tim burrowed deeper behind the pipes, catching his jacket on one of the posts that held them in place. Unfortunately for him, the stack was on top of the collapsed bomb shelter, and the posts were in unstable ground. His desperate tugging dislodged one post – chance, or maybe a ghostly hand, moved another and then, with a rumbling roar of triumph at finally claiming its victim, Death rolled the entire stack down to crush him.

Back in the farmyard, ghosts swirled as if they had been stirred with a stick. Clara held Annie even closer, pulled herself up to her full height and addressed the ghosts directly. "You took our great-grandparents and now you've got Mama. You've taken enough – leave us alone now!"

Gypsies clutched their talismans as the temperature in the farmyard dropped even further, and a sudden chill breeze swirled wisps of straw into a spiral. Ben and Davy clung to Joey, and Fleur stood beside Clara, slipping her arm through hers.

Clara looked into Fleur's face, brown eyes searching blue. "You see them too?"

Fleur bared her teeth in a parody of a grin. "I see them."

The Smith girls looked at their dead mother and their brothers, at the baby sister they held, and then back to see in each other's faces the same determination that had conquered the school bullies. Standing shoulder to shoulder they faced the ghosts together and raised their voices in one defiant shout. "Leave us alone!"

## CHAPTER SEVENTEEN – CORONATION

After the tidal wave the Fire Service had pumped out the basement of the Market Hall but, thanks to its elevated position, the ground floor had remained undamaged. In May, Lillian Smythe was crossing Market Square when bright sunlight flashing from the tall windows caught her eye. "Why didn't I think of that before?" she said to herself. "It's the perfect place."

In the butcher's shop, Bert served her with a pound of sausages and a piece of steak for Gerald. "That'll be one pound, four shillings, Mrs Smythe."

"Thank you, Mr Daly. Now, may I ask Councillor Daly a question?"

Bert grinned – she never showed any resentment that he'd beaten her old man to the Council. "Fire away, missus – what can I 'elp you with?"

"The Market Hall – could the WI use it for a children's party on Coronation Day?"

"Golly – that's only a month away. God only knows what state it's in."

"I apologise for the short notice, Mr Daly, but I have only just had the idea. Perhaps with the help of volunteers we could spruce it up?"

Bert pondered for a minute and then his face lit up. "I know just the chap! Luke Finch helped me with the election – if anyone can get it done, he can."

***

A week before Coronation Day, Lilian bought her vegetables from the market before stopping in the Olde Tea Shoppe for a cup of tea and a slice of coffee cake. From her table in the window she could see over the half-curtains to the men painting the Market Hall windows. Mr Daly kept her up to date on progress, so she knew that the roof had been mended by a jobbing builder, the interior painted, and Mr Finch had even had the old gas-lights converted to electricity.

Obsessively she ran over her list again in her mind. The interior was shrouded in dustsheets to keep paint off the floor, but her WI ladies would need more than one session to bring those tiles up to an acceptable standard. They had already collected children's names for the party, planned the entertainments and drawn up a food rota. This Coronation would be the biggest event of Lillian's Chairmanship of the WI and the responsibility was daunting.

She checked her watch and called hurriedly for the bill – she would only just be in time to catch Mr Daly before lunch.

"Morning, Mrs Smythe," Bert said as she entered the shop. "I'd nearly given you up."

"I apologise if I have delayed you, Mr Daly – I'm afraid I was daydreaming."

"No problem, missus. Your chicken is ready for you. Now, what'll it be for today's dinner – lamb chops? Or I've got a nice bit of liver left."

"Anything, Mr Daly – whichever is easiest."

Bert was surprised – Mrs Smythe usually knew exactly what she wanted – but he wrapped up half a dozen lamb chops and put them into her basket with the chicken for Sunday. She was his last customer – he'd already scrubbed the chopping-block and swept up the sawdust from the floor – so he removed his apron and escorted her to the square. As Lillian hurried away down Market Street towards the promenade, Bert turned into the pub.

"Does Alice know you're chatting up other women, Bert?" Albie asked.

"That ain't a woman – that's a lady customer – she's Smythe's missus."

"She's married to him? Poor woman." Albie buried his nose in his pint.

Talking to Albie was uphill work, Bert thought. "She's organising next week's party."

"What party?"

"For the Coronation, Albie – your kids are coming."

"Oh – that party." Since Maria's death Albie seemed to have lost interest in everything. Bert suspected he only came to the pub because George insisted, and as if to prove it, as soon as George had finished his customary two drinks, Albie hustled him into the van and drove off without having spoken a word for a full half hour.

***

Coronation Day was damp, with a breeze that snapped the red, white and blue bunting and turned the Mayor's speech into disjointed staccato phrases, but no-one minded – they were determined to enjoy their day-long party.

A few houses in the streets adjoining the square had their television sets switched on to show the broadcast, and throughout the day people popped in, whether invited or not, to watch the tiny black and white pictures of the young and lovely Queen Elizabeth. Television cameras were stationed from Buckingham Palace to Westminster Abbey itself, with BBC commentators maintaining a running commentary that drew the townsfolk back time and again, to jostle for positions in dimly curtained living-rooms and comment on the splendid clothes of the Coronation guests.

Dozens of women made mounds of sandwiches in the sparkling interior of the Market Hall, covered them with damp tea-towels, then hurried away for a glimpse of the Royal processions. Men who had served in both World Wars set out long trestle tables and chairs on the gleaming black and white tiles, then were pulled back by the sound of military bands to watch troops of soldiers in full dress uniform ride their polished horses between crowds of cheering thousands.

When the glittering congregation inside the Abbey cried out with one voice, "God save the Queen!" women in Thambay wept openly and men coughed to clear lumps from their throats. The Queen's young voice asserting "I am willing" prompted more than one woman to exclaim, "Ah, God bless her – she's such a little thing for the job!" The Queen seemed far too slight to wear the heavy Robe, and when the Archbishop of Canterbury held the Crown aloft, everyone held their breath for fear that her slender neck would be unable to support the weight – even the children were silent until it was safely on her head. Then the Duke of Edinburgh paid homage to his Queen and one woman told her own husband, "See, Henry – that's a man's rightful place – at his wife's feet!" and the tension was released by laughter.

The queue of Dukes, Marquises and Lords seemed interminable, and many people took the opportunity to visit the bathroom or to go outside for a smoke. A fair number nipped into the pub for a quick one, but then the well-known strains of 'All people that on earth do dwell' rang out at full volume from the loud-speakers fixed to the lamp-posts and half the town of Thambay joined in.

When the Coronation itself was over, there was a concerted dash to fill kettles before sitting back down with a cup of tea to watch the triumphal progress back to Buckingham Palace. Anyone without access to a kettle lined up in the square in front of a battery of tea-urns, and May said to Paddy, "I bet Her Majesty's dying for a cuppa – I know I am."

Two hundred children clad in red, white and blue, scrambled to find seats in the Market Hall. As soon as they were all seated, the WI ladies passed round jugs of squash to fill the Coronation mugs that the Council had bought for every child. The centre of each long table held plates of sausage rolls, paste sandwiches, homemade cakes and biscuits, and even the hungriest child could see there was enough to go round. The noise level was almost painful, but it was not the mayhem Lillian had feared – eagle-eyed mothers ensured that their own children didn't grab more than their share, and she noted that even the group of gypsy children were well-behaved. She relaxed enough to join Gerald for a cup of tea at the Mayor's balcony table – a privilege her husband only enjoyed because Lillian was running the show.

Down in the body of the hall, Annie started grizzling, and Clara, who had the baby on her lap, said, "It's time we went home – it's been a long day for her without a proper nap."

Ben and Davy grabbed one more cake each before following their sisters out of the hall and ran across to the King's Head to find Albie.

"Mama was here today," Fleur said to Clara. "Could you feel her?"

"She's here all the time," Clara replied. "I just can't get used to you feeling it too."

"*You* think it's strange? Imagine what it's like for me, and I'm not even a proper gypsy."

"Gypsies aren't the only people who can sense things, I suppose," Clara conceded. "And you could be one for all you know."

"Could be one what?" George asked, taking his usual place in the front seat of the van and holding his arms out for Annie. Clara handed her over and climbed into the back next to Fleur, who said, "I could be a real gypsy – not even Dad knows who my mother really was."

"Maria was your mother," Albie snapped, starting the engine. "And that should be enough for anyone."

"Maria was her mama, Albie," George said. "Same as she was for the rest of 'em, but Fleur's bound to wonder who her natural parents were."

"But we've had her from a baby."

"Makes no difference, son – she'd still like to know, same as you did till you found Nate."

"We've no way of finding out, so she'll have to make do with what she's got," Albie said, his jaw muscles tightening visibly. "Which is only me now, in case you'd forgotten."

George's next words dropped into a pool of silence.

"There's no call to speak to me like that, Albert Smith. We're all grieving, not just you – summat *you* seem to have forgotten. These kids need you to step up and be a proper dad."

Albie's knuckles whitened on the steering wheel, a vein throbbed in his temple, and the van leapt forward, narrowly missing another car. When he stamped on the brakes the engine stalled and Davy wailed from the back, "I fell over!"

George had clutched Annie so tight that she began crying too, and the realisation that he had frightened his children brought Albie to his senses. Clearing his throat he said, "All right – everyone settle down – there'll be no more arguments today," restarted the engine and drove home more sedately.

## CHAPTER EIGHTEEN – SNOW AND ICE

Work on the water mains restarted after the Coronation weekend, and the spur to supply George's cottage was installed at the end of the month. The foreman called round and offered to remove the backyard pump but George sent him packing. "I've seen them pumps going for silly money in antique shops," he said, noting from the foreman's expression that he'd hit the mark. "Besides, how do I know you've buried them pipes deep enough not to freeze?"

So the pump stayed, and George continued to fill his kettle there, claiming the tea didn't taste right with "that piped stuff". The Water Board's machinery and surplus pipes vanished overnight and the old campsite was abandoned to nature, some of its new growth nourished by the blood of the man who had dared to kill a gypsy.

***

One hot July day Paddy came home from work to find Raymond sitting in May's kitchen waiting for him. As soon as Paddy had washed the garage grease from his hands, Raymond broached the subject on his mind. "I've got a problem, Paddy, and a proposition. You're under no obligation to accept but I hope you'll give it serious consideration." Paddy tensed, wondering if his comfortable life was under threat, but Raymond raised his hand. "Don't look so worried, man – nothing has to change if you don't want it to. The thing is, I've lost two farmhands recently – the factory pays better wages – and we can't manage with so few. I could go to the Labour Exchange and get some pimply youth to help out, but I'd rather have a man I know and trust. Would you consider leaving the garage and working on the farm?"

"What, as a farmhand, you mean?"

"As assistant manager under me and Carl, I was thinking, though we both work as hard as the farmhands."

"What's Carl got to say about it?"

"He agrees with me. The farm will be his and his cousins' eventually, of course, but right now we need an older man we can trust. So what do you say?"

Paddy put a trembling hand over May's and felt how tense she was. "What do you think, me darlin' – could you be doin' with me under your feet all day?" Her broad smile and shining eyes were answer enough and Paddy released her hand to shake Raymond's. "'Tis a dream I'm having, so it is. All I know about animals is the pig me auld feller used to keep – and a little goat, but that's another story. I'm your man."

\*\*\*

Clouds scudded across the October skies, all the blackberries had been picked long ago, and dead leaves were piled high beneath the hedges. To celebrate Albie's fortieth birthday they had a bonfire party in Perez Field, at which they also bade farewell to Josef and the other gypsies who would leave the next day to spend winter in Ruxley. Josef made one last effort to persuade Albie to join them, but he'd already decided to stay.

"Mr Finch needs me on the farm. Annie's used to going to May's every day, and the kids are getting a proper education at last."

Josef could see George was pleased not to be left alone – it was clear from the relief on his face when he heard Albie's words. Looking round the birthday bonfire at the grandchildren he shared with George, Josef saw Maria everywhere. Clara was her image and, although the boys and Annie had Albie's sturdy build, they had all inherited Maria's curly hair – even blonde Fleur had absorbed Maria's smile and mannerisms. Josef, as king of his tribe, was expected at the winter council meetings, and the children's place was wherever their father chose to stay, but he was going to miss them badly. The thought occurred to him, not for the first time, that he really ought to have married again – it was going to be a lonely winter.

***

That December a heavy fall of snow covered the miles of filled-in trenches that hid the water and drainage pipes, and soft flakes blanketed the small square slab in the churchyard where Maria's ashes lay buried. Despite the cold, Albie sat on the nearby bench each Saturday morning to talk to her, hoping for a sight or even a sense of her spirit. He would have stayed there all day if George, Bert or Paddy hadn't come after half an hour to take him to the King's Head, where he would lean against the bar watching a darts match or a game of dominoes from inside a barrier of grief that none could penetrate.

As snow continued to pile up, labourers on the dole were issued with shovels and sent out in teams to clear the roads, and vehicles clanked along with chains wrapped round their tyres. Traders shovelled the trampled snow from the pavements in front of their shops, and their customers crept cautiously along the narrow, ash-strewn pathways to buy necessities before scuttling back to their firesides. Burst pipes and ponderous, slow-motion car-accidents were a daily occurrence. Old people slipped over on patches of ice, and the brand new Health Centre was inundated with patients injured in falls. It was so cold that the harbour froze, and those boats whose owners had not had the foresight to lift them into cradles cracked in the grip of the ice. Fishermen who had moved their boats outside the harbour had to chip ice off their rigging before they could set out to sea, and work on decks that were lethal with frozen spray.

Anyone driving on the out-of-town roads faced a nightmare of skidding between snow-ploughed walls. Over-laden trees cracked under the strain, and when the school bus was put out of action after hitting a fallen branch, Paddy ran the farm children to school in a heavy-wheeled army surplus lorry. They sat on hay bales in the back, looking out over buried hedgerows and snow sculpted by the wind into caves and wave-crests, gleaming arctic-blue in the winter sun. On his return trips Paddy brought any essential supplies from town for Coppin and Pinetree Farms, both of which faced a daily challenge just to keep going – simply sheltering and feeding the livestock in these extreme conditions was a dawn-to-dusk task. The only relief from the cold was in the kitchens, where the old-fashioned ranges maintained a steady heat day and night.

One afternoon, having collected Annie from May's home, Albie found George sitting by the fire watching Clara prepare supper. As he removed Annie's coat, Albie asked, "Where are the others?"

"Fleur went to Linda's," Clara told him. "I don't know where the boys are."

"They're playing by the stream," said George. "I'm surprised you didn't see 'em. They asked if you'd go out when you got home."

"I'll play with them tomorrow," Albie said, letting his gaze wander round the kitchen. Despite the fact that he and his children were living in the cottage too, this room remained unmistakably Dad's. The dresser displayed the same china he had used as a boy, and the big old wireless still waited to be switched on for the football results. The coal-scuttle now contained logs, but the dents from when he'd dropped it were still there. Whatever Clara was cooking smelled like something Mum used to make, and he wished he could bury his face now in Mum's apron and bawl away the misery that haunted him every waking moment.

Clara put a cup of tea in front of him and Albie picked it up, staring out at the snow-bound garden. A flurry of flakes swirled up in a wayward puff of wind and he watched it absently, then frowned and leaned closer to the window as they formed a familiar shape. "Maria?" he said hopefully and Clara ran to look past him, but the apparition moved down the garden and Clara cried, "Davy – something's happened to Davy!"

Albie scraped his chair back and grabbed his boots just as Ben threw open the back gate shouting, "Davy's hurt!" Albie raced down the cinder path to rescue his son.

The boys had been sliding on the frozen stream until Davy fell, and Albie found him clutching a broken arm, his face as white as the snowy bank he was lying on. While Albie carried Davy indoors to cocoon him in a blanket, Ben ran to Pinetree Farm for help, and moments later Luke arrived with the lorry.

Alerted by a telephone call from Daisy, the doctor was waiting at the Health Centre. "There's no way you'll get him to hospital on these roads," he said after he'd examined Davy. "But it's a clean break. I can fix it but it'll be the old-fashioned way, I'm afraid." He tilted Davy's chin up and looked him in the eye. "You're going to have to be a brave boy – this will hurt." Davy nodded, wide-eyed, and Albie held him still while the doctor pulled his arm straight. There was an audible scrape when the bone moved back into position and Davy whimpered, but as the doctor splinted and bandaged it he made no further sound. Seeing Davy's gaze fixed on the foot of the couch, Albie saw Maria standing there, with her hands on her hips and her eyes darting from the doctor to her son's face. When the last piece of sticking-plaster had been applied, she brushed a kiss on Davy's forehead before looking angrily at Albie. "Why weren't you watching him?"

Albie flinched – after months of sitting beside her grave marker hoping in vain for a sight of her, the first time he saw her she was telling him off? "That's not fair," he muttered.

"The boys asked you to play with them – you should have been there."

"I've been working all week!" Albie was so incensed that he spoke aloud and the doctor shot him a startled look. "What's that, Mr Smith?"

"Sorry, doc – thinking out loud," said Albie and when he

looked again, Maria had gone.

Now the job was done, Davy was biting his lip to hold back tears, so Albie wrapped him up again and carried him to the truck. Luke drove them carefully past the snowy fields and Davy was almost asleep from exhaustion. Albie had to lean close to hear his murmur, "Did you see her, Dad? Mama said I was brave – did you see her too?"

Albie kissed his son's curls and answered softly, "Yes, Davy, I seen her."

"She was by the stream when I hurt myself too." Davy stuck his thumb in his mouth and went to sleep.

"So your children see ghosts too," Luke chuckled. "I suppose it shouldn't surprise me."

The following Saturday Albie paid his customary visit to the churchyard and crouched to brush the snow from Maria's stone, tracing the engraved letters with his fingers. "Davy's perked up today," he told her. "He can't decide whether to be pleased he's missing school or miserable at being stuck indoors." A lump of snow plopped from an over-laden tree and the released branch sprayed him with stinging icy crystals. "What you do that for? Davy's all right. I've got to work during the day, but he's got Grandad till Ben and the girls get in from school." Still there was no reply. "I s'pose you know all this. Everyone sees you but me – I bet you even visit Annie." An icy blast set him shivering but, as he walked to join the others in the pub, he vowed that he'd keep on coming until Maria showed herself to him alone, not just through their children.

***

What Albie had told Maria was true – the extreme weather meant that all the farmhands worked long hours. Albie's superior strength was especially in demand for such jobs as tossing bales of fodder from carts drawn by the shire horses that could go where no tractor could, or for heaving sodden sheep out of snow-drifts.

One evening, only minutes after he'd come in from milking
and collapsed in front of the fire to thaw out, Mike Finch stuck
his head round the back door. "Albie – that ewe you brought
in today is lambing – do you want to help?" Albie had his
boots back on in a flash.

Clara looked up from sewing a button onto one of his shirts
to say, "I'll bring tea if you're not back in an hour," but they
had already gone.

An hour later she made a flask of tea and packed it in a
basket with some tin mugs.

"You're not going on your own," George said. "What if you
fell over in the dark? Fleur can go with you."

The girls took a torch and found their way to the small
barn, where all the ewes in lamb had been brought to shelter
from the severe weather. Most of them were sleeping
peacefully, but one or two were watching with detached
interest through a temporary barrier as their sister gave birth.
Albie was sitting on a bale following the proceedings closely,
waiting to see if he would be needed, and the girls were just in
time to see the first lamb slide out onto the straw. It was
wriggling strongly even before Mike put it under the ewe's
nose to be licked clean of its yellow coating.

"Ugh – that's disgusting," Fleur said, looking away, but
Clara was enthralled. "What are we waiting for now?" she
asked Mike when he made no move to stand up.

"She's got another one in there."

Clara leaned on Albie's shoulder while they waited for the
twin to emerge. He slipped his arm round her waist and Fleur
immediately claimed his other side – Dad's cuddles had been
rare lately – and as his free arm held her close she was glad
after all that she had come. The second lamb was tiny, not
much bigger than one of the cats peering from a nearby
manger, and it wasn't moving at all.

Mike shook his head saying, "I don't think this one's got
much of a chance."

But this was Albie's first lambing, and he felt responsible for the ewe he had rescued from a snowdrift that morning. "Give it here," he said, holding out his big hands. "It can't be much different to a foal, and I've seen enough of them born." He massaged the lamb with gentle fingers while his girls watched, and after a couple of minutes it kicked feebly and drew a breath that was clearly visible through its thin ribs. Beaming all over his face, Albie knelt in the straw and slid it under its mother's nose, but the ewe refused to acknowledge it. Albie only just whipped it out of her way in time when she got to her feet. He tucked it inside his coat for warmth and grinned at Fleur. "I done this with you once a long time ago," he said, sticking his finger in the lamb's mouth.

As it sucked frantically, Fleur giggled, but Clara looked thoughtful. "Mike – do you think it'd take a bottle? We've still got Annie's somewhere at home."

Mike smiled at the girls' eager faces. "It's worth a try but don't expect too much – I've rarely seen a lamb this small."

Tommy and Tuppence, George's cats, were not over-impressed with the new addition to their household, especially when it was given a basket by the range, but within days they had taken to sleeping against the lamb's soft white curls. Two weeks later, after two-hourly feeds from George and some cross-species mothering from the cats, the lamb had doubled in size and was strong enough to withstand Annie's intense interest. She discarded her teddy bear in favour of this real live soft toy and on a bitterly grey day, when George and Albie came in after their Saturday pint, Annie staggered over to Albie with the lamb draped over her chubby arms and said, "Baa."

"She said 'Da'!" Albie exclaimed in delight.

Annie stamped her feet in frustration. "Baa," she insisted. "Baa."

"She's been saying that all morning," Fleur told him. "Isn't she clever?"

Albie's face fell. He had been so sure she was saying 'Da'. Then he remembered his other children's first word had been 'Mama' – if he wasn't careful, Annie's next word would be 'May'. Dad had tried to tell him the kids needed him, Maria had been angry with him over Davy, and still he hadn't stepped up to the mark. Well, things were about to change.

After tea that evening, when Linda came round to see Fleur and Clara, Albie said, "You girls go upstairs and leave Annie to me." Clara opened her mouth to protest, but George made frantic signals behind Albie's back, so they left the men in charge.

Albie had seldom washed a baby before, let alone changed a nappy, but somehow, under George's amused supervision, he managed to get Annie ready for bed. Her nappy would not have stayed up without the rubber pants, but she bore her father's inexpert fumbling with her usual calm, and rewarded him with chortles of glee when he kissed her clean pink tummy before pulling on her flannelette nightgown. Once she was settled in her cot, Davy and Ben demanded their share of his attention and, with George taking the fourth side of the board, they played Ludo until bedtime.

After all the children were in bed, Albie sank back against the cushions of the rocking chair and closed his eyes and sighed, "God, I'm knackered!"

"Stop moaning, Albie," George said briskly. "You're half my age and I'm still going strong." Albie scowled but said nothing as George brewed a pot of tea and stirred it vigorously before pouring out two mugs. "It's weak as dishwater," he said apologetically, putting Albie's mug on the range within his reach. "I forgot to put tea on the shopping list."

The innocuous little remark pulled Albie up with a jolt. He stilled the rocker to lean forward with his elbows on his knees, staring at George through the steam from his tea. "You've been doing the shopping all this time, ain't you, Dad?"

"I used to take Blossom and the cart, but Paddy's been fetching our rations since the snow," George replied. "And Daisy makes us a few loaves on baking day. I wondered when you'd notice. It's been seven months now and this is the first time you've shown any proper interest in me or your kids. I thought you were never going to pull yourself together."

"But I miss Maria so bad!" Albie wailed, dashing angry tears from his cheeks. "The only time I seen her was with Davy at the doctor's."

"So that's why you've been even more dismal these past couple of weeks. Did she say anything?"

"Give me a bollocking for not looking after Davy better."

"There you are then – snap out of it and do like she says. Maybe she'll come again when you've turned into a proper dad." George poured the last of the tea into their mugs, ignoring Albie's indignant gasp, and passed over the big round biscuit tin. "The tea's stewed and the biscuits are soft, but we've got to make the best of it," he said, and Albie knew he wasn't just referring to the tea and biscuits.

That night, for the first time since her death, Maria crept into his dreams in the bed he had bought for them to share. He half-woke, feeling her presence so strongly that he reached out to touch her. When he encountered only emptiness he could have wept, but he was afraid of waking Annie. Even so, the small visitation was a comfort to his bruised spirit, and the next day he responded to Luke's cheerful "Morning!" with a passable attempt at a smile.

***

On Christmas Day 1953 Albie's children – all six of them – found their stockings filled with the usual Woolworth's oddments. Albie had never forgotten his own first stocking at the grand old age of twelve, two months after George and Dot Smith adopted him. He had heard Mum saying she'd give him a stocking till he stopped believing in Father Christmas. Now he was a father himself and he knew Joey, Clara and Fleur must be keeping up the pretence for the sake of the little ones, but he'd keep on filling stockings till the last one said stop.

At the dinner-table later on they were all expecting him to produce the customary larger boxes, but when Joey had distributed the gifts he'd bought with his wages and the others had exchanged their home-made presents, the only big parcel was for Annie – Albie merely gave each of the others an envelope.

Davy's face fell comically. "What's this, Dad? I wanted Meccano!"

Joey slapped the back of his brother's head. "'I want' doesn't get – open the envelope!"

He had already opened his own envelope and seen the ten-shilling note – when all the others found the same, Albie explained. "That's spending money for our holiday. I'll get a passport for all of us in the new year. We're going to France to find Fleur's farmhouse."

Fleur squealed with delight and rushed round the table to fling her arms round him. "Dad! Do you mean it? When are we going?"

"Not till the summer, when school's closed and Joey's free. The weather'll be better then, too – we don't want no-one getting seasick."

"Is Grandad coming?" Davy asked.

"No I ain't," said George, carving slices of beef and passing plates round the table. "I've never left England in me life and I'm too old to start gallivanting about now."

"How much is it going to cost?" asked Joey. "Can you afford it? I'll buy my own ticket."

"Bless you, Joey, no need to do that – I've got some saved. But them ten-bob notes are going in your jam jars – if you want more to spend you'll have to earn it."

"I'll get a job tomorrow," Fleur declared. "I'm not going to France with only ten bob."

"I could ask Alice if she wants help on Saturdays," said

Clara. "I like her hat shop."

"What about me and Davy?" wailed Ben. "We're not old enough to work."

"You don't know till you've tried," George said. "You could ask at the farm – offer to muck out the pigsties or something."

"Yuck!" the two boys cried together, but the seed had been sown, and George and Albie both knew how persuasive Ben and Davy could be if they teamed up to get what they wanted.

## CHAPTER NINETEEN – FRANCE

When spring brought the tourists to Thambay, Clara started helping Alice Daly in her shop. She loved tidying the rows of shallow drawers under the glass counter, and selling the gloves, scarves and brooches with which Alice supplemented her income from making hats. Fleur secured a waitressing job in a seafront café, where the homemade cakes and scones drew local customers during the week and tourists at weekends. Ben and Davy, faced with the unsavoury prospect of mucking out pigsties, talked the manager of the ironmongers into letting them sort out the thousands of oddments that filled cardboard boxes under the counter, and which he could never find the time to go through.

Every bit of their wages went into the row of jam jars on the dresser, and one day Ben looked at the growing amount in his and asked, "How do you say 'sweets' in French, Dad?"

"Bonbons," said Fleur unexpectedly. "*Bonbons s'il vous plait* – that's 'sweets please'."

Albie gaped at her in astonishment. "Where did you learn that?"

"There's a French lady comes into the café," Fleur said smugly. "I've been learning a few words every week."

"I was wondering how we'd manage when we got there."

"I'm going to buy a phrase book next week. If I ask Madame how to pronounce things we could all practise on Saturday nights. Clara will have to learn them later, of course," she added slyly. "She'll be too busy canoodling with Frank."

"We do not canoodle!" retorted Clara hotly. "We just go for a walk."

"What, no romancing at all?" asked George, noting his granddaughter's pink cheeks. "I'll have to have a word with that boy."

"Grandad! Don't you dare!"

"I'm only teasing, child, but if he don't at least hold your hand then young men ain't what they was in my young days."

Clara responded to the twinkle in his eyes. "Well, we do hold hands – and sometimes I let him kiss me goodnight. He says he's coming to France with us."

"How come?" asked George.

Albie answered him. "Paddy and Bert said they fancied coming along too. We've heard them war cemeteries are something special, and maybe Bert can find out where his brother Eddie's buried. May wants to try French cooking, and Alice is going to look at French hats. There'll be sixteen of us counting Josef."

***

On the morning of Friday 6th August 1954 the usual queue of cars waited in brilliant sunshine on the dock at Dover to board the ferry to Dunkirk. Among them was an unusual mixture of conveyances – a Jowett Bradford van of uncertain vintage lined with old floorboards and towing a caravan, a white butcher's van, and a farm truck laden with camping stoves, saucepans and sacks of vegetables among the tents and sleeping bags.

A Customs officer peered into the back of Bert's van. "Who's the butcher?"

Bert owned up nervously. "That would be me – is there a problem?"

"You've got enough meat here to feed an army."

"Well, there's sixteen of us, so we brought the 'ole pig."

"Nice looking meat, too," said the officer. "Don't often see meat this good, even now it's off ration."

Bert hurriedly slipped him one of the wrapped packages. "I expect you could use a couple of chops? Only killed Tuesday so they're lovely and fresh."

"Fed on our farm, too," said Paddy, looming large beside Bert, and the officer quickly waved them on.

Albie heaved a sigh of relief that another hurdle had been

crossed – Josef had told him at the last minute that he hadn't got a passport, and they had managed to slip him through while the officer was distracted. He negotiated the ramp into the ship cautiously with Josef's caravan in tow, and soon everyone was climbing the steep echoing stairs to the upper deck.

Immediately the older children scattered, leaving the adults to spread their coats and picnic baskets over an entire corner. Annie, who had slept all the way down the A2 in May's arms, was now as lively as a puppy, so May took her for a walk round the lounge. Most of the passengers seemed content to leave their things unattended, but Albie was reluctant to do that until an elderly woman indicated with a gesture her willingness to look after them, so Albie took Davy to join the others on deck while Paddy kept a firm hold on Ben.

"I can't believe we're actually going!" Fleur said, hugging Clara ecstatically.

"Nor me," Clara replied as the bubble of excitement threatened to burst in her chest. They watched the ramp being raised and the dockside men lifting the thick mooring ropes from the bollards. Then the vast engines shuddered beneath their feet and the scummy water between the ship and the dock churned to froth. At first the movement was almost imperceptible, but gradually the gap between ship and shore widened.

"*Adieu*, England!" they shouted together, waving at the spectators lining the quay.

"Goodbye!" Ben and Davy yelled at the fishermen holding rods over the harbour wall.

When the prow of the ferry lifted to the first wave outside the sheltered harbour, Bert disappeared hurriedly to the toilet, but Josef and the Smiths had spent their lives in swaying wagons and hardly noticed the movement of the ship at all. Later, when Bert emerged green about the gills and very embarrassed, he said to Albie, "You could've reminded me 'ow bad I was last time we went to France."

"That was a troop-ship in the middle of winter with huge waves."

"I know – don't remind me."

"But you just said…"

"I 'ardly know what I'm saying – just leave it, right?"

Alice took her daughters and Clara to look round the duty-free shop, but Fleur remained with Albie. Dover was just a smudge in the distance when she asked him, "Can we go up front and see if France is there yet?"

"Course it's there, lovey, but we can go and look if you want." He turned to the woman who had guarded their possessions earlier and asked, "D'you mind watching our stuff again, missus?"

She shrugged and spread her hands expressively. *"Monsieur – je ne comprends pas."*

"She doesn't understand, Dad," Fleur said, and then, taking a deep breath, she said carefully, *"S'il vous plaît, Madame – pouvez-vous guarder* our things?"

*"Ma petite! Tu parle francais?"*

"Only a *petit peu, Madame."* But a little bit of French was all it took and the woman smilingly agreed.

Fleur and Albie went on deck to discover that France was indeed there, although still indistinct. Albie hugged his daughter. "You talk French like a Froggie already – it must be in your blood."

"It scares me a bit, Dad, now we're actually going. What if I find out something awful? I mean – no-one really knows who I am, do they?"

"You're Fleur Smith, that's who you are – my little girl from when you was small enough to hide in me jacket. Finding out who your first mum was won't change that – I was still George's son after I found Nate."

But Fleur remained worried. "Do you think we will? Find out, I mean."

Albie drew her down beside him on a bench in the sun and looked into her troubled eyes. "We'll do our best, lovey, but I can't promise. We've got to find the right road first, then the farm, and that were burning fierce when we left so it's probably a ruin. What are you hoping to find – that you're a princess like Linda says?"

Fleur couldn't even raise a smile – she shook her head slowly as tears threatened to spill over. "I don't know what I want, Dad, that's the trouble. I don't need another family, I've got you." But even as she buried her face in the familiar comfort of his chest, the thought that Linda had planted years ago buzzed in her mind like a wasp in a jam jar.

Back in the lounge, Albie spread a large-scale map of northern France out on the table. "Bert, can you read a map? Luke says the British army retreated between Arras and Amiens, so we've got a rough idea where to look, but I could never get the hang of map-reading."

Bert seized on the distraction with relief and ran his finger along a road. "I think we got to Dunkirk this way, but it was fifteen years ago. I do remember the sea was on our left, so if we start driving south we should be OK. After that, I dunno – we weaved about a fair bit."

"I was good at Geography at school," Alice said. "I think I could read that map."

"In that case you're in the lead," Albie said instantly. "Me and Paddy can follow you. Just remember the Froggies drive on the wrong side of the road."

Fleur was talking to the old lady again. With frequent reference to her phrase book, she discovered that her new friend was called Madame Gerets.

"I am Belgian," Madame Gerets told Fleur. "But now I live in France with my son."

As she spoke, her son appeared from the direction of the bar – a thin balding man with a neat blond beard. To Albie's consternation he bowed and said, "A thousand apologies, monsieur, that my mother is molesting you."

"Your mum and Fleur are getting on just fine," Albie said sharply. "My daughter's practising her French."

The man bowed again. "Permit me to introduce myself – Henri Gerets, manufacturer of clothing." He peered at Fleur short-sightedly. "*Mais mam'selle!* Surely we have met?"

"I wouldn't think so for a minute," said Albie. "She's only fourteen."

Henri hurriedly backed away from the menace in Albie's voice and Fleur returned to her French conversation. She was enjoying herself, and her gestures became more animated and very Gallic as she spoke. Every so often Mme Gerets' brow furrowed – there was something curiously compelling about this English girl.

Fleur was so engrossed in their conversation that it was only when the ship slowed down that she realised the voyage was over. Alice and the other girls returned from their extended window-shopping, Josef herded the boys into the lounge to collect coats and bags, and Fleur said "*Adieu*" to her new friend. The loudspeakers called drivers and passengers down to the car deck and Fleur turned at the top of the stairs to wave. Catching sight of her profile, Mme Gerets clutched her son's arm and cried, "*Chantelle!*"

"*Maman* – if Chantelle was still alive she would be over thirty by now," Henri said dismissively, and hustled her towards the opposite staircase.

Clara sensed rather than heard Mme Gerets' cry and tried to turn back, but the press of people forced her down the stairs, then regaining their vehicles overrode anything else. They had a tense few moments slipping Josef past Immigration, but finally they were through, driving on the wrong side of the road onto French soil.

Clara grabbed Fleur's hand. "We're here! Do you feel any different?"

"Give me a chance!" Fleur laughed, but her nostrils flared

as she took in the scents of France that were, oddly, not as alien as she had anticipated.

## CHAPTER TWENTY – THE SEARCH BEGINS

The brand new harbour at Dunkirk bore no resemblance to the smoking mess Albie, Bert and Paddy remembered. A whiff of garlic and Gauloises evoked vivid memories of their arrival at Cherbourg at the beginning of 1940, but there was no time for reminiscences – they were far too intent on trying to follow the unfamiliar road signs.

As Bert's butcher's van led the little convoy through the town, Rita, squeezed onto the front seat between her parents, asked why Dad was driving on the wrong side of the road.

"'Cause everyone else in France does," he told her. "Now pipe down – I'm just 'oping I don't 'ave to overtake anything with only your mum's eyes to rely on."

Albie's van brought up the rear of the trio of vehicles, with Clara and Annie sitting between Albie and Fleur on the front seat.

"Which way are we going, Dad?" Fleur asked.

"We're going to drive past St Omer and turn round – we're more likely to recognise places if we're pointing the right way."

"Mama will help us," Clara said. "She hid Grandpapa from the Immigration men. He sort of faded when they looked in the back of Uncle Paddy's truck."

"Well, I hope she carries on doing it," Albie said. "'Cause all we've got is guesswork – we drove about fifty miles that day, but it was all on little country roads to avoid the Jerries."

A car nipped in between them and Paddy's truck and Fleur flew into a panic. "What happens if we lose the others?"

"We're gypsies," Clara said. "We're never lost for long."

A moment later the invading car passed the farm truck and Albie relaxed. "You can see Dunkirk took a right battering," he said. "There ain't a building not damaged. Mind you, it's miles better than it was – we had to dodge broken walls at every turn to reach the beach."

"It looks peaceful enough now," said Fleur, but Clara said nothing – the dramas of the past were still visible for those who could see them. Instead of housewives with shopping bags and children on holiday, she was seeing thousands of wounded and defeated men struggling to reach safety. Today's bicycles and little corrugated Citroens were replaced in her mind's eye by wrecked and abandoned army vehicles. On the bombed buildings she saw wooden shutters hanging askew, shop windows lying in shards of shattered glass, and the men sitting at pavement tables were blood-stained and grey with fatigue.

She snapped back to the present when Albie said, "It's a different world from 1940, that's for sure, and I only remember bits 'cause I was dopey with morphine. I wonder what Bert thinks about it now."

But Bert wasn't thinking about the state of Dunkirk. The responsibility of leading weighed heavily on his mind, and when Alice clutched his arm exclaiming, "Bert – we nearly missed it – that's the road we want," he actually swore.

"There's no call for that, Bert, not with Rita in the van," Alice scolded, waving furiously to catch Paddy's attention as Bert swung the wheel hard over to take the road south.

In the farm truck behind them Paddy stamped on the brakes and hauled the heavy vehicle round the corner, also cursing as his hands slipped on the steering wheel. May refrained from comment, but a chorus of complaints erupted from Susie Daly and the boys in the back.

"Sorry!" Paddy yelled over his shoulder before saying anxiously, "Don't lose sight of Bert's van, May, or we're done for."

"He's my brother – he wouldn't leave us behind," May said, patting his arm. "Besides, I haven't taken my eyes off him since we left the boat."

Once they were outside the environs of Dunkirk the convoy slowed to a sedate crawl, pulling over occasionally to let other vehicles pass. Apart from their quest this was a holiday – the first trip abroad for everyone but the old soldiers – and they were anxious not to miss a thing in the short week before their return ferry crossing.

The flat straight road was bordered by open fields of ripening wheat and maize – the broad sweep of countryside seemed limitless after the hedged patchwork of Kent. Fleur opened her window wide to take in the perfume of the countryside – the very smell of France striking a chord deep in her subconscious. "I was born here," she whispered. "This is my place."

Clara shivered, holding Annie as a shield between herself and the vast alien landscape.

A couple of hours later they were heading towards Aire when Annie announced she needed a wee. Albie leaned on the horn to warn the others, drove onto the grass verge, and the boys tumbled from the back of the truck.

Clara looked round in dismay. "There's nowhere to hide here, Dad – not even a shrub."

"You girls use the ditch and we'll promise not to look," Joey grinned, herding his younger brothers and Ted Daly away. The road was quiet, but Clara was thinking about more than a toilet break – the wide open spaces of France made her uneasy. She was an English gypsy, all her instincts geared to seeking out hidden places.

When they returned to the van she pointed to a green haze on the eastern horizon. "That might be a forest, Dad – we could camp there."

"Yeah, Dad – we're tired of sitting," Ben said, rubbing his backside.

Josef said, "We must make camp before it gets dark – we can take this side road."

"We'll have to buy bread and milk first," said May, and in the next village they were just in time to buy all the remaining baguettes. Fleur obtained directions to a farm to buy milk, after which they drove into the forest just far enough to be hidden from the road.

Josef took charge. "You boys can go and gather wood."

"What – you mean leave Mum and Dad?" Ted said. "What if we get lost?"

"We won't," Ben said confidently. "And anyway, Clara would find us."

"Just don't lose sight of Grandpapa's caravan," Clara said. "We're going mushrooming."

So while Ben, Davy and Ted circled the camp collecting wood, Clara, Fleur and Susie Daly headed further into the forest to forage.

Susie eyed the fungi suspiciously. "These look like toadstools to me – are you sure they're not poisonous?"

"We've been eating these since we were babies," Clara said, adding wickedly, "We're probably immune by now."

Fleur grinned at Susie's expression and swooped on a patch of nettles with cries of delight. "We'll need greens too. Nettles taste just like spinach – and they're free."

"Well you won't catch me eating nettles – or those toadstools."

"They're as safe as your dad's sausages," Clara said, taking pity on her. "We wouldn't take risks with Annie, would we? Mama would never forgive us."

The undergrowth rustled briefly and Susie jumped as a mouse shot across their path. "I'm going back now," she said, starting to walk away.

Fleur caught her arm. "You're going the wrong way – the camp's over there."

Meanwhile Paddy was erecting the tent he had found in an army surplus store. "Never thought I'd be putting one of these up again," he said to Bert as they slid the tent out of its tubular sack. "They're a fierce weight, so they are."

"We ain't as young as we were, neither," Bert replied, slotting poles together. "But I'd sooner do this than sort out one of them gypsy things!"

Albie and Joey were unrolling what appeared to be nothing more than a heap of cloth and some hazel sticks, but before long they had created a tent large enough for their entire family. Meanwhile Josef had started a fire, Frank had found a stream and fetched water, and the stew was beginning to simmer. When the foragers returned, the camp had taken on a comforting air of safety.

One of the abiding memories of the trip would be that forest camp on their first evening. They sat on rugs in the shelter of the trees, listening to birds settle down for the night. The only other sounds were the fire crackling under the big cauldron and bubbles popping in the stew. While potatoes baked beneath the cauldron, Josef showed the children how to weave twigs and leaves into bowls that they could discard after they had eaten.

"No washing up!" Rita said gleefully, and Alice smiled – it was clear that this would be the highlight of the holiday for her ten-year-old daughter.

After supper, as the slow August twilight deepened, they sat around their discreet bonfire listening to Josef's stories of his travels since his birth in the final year of the last century. Clara and Frank held hands, Fleur snuggled into Josef's chest listening to the comforting rumble of his voice, and Annie lay in Albie's arms sucking her thumb. Bats swooped in the dusk, sparks flew and flames danced, and their eyelids grew heavy. The mere fact of being on foreign soil was tiring, and when Albie said, "Bedtime, I think," there were no protests. They banked down the fire, Alice and her daughters retired to Josef's caravan, and the others crawled into their tents.

For a while the groundsheets rustled as bodies shifted around trying to find comfortable hollows, but eventually all was still and the night sounds crept in. The call of a tawny owl, the churring voice of a badger, the small scream of a tiny death – they were strange to the town-dwellers drifting off to sleep in caravan and army tent, but infinitely comforting to the family of gypsies in their familiar bender shelter.

***

"This French bread is like wood," May complained the next morning. "We only bought it yesterday."

Paddy squeezed the baguette and was instantly transported back fourteen years. "'Tis as hard as the bread we ate on Dunkirk beach," he said. "Bert remembers."

"Too damn right I do," said Bert. "And Albie'll remember where we nicked it from – Ratty's jacket front were bulging with bread."

"Bert was too busy nicking bottles of wine." Albie laughed. "That was the town where I got hit – all 'cause I couldn't resist a stupid carousel."

"What – a carousel like the one in Thambay, Dad?" Davy asked. "The Gallopers?"

"It was exactly the same, son, except it had a Froggie name. That's why I stopped to look, then the Jerries bombed it."

"And who was Ratty? That's a nasty name."

"He was a horrible little man who got his comeuppance in the end." Albie grimaced at Paddy for help.

The Irishman jumped in. "It was a long time ago, so it was, and we've got breakfast to think about now. Will I be going back to that bakery, May?"

"No need for that, darling – we'll just dunk the bread in milk."

After breakfast Albie and Bert joined Paddy in the high cab of his truck, while Fleur and Clara, Joey and Frank sat on hay bales in the back with the canvas sides rolled up. Leaving the others to relax in the sunshine, they spent the morning zigzagging across the countryside between Bethune and Aire, searching for one particular ruined farmhouse among many, but although the three veterans looked over every hedge and peered down every driveway they saw nothing even vaguely familiar.

After several hours without success they returned to Aire and invaded a Café de Sport, where Fleur opened her phrase book and ordered beer, lemonade and omelettes and chips – the only food she recognised. The owner hurriedly sent a lad to fetch his wife to cook for the unexpected crowd of English customers, and ushered them to a pavement table.

"Tablecloths must be the same all over France," Bert remarked. "That café in the carousel town had some like these."

"It were a lot quieter there, though," Albie replied. "And scarier. There won't be Jerries behind these shutters." He smiled at his daughters. "Do you feel like you're on holiday now?"

"It's so foreign," Clara said, looking at Fleur. "Does it feel foreign to you?"

"I can't tell yet. It's weird to think if Dad hadn't found me I could've grown up here."

"Do you wish you had?"

Fleur bit her lip but didn't answer, and ripples of an uneasy silence spread, but fortunately the café owner chose that moment to deliver a tray of glasses.

Albie picked up one of the beers, which almost disappeared in his large hand. "This ain't a man-size drink," he said, knocking it back in two swallows. "It tastes like gnat's piss too."

As if to compensate them for the weak beer, the omelettes were the best they had ever eaten, the chips were fresh and hot, and they set off again feeling refreshed.

It was the height of the holiday season, and the boys were blissfully happy spotting the tourist cars. Cries of, "Look, that's one of the new Citroens" and, "Oh my God, that's a Mercedes-Benz!" filled the rear of the truck, while Clara and Fleur watched the road unfurl from beneath the tailgate and ignored the boys completely. They weren't interested in the latest models of motorcars – they were hoping to spot that one clue that would tell them they were on the right track.

"We don't even know if we're in the right part of France," Fleur said at one point.

Clara replied, "Yes we do – there are soldiers everywhere. Can't you see them? They're all grey and dirty as if they haven't washed for weeks, and a lot of them are wearing bandages."

Then Fleur saw them too – thousands of long-gone soldiers thronged the peaceful country roads, limping along in a never-ending stream of dejected humanity. She poked her head through the cab's back window. "Dad – can we stop and help them?"

"They ain't real, love – these roads are bound to be haunted after all that killing."

"A happening as desperate as a war leaves a memory behind," Paddy said. "Like a stain on the land – it'll be that you're seeing."

Bert stared at his friends. "You're all off your 'eads – can you see 'em too, Paddy?"

"God love you, no, but I can feel them." He stood on the brake suddenly. "But your fella out there is real enough, and so is that bread he's got under his arm. May said we should fetch some back with us. Fleur, me darlin' – ask him where he got it."

Fleur called to the man and relayed his instructions. "The next turn on the left," so Paddy drove down the street, turned left, and stopped in a small square dominated by a church.

"I know this place!" Albie exclaimed, but Bert had already wrenched open the door and stumbled to the church where he stopped, tears streaming down his face.

"What's the matter with him, Dad?" Joey asked.

"This is where a German plane killed his brother Eddie."

"How old was Eddie?"

"Eighteen," Albie said. "Only a year older than Joey and Frank are now."

The two boys blanched – a generation ago they could have been like Eddie, dead before their lives had even begun.

Paddy pushed open the door of the church and walked inside, dipping his finger into the holy water to cross himself before looking at the altar, half afraid of what he might see. But there was no dead priest sprawled on the sanctuary steps, the bomb-hole in the roof had been repaired, and the church was once again just a church, albeit one with some dreadful memories.

Bert walked past him to lay his hand on a large stone tomb. "We 'ad to leave our Eddie 'ere – remember?"

"And the Corp and Toff Steele, God rest their souls – I wonder who buried them?"

The girls and the younger boys, uncomfortable in the church with its gilded saints and smell of incense, had retreated to the porch, while Joey and Frank slipped away round a corner for a smoke.

"We'll find my mother if we start here," Fleur said, watching the activity in the square. "She might have done her shopping in this town." She stepped off the worn kerb onto the cobbles. "She could have walked on these actual stones," she said and danced away, skipping joyfully from one cobblestone to another. Clara caught the mood and danced with her sister, to the evident amusement of some French housewives.

"We're getting close – I can feel it," Clara crowed, swinging Fleur round and round until they were both dizzy.

"What are you two up to?" Albie called, catching their staggering figures. "We walked all the way from this town to that farm, so we're bound to find it soon."

Back in the church porch they found Paddy trying to talk to the parish priest. Once he understood that the Englishmen had been here when his predecessor was killed by the German bomb, he dragged them to a small café where the owner, Nicole, spoke some English. Word spread rapidly through the small town, and Nicole's son Philippe arrived, then several farmers, who clambered admiringly all over Paddy's truck. One man even offered to buy it, pulling from his back pocket a fat roll of thousand-franc notes.

Paddy laughingly declined. "'Tis me brother-in-law's truck – if I went back without it I'd be a dead man, so I would!"

After an animated discussion with her customers, Nicole told Bert that the three dead soldiers had first been buried in the town's *cimetiére*, but had been taken away later and were probably buried at Dunkirk. Bert sagged in disappointment, but after a whispered prompt from Fleur he said, "*Merci, madame.*"

The group of farmers laughed and one corrected him, "*Mam'selle – elle n'est pas mariée!*"

Nicole joined in the laughter, totally unconcerned. "I was housekeeper for English milord before *la guerre* – Philippe is his son."

"That explains his fair skin," Fleur said and Nicole turned a quizzical gaze on her. "And yours, *ma petite*, you are different too. Was your father also an English milord?"

So Fleur told how Albie had rescued her and asked where they would find a farm that burnt down in 1940.

"*Ma petite Fleur*," Nicole said, "there are many burned farms – *la guerre* went through our land like a band of wild pigs – but I know nothing of a mother and baby who were lost."

"What about that tank we got with our mortar?" Paddy said. "Anyone remember that?"

"You were mortar-men?" one farmer asked with delight. "So was I! I am deaf thanks to those Boches," and he spat with nonchalant accuracy into the spittoon. But despite the camaraderie of fellow veterans, the juxtaposition of farm and tank raised no memories either.

Albie hugged his woebegone daughter. "We'll find it, Fleur, don't you fret – starting again tomorrow morning from this square. But now the sun's going down and we must be getting back – Josef'll think we've got lost."

"You must have *le petit déjeuner* here tomorrow before you start," Nicole said. "You and all your family."

"Tomorrow is Sunday," said the priest. "You will attend Mass first."

It was obviously an order, so they enquired what time they should arrive, got into the lorry and drove back to the forest.

## CHAPTER TWENTY-ONE – THE FARMHOUSE

They struck camp in the morning, and the convoy of vehicles trundled into the town square in time for Mass. The priest ushered them into seats at the rear of his church, aware that most of them were Protestants, but sure that *le Bon Dieu* would forgive him in view of the fact that their friends' bodies had lain in front of this altar. He kept the sermon mercifully short.

Immediately the service was over Nicole hurried out, leaving her son Philippe to escort the visitors outside, where the café tables, supplemented by ones borrowed from various houses, spilled halfway across the square. Beneath the dappled shade of the plane trees a long trestle covered with a white cloth bore a breakfast feast – fresh baguettes, croissants and brioches, pale farm butter and ham and cheese, with big jugs of fragrant coffee and hot milk. As the square filled up, the noise intensified until it seemed that all the inhabitants of the town had come to see the visiting English. Philippe ushered them to tables just outside the café and Nicole put big cups full of milky coffee in front of them.

Susie wrinkled her nose. "Do you suppose they have tea?"

"The French don't do tea," Fleur said curtly. "And I can't think why you came at all if you're not prepared to enjoy different things."

Susie's eyes flashed, but when she saw Philippe watching her she swallowed her angry retort. Fleur nudged Clara. "That French boy's got his eye on Susie."

"He's not the only one," Clara said. "It must be her red hair."

Their French hosts made a great fuss of the children, especially baby Annie. When it emerged that Albie was the father of six of them he was the recipient of several hearty back-slaps from the men, and more than one speculative glance from the local war widows. Philippe tried his few words of English on Susie, whose hair flamed exuberantly in the morning sun. She flirted with him shamelessly – although he was too young for her, his accent was delicious and it would be fun to tell her friends she had been chatted up by a Frenchman. Joey was similarly engaged in flirting, though his conversation with three olive-skinned girls was conducted mainly in smiles and giggles under the watchful eyes of two black-clad elderly women. Even Ted, with his ginger hair and freckles, attracted several admirers.

Frank's hovering presence informed the young men that Clara was already spoken for, but Fleur was surrounded. Her face glowed with the thrill of understanding some of what they said, and she made up for her lack of vocabulary with animated gestures. Her blonde hair shone almost white in the strong sunlight, and the contrast between her fair skin and the darker skins of her suitors was very marked.

Albie said to Bert, "She's having the time of her life, ain't she? She's going to come down with a bump if we don't find her mum. Nicole says there were thousands of refugees, and she was most likely one of them if she were sleeping in a barn."

Bert nudged him. "You been chatting up Nicole, 'ave you?"

"Not me – my crowd of kids would put anyone off – but I reckon she's after my father-in-law."

Josef was sitting outside the café with the baker and a couple of farmers, sipping coffee heavily laced with cognac and revelling in the atmosphere of unconditional acceptance. He had heard that the French were an unfriendly race, but their reception today couldn't have been more welcoming. The life of a gypsy in England had become much more difficult in the years since the war – he was thinking he could do worse than stay in this little town. All he'd need was enough work to put food in his mouth, and a permanent spot to park his caravan. He watched his grandchildren and Albie enjoying the party – they were recovering from the loss of

Maria and could manage very well now without him.

Sensing someone was staring at him, he turned his head to see Nicole standing in the doorway of her café holding a jug. She smiled – a flash of white teeth in a dark face that could have been gypsy-bred – and Josef felt a surge of life rush through his veins. He lifted his cup and his eyebrows in a salute and she responded with an unmistakable wink, brought the jug over, and rested a hand on his shoulder as she refilled his cup. "You are the *grandpère* for the six children of Albie?" she asked in her husky voice. "*C'est incroyable* – you are too young!"

"I am fifty-six," Josef replied.

"And I have forty-three years – as I say, we are young. Your wife is not here?"

"My wife died many years ago," Josef told her and she squeezed his shoulder in a gesture that could have been merely condolence but somehow meant more. This was all they said, but a kind of understanding had been established.

A little later, after the Mayor had made a speech, Nicole brought a farmer across to meet Josef. "Jacques has a field not used, with water near. You make *le camping* with him, *non*?"

"Show me this field," Josef said instantly, and went off in Jacques' battered Citroen. He returned twenty minutes later and told Albie the field was perfect – south-facing with woods behind it for a wind-break, and there was a stream that trickled clean and sweet from a fern-clad rocky bank. "If we camp there we won't need to find another forest tonight."

So agreement was reached with Jacques on a handshake, and they took their tents and caravan to the field. Leaving May and Alice to organise the camp, the ex-soldiers, with just Clara and Fleur this time, set off again to explore.

Back in 1940 they had been too stunned by the loss of three comrades to notice their surroundings, and they were afraid they might miss a turning, so Paddy drove at walking-pace. At the crossroads he speeded up a little – with only one road leading north there was no chance of them taking the wrong one out of town.

Bert sat in the back with the girls, leaning against the rear of the cab and letting his despair at having left Eddie lying dead in that church wash over him anew. Waves of his misery lapped at the edges of Clara's consciousness, but she shut them out – Bert's old grief was less important today than Fleur's search. She and Fleur stood, holding onto a roof support and watching the scenery unfold, all senses alert. The broad sweeps of golden crops were intersected by green strips where streams ran, and by the dusty ribbons of roads and farm tracks. Occasionally a building came into view – a farm or an isolated storage shed – but they saw nothing that might be the farm where Albie had rescued Fleur from a burning outhouse.

"Do you see anything you recognise?" Clara asked Bert.

He made a visible effort to concentrate on the present. "Sorry, lass, I don't remember much. I wasn't thinking straight then – to be honest I still ain't."

"Don't worry, Uncle Bert – Dad will see something," Fleur said confidently.

She was proved right when Albie exclaimed, "We went through this wood."

A little later Paddy said, "I remember that crooked chimney," and then he slammed on the brakes with such force that Bert and the girls ended up in a heap on the floor of the truck.

"Watch it, Paddy!" Bert shouted. "We could've broken summat then."

"Sorry, boyo!" Paddy yelled back. "But this is as far as I carried Titch – I remember Auntie standing in the road just by that gate to stop the ambulance."

"The driver didn't want to stop, did he?" Bert recalled. "Then Albie put a curse on 'im and 'e couldn't move till after Paddy got Titch into the back."

"I only looked at him," Albie protested, shooting a guilty glance at his daughters.

"Well, he had a face on him that said different," Paddy chuckled. "Fair shook up, so he was."

He put the truck into gear and drove on slowly with everyone now looking even more carefully for signs of a ruin, and a few miles later Fleur asked, "Could that be it?"

"I do believe it is," Albie said as Paddy drew the truck to a gentle halt. Across a wide field of stubble stood a large ruined building, its smoke-blackened walls still supporting a few fragile roof-beams. "Reckon we found it," Albie said in awed tones. "That's the house and the hill the Sarge climbed to look for the Germans."

Two hundred yards further along the road they turned into a farm track.

"Somebody's still living here," Paddy said. "There's fresh tyre marks."

Barking dogs confirmed this surmise and they proceeded cautiously, wondering how they would explain their presence.

"Should've brought that café woman along to translate," Bert said.

"She'll be busy washing up after our breakfast," Albie said, hiding a smile – he'd seen Josef setting off towards the town, and suspected he had more in mind than helping Nicole with the dishes. Suddenly a man barred their path, a shotgun propped against his shoulder.

"Your man looks ready to use that," Paddy muttered to Albie and stopped the truck, slipping it surreptitiously into reverse for a quick getaway. Before anyone could stop her, Fleur had leapt over the tailgate, stopped a yard away from the man, and waved her arm at the house. "*S'il vous plaît, monsieur – est votre maison?*"

Clara came to stand beside her sister and the man looked from one to the other, clearly nonplussed to be confronted by two excited girls. "*Oui, c'est à moi,*" he admitted.

Fleur leafed through her phrase book and explained haltingly that her mother had died here, killed by the Germans in the war.

"*Les allemands!*" the farmer spat. "*Vous etes anglaises?*"

"*Oui, monsieur,* we are English – my father was a soldier."

"And the other men?"

"Soldiers also."

When Fleur said they only wanted to look at the ruin, the farmer directed Paddy into the littered yard, where they drew up between the ruin and a new-looking barn. Hens scattered away crossly at their approach and a pair of geese stretched their necks, but the farmer hissed at them and they flapped away. When the engine noise stilled, the usual farmyard sounds took over – grunting pigs, clucking hens and the bleat of a goat.

"Bit of a mess, ain't it?" said Bert. "Still, I suppose 'e only uses it for the land."

The farmer remained lounging against the barn door holding his gun. He might simply have been protecting his property, but the combination of this farmyard and a gun made the veterans uneasy. Relapsing into their old army ways, Albie took charge. "Bert – you and the girls stay by the truck – just lean on the horn if he makes a wrong move."

Just to confirm they had the right place, Albie ran through the stubble to climb the small hill behind the farm. Because he knew where to look, it was just possible to make out a discolouration in the soil where the German tank had exploded. He remembered the fierce joy when their mortar-bomb had dropped straight into the open turret. On his way back to the others he passed the shed where they'd found the van in which they reached Dunkirk, but Fleur's book had no word for 'tank' and they agreed it was better not to mention the van – it might have been fourteen years ago but they had still taken it without permission.

Meanwhile Paddy had tracked down the goats by their

smell, and returned to the truck carrying one. He dropped it hurriedly when the farmer raised his gun. "That one's exactly the same as yours was," he told Fleur. "Small, noisy and shitty."

"They're smelly, too – and how did you milk it?"

"God love you, child, you sucked your milk straight from its titty."

Fleur wrinkled her nose in disgust and Clara giggled, but Albie said, "We need to find that outhouse. You two girls come with me – your mama will help us find it."

The three of them circled the ruin, their nostrils full of a mingled smell of ancient soot and livestock. Albie tried to work out logically where the outhouse had been but, with all the walls collapsed and the timber burnt, he found it impossible to tell. The sisters held hands, hoping Mama would help them, and whether it was Maria or chance, they both stopped abruptly in the same place. The twelve-foot square, enclosed by low walls of scorched stone, looked no different from half a dozen other ruined rooms, but they were certain.

"This is it," Fleur said. "My mother died here." Every shred of colour had drained from her cheeks and her eyes were wide with shock. She touched a broken door post but snatched her hand away as if it was still burning.

"Dad found you just in time," Clara said to give her courage, then they both flinched as flames roared and the ghost of a beam fell.

Albie didn't even question their conviction. They were Maria's daughters, she had nursed them both at her breast, and besides, he could feel it too – this was the place. He fought down the urge to scoop Fleur up and carry her away as he had done before, but Maria was clear in his mind, telling him that Fleur was on the verge of womanhood and must cross this bridge without him. "Go on in," he said, "This is why we come to France, after all."

"I can't do it," said Fleur with a haunted expression.

Clara said, "There's nothing to be scared of, Fleur – it happened a long time ago."

Together they stepped gingerly into the ruin of the outhouse where Fleur's mother had died. With a whimper of distress Fleur went straight to the corner where Albie had found her wrapped in a fold of her mother's skirt. A grey hen scuttled away from the heap of straw, leaving behind some pale green eggs, but Fleur didn't even notice. Clara hovered protectively, watching as a ghost wrapped her translucent arms round Fleur. For a moment they all felt the heat of the flames and Albie tensed to rescue them, but the phantom fire died.

Feeling blindly behind her for Clara's hand, Fleur said, "I'm glad I came. I wanted to and at the same time I dreaded it, but it's all so peaceful."

"Did you see your mother?"

"I think I did, for a second."

The girls were so quiet and still that the grey hen returned to her nest and began to rearrange her eggs with irritated little movements.

Returning to the lorry, Fleur asked the farmer what had become of the bodies that had been removed from the farm during *la guerre*, but she got nowhere. Telling him, "We will return soon with a Frenchwoman to speak for us," they left the ruined farmhouse and drove back to the camp in Jacques' field.

Josef had spent a delightful couple of hours with Nicole in her *appartement* above the café, before persuading Joey and Frank to help him erect the tents and move his caravan into the skeletal remains of a cattle shed to make it less conspicuous. From his doorway Josef would have a clear view down the sloping field to Jacques' small farm and the town beyond, whilst remaining virtually invisible.

"Looks like you're planning to stay a while," Albie

remarked when he saw it. "Getting on that well with Nicole, are you?"

Josef gestured across the countryside basking in the August sun. "There is plenty of space here, Albert – enough for me not to be noticed. I have lost count of the number of times I have been moved on in England since the war. Now I am here I might stay."

"The kids'll miss you – and the tribe."

"I will be back to see you, do not worry about that."

"You won't get through on your own without a passport."

"Nicole's brother has a fishing boat in Boulogne – he goes across all the time."

"Got it all worked out, ain't you?"

Josef refused to rise to the accusation in Albie's voice. "I am not getting any younger, Albert – it is time I started living again. Besides, now you have your passport you can come and see me."

"It's obviously a done deal," said Albie with grudging acceptance. "Find you here, will we?"

Josef smiled a smug, satiated smile. "Oh, I think there is no doubt about that."

Nicole was smilingly helpful and said it would be *un grand plaisir* to accompany them back to the farm where *la pauvre petite Fleur* had lost her mother, but not until tomorrow. They were on holiday, *non?* and they must also enjoy themselves. Tonight they must come to her café to sample the local *recette* for rabbit, then there were the shops in St Omer that must be visited, and on Wednesday there was to be a *fête* to celebrate the birthday of the wife of the *Maire* to which they were all invited.

The rabbit – fried with garlic and herbs – was delicious, and so cheap that May said, "Even if we ate here every day there'd be enough money for a bit of shopping."

"We can go to St Omer tomorrow," Susie said happily.

Fleur gaped at her in disbelief. "But we're going back to the farm tomorrow with Nicole."

"Only you and your dad – there's no reason the rest of us can't do something else."

Alice jumped in quickly. "The shops will still be there on Tuesday, Susie – you can spend the day with Philippe."

Susie flushed and sulked, but the mention of his name had alerted Philippe. He refilled her wine glass, raised his own glass to her in a toast, and then lifted one of her red curls to murmur incomprehensible French love-words into her ear. Observing their interplay, and the sparks flying between Nicole and Josef, Frank thought ruefully that these French had the knack when it came to romance – they didn't have gypsy fathers watching their every move.

## CHAPTER TWENTY-TWO – THE GRAVE

The shotgun-toting farmer turned out to be a distant cousin of
the previous owner of the farm. He had inherited the place by
virtue of being the only male member of the family to have
survived the war. Nicole learned that the dead Germans and
one English soldier had been taken away by the army after the
war.

"Only one Englishman?" Albie asked. "We lost two men
here – Ken Coppin and Sergeant Davis."

"*Le Sergent Anglais*? I found him in that field last year."

"Last year? I thought the army was more organised than
that." Albie was visibly shaken, until the farmer told him that
the Germans had dragged away their useless tank in 1940, but
it was not until he ploughed that field last winter that he
unearthed the sergeant's body.

"That bloody tank must've driven right over him and
squashed him into the ground," Albie said. "What a horrible
way to die."

The farmer told Nicole, "They took what was left of the
sergeant to bury at Dunkirk with all the other English
soldiers."

There was a small respectful silence which Fleur cut short
with the question she had been bursting to ask. "What
happened to the bodies from the farmhouse?"

The farmer looked surprised that she was interested but
said, "My cousin and his wife are buried with the family in St
Omer."

"But there was another woman – a stranger," Nicole said.
"Possibly a refugee."

"Oh, her – I expect she went to the village," he said
dismissively, pointing to some roofs a mile or so north of his
land. "You'll have to ask the priest."

So they got back into the truck, aimed for the church tower,
and tracked down the village priest. When he heard Fleur's

story he crossed himself and unearthed from a shelf in his study a tin box, opening it to show them a few bits of twisted jewellery and a charred metal case wrapped in a piece of blackened cloth. "This case is silver and the cloth was good quality once," he said. "It was clear the woman was not a poor farmer." He opened the case with infinite care to reveal a photograph and there, staring at them out of the past, was Fleur.

Albie gasped with the shock of it and Fleur touched the faded face with a trembling finger, murmuring, "My mother." Beside the girl in the photograph stood an older woman and, when the priest turned the picture over, on the reverse was written '*Maman et Chantelle*'. Fleur raised swimming eyes to Albie. "Chantelle – I know her name now."

Albie hugged her and asked the priest, "Did you bury her here?"

"Come with me," the priest said, taking Fleur's hand, and led them into his churchyard where he showed them a grave set against the wall as if for protection. "*Voilà! Tu maman!*"

Fleur traced the mossy lettering with her finger – '*Chantelle – Avec le Bon Dieu 1940*'.

"It ain't much, is it?" Albie said. "Just Chantelle – didn't she have no other papers?"

The priest shook his head and spoke rapidly to Nicole, who explained, "The fire burned very hot – he saw it with his own eyes – but the photograph was underneath her."

"Then we're lucky it survived," Albie said. "Something about that picture's bugging me – ask him if I can have another decko at it." Back inside the priest's house he examined the sepia print and nodded slowly. "Thought the face was familiar. Look at this, Fleur – ain't that the old dear from the ferry – the one with the smarmy son?"

"Madame Gerets?" Fleur snatched the photograph and peered at it intently. "You're right, Dad, it *is* her – I met my grandmother and I never knew!"

"You'd think Clara would have seen it," said Albie. "This woman could be your nan and we don't even know where she lives!"

"It doesn't matter, Dad," said Fleur, slipping her arms round his middle. "I know my mother's name and I've seen her grave – I don't need a grandmother as well."

The priest gave Fleur her mother's picture and jewellery, kissed her on both cheeks and saw them off with a blessing, before retiring to his altar to offer a prayer of thanks for the baby who had lived and for the English soldier who had snatched her from death. Glancing over his shoulder as if afraid of being overheard, he added his own heartfelt gratitude to *le Bon Dieu* for staying his own hand last year when he had almost discarded those war-time relics.

*** 

Meanwhile, fifteen miles to the south, Paddy and Josef were standing in the middle of Farmer Jacques' courtyard surrounded by brown hens. Warm stone walls enclosed the straw-littered cobbles, a boy wearing wooden *sabots* watched them from the top of a short flight of steps, and two horses snorted a greeting from their stable. Jacques hurried out of the barn to shake Josef's hand in a hearty two-handed grip, and launched into a voluble, arm-waving speech, much of which Paddy, to his own astonishment, understood.

"'Tisn't that much different from Coppin Farm," he told Josef. "Though 'tis a long time since I saw a cub wearing clogs."

"He is not a very tidy man, but I think I will like working here," Josef said.

Paddy raised his eyebrows. "He hasn't asked you yet."

"He will – it's written on his face."

"You could be right, Josef," Paddy said. "His yard's in a shite state and those horses are manky – your man needs some help, right enough."

Jacques was roughly the same age as Josef and had lost

both sons in the war – only he and his daughter had survived.
To his intense disappointment she had not married a farmer,
but Jacques was determined to keep the farm going for his
grandson. He had taken an instant liking to the wiry *gitan*,
which was why he had suggested his field as a campsite.
Now, again using sign-language that was as voluble as his
speech, he offered Josef one meal a day and a miniscule wage
in return for his help on the farm.

"He's not offering you much money," Paddy said. "He
thinks he can get you cheap."

Josef's black eyes flashed. "Because I am Roma?"

"He just reckons he's got the upper hand because you're a
foreigner. Ask Nicole to help – she won't let him cheat you."

Indicating they would consider Jacques' proposal, they
promised to buy him a beer later in the café, walked back over
the fields to the village, and went straight to the square, where
Paddy's truck was ticking as it cooled beneath a plane tree.
Josef gestured 'talk later' to Albie and hurried inside the café,
where he found Nicole preparing snacks of sliced ham and
cheese. He kissed her cheek and said, "Jacques has offered me
work on his farm – if I stay here will you be happy?"

Nicole dropped her knife, seized his face in hands still
greasy from the ham, and kissed him thoroughly. "Josef – *mon
amor* – very happy! How much will he pay?"

"Two thousand, I think he said, and one meal a day."

"The daughter of Jacques cannot cook. You will eat here
and he will pay four thousand francs – two thousand is only
two English pounds."

"But I have no papers – what if the police come?"

"*Pah! Les gendarmes!* They will not be a problem," Nicole
said with a shrug. "A man drinks here who will make you
documents – he had much practice during the war." She
kissed him again and returned to her task. "Do not concern
yourself – all will be well."

Josef could see that all would indeed be well – after half a lifetime with no woman to call his own he had landed in paradise. He took a dish in each hand and took them outside, already looking more like the *patron* of the *café* than a customer.

Fleur guessed as soon as he appeared. "You're staying here, aren't you? I find my mother and lose my grandpapa all in one day." Her bottom lip wobbled.

Josef put the dishes on a table to sit down, pulling Fleur onto his lap and blowing her nose as if she was still a little girl. "You, *cariño*, will never lose me. Sometimes in England I do not see you for months but I am always your grandpapa." He looked at all his grandchildren in turn, his eyes asking them to accept his decision. "This is where I belong now – you must understand that?"

Clara ran to wrap her arms around him and the boys' faces fell. When little Annie caught their mood and started to whimper, Josef sent an anguished look to Albie, who said with determined cheerfulness, "We've got a passport now, kids, and a holiday home in France – your pals will be dead jealous."

"That's true," Joey said, and Ben promised, "We'll come over every year – I'll start saving as soon as I get home."

"How will you be managing the lingo?" Paddy asked.

"I will learn," Josef said confidently. "It is a little like the Spanish my grandparents spoke, and farms are farms wherever you live."

"It's every man's dream, so it is," said Paddy. "A grand-looking woman and a pub into the bargain." He caught sight of May's expression and added hastily, "Or a farm, of course."

"But we are forgetting Fleur," Josef said. "What happened today, *cariño*?"

Fleur described their discovery of Chantelle's grave and produced the jewellery and the photograph. Clara held the jewellery, her mind flying back fifteen years to the woman who had worn it. The earrings were valuable – twisted by the heat of the fire but undeniably gold. They held no fond memories, but the pendant – merely a smooth stone wrapped in silver wire – that had been precious. She felt a lover's touch on her bare neck as he fastened the clasp and she turned to kiss him, but then there was a beam falling on her head, and she had no time to do more than push her baby out of danger before the beam crushed her.

Clara jerked backwards instinctively and Albie caught her. "What did you see, Clara?" he asked. "Anything that will help us find Fleur's other family?"

"The earrings are valuable but the pendant..." Clara rubbed it on her shirt to reveal a striped tiger's eye stone. "The pendant was a gift from her lover." She handed it back to Fleur. "I think your father gave this to your mother – he had blue eyes just like yours."

"So we've still got no way of finding Fleur's nan," Albie said.

"Didn't her son say he was a factory owner?" said May. "That might help us track them down."

"I remember now," Albie said and he sketched a bow, waving his glass of beer in a parody of the prim little man on the ferry. "Henri Gerets, manufacturer of clothing."

"Gosh, Fleur, you could have a rich uncle!" exclaimed Davy. "Wonder if he lives in a castle?"

"They call them *chateaux* in France," said Fleur. "And who wants an uncle like him?"

Later, taking a rug to a secluded corner of the field, the girls lay on their stomachs and dozed, letting the hot sun bake away their stress. After a while Clara asked gently, "Do you want to talk about it?"

"No, not yet," Fleur mumbled into her arm. "I've got to sort it out in my own head first." She rolled onto her back and gazed unseeing at a lone fluffy cloud. "I'm glad it's you here and not Linda – she would have talked about it non-stop."

Clara tucked the compliment away to enjoy later and said,

"She makes a drama out of everything, Linda does, but you must admit this is bigger than most things that happen in Thambay."

"I know. I wish I was there now – I need one of Grandad George's cuddles."

"Only a few more days," Clara said comfortably, peering sideways at her sister's profile, and soon they dozed off again. Thinking about the implications of what Fleur had discovered could wait until they were safely back where they belonged.

***

Having seen the boys off to the woods with Josef, Albie wandered aimlessly along the lane behind the campsite with his mind churning. He was more disturbed than he liked to admit by the upheavals of the last few days. Fleur was his – she had been his since they shared that dugout in the Dunkirk dunes, and he was terrified at the thought that the rich Mme Gerets might decide to claim her granddaughter. If only they hadn't met her on the boat – but that was meant to be, Maria's voice scolded him, and you can't argue with Fate.

"I know – I know," he said aloud, and was startled to be answered by a moist harrumph. A horse was observing him curiously over a fence, and its big black head reminded him of the carthorse he'd ridden as a boy – the one that had shown him he had been born with a way with horses. Holding his fist out for its inspection he approached it confidently, speaking to it exactly as he spoke to the animals in Pinetree Farm's stables. Horse-talk was neither English nor French and it seemed to understand him. While he stroked the big muscles of its neck it stood nuzzling his chest and blowing damply into his shirt-front. "You understand, don't you, boy?" Albie said into its receptive ear. "It's all too much to swallow in one gulp. Fleur's knocked into a heap over her mum, Bert's upset all over again about Eddie, and now Josef's going to leave us for a bit of French skirt."

The horse stamped its foot and Albie pulled himself

together. "Sorry, that ain't fair – he's entitled to some loving after all this time. It's just that I'm used to having him around – he reminds me of Maria." A breeze ruffled his hair and he chuckled. "Alright, me darling, so I don't need Josef to remind me of you. I'll stop being selfish and wish him all the best."

Time slid by for Albie while he talked to the horse, and it was dusk when he returned to the campsite to find a fire burning merrily and supper nearly ready. He sat with Josef outside his camouflaged caravan, watching numerous rabbits making their way home to their burrows and said, in a tacit acceptance of Josef's decision to stay, "No danger of you going hungry while you live here, is there?"

***

Tuesday morning was spent shopping in St Omer, where they filled their petrol tanks using the RAC coupons they had brought with them. May and Alice and the girls trailed round shop after shop, gazing longingly at chic French fashions that they couldn't afford, but Josef, who had paid no more attention to the currency restrictions than he had to the need for a passport, treated them to a scarf each, and a kindly saleswoman demonstrated how to tie them *á la mode français*. Every boy in the party bought a wicked-looking pocket-knife, the men replenished their stocks of tobacco, and just before they headed home Josef purchased a beautifully-arranged bouquet. The moment they arrived at the café he presented it to Nicole with a flourish that rendered her pink with delight, and informed those of her customers who had not already guessed that she had found romance with another *anglais*.

When the bats began to swoop on the insects and moths attracted by the campsite's flaming torches, Nicole, Philippe, Jacques and many more of their new-found friends arrived for a bonfire party in the field.

"Did we ask all these people?" Clara asked Fleur, trying to count heads.

"I think Grandpapa got carried away and asked everyone in the café," Fleur said fondly. "And every one of them has brought their family."

Clara sighed. "Oh well, at least they've brought bottles."

Albie waved the steam away from one cauldron to peer inside. "I hope you've made enough stew?"

Clara stirred the other cauldron with a stick the size of an oar and said, "We should be alright – Uncle Bert chopped up all the meat we had left."

"What – all of it? But our boat home's not till Friday."

"It's summer," Alice said. "We only just caught the meat before it went off, so we threw in plenty of garlic and a fistful of spices to disguise the taste."

"And fresh mushrooms from the woods."

"And Grandpapa poured a whole bottle of wine into each pot."

"Wine in our stew?" Alice said. "These children are too young to be drinking wine."

Albie waved his hand airily. "Oh, you needn't worry about that –alcohol evaporates."

An hour later, with bread to eke it out, every scrap of their stew had disappeared with flattering speed and no ill effects. As everyone relaxed to digest their meal and pass round bottles of wine, Albie said to Josef, "If you're going to live in this field you'll be needing transport. I'll leave you the Jowett and use your car when we get home."

"That is a good thought, Albert, thank you."

"Plenty of room in the truck to get us all home," said Paddy. "Specially as I've sold the petrol cans to your man Jacques."

"Were they yours to sell?" Josef asked.

"Not really – but I'll tell Raymond they were confiscated. A bit of extra French money will be handy with three days to go and all these mouths to feed."

One by one the pine-resin torches flickered and died until the only light came from the fire. Both cauldrons were moved aside to cool, leaving the flames free to dance and flaunt their colours in a foretaste of autumn. Night birds called, the church clock chimed in the distance, and it was almost unbearably romantic.

Paddy lay on his side in the tussocky grass and pulled May into the curve of his body. She resisted briefly – "Paddy – not in public!" – but then, realising nobody was taking any notice, she leaned against the comfortable cushion of his belly. Josef and Nicole sat entwined on the caravan steps, only a yard away from the bed they would use later, but easy in the knowledge that they had many bedtimes ahead of them. Even Bert, a married man for over twenty years, put his arm round Alice as they watched the circle of children playing five-stones on a rug.

The teenagers were sharing a tarpaulin, Fleur's French was improving by the minute as wine loosened her reserve, and the local youngsters were trying out their schoolroom English. When Susie and Philippe silently disappeared from the edge of the group, Clara nudged Frank's knee and tilted her head in a clear invitation to follow their example, but he didn't respond. Clara looked around to see Albie leaning up on one elbow watching them, and Josef's dark eyes equally vigilant.

"You've been warned off, haven't you?" she whispered and Frank nodded miserably. Staring defiantly at Josef she moved closer to Frank, but his entire body stiffened. The chill of his withdrawal made Clara shiver, and she turned away to join the group around Fleur. Frank's face registered his shock – he wasn't sure what had happened but he knew he was in danger of losing something precious.

***

"What has happened between you and Frank?" Josef asked Clara the next day.

"You should know, Grandpapa."

"I have not spoken to him about you," Josef said truthfully.

Clara pinned him with a glare so like Maria's that he winced. "You warned him off somehow – and he is too scared of a gypsy curse to defy you." Her mouth twitched into a grin. "But when we return to England you won't be around."

"Now you have given me another worry, child, so let us talk of something else. Can you get me those earrings of Fleur's mother? I will mend them while you are picking fruit with Nicole."

When the girls returned, laden with apples from Nicole's orchard, Josef presented Fleur with a pair of gold and sapphire earrings that could have been bought that day.

"Gosh, Grandpapa, I didn't think they'd be this pretty!" she exclaimed, holding them up so that they flashed in the sunlight.

"Put them on," Clara said. "They're exactly the colour of your eyes."

Fleur took out the gold rings she had worn since she was a baby and hung the sapphires in her ears, shaking her head to set them swinging. "I'll wear them to the party tonight – isn't it lucky I bought a blue scarf?"

\*\*\*

The Mayor's wife's birthday party was a rather stiff, sit-down affair in the *Hôtel de Ville* but, as Albie pointed out, "The food's free and we've got none left till we shop tomorrow."

After the meal everyone streamed outside for a more informal party in the square. When Nicole tuned her wireless to a music station there was even some dancing, but she concentrated on serving her customers, leaving Josef to spend this final evening with his family.

Ben had worked out, to his own dismay, that Josef was going to be at least a hundred miles away from Pinetree Farm.

"And in a foreign country," added Davy. "What if something awful happens to you?"

"Nicole has a telephone," Josef told them. "And forget about counting the miles, Ben – I could get to you in a day."

"I s'pose so," Ben said grudgingly. "It only took a day to get to that forest the first night."

"Nothing bad's going to happen to Grandpapa," said Clara. "Mama will look after him."

Her assurance would have comforted them more if Annie, whom they had all assumed was asleep on Josef's lap, hadn't opened her eyes, pulled her thumb out of her mouth with an audible plop, and said sadly, "I want Gampa at home." Her doleful little comment stripped away even Albie's pretence of stoicism – they were used to Josef's comings and goings, but the thought of the Channel between them was daunting. Annie plugged her thumb back in, curled her forefinger round her sunburnt nose and snuggled back into her Gampa's chest.

Her warm little body in his arms was almost Josef's undoing. Swallowing hard, he stood up holding her and said huskily, "I think it is time everyone was in bed."

Albie picked up on his cue quickly. "Yes – say your goodbyes, everyone – early start tomorrow." Swinging Davy onto his shoulders, he shook hands all round and followed Josef down the lane to the campsite.

Seeing his mother walk off into the darkness arm-in-arm with Paddy, Frank sidled up to Clara and asked plaintively, "Clara – what have I done wrong?"

He was so clearly puzzled that Clara took pity on him, slipped her arm through his and said to Fleur and Rita, "Come on, girls – let's walk him home," and Frank knew he had been forgiven.

Before Joey ran to catch them up he claimed chaste kisses from all three of his little harem, under the temporarily indulgent eyes of their *chaperones* – even Ted walked back across the moonlit fields with the memory of a soft French mouth tingling on his lips. Susie hung back until the others had gone, then pulled Philippe into a dark corner and kissed him with a thoroughness that left him gasping, thus proving to one young Frenchman that the English were not the passionless race he had been led to believe.

## CHAPTER TWENTY-THREE – YVETTE

By the time the travellers had struck camp, loaded their gear into the truck and Bert's van, and breakfasted in the café, it was mid-morning. They said goodbye to Josef and drove out of the square through a guard of honour composed of French children, their mothers, and all Nicole's regular customers.

Watching the tears roll down Josef's face, Fleur said, "We will see him again, won't we?"

"Course we will," Clara sniffed. "I'm only crying because I love him."

They drove straight past the ruined farmhouse and the nearby village – Fleur didn't want to visit the graveyard again. With Bert's van still leading they motored on slowly, the veterans looking for half-remembered landmarks. Then Bert veered suddenly left, narrowly avoiding an on-coming tractor, Paddy followed suit, and they were driving along a poplar-lined road.

"Why have we left the main road?" May asked crossly. "We won't have time to buy food before the shops shut."

"Whisht, me darlin'," Paddy said. "This is where we hid from the Germans."

"These skinny trees couldn't have hidden anyone!" Joey scoffed.

"You're right about the trees," Albie said. "But we shot along here and just made it to them woods in time."

"And we didn't have a big truck like this," Paddy said. "The only transport we had was a knackered old van we liberated from your farm back there."

As the shadows of the poplars fell rhythmically across their faces, Clara sensed the panic that had driven her father and Paddy to run from the pursuing enemy. None of them really relaxed until they rounded a blind corner between two stone walls to find themselves in another small town.

The buildings on the outskirts were obviously new, but

soon they were driving between the tall shuttered windows and old, secretive archways that had comprised every town they'd seen in the past few days. An unusual number of pedestrians slowed them down to a crawl, and they realised they had arrived in time to replenish their stock of food at a mid-week market. Parking in a side street, they followed the noise to the main square.

"The last time we seen this square it was deserted," remarked Albie, staring at the mass of people and stalls around the fountain. "Everyone seems to have found their way back now."

Bert pointed across the square. "There's the café where I nicked the wine."

"And the baker's," said Albie. "A few stale sticks of bread was the only food we had till we got back to England."

"Except for Fleur," Paddy reminded him. "She had her goat."

They wandered round the market, bemused by the abundance of food available in France after the years of austerity in Britain. They bought cheese and eggs, potatoes and bread, sausages and bottles of wine, and Albie had to fight the urge to take home a box of fluffy brown chicks for George. They had just entered the café so that the girls could use the toilet when Albie said, "There's one more place I've got to see before we go," and left them standing. As he turned down a street beside the Town Hall, Clara saw a huge flash and felt a blast that made her stagger, and she ran to catch him up.

"I'm coming with you," she said, slipping her arm through his. "What was that explosion, Dad?"

He patted her hand absently as they walked together into another, smaller square. "I ain't surprised you felt it. That was the German bomb that damn nearly killed me fourteen years ago – it landed right here."

Every building's façade bore the scars of the bomb, and

Albie wondered how he could possibly have survived such a blast. Naturally there was no sign of the carousel that had distracted him then with nearly fatal consequences, but a twinge in his shoulder brought to mind vividly the weight of the wooden horses that had pinned him down until Bert, Paddy and the others had hauled him free.

Clara shivered too. For a brief moment the square was peopled by ghosts – ghosts of the locals who had been hiding in their homes hoping the war wouldn't touch them, ghosts of the German troops who had flushed them out and picked the Jews from among them – but then there were real footsteps as Bert and Paddy appeared.

"Bloody 'ell, Albie – look 'ow far that explosion went!" said Bert in awed tones.

"Didn't we always say you had the gypsy luck, Corp?" Paddy added.

Albie smiled to hear his old army rank after all this time. "You're right about the luck, Paddy, but it gives me the willies just thinking about that day – let's get out of here." They left the ghosts behind and returned to the main square, to find the others and knock back a much-needed beer.

When Albie paid the bill, the café *patron* was so surprised by the size of his tip that he actually pointed out the error. Albie pressed the money back into his hand. "You keep it, mate – we owe you for several bottles of wine."

***

It was late in the afternoon when Alice's map-reading located the Dunkirk cemetery. They parked their vehicles and entered the gates to be confronted by rows and rows of white headstones casting long shadows over the pristine grass. For some moments they simply stood, hardly able to take in the enormity of the numbers.

"I never expected this," said Bert at last. "They look after it lovely, don't they?"

"There's thousands of graves!" Davy said in awe. "Did you

see all the bodies, Dad?"

"Quite a few of 'em, son," said Albie. "And if it wasn't for Bert and Paddy I could be lying here too."

"Don't say that, Dad," Clara pleaded. "We don't want to think about you not coming back – there's enough sadness here as it is."

"Sorry, lovey, but I'm bound to think about it, same as Bert and Paddy are. The main thing is that we *did* come home."

"Now we're 'ere, 'ow do we find Eddie's grave?" Bert asked, and Alice consulted the wall plan that showed the way to the English section.

*\*\**

In the mill of people threading their way through the graves, none of them noticed Mme Gerets sitting in the shade near the gateway.

Henri Gerets was not the rich uncle Ben imagined – he was not even the owner of the firm *Tissu Gerets* – his mother was. Yvette Gerets, despairing of her son's ineptitude in business, had hoped her daughter would take over the company, but when Chantelle disappeared, even the efforts of several detective agencies had been unable to trace her. Nevertheless, Yvette still hoped to find her, although after fifteen years, she was looking for a woman, not a girl. It was only in that final moment on the ferry, when Fleur waved from the head of the stairs, that Yvette saw the likeness and realised that she could have been talking to her granddaughter.

On the way back to her home on the Belgian border, Yvette had gone over every snippet of information Fleur had conveyed in her stumbling French, and she kept returning to one fact. The Englishmen had all fought in the war and the red-haired one had lost a brother – surely they would not come to France without visiting the Commonwealth War Graves? Also, Fleur had said they would be returning to England the following Friday.

Accordingly, allowing an extra day to be sure of not

missing them, Yvette had summoned her chauffeur to drive her to *le Cimetière de Ville de Dunkirque* on Thursday. While she sat, pretending to read a novel, on a folding chair beneath the shade of a tree, she sent him to book an hotel and ascertain the ferry schedule for the following day. "Take your lunch in town, Pierre – I shall remain here."

Pierre had looked at her affectionately – she was the same age as his own mother and, in his opinion, too old to be sitting here all day on a wild goose chase. "*Et vous, Madame – un sandwich, peut-etre?*"

"*Non merci, Pierre,*" she had said, and shooed him away.

Now, with Fleur within touching distance, she kept silent – after waiting years for this moment, she could afford to wait a few minutes longer while they visited their friends' graves. She watched Fleur closely, becoming more and more convinced that she was Chantelle's daughter, but she was astute enough to know that her obsession could be misleading her. The girl was travelling with a family who looked like gypsies, but what had happened to Chantelle? Had they stolen her baby? Yvette wanted desperately to be right about Fleur, yet there was the nagging doubt that Henri had nourished with drops of poison ever since the ferry – the Gerets fortune must not be allowed to fall into the wrong hands.

\*\*\*

"Found 'im!" Bert said suddenly, laying his hand on a headstone. "This is our Eddie." He covered his face and wept for the brother who had been killed before he could reach nineteen, while his three children stood in a huddle, shocked to see their father in tears.

Albie crouched to pat the grass over Eddie's grave. "Meant to buy you flowers, Eddie – sorry, mate, I forgot."

Bert laughed through his tears. "Trust you to talk to a dead man! Eddie'd think we'd gone soft if we brought 'im flowers."

"The Sarge is over here!" called Paddy, then they found

Corporal Evans and Private 'Toff' Steele, and finally Private
Ken Coppin. "May – here's your old man," Paddy said
shakily, stepping back as if Ken might leap from the grave to
confront him. "It don't feel right me standing here with his
missus."

Seeing Ken's name carved into the stone affected May more
than she had anticipated, and remembering the young farmer
she had loved once, she put her arm round Frank's waist.

"You alright, Mum?" he asked. "Uncle Raymond says Dad
used to bully you."

May fished out a handkerchief and blew her nose to give
herself a moment to think. "He wasn't always like that, Frank,
and he *was* your dad – he didn't deserve to die." She gazed
out over the endless rows of headstones. "None of them
deserved this."

"I ain't so sure about that," said Albie. "The world's a better
place without Ratty Green. I suppose we should look for his
grave too."

Paddy snorted in disgust. "That gobshite! I'd spit on his
grave. When the small boats came he nearly let you drown to
save his own miserable skin."

"Well it didn't work, did it? And 'e got what 'e deserved,"
said Bert venomously. "I'd sooner talk about the others –
remember Tommy teaching Dimbo to drive with three tins of
beans and a floor mop?" and they were off, reminiscing and
laughing and very, very glad that they had come.

"Fleur!" Clara clutched her sister's arm and leaned close to
whisper. "Don't look now but that woman from the boat's
here – what do you want to do?"

But of course Fleur had to turn round to look, and the
stillness of the two girls affected the rest of the group. Their
chatter died away and they all turned to see Mme Gerets
walking slowly towards them, leaning lightly on a slender
walking stick. She was barely a yard away when she stopped
suddenly and smothered a gasp with her hand, then took two

more steps and gently touched one of Fleur's earrings. "Where did you get these, child?"

Fleur's hand shot to her ear – she had forgotten she was wearing the sapphires. "They were my mother's."

"*Monsieur*," Yvette said, turning to Albie, "I believe Fleur is my granddaughter." She hadn't intended to blurt it out like that and blushed painfully, but while Fleur translated Yvette stood her ground – those earrings had been her gift to Chantelle on her eighteenth birthday, and were the final proof she needed.

The moment of truth had arrived and Albie's heart sank. He laced his fingers through Fleur's soft hair and tilted her head to look into her blue eyes. "It's up to you, lovey. She's got no proof she's your nan, and your first mum could have had a good reason for running away." Probably because she was pregnant, he thought, but he turned to Clara and asked, "What do you think, Clara?"

Clara wrapped both her hands round Yvette's hand as it held the cane, and the Frenchwoman froze. These dark-eyed gypsies had thrown her off-balance and she was not used to the sensation – it took all of her resolve not to snatch her hand away. Clara concentrated fiercely – her sister's future happiness hung on this moment and it mustn't be hurried. The blood running through Yvette's prominent veins felt warm and strong – this was a woman accustomed to getting her own way – but Clara also sensed her yearning. Mme Gerets meant Fleur no harm, and of the blood-tie there was no doubt. She released the old hand and nodded at Albie, who lifted Fleur's head again. "This is it, Fleur – Clara says she is your nan, but you've got to decide what you want to do."

Pierre the chauffeur returned just then from his prolonged lunch to see his mistress surrounded. Hurrying to her side, he heard her speaking in elementary French to the blonde girl. Yvette turned to him in relief. "Pierre, please translate for me. I wish to invite this child and her father to dine with me. She is my granddaughter – I have found her at last!"

"Are you sure, Madame? You have been mistaken before."

"Simply invite them, Pierre. We will ask more questions over dinner, but I am not mistaken."

So Pierre, who had learned English during the war, translated the invitation, but Albie refused to be parted from his friends. "We'll be camping on the beach to be handy for the ferry tomorrow," he told Pierre. "You and your boss lady can eat with us if you want."

"Madame is not accustomed to the camping," Pierre said but Albie was adamant. "We'll stick together, just like in the war," and Pierre, who had also been a soldier, explained this to his mistress.

For a moment the decision hung in the balance, but then Yvette clapped her hands and said, "In that case we will eat on the beach – it will be amusing!" She pressed some francs into Pierre's hand. "Buy food and wine – quickly, before the shops shut – and I will ride with Fleur."

"But how will I find you, Madame?"

She gestured at the fifteen English campers and laughed, "Surely there will not be more than one group this large on the beach tonight?"

So Pierre yielded, retrieved her chair and returned to the car. Yvette linked her arm with Albie's – a shrewd business-woman always courted the head of a company – and touched Fleur's sleeve lightly. "*Alors, ma cherie* – I go with you."

By the time Pierre arrived with meat, wine and beer there was a driftwood fire burning cheerfully. One of the English tents was obviously army surplus, and he recalled with a stab of nostalgia his own war service. The second tent was an odd construction of bent sticks and canvas, and a glance inside the farm truck revealed a pile of sleeping bags – these were clearly not wealthy people. He resolved to keep his wits about him even if Madame did not. He unfolded Madame's chair for her and sat on a beer crate among the men, watching sausages being cooked and translating when necessary.

Strangely, under the influence of alcohol and the party atmosphere of the beach barbecue, the conversation moved swiftly from stilted to animated, and soon flowed freely with less and less need of Pierre's services. Before the light faded completely, Fleur showed Yvette the photograph in its battered frame that the priest had given her.

"It is me and Chantelle!" the old lady cried. "This was taken on her birthday – see, she is wearing those earrings. Where did you find it?" She held the photograph against her heart as Fleur told her about the grave in the French country churchyard. "All these years she has been so close!" Yvette said. "Henri was right – I should have known that she was dead."

"Madame," said Pierre gently, "If you had not continued to hope, you would not have found Fleur." Emboldened by the informality of the gathering, he added, "Monsieur Henri is concerned only for his inheritance."

"*Pah*! Which he must now share." A mischievous smile played over Yvette's face as she imagined Henri's reaction to that unwelcome news. She raised her wine to Pierre in a conspiratorial salute. "How I will enjoy telling him of that! But Pierre – you have no beer!"

"Madame – I have never drunk in your presence."

"Tonight is different."

Removing his jacket and cap made Pierre feel less inhibited. He knocked back his first beer in three swallows, before translating for his employer the story of how the English veterans had rescued her granddaughter from a burning farmhouse.

"So that was where Chantelle died?" Yvette asked, sipping her wine as daintily as if she held a crystal glass instead of a sturdy mug, but her hand was shaking.

"She wouldn't've known nothing about it," Albie hastened to say. "It were only 'cause Fleur cried that I found her – she were all wrapped up in her mum's skirt."

Yvette sat up straighter. "So you simply found Fleur? You are not actually her father?"

Fleur went white and said firmly, "He *is* my father. I have an English birth certificate and everything!"

Pierre sucked his breath in sharply at the sudden change in the atmosphere, but Yvette lifted her hand. "A thousand apologies, Fleur. Pierre, please translate this carefully. I see now that we will never know who Fleur's natural father was, but I consider myself fortunate that Monsieur Smith found her."

A little later, as the moon rose over the otherwise deserted beach, Yvette slipped back into her autocratic tone. "Fleur must come home with me and learn about the business she will inherit."

Emboldened by his beer, Pierre told her quietly, "Madame – you will lose her if you insist on that. This man will not take orders, but if you make a friend of him he might meet you halfway."

Yvette Gerets, *doyenne* of *Tissu Gerets*, drew her breath in with a sharp hiss and glared at her employee, but when Pierre refused to lower his eyes her expression softened. "Very well, Pierre, I will take your advice. Kindly tell Monsieur Smith that I would be honoured if he would furnish me with his address and allow us to visit."

"Fleur," Pierre said with a broad smile, "your *grandmère* hopes that you will become friends and therefore she wishes to visit you."

"We've only got two bedrooms."

"For such a big family?"

"The boys sleep in the wagon."

"*Ah, oui,*" Pierre said and told Yvette, "I think they are *gitanes*, Madame – you will be shocked at how they live."

She gestured at the little camp and said, "They are all clean after a week of living in tents. You say Thambay is by the sea –

there will be *un hotel, no?*"

"Course there's 'otels," said Councillor Bert Daly, springing
to the defence of his home town. "The Palace, the Railway
'otel, and boarding 'ouses if you're a bit strapped for cash."

"Madame has no need to concern herself about cost," said
Pierre. "Surely you have heard of *Tissu Gerets*? Madame owns
the factory."

"Tissues? You make paper?" Clara asked.

Yvette laughed. "No, child, we manufacture cloth and
clothing – very fashionable clothing."

"It sounds interesting. I like clothes," Fleur said. "I'm
always getting told off for drawing frocks in my school
books."

Yvette sat up straighter in her chair and said rapidly to
Pierre, "The child draws clothes! *C'est incroyable!* Her mother
designed clothes for us."

"Madame – *s'il vous plait* – slowly," Pierre reminded her.

"Very well, Pierre, I will proceed gently," she promised.
"Now, please ask Monsieur Smith if he would book two
rooms for us in a Thambay hotel for next week."

"For us, Madame?"

"But of course, Pierre, you will accompany me. Henri
would be useless, while you have made it abundantly clear
that I cannot do this without your help."

## CHAPTER TWENTY-FOUR – THE VISIT

If Madame Gerets had expected to be met when she arrived at the hotel, she was disappointed, for by the time she arrived in Thambay the Smiths had settled back into their normal summer routine. Pierre telephoned Pinetree Farm, where Daisy told him that Albie was out in the onion field and would get his message when he came in for his tea, so Pierre left his mistress to unpack and went for a stroll.

The Palace Hotel filled an entire block between the Town Hall and the sea, its pillared porch opening directly onto Marine Drive, on the other side of which was the promenade. Holidaymakers were promenading, their sunburn cooling under the day's cloud cover, while others braved a stiff onshore breeze on the sands.

Pierre, who loved all forms of transport, was irresistibly drawn to the boatyard, where a team of shipwrights was repairing a fishing boat. He couldn't hear the words, but the very cadence of the men's conversation confirmed he was on foreign soil. Pierre had never actually been to England – Henri Gerets usually drove his mother on cross-Channel trips – and he was struck by the difference a few kilometres of sea could make. The shops and cars along Marine Drive were markedly different, the air full of strange smells. He lit a *Gitane* – at least that smell was familiar – and watched the men scraping the boat's hull for a while before returning to the hotel, just as Albie parked his battered Austin in the road outside.

While Clara and Fleur ran up the hotel steps, Pierre shook Albie's onion-stained hand in both of his as if clinging to a rock in a shifting world. "Monsieur Smith – we have arrived."

"I told you before – call me Albie. I wasn't expecting you till later, but when you telephoned, Mr Luke let me off early. The girls were working in town so I picked 'em up and come straight round."

"Your daughters work? They are very young."

"They got jobs to save up for France," Albie said proudly. "Clara helps Alice in her hat shop and Fleur's a waitress in a café – she learned French off one of her customers."

"It is fortunate that she did."

"I ain't so sure about that," Albie said unguardedly, and then blushed as he realised he had said it aloud.

Pierre pretended not to have noticed. "But I regret that we took you from your work – there was no need for you to come here."

"The girls were busting to see inside the hotel – it's too posh for the likes of us. We'll say hello to Madame and then you can follow us in your car."

George had dusted and swept the cottage, and the kettle was boiling when Pierre pulled his Citroen into Perez Field. When he helped Yvette out onto the rough grass, the first thing she saw was the old gypsy wagon. She wondered with brief horror if her granddaughter lived in it, but Fleur ushered her past the wagon and through to the garden, where the full charm of the old cottage and George's neat rows of vegetables was revealed.

"*Mais, c'est charmante!*" Yvette exclaimed, her attention sharpening as George emerged from the back door to put cushions on the bench beneath the kitchen window.

"*Madame Gerets – mon grandpère,*" said Fleur, and George astonished everyone by lifting Yvette's hand to his lips and kissing it.

"Pleased to meet you, Madame," he said and, drawing her hand through his elbow, escorted her with old-fashioned courtesy to the bench and plumped up a cushion for her back. "You sit yourself down there and I'll fetch the tea."

"I'll get it, Grandad," said Clara. "You stay here and talk to Madame."

So George Smith, former helter-skelter owner, sat beside Yvette Gerets, a woman to be reckoned with in the fashion industry, and proceeded to charm her into revising her opinion of Englishmen.

"We weren't expecting you till later," Clara whispered to Pierre. "But we can make supper go round two more – will Madame eat sausages and mash?"

"Madame has reserved a table for dinner at the hotel," Pierre said, smiling down into her worried eyes. "Do not concern yourself, child – all is well."

"All is not well – everything is changing – and I am not a child."

"My apologies, *mademoiselle* – my daughter says the same and still I forget." He glanced across the tea-tray to where Fleur was struggling to translate. "It appears that *grandmère* and *grandpère* will be friends – that is something I did not expect."

He looked meaningfully at Clara. "We must all accept surprises, *mam'selle*."

An hour later Yvette stood up to say her *adieus* and, seeing George accept her kisses on both cheeks, Ben and Davy manfully stood still for theirs. As the family waved goodbye from the lane, George slipped the boys tuppence each. "Well done, lads – there'll be more of those if you keep it up."

On the journey back to town Yvette said to Pierre, "How I wish that I had learned English instead of Flemish in my youth. I cannot ask you to translate everything I wish to say, Pierre – tomorrow I shall purchase a dictionary."

***

The next morning, armed with a small dictionary and phrase book, Yvette found the café in Market Square where Fleur worked and ordered a *café au lait*. When she asked, "Will you take a coffee with me, my dear?" Fleur backed away, her eyes signalling alarm.

Her employer had noted the Frenchwoman's stylish costume and hurried over, gushing, "Take your coffee break now, Fleur, and do introduce me to your friend."

Fleur had never had a coffee break in all the months she

had been working there, but she introduced Yvette to her employer, brought two coffees and a plate of cakes to the small table, took off her apron and sat down.

"You do not tell her I am your *grandmère, ma cherie?*"

"I don't want the whole of Thambay to know my business."

"Ah – the woman is a gossip?"

"Dreadful!"

"But you should be proud to be called Gerets."

"*Madame* – consider! If I am not Fleur Smith then I am a bastard. I haven't decided yet if I want *anyone* to know."

Yvette sat back and looked at Fleur – really looked at her – and saw she had inherited not only Chantelle's looks but also her stubbornness. "It is possible that your parents were married," she ventured.

Fleur shot that hope down in flames. "Hmph! So why did my mother die alone on that farm? No – the name that Dad and Mama gave me is good enough. Now I must get back to work," and she got up, tied her apron strings and began to take a customer's order.

Yvette was left to digest a cupcake along with the unwelcome knowledge that her name alone could not open this, the most important door she had encountered in all her sixty-eight years.

At five o'clock Fleur found Yvette's car outside the café with Pierre holding the door open, and she was sinking into the soft upholstery before she could draw breath. "Where are you taking me?" she demanded, suddenly suspicious.

"Home, of course," said Yvette.

"*Your* home," Pierre added when he saw the panic on her face.

"I usually get the bus with Clara."

"Then we will take Clara also." Five minutes later the queue at the bus stop watched in silent awe as the two Smith girls were driven away in chauffeured luxury.

They caught George on the hop, happily gardening and

mucky to the eyebrows, but he doffed his ancient hat to Yvette and hurried into the scullery to wash while the girls put the kettle on. Yvette was comfortably ensconced in Dot's old rocking chair when Pierre came in, staggering under the weight of a large travelling chest which he placed on one end in the middle of the floor. "Madame brought some clothes."

George immediately panicked. "She can't stop here – we ain't got the room!"

"No, you misunderstand, *monsieur*, these are for the girls." Pierre didn't know what angel prompted him to imply that his employer had been thinking of both Smith girls, but he earned a look of gratitude from Yvette, who waved her be-ringed hand at the chest.

"Fleur, Clara, see if you like them."

The chest opened like a wardrobe and there, catching the light from the window, were two rows of clothes, carefully arranged on hangers and held in place by straps.

Fleur gasped, "Did your factory make these?" and dived in head first, inhaling the scent and luxuriating in the touch of fine fabrics. "Feel this, Clara! Look at these colours! Here – this one would suit you," and she ripped a dress off its hanger to hold it against Clara. The rich blend of russet and orange wouldn't have been a natural choice for a young girl, but Yvette realised that Fleur was right – the colours were perfect against Clara's olive skin and black hair. Soon the kitchen table, the chairs and even the dresser were draped in fabulous dresses, and Fleur was running from one to the other, rubbing a skirt between her fingers, stroking an embroidered bodice, inspecting a braided hem. Never had *Tissu Gerets'* fabulous gowns been treated with such disrespect, but Yvette was thrilled – her plan to dazzle her granddaughter was working.

Then Clara asked, quietly but clearly, "How much would one of these frocks cost?"

Yvette waved her hand in a careless gesture. "Two or three hundred pounds, perhaps."

Fleur stopped spinning, suddenly sober. "Clara – help me put them away."

"*Mais ma fille!*" Yvette cried. "Do you not like them?"

"They are beautiful, but where would I wear a silk dress?"

"To a dinner party, perhaps," Yvette said desperately as Fleur hung the dress back in the chest. "Choose one, *ma fille*, and come to dinner with me in the hotel."

"We've got shepherd's pie in the oven," Clara said.

Fleur's face lit up. "Grandad makes the best shepherd's pie ever!"

Yvette sank back in her chair, defeated – her strategy had failed. She was so disappointed that she drank her cup of dark, lukewarm tea without even noticing, but George opened the oven door, releasing a delicious smell. "Eat with us, Madame – there's plenty to go round."

For a moment it was touch and go, but then Davy bounced into the room and said, "*Hallo madame,*" with such a brave attempt at a French accent that Yvette sat back in her chair in tacit acceptance of George's impulsive invitation.

The table was crowded and noisy, but the shepherd's pie was excellent. Watching Clara help Annie with her food, Yvette asked George quietly, "What happened to the mother of these children?"

He brought a framed photograph from the dresser. "She died last year – this was taken on their wedding day."

She studied the photograph carefully, her designer's eye mainly on the wedding outfits. Even in black and white she could see that the white bridal gown was simply glorious. "Their mother was beautiful – and such a dress!"

"I will wear that dress when I'm married," Clara said. "And so will Fleur – it's a family heirloom." Her expression reminded Yvette, as clearly as if she had said it, that Fleur was her sister and belonged to the Smith family.

Then Fleur asked, "Have you got any photos of my mother when she was young?"

Yvette seized her chance. "I have an album of photographs at the hotel. If you would dine with me tomorrow we could look at them together."

"Can the hotel fit us all in?"

Yvette had not intended the invitation to be a general one but she rallied magnificently. "*Bien sûr, ma fille – c'est un hôtel.* Shall we say seven o'clock?"

\*\*\*

Mme Gerets hadn't enjoyed a hotel meal so much in years. The formal dining room briefly overawed her guests, but the waiter was patient and eventually their food choices were made. Yvette pulled a face when the prawn cocktails arrived – tiny tinned prawns on a bed of limp shredded lettuce – but she ate her own without comment.

Albie and the boys had ordered soup, and when he saw the tiny pats of butter that came with the bread, Albie called the waiter back. "These are the size of a shilling and there ain't enough even for one of us, let alone four. Now bring us a bigger lump – butter came off ration months ago."

A woman at a neighbouring table tutted, but her husband said, "Hear! Hear! Well said, sir! Waiter – we'll have more butter here as well."

The main course passed without comment, although the meat was grey and tough, and the fruit salad was clearly out of a tin. There was an awkward silence when they had finished – clearly no-one knew what to say until Ben looked at Yvette and said, "You should've gone to Charlie Warren's mum's boarding house – they give you proper dinners there."

"Proper dinners – what are these?"

"Well, for a start his mum buys her meat from Uncle Bert – *and* she makes her own puddings."

"Ben's right, Madame," said Fleur. "Even Grandad cooks better than this hotel, and he's only learned since Nan died. You'll have to go to Mrs Warren's next time."

Yvette felt as if a balloon had inflated beneath her ribs –

'next time'. It was with a joyous heart that she sent Pierre to fetch the album so that she could show Fleur the carefully preserved photographs of the mother she had lost.

Fleur gazed and gazed at the face that was so like her own – the photograph she had brought home from the French church was half-burnt and faded, but these images were sharp and clear. "Why did she run away – did you have a fight?"

"No fight – I do not know why she went. We assumed she had gone with a lover who abandoned her. Perhaps because she was *enceinte*? Men can be cruel."

Fleur leaned against Albie's arm. "I ended up with the right Dad in the end."

"Well," Albie said, sensing the moment had come to leave, "thank you for inviting us to dinner, Madame, but it's time these boys were in bed."

As the family said goodbye, Yvette had difficulty holding back the tears. In the days since Dunkirk her spirits had gone up and down like the horses on a carousel. She had arrived in Thambay full of hope and confidence but it seemed she had lost. Finding Fleur had been a miracle – but now she felt as if the gypsies really had stolen her grandchild.

Then Davy offered his hand. "We're not supposed to tell fibs, so I won't say dinner was lovely 'cause it wasn't – you'd better come to us tomorrow."

Fleur said, "She's *my* grandmother – *I* was going to ask her."

Ben said, "Can't we share her? We haven't got a grandmother."

Clara said, "Yes, do come – it's Annie's second birthday tomorrow."

Albie held his arms out in mock surrender. "See what I've gotta put up with? We'll expect you tomorrow about five."

***

Madame Gerets arrived for the birthday party in style, stepping out onto the grass of Perez Field as if she were attending a society function, and managing to conceal her shock at the number of wagons which had appeared overnight.

As Pierre shut the car door, a dark brown hand took hers, a dark brown voice said, "This way, Madame," and she was looking at an older version of Albie. Nate laughed at her confusion. "Yes, I am Albert's father by blood – didn't they tell you George adopted him?"

He escorted her to a chair in front of Rosanna's wagon and Fleur moved towards her, but Nate stopped her. "Leave her for a few moments – Rosanne speaks excellent French." When Fleur looked again, Rosanna was already pouring wine into two glasses. Yvette didn't even look out of place – her silk paisley costume was nothing remarkable among the colourful clothes of the gypsies, and the glint of firelight shone equally from her jewels and theirs.

After the birthday cake ceremony the party gathered momentum. There was quite a crowd, and not just for Annie's benefit – the mixture of gypsies and farming folk had worked together for generations, and conversation flowed freely. With Joey's imminent return to Margate to play in the Kent League Cup, the men were talking football, while the women naturally congregated around Rosanna and the elegant Frenchwoman.

As Fleur and Clara had anticipated, Linda's antennae were working overtime. Linking her arm through Fleur's, she lowered her voice to an excited whisper. "I heard you found a long-lost relative in France – tell me all!"

Realising there was no point in concealment, Fleur introduced Madame Gerets as her grandmother without a hint of hesitation. Yvette raised a quizzical eyebrow. "It is no longer a secret?"

Fleur spread her hands in a gesture so like her mother's that Yvette's heart turned over. "Nothing is a secret for long with Linda."

"She is the daughter of Daisy and therefore your cousin?" Yvette smiled with pleasure at Fleur's surprise. "Rosanna has been educating me – you have a large family."

Linda had only had a year of French lessons at school but she seized on the word '*cousine*' and used it as an excuse to move closer. "I love your jacket," she said now, stroking Yvette's sleeve reverently. "It looks like that design you did last term, Fleur."

Yvette took a careful sip of her wine – she did not want to make any more mistakes with her granddaughter – and said, "Fleur – will you show me your designs, *ma cherie*?"

Treating Linda to a killer glare, Fleur protested, "They're only scribbles."

"All designs begin as sketches," Yvette insisted and sent her to fetch them.

As Yvette leafed through the scrapbook, Fleur looked everywhere but at her face, dreading ridicule – whatever had possessed her to show her scribbles to a professional dress designer? But Clara watched Yvette closely, and knew her professional interest was aroused. Drawing after drawing sprang from the pages as if already transformed into clothes, and as Yvette flicked back and forth the excitement rose in her chest until she could barely breathe. The drawings were crude, naturally, but this child had a rare talent which she must snap up before anyone else did. Yvette was a heartbeat away from repeating her wish to take Fleur away with her when she caught Clara's eye and merely said, "Fleur – these are excellent. This one would look wonderful in pink silk, and this in gold brocade."

But Clara had seen enough. "Come on, Fleur – Annie's nearly asleep. Let's put her down in Olivia's bed for a while."

As the girls took their sleepy little sister into the wagon behind them, Rosanna said to Yvette, "Fleur is only fourteen and still a child – do not push too hard."

"But her talent will be wasted here." Rosanna followed

Yvette's gaze around the gypsy camp and said nothing, but her eyes glittered and Yvette felt her disapproval. "My apologies – I did not mean…"

"I know exactly what you meant, Madame. You would do well to remember that although Fleur was not born Roma, she drank Roma milk and is one of us." Rosanna's words held a stark warning. "We love her for herself, not for her talent, nor for who her mother was. Perhaps one day she may accept the future you offer, but only if you respect this family." Flicking her shawl emphatically, she turned away to talk to Nate, leaving Yvette chastised.

Nevertheless, the *couturier* wondered what there was to respect here. The Smiths were an uncultured family, their home was tiny and poorly furnished, and their nearest relatives were common *gitanes* who had no fixed home at all. Ben and Davy were at this very moment lying beneath one of the wagons on what appeared to be somebody's bed, the men were passing a bottle from hand to hand as if glasses did not exist, the women's skin was so weathered that they had obviously never used face cream, and Albie, the man who had taken Fleur from Chantelle's side, was talking to a horse.

She turned with relief at the sound of George's voice, and was drawn into conversation with him and Daisy. It was a good half hour before it dawned on her that the uneducated gypsy Rosanna had been speaking pure, aristocratic French.

When Annie appeared at the top of Olivia's wagon steps to rejoin her birthday party, Nate brought out his fiddle and began to play. At first the music was only in the background, but as the yearning tune seeped into the night air all the separate conversations gradually petered out, and there was a subtle swirl of movement that ended with everyone sitting in a circle round the fire. The music, speaking of love and loss, drew them closer together, and without it appearing deliberate the gypsies formed an inner circle, with their friends making an outer ring. Yvette looked down on the bright head of her granddaughter, hand-clasped with Clara on one side and Davy on the other. She experienced a chill sense of exclusion until George laid his hand on her shoulder, murmuring in her ear, "You get used to it in time," and unconsciously she leaned her cheek against his solid forearm for comfort.

Nate's fiddle called into the dark, a low hum of gypsy voices rose from the inner circle, the bonfire flickered, and the space filled with ghosts. Maria kissed her children and wound her arms around Albie's neck, Olivia's lost baby lay once more at her breast, and Mateo and Lydia greeted with a feather touch every member of the family they had left two years before. Older ghosts swirled into view – generation before generation of them – while Rosanna wove each name into the tribal chant. Finally Yvette Gerets, *doyenne* of an ancient French family, saw that money and power were not necessary to command respect – this proud Roma tribe could trace their ancestry back hundreds of years.

Between one breath and next Nate's playing became a lively, foot-tapping tune and the circle expanded to include everyone. Clara and Fleur turned round to face Yvette, and she fancied she still saw Maria hovering protectively. She chose her words with care. "That was remarkable."

"And private," Clara said, the warning implicit in her tone.

"I could not begin to describe to anyone what just happened," Yvette said, smiling at the two faces that were, in some way she couldn't fathom, so similar. "You have a family to be proud of. One day I hope Fleur will also be proud of her other family."

Clara took Yvette's hand, searching her heart while the Frenchwoman forced herself to remain calm, sensing another deciding moment in this week of trials. When Clara smiled and said, "Fleur is lucky to have two families," Yvette felt as if she had been given a crown.

A zephyr breeze blew, and a papery fluttering at Yvette's

feet reminded her she had left Fleur's scrapbook under her chair. She picked it up and leafed through it, though it was now too dark to see. The bonfire flared suddenly and a voice in her ear whispered, "Now!" She glanced apprehensively behind her but there was nobody there.

Clutching the book so hard that her knuckles creaked, she said, "Fleur – I believe you still have two weeks before you return to school – would you care to come to Belgium with me for a visit?"

Fleur looked at Clara, Clara looked at Fleur and they both looked at Albie. While he hesitated, still afraid that Fleur might not want to come home again, the seconds stretched to breaking point.

Then Linda said, "I'm her cousin – can I come too?"

"For heaven's sake, Linda!" Daisy cried, blushing scarlet with mortification.

Yvette laughed with genuine amusement. "No, child – this time I am inviting only my granddaughter."

## CHAPTER TWENTY-FIVE – CHANGES 1954-61

Fleur came home after her fortnight with Yvette sporting a very chic hairstyle, and a determination to study fashion design that made her apply herself to her books as she had never done before.

Two years later she took more GCEs than any of her classmates, and after the exams Yvette whisked her off to the South of France for a holiday. When Fleur returned in August to learn that she had passed every subject, she told Albie it was time she moved to Belgium.

"I can learn about the fashion business from the inside if I'm living with *Grandmère*," she said nervously, unsure of how he would react.

Albie looked lovingly at his foundling child. "You'll be home for holidays though, won't you, lovey?" he said, and she flung her arms round his expanding middle in gratitude for letting her go without a fuss.

"The house is emptying too fast for comfort," Albie complained to George when he came home that night after his day's work at the garage. "First Joey and now Fleur – it'll be Clara next, I shouldn't wonder."

"Frank looks like a fixture, don't he," George replied comfortably, scratching Tommy's head in the just the right place to make the cat stretch his neck in ecstasy. "They'll be making you a grandpa before you know it."

"God – I hope not!" said Albie. "That'd really make me feel old."

Clara had left school the year before to work full-time for Alice Daly, selling hats and accessories in her little side street shop. She and Frank met for lunch every day, and at weekends they would go to the cinema. Their romance, which had limped along while Clara was still at school, was now blossoming into full-blown love.

George's light-hearted remark niggled at Albie all day.

Frank was nearly twenty, and now Clara was working, Albie couldn't keep her under his eye like he used to – the pair of them could be getting up to all sorts of mischief. That evening he was so subdued that George was worried.

"Got summat on your mind, son?" he asked when they were having a smoke in the garden.

"Clara and Frank," Albie said. "D'you reckon they're – you know – doing anything they shouldn't?"

"Depends what you mean," George replied. "The sort of things you and that Ellen got up to when you was fifteen?"

Albie choked on his cigarette. "You never said nothing! But it's different for a girl – I don't want her pregnant at seventeen. She needs a woman to talk to – I wish Maria were still here."

"So do we all, son. Have you thought of asking Rosanna to have a word?"

When Albie went through the gap in the wall to Rosanna's wagon, she took one look at his serious expression and said, "Come on in, Albie – I'll make some tea. You've come about Clara, haven't you?"

"I ought to know by now," Albie said, sitting on a bentwood chair to watch while she busied herself at the little pot-bellied stove. "Nowt gets past you, does it?"

Rosanna poured them each a cup before sitting opposite him. "Clara talked to me a year ago – you've no need to worry about her."

"You mean she asked about babies and stuff when she were only sixteen?"

"Albie – what she asked was private, but she won't have babies till she's ready. The right herbs keep a girl safe."

"I'll bloody kill that Frank!"

"You'll do no such thing! In fact, it's more likely to have been Clara's idea – it's in her blood, after all, isn't it?"

A slow blush suffused Albie's face. "You been watching me in the fire?" he asked.

"Of course not – your private life's your own business," Rosanna said, leaving Albie to wonder how much she had seen of his afternoons with a lady customer whose car regularly needed his assistance with a home start.

*** 

On Clara's eighteenth birthday, Frank presented her with a tiny diamond set in an engagement ring, and a year later they were married in Thambay church. To make sure Joey could come they chose a weekend in mid-summer, when cricket, not football, engrossed the sports-loving public. Luke Finch arranged for a marquee to be erected in Perez Field, and in the week running up to the wedding the usual procession of wagons and caravans trundled down Farm Lane, drawn by word of mouth and instinct, to attend the wedding.

Fleur flew over from France with bridesmaid dresses for herself and Annie, and one night a French fishing boat slipped into Thambay harbour to drop off a couple of passengers. The harbour master accepted a bottle of cognac and returned to his office without asking for passports, Josef and Nicole climbed into Albie's car, and the family was complete.

On the morning of the wedding Albie, uncomfortable in a Moss Bros suit, leaned against the back wall of the cottage smoking a calming cigarette. The field beyond the wall was colourful with wagons clustered around the marquee and hung with strings of bunting, but it was quiet enough to hear the crackle of wood burning on the campfires – nearly everyone was on their way to the church. He walked through to the old wagon that had been Maria's home when he first met her. "Twenty-four years ago," Albie whispered, "yet it feels like yesterday – I still miss you."

A zephyr breeze kissed his cheek. "Miss you," it echoed.

"Dad – we're ready," Annie called and he turned round to see his three girls standing in the yard – tall, blonde Fleur, elegant in a slim yellow dress, Annie looking like a plump hazelnut, and Maria between them. As if in a dream, Albie walked towards them and his vision cleared. It was Clara, of course it was Clara, looking so achingly lovely that Albie had to swallow hard. "I wish your mama was here," he said as Clara took his arm.

"She is," said all three girls in unison.

The Saturday lunch-time crowd stopped what they were doing to watch the colourful procession. Real gypsy wagons were a rare sight these days and these wagons, horses and harnesses had been polished until they gleamed. Traditionally-painted pots and pans clanked, bells on harnesses tinkled, wagon springs creaked, hooves rang on the road surface, and the gypsies themselves were transformed by the occasion into people of legend and romance.

Last to arrive was Albie, who drove his refurbished and decorated cart into the churchyard through a chorus of oohs and aahs from the crowd. Clara took his hand and seemed to float down from the cart, Fleur adjusted her veil, and Annie passed her the bridal bouquet. Albie proudly escorted his daughter into the cool church, down an aisle splashed with pools of brilliant primary colour from the stained glass windows, to marry Frank Coppin.

The ceremony brought Albie such a flood of memories that it passed him by like a dream. Before he knew it he was standing in the churchyard under a vast yew tree for the photographs. During one of the interminable waits while the photographer positioned another pose, he moved aside for a quiet smoke and a voice beside him said, "Your daughter is a beautiful bride, Mr Smith."

Albie looked down into a pair of lovely violet eyes and replied, "She's pretty as a picture, ain't she? The spitting image of her mama when we was wed."

Lillian Smythe looked around for Clara's lookalike. "Which lady is her mother?"

"Maria passed away five years ago, Missus Smythe."

"Oh dear – I do apologise – I had no idea!" Lillian was so

flustered she touched Albie's hand. He liked the feel of it – small-boned and smooth without being soft.

"Don't you fret about it, missus, it don't hurt so much now." He dropped his cigarette to cover her hand with his other one. "I heard you lost your old man too."

Albie's big, warm paw sent such a pleasant sensation up Lillian's arm that she withdrew her hand before a blush could betray her. "I did indeed – a heart attack. Your daughter must be missing her mother, today of all days?"

Albie pointed to the row of small memorial slabs by the churchyard wall. "See them flowers? Clara's left her bouquet for her mama – she ain't forgotten." A shout from Joey recalled him to his duties. "Gotta go, missus – been nice talking to you – very nice." As he turned away he smiled a slow, deliberate smile which left Lillian blushing so furiously that the wedding procession had gone by the time she emerged from the churchyard.

***

Once the brief speeches had been made and the present-giving was over, the older men retired to the backyard of the cottage, where they could sit in comfort yet still enjoy the party. Rosanna held a similar female court around the steps of her wagon, but nobody could resist for long the insistent rhythm of the gypsy violins.

Albie danced with everyone – his daughters, his cousins, his neighbours – but he singled out no-one in particular. Rosanna watched him, wondering how long it would be before he fully recovered from the loss of Maria. She sensed a new love around the corner for Albie. She frowned, sure that she'd seen the woman today, but the face refused to come into focus. Then Nate broke into her reverie by claiming her for a dance, and she let the thought go – if she couldn't see the woman clearly then it wasn't going to happen yet.

The departure of Frank and Clara for a weekend's honeymoon in Margate was the signal for the townsfolk to drive carefully home, hoping no police were lurking round corners, but the festivities weren't over yet. Many of the gypsies planned to leave at first light, which would be around four o'clock, so it was hardly worth going to bed. The men who had to drive the next day snatched an hour or two of sleep, but those who still owned horses could safely leave the reins in their children's hands, and carried on drinking. Children slept where they dropped – Albie found Annie under a trestle table in the marquee. Ben and Davy got quietly drunk and fell asleep under a wagon on a couch of long grass, and people dozed in wagons or on rugs in the warm night air, lulled by the murmur of voices.

When the sky began to lighten and the first early bird sang its praise to the morning, fires were smothered, horses were caught and harnessed, engines coughed into life, and by the time the Pinetree Farm cowman drove his herd past for their early milking, Perez Field was almost empty. Josef and Nicole stayed another day, but Nicole had left Philippe to run the café and she was anxious to return. Her cousin's boat arrived, again under cover of darkness, to whisk them away, and the cottage seemed suddenly very quiet.

***

Clara gave birth to her first child eighteen months later, a little girl they christened Lydia after her great-great-grandmother. Albie gazed down into the dark brown eyes and saw Maria's soul looking back. "Your mama's in there," he said softly.

Clara nodded. "Can't miss it, can you? Mama keeps coming back – in me, in Annie, and now in little Lydia – we'll never lose her."

Ben, who had always been good at figures, passed his O levels with respectable enough grades to secure a position at the Midland Bank opposite the Town Hall. Now that Clara was living in town, it was Ben who rode in with Albie each morning, and when the bank manager arrived with the keys Ben was always on the steps, waiting for the daily thrill of entering the quiet banking hall.

Davy, not having an academic brain, left school at fifteen for a job at Wilson's brickworks and cycled in for his early start, so Annie, the last one at school, went to Thambay on the school bus.

Annie and George always had supper ready when Albie and the boys came home from work, but one warm July evening in 1962, they found Annie waiting for them outside, the tracks of dried tears visible on her cheeks. "Mama and Nan came for Grandpa half an hour ago," she said calmly. George, having sown parsley for the winter and mulched his runner beans, had sat down on his bench in the garden, leaned back against the warm brick wall, and closed his eyes for the last time.

*\*\*\**

*I'm an orphan*, thought Albie the following week, standing beside the grave that now held both his parents – *forty-eight years old and I'm an orphan*. He knew it was silly to think that way – George had lived twenty years past his three-score-and-ten – but still he felt bereft. George had been his father since he was eleven – only a year older than Annie was now – and the space the big man had left would be impossible to fill.

*What I need*, Albie thought as he walked slowly to the car and nodded at Joey to drive him home, *is something to take me mind off things.* A different job would be a good start, because he was bored at the garage. It had paid the bills while the kids grew up, but now all except one of them was earning a living, Harry Craig could do without him. When Joey turned the car onto Marine Drive, Albie spotted the travelling fair and his mind shot into over-drive. He was a good mechanic, and Fred Babcock was sure to remember him from his days as a rigger – he could probably get a job with the fair. Then he put the brakes on his racing thoughts – he shouldn't even be thinking of abandoning Annie and the boys.

Annie, squashed between Ben and Davy on the back seat,

smiled as she read his thoughts. If she didn't move fast, Dad would think of a dozen reasons why he couldn't follow his dream – she must talk to the others. That evening, when all the Smiths were sitting round a fire in Perez Field with Paddy and May, his children told Albie what they had decided.

"Ben's going to come and live with me and Frank," Clara said. "It'll help us with the mortgage and he won't have to pay bus fare to get to work."

"But he comes into work with me and Davy." said Albie, "It don't cost him owt."

"That's all going to change, though, isn't it?" said Ben. "You're going to do the fairs."

"What makes you think..." Albie began, until he saw his daughters' faces. "You girls have been reading me mind again – how many times have I told you about that?" Albie shook his head at the smug expressions surrounding him. "You'd better tell me what else you've been plotting."

"Annie can stop with us – and George's cats too – if you'll let us have them," said May. "They can come back to you in the winter."

"I'll be keeping an eye on the cottage," added Paddy, "and the garden."

"And what about Davy?" Albie asked, although he already knew the answer.

"You're not leaving me behind, Dad," Davy said emphatically. "I'm coming with you."

# CHAPTER TWENTY-SIX – OFF TO THE FAIR – 1962

Albie had flatly refused to accept rent from George after the family moved into the cottage, saying that sharing his bedroom with the boys was a high enough price to pay, and he had assumed he spent his pension on tobacco and the presents he showered on his grandchildren. It was a shock to discover that George's Post Office account held an incredible £572, which, added to Albie's own savings, would be enough to buy a caravan.

Before the fair left Thambay, Albie had a word with Fred Babcock, who said he would be happy to have him around again. In fact, if Albie could catch up with Babcock Fair before the August Bank Holiday, the Gallopers carousel needed someone to run it.

Harry Craig at the garage was sorry to lose Albie, he said, but not surprised. "You've worked hard enough, don't get me wrong, but your heart's not in it. I might take on an apprentice if you're leaving. There'll be the odd day's work in winter if you need it – come and see me when the season's over."

"I'll do that, Harry, ta very much – you've been a good boss." Albie stuck his hand out but Harry waved it away. "Get on with you – you'll have me blubbing! We'll be having a farewell drink before you go?"

"Course we will – tomorrow evening in the King's Head."

Albie left early that day, an hour before he was due to meet Davy, and drove out to Cliff Road to visit his latest lady friend – Iris was a nice woman and deserved to be let down gently. Iris saw his car pull up, dragged him inside the house and was tugging impatiently at his clothes before she'd even shut the door properly. "My husband gets home at six," she panted. "You're taking a chance coming this late."

"I come to tell you I'm going away, Iris," said Albie, lifting her easily in his strong arms to press her against the flock wallpaper. "This is the last time."

"Then you'd better make it one to remember," Iris replied, digging her heels into his back, so Albie set out to do as she asked. Iris liked it rough, though how she explained the finger-marks to her husband Albie couldn't imagine. *She'll have the pattern of this wallpaper all over her bum today as well,* he thought, as he pinned her against the wall.

When they'd finished, Iris slid gently to the carpet. "God, Albie, that was a real knee-trembler!" she gasped, hanging onto the banister rail to tug her skirt down, then she looked at her watch and pushed him urgently to the door. "Go quickly – he's due home any minute – phone me when you get back," and as Albie went down the steps she slammed the door behind him.

*She never even asked where I was going,* he thought – *shows how much she cares* – and a voice from the past echoed through his brain – "You waste your seed on those not worthy." He stopped with his hand on the ignition – an old gypsy had said that to him once – was she telling him off again? He shrugged. "What else can I do?" he said aloud. "The only women I meet are snooty ones after a bit of rough."

\*\*\*

Very early two days later, Albie and Davy locked the cottage door, hung the key on a nail in the outside toilet for May to collect later, and went through to their new caravan which was already hitched behind the Austin.

"Well, Davy, we're off," Albie said. "You OK?"

"I'm fine, Dad – it weren't me who got drunk last night."

"Did go a bit over the top, didn't I?" said Albie contritely, manoeuvring through the gate. "I were still in two minds about doing this. I'm as excited as a kid running off to join the circus, but I'm worried about Annie – I should be here to see her back to school."

"Don't worry, Dad – you know she loves it with Paddy and Auntie May." Davy got out to shut the gate, but before they could move off, a crowd of people jumped out of the hedge

and there, proudly holding up a huge banner with the words
'GOOD LUCK' painted on it in wobbly letters, were Annie,
Paddy, May and all the Coppin and Finch families. "Goodbye!
Good luck! Remember to phone!" The voices floated through
the open windows of the car as Albie drove up the narrow
lane, and the last vision in his wing mirror was of Annie
standing in the middle of the lane, waving both arms and
shouting, "I love you." Flanking her were the solid, reliable
bulk of Paddy and the motherly figure of May and behind
them, shadowy but unmistakable, stood Maria.

***

Babcock Fair travelled all over the south-east every year from
Easter to the beginning of October. There were still some
gypsies who followed the fairs, though they drove cars and
modern caravans more often than the slower horses and
wagons. Albie and Davy spent many an evening around a
campfire with distant relatives or members of other tribes.

At the close of the season, several of these families followed
Albie home to Perez Field. The Government Act, that had
closed many of the gypsies' traditional stopping-places, had
been unable to touch their out-of-the-way haven on Pinetree
Farm, mainly because Adam Finch had ensured that Albie's
field had a caravan site licence.

That Christmas there were several inches of snow all over
the south-east. It drifted deep around the caravans and froze
the pipes in the toilet-block, so the cottage toilet was well-
used. Albie lifted Maria's old cauldron onto the range, and
each morning Annie stood on a chair beside it to stir porridge
with a big wooden spoon, clearly thrilled at having so many
mouths to feed. When the snow melted, the field became a
quagmire, and the cottage with its hot water from the copper
and its cosy kitchen was always full of people.

The gypsies were so grateful for the shelter freely offered
by Albie and his family that, just before they left in April, a
delegation visited Luke at Pinetree Farm to give him a

surprisingly large wad of cash. As soon as Albie and Davy had driven off to rejoin the fair, Luke moved workmen into the cottage to install a bathroom off the scullery.

Annie was sworn to secrecy, so it was July – the week of Thambay Fair – before Albie discovered the delights of his own bathroom. He was almost tempted to stay put, because the weather was terrible, but he wouldn't let Fred Babcock down.

The town fair's procession of floats that year was a sadly bedraggled affair of torn crêpe paper and damp costumes. When the tea-tent almost took off in the gusty wind, the local stalls packed up early, and rather than waste the food, the WI ladies carried trays of unsold sandwiches and cakes to the fairground. Lillian Smythe discovered Albie occupying a pay-booth, the horses of the carousel empty of riders.

"Why, Mr Smith – I was not aware you were a travelling fair man," she exclaimed, offering him her tray. "Although, now I come to think of it, I haven't seen you in town lately."

"I was a traveller till ten years back," said Albie, surprised that a lady like Mrs Smythe had noticed his absence. He opened a sandwich to peer inside. "Cheese and chutney – me favourite – ta very much," he said appreciatively.

"You're very welcome, Mr Smith – do please take more than that – I would hate to see them wasted. Tell me, what made you take up the wandering life again? It can't be very pleasant in weather like this."

"There are days when I think I must be off me rocker," Albie admitted, just catching a wind-blown shutter before it slammed into Lillian. "But you have to take the rough with the smooth. I get to breathe fresh air instead of garage fumes, and it's worth it for the freedom."

"Freedom," Lillian repeated wistfully. "I could almost envy you that, Mr Smith!" Then a rain-laden gust whipped her headscarf and she shivered. "I must be going now, and I wish you luck, although I doubt you will have many customers this evening." Leaving Albie to consume his sandwiches, she battled her way back to her car.

Lillian had been right. That evening – and indeed the remainder of the miserable season – barely covered costs. Albie and Davy arrived home early at the end of September, collected Annie from Coppin Farm and moved back into the cottage.

Although they declared they were half-inclined to get regular jobs, there was plenty of casual work on the farms to keep them busy. They worked with Paddy to clear clogged ditches, picked up potatoes so caked in mud that each load was reduced to half its weight after hosing down, and mended fences and laid hedges battered by wind and rain.

Then a thick yellow fog drifted down the Thames Estuary from London, choking people in the streets and animals in the fields, and rendering the roads lethal. Harry Craig employed Albie and Davy to help his three-man workforce repair the victims of crashes. When the fog cleared, only to be followed by thick snow, once again the cottage hosted a crowd of gypsies.

"We must be bloody mad not to live like this all the time!" said one man as they sat in the warm kitchen, but as soon as the snow melted, people drifted back to their caravans to cook their meals over the familiar flames of a bonfire beneath a limitless sky.

Then spring came in on a burst of daffodils. Fred Babcock phoned Pinetree Farm to say he'd booked a site for the Easter weekend, and yet again Albie and Davy were drawn by the lure of the open road.

***

The Beatles rocked the world that year with 'I Want to Hold Your Hand', and Davy was eighteen, old enough to be left in charge while Albie nipped home to celebrate Annie's twelfth birthday. He arrived carrying a Dansette record-player for which he and Davy had saved up, Fleur sent over from France a wonderful froth of a petticoat to fill out Annie's circular skirts, and everyone else, forewarned, gave her records – Paddy and May's home throbbed with music all afternoon.

"I never thought about the noise when I bought the Dansette," Albie said ruefully.

Paddy simply laughed. "'Tis grand to be having a bit of life about the place, Albie."

"Talking of 'aving a bit," Bert said, "been meeting any wanton women on yer travels?"

Albie glanced around and confided in a whisper, "Since you ask, I were doing better at the garage. They still give me the eye, but having Davy around cramps me style."

"Me and Alice have to keep it down with Rita still at 'ome," Bert said. "And thinking of that – did you 'ear William Smythe chucked 'is mum out to make room for 'is twins?"

"Like father, like son," Albie said. "But what d'you mean, chucked her out?"

"She were in me shop the other day," said Bert. "Told me she's moving into one of them flats on Marine Parade – Sea View, I think she said."

"That's where Norah lived!" exclaimed Albie. "Wonder if it's the same flat?"

Bert shrugged. "Could be. She said it'd be much more 'andy for the shops."

Bert drove Albie to the station later to catch the train back to Canterbury, and as they passed Sea View Albie looked up at the flat that Norah had left to him in the early days of the war – since he'd sold it to buy the cottage it had changed hands several times. The balcony door was open and he could see a man in overalls hanging wallpaper. Bert must be right – Lillian Smythe was moving into Norah's old flat.

***

On her first night in her new home, after shutting the door firmly on her son, Lillian made a cup of tea in the neat little kitchenette, opened the curtains to dispel the smoke from

William's cigar, and took her tea out onto the balcony. The only furniture she had kept from the previous owners was the dear little set of wrought-iron table and two chairs, which she had repainted white, adding deep-buttoned purple cushions to soften the seats. They gave the balcony a continental air, she thought, although the actual air was decidedly autumnal. She pulled her cardigan closely across her bosom before sitting down to gaze out over the promenade. As she sat there, taking sips of tea and watching the mesmeric curves of surf nibbling at the shore, the tensions of the past few months drained away as if being drawn out on the ebbing tide.

Gerald had not been an easy husband, but his sudden death had left her drifting like a rudderless boat. He had always managed their finances, and it had seemed the ideal solution when William offered to move into the big house on Cliff Road with his family. Lillian couldn't recall whose suggestion it had been for her to move into the converted garage that William referred to as The Annexe, but when she had surfaced from a totally unexpected black well of misery, it was to discover that she had been ousted from all but those two charmless square rooms.

Strangely enough, it had been a chance remark by that nice Mr Smith that opened her eyes. When he had spoken of freedom as if it was there for the taking, Lillian had realised that she had none. William or Sadie oversaw her every move – each small expenditure was questioned – and at forty-eight she deserved some of that freedom.

After a private meeting with her solicitor, she had fortified her resolve with a small glass of sherry and bearded the lion in his den. "William, I wish you to purchase a flat for me."

Her bald statement had rendered William momentarily speechless, but when he'd stopped gasping like a landed fish he'd objected strongly. "Mother, this is your home."

"This is no longer my home, William, it is yours. I will not spend my remaining years in a converted garage."

"But I thought you were happy here with your grandchildren."

"The twins will be welcome to visit me at any time, provided they telephone first to ensure I will be at home."

"But Mother – I can't possibly afford to buy you a flat – the business swallows all my capital."

Lillian had raised one eyebrow in an expression he knew all too well. "That, William, is not strictly true. The sale of your own house will soon be completed, which will release sufficient capital to buy me a sea-front flat."

"Sea-front? They cost a fortune!"

"I have already enquired at the estate agents, William. The price of one would be well within your means." Then Lillian delivered her *coup de grâce*. "Of course, I could easily afford to buy one myself if I were to sell this house – after all, your father did leave it to me."

After that it had simply been a matter of digging her heels in and refusing to be bullied – something she should have done years ago with Gerald – but it had been nearly a year before a sea-front property became available.

Lillian had loved the little flat as soon as she set foot in it, but she managed to conceal her delight while William bumbled round importantly, opening cupboards and drawers. "These want easing a bit," he said. "Drop of oil on the hinges and they'll be good as new."

"I will have new cupboards," Lillian said firmly. "And the entire flat needs redecorating."

"Mother – the agent assures me it was done last year, and this carpet is hardly worn at all."

"Not only is the design offensive to the eye, William, but the previous owners obviously had a dog they failed to house-train properly." She walked into the front bedroom, visualising a three-quarter-sized bed and her dressing-table in front of the window. "I'll have pale lilac in this room, and curtains in lavender – I saw just the fabric in Whitstable last week. And those electric fittings are Bakelite – the flat needs to be rewired."

"I'm not made of money, Mother!" William protested.

Lillian fixed him with a look he remembered from his youth. "You are just like your father, William – he was also mean with money. You have his business and now you are taking over the home I shared with him. You will renovate this tiny flat exactly as I require or I will refuse to live here – I dread to imagine how you would explain that to Sadie."

By early October the work was finished to Lillian's satisfaction and she moved into her new flat with relief. Now, at last, she was here, sitting on her own balcony watching the ever-changing sea. The summer season was over, tourists no longer crowded the promenade, and the town had reverted to its winter peace. The couples sitting in the seafront shelters would be local, a man walked his dog along the otherwise deserted beach, and the only movement on the recreation ground was from an elderly couple leaving the Legion Club.

Maria sat on the other chair and studied Lillian. After twenty years of unsuitable occupants, Norah's flat had finally fallen into the right hands, and Norah's love of lavender was reflected in the colour scheme. Maria laid her fingers on Lillian's wrist and sensed her loneliness, her loving heart, and the touch of fire that Albie needed. Albie, who had lost his way over the past few years, relieving his body without easing his heart, should be looking for love again to take him into old age. This woman, whom he had met long before either of them was ready, would fill his heart as well as his bed until he was reunited with Maria, his true bride.

Lillian rubbed her wrist absently, hoping that its sudden warmth was not an indication of the beginnings of arthritis, and took her empty cup indoors. As she closed the door she fancied she saw a figure on the balcony, but when she blinked it had gone. She drew the curtains, and could have sworn the little sprigs of lavender with which they were decorated released a waft of perfume. *For Heaven's sake, Lillian, don't start imagining things*, she scolded herself – *you've had a tiring day.* She undressed quickly, dropping her clothes in a disgracefully slovenly fashion over the chair, and slid gratefully between the crisp sheets of her new bed. Within seconds she had fallen into the best sleep she had had in years and dreamed, as she often did, of Coronation Day in the Market Hall and a big, darkly handsome man with a tribe of gypsy children.

***

In the spring of 1965 Frank and Clara's son was born, weighing in at a hefty eight pounds.

"Going to take after his grandpa," said Albie smugly as he inspected the baby's sturdy little limbs.

"We're going to give him my grandpa's name," said Clara, smiling adoringly at her son. "George Patrick Coppin, and we'll call him Georgie."

"A good, strong name, that is," said Albie approvingly. "Dad would be proud, and I bet Paddy's chuffed. Your house will be crowded when he starts running around with Lydia."

"Our Ben's moving out – didn't he tell you? He's got a bedsit over the shops behind the Royal George."

"What – he's going to live on his own? Why not move back into the cottage?"

"Ah well, that'd be too far away from town for Ben," said Frank, but Clara shot him a look that said "Shut up" as clearly as words and they refused to say more.

That evening Albie met the old crowd in the King's Head to celebrate young Georgie's arrival, and Ben came in with a girl on his arm. "This is Audrey, Dad – she's a friend of Rita Daly's."

Audrey smiled shyly at Albie. "Pleased to meet you, Mr Smith," she whispered, and spent the rest of the evening hovering silently at Ben's shoulder, sipping a Babycham and never taking her eyes off him. *Pretty little thing*, thought Albie – *a bit quiet for my taste, but seeing the way our Ben's looking every*

*few minutes to make sure she's still there, he's obviously got it bad.*
***

A year later Ben and Audrey were married. Audrey's parents hosted a luncheon reception in the Station Hotel, with tablecloths and sparkling wine, which they restricted to family. The presence of Joe Smith the England footballer with his glamorous girlfriend was a feather in their cap, Ben's grandfather sailing over from Boulogne with his French wife added a touch of continental panache, and Ben's brother Davy, looking very uncomfortable in a suit that strained to contain his muscles, delivered an acceptable speech.

But to their dismay, Ben's sister Fleur, the glamorous fashion designer, brought a female partner and then, to add insult to injury, the bride and groom insisted on going to the evening party as well. Instead of a sedate drive to the station to catch the London train, the limousine led a procession of vehicles miles out into the country, where Ben ceremoniously introduced his bride to an entire field full of gypsies, and their darling Audrey's expensive wedding-dress was irretrievably ruined by grass-stains as she and her new husband danced to strange, uncouth music and drank strong wine straight from bottles.

After several futile attempts to include Audrey's parents in the festivities, Albie left them sitting disapprovingly on two folding chairs and danced with Annie, made sure wine was circulating freely, had a good long talk with Josef, and finally found a moment to sit down on the steps of the old wagon.

"Giving up on us, are you, Dad?" called Davy as he swung past.

"Can't keep up with you kids no more," Albie called back.

Clara brought Georgie to sit beside him and Albie observed, "There must be summat in the air at weddings – our Davy's danced with that girl half the night."

"Her name's Tammy," Clara replied, shifting her sleeping son to her other shoulder. "Davy says her family arrived here yesterday."

"I've been too busy to notice 'em," said Albie. "But Davy looks quite keen on her."

A surge towards the road alerted them to the departure of Ben and Audrey, closely followed by her family, and then the party settled into the familiar pattern of circles around bonfires, tired children being tucked into caravans, and the murmur of conversation under a night sky.

***

Tammy's family faced the same predicament as many other gypsies – being driven out of their lifestyle by the Caravan Act and the increasing mechanisation of agriculture. After talking to Albie and Davy, they tagged along with them when the travelling fair restarted, and Fred Babcock took Tammy's father on as a rigger.

Davy and Tammy were inseparable from the start. Albie watched the pair indulgently, remembering his own courtship. He'd fallen in love with Maria the instant he'd set eyes on her, so he could hardly complain if his son was just as quick off the mark.

One evening, when they were all sharing a meal, Tammy's father said suddenly, "If you two are getting married you'll have to find a way to earn more money."

Tammy held Davy's hand tightly. "How did you know he'd asked me? We haven't told anyone yet."

Her father winked. "You should know by now you can't keep secrets from your mother."

Davey blushed – a tendency he'd inherited from Albie – but he spoke up like a man. "We thought I might try a strongman act. It wouldn't take much – just a tent and a few props."

"You'll need a caravan as well," Tammy's mother said. "And the sooner you two are married the better – I want my grandson to be born legitimate."

"Grandson?" Albie exclaimed, glaring at Davy. "What've you been up to?"

Davey mumbled, "Nowt much," but Tammy stared at her mother. "I can't be – it was only the once – last week!"

"Once is all it takes sometimes," said her mother. "It's the Registry Office for you, my girl. We can have a party next winter when a month either way won't cause comment."

By the end of that month Davy had a red-and-yellow striped tent, a leopard-skin tunic and a set of weights. He had also constructed a boxing-ring in which he took on any local youth who wanted to impress his girlfriend, while his new father-in-law took the money and kept the spectators under control. Tammy and her mother occupied an adjacent small tent, where they told fortunes surrounded by incense-perfumed drapery, and from which they could warn their men-folk if they sensed trouble brewing.

## CHAPTER TWENTY-SEVEN – THAMBAY FAIR 1966

Babcock Fair's trailers trundled onto Thambay recreation ground after dark, and the town awoke on the first Friday morning in July to the annual thrill of discovering the fair gradually taking shape. Bare-chested men bolted metal sheets in place for the dodgems, agile youths climbed wooden A-frames to attach swing-boats, striped circular booths appeared for roll-a-penny or hoopla, and in the middle of it all stood the carousel with its galloping horses.

Lillian Smythe's kitchenette was full of WI ladies making sandwiches. Her flat was handy for the recreation ground and it would be the work of moments to carry the results of their labours across the road to the tea tent. When the sandwiches had been covered with damp tea towels and her ladies had gone, the sound of the waves was drowned by the deep thumping noise of the fair. Drawn by a strange urge to be part of it, Lillian took her supper onto the balcony and sat to watch.

Albie, after making sure only one rider was on each horse, glanced across the road and noticed Lillian silhouetted against her curtains. The slim figure could almost have been Norah, whom Albie had first met on the pier when he was a boy. He hoped that nice Mrs Smythe would be happy in Norah's old flat.

***

Market Square was packed with spectators for the judging of the Float Competition on Saturday, and then the winning float – an Enid Blyton themed one full of infant-school children dressed as Noddy, Big Ears and Wishing-Tree fairies – followed the Boys' Brigade Band as it led a procession along Marine Parade to the recreation ground.

Between Babcock Fair and the tea tent, a roped-off arena was surrounded by stalls such as guess the weight of the cake, bat the rat, tombolas, handicrafts, bric-a-brac and second-hand books. Chipped cups and cracked plates were lined up for a sacrificial death on the shelves of the crockery smash stall, and eager children queued up for the chance to aim a rounders ball at a target to duck the teacher. There were races for all ages from toddlers to adults, and a fiercely-contested tug-of-war between pub teams. At the end of the afternoon, the Fair Queen drew raffle tickets to decide who would win the first prize of a television donated by Biggins Electrics, or lesser prizes such as a Sunday joint from Daly's Family Butcher, a permanent wave at La Mode Hair Salon, or a nicely arranged basket of fruit and scrubbed vegetables from Coppin Farm.

Throughout the afternoon Babcock Fair did a steady trade with crowds composed mainly of parents and children, then the town's stalls packed up, the WI sold their last sandwiches and butterfly cakes at half price, the lights on the fair rides and sideshows glowed more brightly in the dusk, and the atmosphere changed.

As the younger children were taken home by their parents, the teenagers and courting couples arrived. Albie increased the speed of his ride, watching carefully to ensure no-one got on carrying a bottle. Davy the strongman oiled his muscles so that none of his opponents could get too much of a grip, and outside the fortune-teller's tent Tammy's father changed his patter from "Learn what the future has in store!" to "Madame Stella sees love in her crystal ball!"

Young men keen to impress their girlfriends crashed the dodgems, hauled on the swing- boat ropes in attempts to make them loop-the-loop, or spat on their hands to grip a mallet and ring the bell on the try your strength machine. Girls squealed as their skirts flew up on the twister, the hot dog stall did a roaring trade, as did the candyfloss machine, and shouts of triumph or groans of despair came from the shooting gallery.

When Davy's challengers became increasingly drunk and belligerent, he closed his booth and moved to help Albie with

the carousel: a pair of policemen patrolled the alleyways
between the stalls at a measured pace, smiling but watchful,
and the black waters of the bay reflected a thousand twinkling
lights.

Albie was in the ticket-booth when a premonition fizzed
through his veins like an electric shock. He counted the bodies
in the queue – fourteen, nearly a full load – and said to Davy,
"I'm shutting the ride after this lot – lock the gate when
they're inside the fence."

"But the evening's only just warming up," said Davy.
"We'll lose a lot of money."

"Don't argue, Davy, just do it – I can feel summat's
brewing."

Davy said no more – he'd learned to trust Dad's instincts –
and Albie rushed the last customers through before shutting
the ticket window decisively and standing outside the booth
to keep an eye on things.

The whine of a dozen scooter engines was the first
indication of the coming invasion. To begin with the neatly-
dressed riders and their girlfriends behaved like any other
couples, riding the thrill-rides and eating candyfloss – but the
bottles the youths carried in their pockets spread unease
among the stallholders. Music blared as usual, but it failed to
hide the too-loud voices and a sensation of mounting tension.
The two policemen spoke quietly into their radios – this bunch
of Mods exuded an air of anticipation that was worrying.

Albie wasn't the only one to sense trouble. The Shooting
Gallery proprietor dropped his shutters and removed his guns
to safety, prompting a few more to close their booths, and the
men who ran the swing-boats brought them to a halt. Then the
air was shattered by the deep-throated roar of motorbike
engines, and the scooter-riders instantly clumped together like
pins round a magnet.

Davy shot an agonized glance at the caravans and Albie hit
the emergency stop button on the carousel, shouting, "Make

sure Tammy's OK – I'll sort this out." Davy vaulted the fence to check on the campsite while Albie ushered his passengers out of the enclosure, silencing their protests with promises of free rides tomorrow.

A score of bikers and their girlfriends swaggered into the fair, revelling in the wave of alarm they caused, the studs on their leather jackets shimmering under the lights. They congregated by the Hot Dog stall, where one youth with long, greasy hair raised his voice above the background noise. "Hot dogs all round, mate, with lots of onion and mustard."

The cook began putting sausages into rolls while the youth leaned one elbow on the high counter and surveyed the group of Mods. "You lot live in this dump?"

"Just passing through," said a tall boy wearing a short jacket. "Out for a peaceful ride and saw the fair – we ain't looking for trouble," but as he spoke his hand was creeping stealthily towards his back pocket.

The Rocker lunged forward so fast that a girl squealed, but the Mod was quicker – there was a small but audible click, a blade flashed and the Rocker stopped dead. "We ain't looking for trouble neither," he said with studied calm, reached behind him to take a filled roll from the cook's trembling hand, and bit into it. The slow, deliberate movement with its undertones of menace mesmerized the onlookers, then suddenly he tightened his fist and half a sausage smothered in greasy shreds of onion and yellow mustard shot onto the Mod's jacket. "Oops! Sorry, mate," said the Rocker, taking hold of the Mod's lapel as if to wipe it clean, then he yelled, "You sneaky bugger!" and snatched his hand back, displaying torn fingertips to his gang. "Fish-hooks!" he hissed, and all hell broke loose.

Lillian had had a busy day in the hot marquee, serving tea from the big urns that made the tent even hotter, and she had been sitting on her balcony enjoying the sea breeze. When the Mods' scooters arrived she sensed the change in the atmosphere – everyone was nervous of large numbers of youths after the riots of last year. Feeling rather exposed on her balcony, she went into her sitting-room and closed the doors, but the roar of the motorbikes brought her running back to lean on the rail, hand over her mouth in alarm, straining to see what was happening through the dazzle of fairground lights. Then the volume of noise increased and she heard the unmistakable piercing call of police whistles.

Sergeant William Daly had reacted quickly to his Constables' radio message, but several of his men had been on extra traffic duty during the float parade and he'd given them the evening off in lieu. He managed to contact some of them and then, hoping they wouldn't be far behind him, left the elderly Desk Sergeant in charge at the Station, and marched briskly towards the promenade. At the corner he met Bert and Rita coming out of the fish and chip shop carrying fragrant newspaper parcels.

"What's the rush, Billy?" Bert asked his brother.

"Trouble at the fair, Bert – Mods and Rockers by the sound of it," replied Billy and strode bravely on – one policeman with a truncheon marching to face an unknown number of knives and coshes.

Bert thrust his fish and chips at Rita, saying, "Run 'ome and phone Paddy – tell 'im to get 'ere double quick."

"What are you going to do, Dad?" Rita asked fearfully.

"Round up a few of the lads, that's what," Bert replied with the glint of battle in his eyes, "This is our town."

In a matter of moments he had collected several volunteers from the King's Head and the Royal George. The landlords phoned the Station Arms and the Harbour Tavern, and a crowd of locals ran to catch up with Sergeant Daly. He paused for just long enough to issue instructions to stick together and not to kill anyone if they could help it, then the constables' whistles sounded, 'Get here right now!' and the men of Thambay pounded after the Sergeant to reclaim their territory.

When Paddy got the message that Albie was in trouble, he phoned Pinetree Farm before he got the truck started, and May ran across the fields to the gypsy camp. Half a dozen men piled into the truck, armed with a fearsome collection of agricultural tools, and Paddy drove at a hair-raising speed towards town.

The rapidity with which the stand-off between Mods and Rockers escalated into full-blown war was frightening. Within seconds a dozen flick-knives flashed, coshes were raised and fists were sporting knuckle-dusters. The two constables jammed their helmets on tighter and drew their truncheons to wade into the melee, aiming at forearms and wrists to disarm rather than to maim, but without the assistance of the stallholders they wouldn't have stood a chance. The hot dog seller tipped a pan of fried onions over a couple fighting by his stall, scalding their exposed skin and turning the flattened grass beneath them into a greasy mud-bath. The man in charge of the Twister turned his ride up to full power, making it impossible for those fighting on its undulating surface to keep their balance, let alone land a punch. Three riggers grabbed the slotted slides from the Roll-A-Penny stall to use as clubs and swung them with muscles tuned by months of lifting heavy weights, and every man who relied on the fair for his living defended his property with any weapon at his disposal.

The arrival of Sergeant Daly and his volunteer troops turned the heat of battle up a notch as the townsmen vented their anger on both gangs of outsiders, and the local youngsters who had come out for an evening of fun and romance milled about in panic, trying to avoid getting caught up in the fight. What shocked Albie more than anything else was to see the Mod and Rocker girls fighting as fiercely as the boys – he lifted several Thambay girls over the fence into his enclosure and stood guard in front of them. One Mod tried vaulting over the fence only to be stopped in mid-flight by the rock-like arm of Davy, and two leather-clad girls demanded entrance to Albie's sanctuary.

"You're part of that mob, so bugger off," he told them and both girls leapt at him with their claws out. Despite being taught never to hit a woman, Albie grabbed the two heads of tangled hair and banged them together, dropping their dazed bodies on the grass just as Paddy's truck sped across the recreation ground and disgorged its occupants.

"'Tis a grand fight you're having here, Corp!" Paddy yelled in Albie's ear. "Got here as quick as we could – what needs doing?"

"I'm guarding this lot," said Albie, indicating his pen of frightened girls. "Reckon Bert could use a hand though."

Paddy looked across to where Bert was trying to restrain two bikers at once. "Right you are, boyo – on me way!" and with a whoop of sheer glee he threw himself into battle.

White teeth gleaming in their dark faces, the gypsies followed his example and attacked the combatants of both gangs indiscriminately, confiscating in the process various weapons that might come in handy later. The farm-hands herded a group of Mods into a circle and held them captive with pitch-forks, Bert's drinking pals caught six of the Rockers and subdued them by sheer weight of numbers, and Sergeant Daly collared one ringleader while his constables stripped the fish-hook jacket from the other. Several gang-members decided that flight would be wiser than fight, only to discover their scooters and motorbikes had been tied together with ropes, and toppled like rows of dominoes at the slightest touch.

And then it was over – both gangs overcome by the determination of Thambay's residents and the fair people. Thambay's police cells couldn't cope with the number of arrests, so Sergeant Daly summoned a pair of Black Marias from Whitstable to cart the gangs away. By mutual consent the fair closed down for the night – it was nearly eleven o'clock anyway – but the police turned a blind eye to the fact that the pubs stayed open till well after midnight, serving pint after restorative pint to the flushed and battered victors in what the local papers later dubbed 'The Battle of Thambay Fair'.

## CHAPTER TWENTY-EIGHT – LILLIAN

Lillian Smythe spent her Monday morning in the Market Hall with the WI ladies, re-washing the crockery that had only been given a cursory rinse in buckets in the marquee. Then she had to make sure that every cake-dish was restored to its rightful owner, and by four o'clock she was weary of standing. Turning down the offer of a lift home, she took a stroll along to the harbour before turning for home.

At the door of Sea View flats she paused, drawn by a curiosity she told herself was concerned rather than vulgar, and crossed Marine Drive towards the quiet fairground. She wandered without any real purpose between the deserted stalls and rides until she saw lines of washing flapping in the breeze and stopped, touched by the domesticity of the scene that met her eyes.

Albie dozed in the sun like a carthorse at rest, the white wall of the caravan at his back. The muscles of his body were only slightly blurred by age, and his checked shirt, although clearly the biggest available, was just a touch too small. He wore faded jeans, and his massive, dusty boots were planted firmly in the centre of a ring of roll-up butts on the scuffed grass. An ancient, stained hat completed his outfit, tilted to shade his eyes and storing his cigarette papers in the band.

Lillian looked with longing at the other chair beside him. It was an old Lloyd Loom chair, painted green at least twenty years ago, containing two soft old cushions with crocheted covers. Her body suddenly ached to be embraced by their comfort, and she had actually taken a step forward when Albie spoke. "Go ahead, missus, take the weight off."

"Oh but I couldn't, you're too kind, but really…" Her protest, feeble at best, trailed off when he reached across the little table, grabbed the seat cushion by its centre, gave it a shake, and dropped it back in place. Lillian could resist no longer – in a second she was sinking into the comfort of an earlier age, and as she adjusted her hat-brim against the sun's glare, Albie watched her from under his own hat.

He wondered if she remembered him – *it must be three years since she brought me them sandwiches – cheese and chutney, if I remember right – and probably made with her own hands.* He looked at her hands as they rested on soft leather of her handbag – *she must be near enough my age, give or take a couple of years, but she's still a fine-looking woman – comfy body and not too skinny. Good legs too.* He ran his eyes appreciatively down to the neat shoes, then slowly back up to the silky fabric of her dress. Reminded him of a cottage garden he'd seen once from a back bedroom window – all overblown roses and green leaves and constantly shifting light. He remembered the woman in the bedroom too, who had turned from pussy-cat to tigress in the arms of her gypsy lover. *Wonder if this one's got the same fire?* His body stirred, taking him by surprise – *long time since that's happened* – and all in a rush he realised he had been staring at the lady's bosom for far too long. He blushed furiously, raised his eyes to her face, saw the amused glint in her own eyes, and blushed deeper. He coughed and started fumbling with fag-papers and tobacco. "Sorry, missus, forgot me manners for a minute there."

"That's quite all right – it's a long time since a man's looked at me like that. I take it as a compliment, especially at my age." Lillian wondered if Mr Smith remembered her. *It's a long time since that dreadfully wet summer when we had to give away half the WI's refreshments – even longer since the day we met in the churchyard.* Surprised at the direction her memory was taking her, she watched his hands as they steadied under the familiar task of rolling a cigarette.

Albie licked the edge and stuck it down. "You're no age at all," he said. "Just a bit of a girl, and a good-looking one at that. You're Missus Smythe, aincher? Seen you over in that flat – on your own, are you?"

He was blatantly fishing for information and Lillian leaned back in the comfortable chair, ready to enjoy her first real flirt for years. "On my own, Mr Smith – my gadfly days are long gone." She smiled, thinking back to those carefree days, and Albie watched the thoughts flit through her beautiful violet eyes. "My father was appalled when I accepted Gerald's proposal," she confided. "Naturally, their opposition only made me more determined, and I insisted on marrying him." Lillian couldn't believe she was telling all this to a virtual stranger, but somehow this big, handsome man had cut through the years straight back to her girl-hood, and she was enjoying herself.

Albie was unaccountably jealous. "Your Gerald bought you a big enough ring," he blurted out, then could have swallowed his tongue.

"It is rather vulgar, isn't it?" Lillian said. "But it reminds me that he loved me once, and he gave me two sons, so I was lucky in that respect." Recalling what had drawn her to the fairground in the first place, she said, "Forgive me, Mr Smith – I meant to enquire about your welfare after that dreadful fight on Saturday. Was anyone injured?"

Albie chuckled – a lovely deep rumble that set Lillian's senses quivering. "Our lot got nowt but a few bruises and me mate Bert got a black eye – some of the gang lads were a bit the worse for wear."

"It would appear you all know how to protect yourselves," said Lillian, admiring the broad chest under Albie's shirt. "I need not have been so concerned for your safety."

"You was watching? You must've seen the whole thing from up there – half the town turned out to help or it might've gone different."

"So I gathered from the newspapers. I am relieved you came to no harm."

Some small movement of her body warned Albie that she was going to get up, and he reached behind his chair to bring out a brown Thermos which he plonked on the table. "Fancy a cuppa? I'm sure I could dig out a spare cup."

Lillian saw the blatant longing in his grey eyes, and hesitated. *He's as lonely as I am,* she thought. "Thank you, that would be lovely." She sank back into the cushions and put her handbag under the chair. "If I am to impose further on your hospitality, we should introduce ourselves properly – my name is Lillian."

Albie looked at her outstretched hand, then at his own none-too-clean one, and wondered whether a bit of spit would help. Lillian watched and waited. Albie coughed, embarrassed, but still she waited, smiling at him encouragingly. *A little dirt has never worried me – I was the mother of two boys, after all – but Mr Smith must decide for himself.* As the seconds stretched almost to breaking point and Lillian was wondering if she had pressed him too far, Albie let out a great gust of held-in breath, wiped his dusty hand on his equally dusty shirt, and swallowed her delicate pink hand in his brown paw. "Mine's Albie – Albert Smith." He held on to her hand, liking the feel of the small bones and delicate skin, and grinned a huge relieved grin.

Lillian let her hand lie, feeling somehow that her entire body was enclosed by this enormous man, and smiled broadly back at him. "Albert Smith, Lillian Smythe – why, we could practically be related!" Suddenly she felt very shy, and gave her hand a little tug. "That cup of tea would be most welcome, Albert, after walking in this hot sun."

Albie dropped her hand and fumbled for the Thermos. *Here I am, a grown man, a grandpa for Pete's sake, behaving like an ignorant lout.* He half-turned his head and yelled, "Davy! Fetch another cup – a clean one, mind!"

A moment later a shadow fell over them and a cup appeared almost under Lillian's nose. It was clean, white, thick, and had a British Rail crest on the side. Albie snatched it away. "Not that one! Get one of your mama's best, and the biscuit tin."

Lillian looked up into the astonished gaze of another giant. "Really there's no need to go to all that trouble. I have drunk from British Rail cups on many occasions – this one will do nicely."

And Albie could see that it *was* all right. *She's sat in my chair, on my patch – she'll take me as I am.* "OK then, if you're sure, but a biscuit would go down nice. Davy!"

Davy visibly shook himself and disappeared round the corner, to reappear holding a round tin which he put on the table between Albie and Lillian. Albie removed the lid with a practiced twist and tilted the tin towards Lillian. "There's not much left. Davy can't be trusted inside the van with a tin of biscuits. His mama was always finding the tin empty."

"You was just as bad, Dad." Davy was leaning his broad shoulders against the caravan wall, smoking a cigarette and watching them. Lillian could see how obviously he was Mr Smith's son, in the shape of his big body and the glint in his eye. His mother's input showed clearly too – he was black-haired and olive-skinned, and those flashing black eyes were pure gypsy. Albie pushed the cup of tea towards her, then a bowl of sugar with a spoon sticking out. Lillian began to form the words 'no thank you' until she looked at the dark brown liquid, so she helped herself to a spoonful of sugar and returned the spoon to the bowl.

"Not going to stir it, then?" Albie leaned over and stirred her tea, an action so intimate that Lillian experienced a rush of warmth for this big, gentle man. When he removed the spoon to plunge it straight back into the sugar bowl and help himself, Lillian pulled the tin of biscuits towards her and selected a digestive. Albie's hand dived in to pick out a ginger nut, then Davy leaned over to grab a couple for himself.

Albie smacked his wrist. "Can't a bloke entertain a lady friend in peace? Go and find summat useful to do." Davy grinned, snatched a couple more biscuits, winked at Lillian, and ambled off. "Kids! Always the same, ain't they?" grumbled Albie fondly.

Lillian thought of her own very proper sons, who would be

shocked to the core to see her sitting here in this company, and smiled back at Albie. "Yes, they're always the same. Mine loved biscuits too. They may still do, for all I know." She faltered as she realised how little she knew about the adult tastes of those two little blonde boys she had mothered. "They were very like their father," she continued, not realising how bleak she sounded. "And they grew more like him every year. Now they are both successful, with work and their own families to occupy them, and I don't really know what their tastes are these days."

*So she's lonely too – doesn't even have her boys popping their heads round the door regular.* "Live far away do they, your boys?"

"John lives in London. Sometimes he collects me in his motorcar and we have tea in an hotel. William lives on Cliff Road and I see him more frequently."

*Bet this William comes round once a month at most, and him only up the road,* Albie thought. "Ain't they got room for you? Their places too small?"

"Oh dear me, that would never do! I like my little flat, and now I have my independence I couldn't abide either of my daughters-in-law for more than a day." *Did I really just say that out loud?* "Do you know, Albert, I do believe that's the first time I have admitted that I don't even like them – you really are bringing out the worst in me!"

*She must've picked up some of Norah's bluntness from living in her flat,* Albie thought – *Norah could tell you off in a lady-like way just like that.* "Nowt wrong with the truth, Lily, and it's just between friends, ain't it?"

Friends! A warm glow suffused Lillian's soul – she had loathed Gerald calling her Lily but on Albert's tongue it sounded right – as if by giving her another name he had released her from her old life. She smiled happily at him. "Friends indeed, Albert."

Albie covered the deep pleasure this gave him by emptying the flask into their cups, sugared Lily's as a matter of course, and tilted the tin towards her once more. "If you fish around a bit, I reckon there's a couple of ginger nuts left."

"Oh I can't manage those nowadays, my teeth are too fragile."

"You want to dunk them like me," Albie said and suited the action to the words.

Lily watched the look of ecstasy on his weather-beaten face and thought, *Why not? This whole afternoon is extraordinary.* "Do you really think I should?"

"Go on Lily, enjoy life while you can!"

Lily, amazed at her own temerity, unearthed from the crumbs the very last ginger nut, tapped it clean on the side of the tin, and dunked it in the sweet, strong tea. She just managed not to make an unladylike slurping noise as she sucked the limp crescent into her mouth, but she couldn't suppress the little moan of pleasure that escaped her as the wonderful flavour assaulted her taste buds. She shut her eyes in sheer delight and Albie thought, *I reckon she'd moan like that in bed, there's fire there all right. Bloody Hell! What is this woman doing to me? I've two grandchildren and a third on the way and here I am, can't even control me own thoughts. Get a grip, Albie!*

A sudden gust of wind blew, and the clatter of a rolling beer bottle made Lily look at her watch. She began to gather herself together – handbag, cardigan, wandering thoughts. "It really is time I should be going home," she said, getting to her feet. "I have taken up far too much of your time, and I believe that is William's motorcar I can see on the promenade." She had completely forgotten that William was to collect her for a 'light supper with a few friends'.

Albie levered himself out of his own chair – *if I'm not quick she'll be off before I've said me piece.* "Missus Smythe – Lily – you will come back? Tomorrow? I'll get more ginger nuts." *Dammit – I'm rambling! And here comes her son, striding across the fairground, red as a beetroot and yelling summat.*

Lily looked at William – *So ridiculous to be wearing a topcoat in this heat, and he really should not get so agitated with his blood-*

*pressure.* "I would love to come again, Albert. Tomorrow at the same hour? I shall look forward to it."

William's voice finally reached them. "Mother! Are you ill?"

"No, dear, I am quite well, thank you."

"Then why were you sitting here with this – this – person?"

"We were enjoying a cup of tea and becoming acquainted, dear." She turned to Albie. "Albert, this is my son William Smythe. William, allow me to introduce Mr Albert Smith."

*So this is the son – dead spit of Gerald who always was a pompous arse.* Albie grabbed William's hand and shook it firmly. "Lovely lady, your mum."

William grasped his wayward mother firmly by the elbow and almost frog-marched her away towards the road, thinking furiously, *I really am going to have to insist she sees that specialist – she's been behaving more and more irrationally of late. At least she's still wearing all her jewellery. And who is this Albert Smith person?* But he found Mother was impossible to talk to, refusing to answer his perfectly reasonable questions.

"Really, William, I will not be interrogated like a junior clerk in your office. I am entirely at liberty to choose my own friends, as you are to choose yours. Also, I feel obliged to say that Mr Smith is infinitely more interesting than anyone I have encountered in your house, and I would prefer to stay at home this evening and watch television – I believe there is to be a play on the BBC."

William drove home, much too fast, and downed a couple of quick gin and tonics to calm his nerves. When his guests arrived he felt pleasantly mellow, and by the time a large brandy was warming in his hand and a cigar clamped between two fat fingers, he had totally forgotten his mother's intransigence.

Lily found she was unable to concentrate on the television that evening. As she prepared supper in her kitchenette she wondered who cooked for Albert and his son; when she took it outside to eat on the balcony, it was to the background music of the fair; and when she raised her delicate porcelain cup of Earl Grey to her lips, she recalled the sweet, thick brew she had drunk beside a caravan.

Maria sat on the other chair, watching her. Things were going well so far – turning Lily's footsteps towards the fairground this afternoon had just been the start – but in ten days' time the fair would leave Thambay. Ten days were not many in which to change a staid middle-class lady into a gypsy.

When Lily laid her head on her pillow that night, a whiff of lavender wafted her into a dream of Thambay as it had been when she was a little girl, playing on the sands with her nursemaid while her parents breakfasted. To protect her fair skin from the sun, Hetty had kept her in a patch of long shadow cast by the helter-skelter on the pier, and in her dream she felt again the deliciously cool sand between her toes. Then she was riding a mat down the helter-skelter with a boy who had Albert's sea-grey eyes, and Lily felt quite safe in his arms as they zoomed off the slide, across the beach and the bay, to soar high over the downs towards a hitherto unimagined freedom.

## CHAPTER TWENTY-NINE – COURTSHIP

Albie stood on the pavement by the recreation ground, as he did every morning, to wave to Annie as Paddy drove her to school. On his appearance in Thambay this summer, Annie had told Albie firmly, "It isn't worth opening up the cottage just for the two weeks of the fair – I'll come over on Saturday." Accepting this was the price of his freedom, Albie had agreed – at fourteen Annie definitely knew her own mind.

Once they had gone by he made his way to Bert's shop. "That shiner's coming on a treat!" he greeted his friend. "You been putting steak on it?"

"Bag of ice does the job just as good," Bert replied, deftly twisting a rope of sausage into links. "Can't afford to waste good steak, anyway. What can I get you?"

"Give us two pound of them bangers, they look tasty."

As Bert served Albie a generous two pounds of his hand-made sausages, the door pinged open and Lily said, "Good morning, Albert, we meet again!"

Bert raised an eyebrow as Albie went bright red and said, "Morning, Lily – you buying bangers too?"

"I believe I will, Albert," she said. "They look very appetizing. I will take half a pound please, Mr Daly."

Albie stood by while Lily was served, and then his hand moved of its own volition to take her shopping basket.

"Why, Albert – how kind!" Lily dropped her purse into her handbag. "I was about to go to the café – would you accompany me? I usually take a cup of coffee at this hour."

Bert leaned both hands on the foot-thick butcher's block and gaped, uncharacteristically speechless as they left the shop.

Albie and Lily raised a few more eyebrows that morning – the big fairground gypsy in his waistcoat and check shirt, sitting at a small table in earnest conversation with the small, neat woman – but they were oblivious to the stares or the whispers.

At midday Albie looked at his watch and exclaimed, "I must get back or they'll think I've been run over!" pulling some coins from his pocket to pay the hovering waitress.

Lily picked up her shopping basket and smiled uncertainly at him. "Perhaps we shall meet again soon, Albert?"

"What d'you mean – perhaps? I hope you're coming this afternoon for tea – I bought more ginger nuts specially."

All the gifts she'd been given over the years paled by comparison with Albie's purchase of ginger nuts especially for her. Lily laid a hand on his arm in full view of the WI ladies at a neighbouring table and said, "I am looking forward to it."

That day set the pattern for the following three, but on Saturday morning, knowing that the fair would be open all day, Lily stayed at home. She was just about to take her coffee onto the balcony when Albie bellowed from the street below, "Lily! Have I upset you or summat?"

Lily rushed outside to peer down at him. "I thought you'd be too busy today, Albert."

Albie laughed. "I hope so – we need the money – but I'm never too busy for you. Tell you what – why not come over and give us a hand? You could sell tickets till Annie gets here."

Lily had already met Davy and Tammy – that Saturday she was introduced, with an airy wave and "This is me friend Lily" to a bewildering array of friends and family.

Paddy and May arrived first with Annie, who smiled at Lily as if she recognised her and kissed her cheek, saying oddly, "I'm glad Dad's found you at last."

With total lack of ceremony, May enlisted Lily's help to make a mountain of sandwiches. As they worked side by side at a folding table, Lily asked, "Are we preparing food for the entire fair?"

"Bless you, no!" May replied. "Just the family – it'll all get eaten, you'll see."

And Lily did see when, at lunchtime, the rides closed for an hour. Albie flopped into his usual chair and waved Lily to the second chair as a matter of course. "You've spent half the morning making the sandwiches – Annie'll hand 'em round."

Within moments Ben arrived – "My son the bank cashier," Albie said proudly – closely followed by Clara and Frank and their two little children, then a van veered off Marine Drive and aimed straight for the caravans, where it disgorged more gypsies than Lily thought the van could possibly contain.

Olivia put a basket full of strawberries on the picnic rug. "Still warm from the field, these are – Luke and Maisie'll be here in a minute with the cream," she said, then she took Lily's hand and said, "So you're the one."

Another comment Lily didn't understand, and there were so many different faces that she couldn't keep track but, as she dipped a plump strawberry into the bowl of thick cream, she felt included in the crowd of people who seemed to have known each other all their lives.

Throughout the long, hot afternoon the rides were constantly full and Albie was busy, so Lily offered to make him a cup of tea, entering his caravan for the first time to boil a kettle. She was fascinated by the neat interior; a cupboard under the two-burner hob concealed a gas cylinder, others held pots and china slotted into racks; at the rear of the caravan was a table surrounded by a padded bench, and that was it – a six-by-eight-foot home for one very large man. Lily unhooked a tin tray from its hook and carried the tea outside; now she understood why the worn tartan rug with its folding table and Lloyd Loom chairs had the air of a living-room – that was precisely what it was.

"Where do you sleep?" she asked Albie when they were alone.

Albie pulled her to her feet. "Come and see," he said, and she watched as he dropped the table level with the bench and padded it with the back cushions. "There!" he said, winking at

Lily. "A cosy bed for two – want to try it out?"

"Certainly not!" Lily gasped. "Anyone could walk in!"

"Not if I shut the door," said Albie, reaching behind him to do so while he registered the fact that she hadn't actually turned him down flat. The exterior sounds faded as he drew her into his arms. "You and me are meant to be together, Lily. If not here and now, then soon."

Lily snaked her arms round his middle and looked up into his twinkling eyes. "I believe we are, Albert, but I am far too conscious of the lack of privacy here."

"Well, we'll have to do summat about that, won't we?" said Albie and covered her willing lips with his mouth.

When Lily came up for air, she trapped his wandering hands and held them away from her, deliciously aware that she could only do so with his co-operation. "Albert Smith! This is all happening much too quickly."

"Too quick? Lily, I've fancied you ever since I first set eyes on you after Clara's wedding – ain't eight years long enough?"

Lily's heart was beating so fast she could scarcely breathe. Eight years? She moved back into Albie's embrace, pulled his face down to her own and kissed him with the passion he had sensed was waiting to be tapped.

"The fair's open till late tonight, me darling," he murmured in her ear before releasing her, "but I could get Davy to cover for me. Will you be home if I come over?"

"I'll be there, Albert," Lily said. "I'll be waiting for you."

Lily was relieved to find the tartan rug deserted when Albie opened the door and returned to the carousel with a cheery wave and "See you later." She made her way through the bustle of the fairground to the peace of her flat, where she sat in her armchair and stared unseeing at the walls, replaying in her mind those five minutes in the caravan that might have changed her life. Albert, unlike Gerald, was a true gentleman despite his upbringing. She was rapidly falling in love with him, and those two kisses had sent her body into turmoil. She knew what would happen when she let Albert into her flat – what she wanted to happen, to tell the truth – but where could it lead?

She took a long, hard look at her life as it had been before this week – shopping every day just to get out of these four walls, WI meeting, Bridge Club, tea with friends – predictable and, if she was honest, boring. The life offered by Albert's words "We're meant to be together" would be a leap into the unknown, and did she want that much upheaval in her life? What would people say? And, more to the point, what would William and John say?

Her mind jumped back and forth between comfortable flat and cramped caravan – between loneliness and love – until she was worn out. She stretched her neck to ease the tension, shut her eyes and sighed, "Oh help! I don't know what to do!" There was the merest whisper of a sensation of someone stroking her hair and a hint of lavender perfume. "Albert's a good boy," she heard someone say, but her eyelids were heavy and she drifted into sleep.

She dreamed again that she was riding the helter-skelter mat, but this time it was being drawn along a leafy lane by a dappled pony. The mat became a creaking wagon and rain blew in her face, but Albert found shelter under some trees and inside the wagon everything was dry and cosy. The door crashed open and William boomed, "What are you playing at, Mother?" grabbing her arm to pull her outside, but there on the tartan rug was Albert holding a tin of biscuits – "You can't go, there's a ginger nut left." Behind him were all the fairground folk, the gypsies from the van, Paddy the Irish farmer, every one of Albert's friends saying, "She belongs here with us." Then Davy in his leopard-skin tunic hoisted William over his head and tossed him away – "See, he's no weight at all!"

"No weight at all." Lily woke up with those words echoing

through her mind and looked at the clock. *Dear merciful heavens – it's eight o'clock!* She turned on the bath taps and scurried round the flat, plumping up cushions and closing curtains, then she bathed rapidly and was just towelling herself dry when the doorbell rang. She dragged a dressing gown on and ran to look over the balcony into Albie's upturned face. "Albert – I'm not dressed!" she hissed in a stage-whisper.

A huge grin spread over his face. "Suits me fine, Lily! Chuck the keys down," and, with every nerve-end tingling, Lily did just that. For a big man, Albie moved fast, and he was in the flat with the door shut inside a minute. Then, seeing how flustered she was, he gave her a quick kiss, pushed her gently into her chair and asked, "OK if I take me jacket off?"

Lily nodded and wrapped her dressing gown primly around her legs, wondering if Albert's restraint meant that she had misjudged the situation, while Albie hung his jacket on the back of the door and turned round holding a bottle of wine. "You got a bottle opener, Lily?"

"In the top drawer by the stove," she told him, noticing that his hair was damp and he had put on a clean shirt. "There are glasses in the left-hand cupboard."

Albie handed her a glass and sat on the sofa facing her, waiting for her to stop looking like a frightened rabbit. He'd caught her on the hop – *not a bad thing in a way, saved fumbling around with buttons and hooks – but she'll need to be gentled into it.* "Place looks nice," he observed, looking round. "Told you me godmother used to live here, didn't I?"

"Yes, Albert, you did. Twenty years ago, I think you said?" Lily sipped her wine and forgot her state of dishabille enough to sit back in her chair.

"Norah would've loved the colours you've picked," Albie said. "She always wore lavender – even had lavender perfume."

"That is strange!" said Lily, sitting forward and

unconsciously revealing her cleavage. "I have often detected a scent of lavender here."

Albie looked at her bosom, but the few feet between himself and Lily was a yawning chasm he couldn't work out how to cross. He could have kicked himself for putting her in that chair instead of on the sofa. As his legs began twitching nervously, Maria lost patience with him and nudged him in the back. He shot to his feet, but the surge of movement startled a squeak out of Lily.

"Sorry, Lily – need a smoke," he blurted out and bolted for the balcony.

Lily hurriedly turned off the light, leaving just a small lamp burning – it would never do to be seen in her dressing gown – and peered round the curtain. Albie was leaning on the rail, smoking a cigarette in deep drags. Every muscle in his back was tense – she could see them jumping under the stretched fabric of his shirt – and a voice in her head prompted, "He's as nervous as you are – go and get him." Taking a deep breath, she threw caution to the winds, stepped out onto the balcony, and began to smooth her hands over Albie's quivering back in a mixture of massage and caress. Albie eased upright slowly, luxuriating in the touch of her hands, then flicked his cigarette into the street with a brief display of sparks, turned round and gazed into her face.

Lily's lips trembled in a half-smile. "I'm not used to this, Albert – you'll have to forgive me."

Albie laid a finger on her mouth. "Shush, me darling, it's been a long time since I made love with anyone either," and the words 'made love' were enough to convince Lily she was making the right choice. Watching her face all the time, Albie untied the cord of Lily's dressing gown and slid his hands inside.

"Albert! What if someone sees?" she protested.

He chuckled. "I'm too big for anyone to see round," and moved his hands lower to cup her buttocks. Feeling very bold,

Lily unbuttoned his shirt to stroke the curly hair on his chest, and Albie pulled her closer. Skin to skin, right out there in the open, they kissed, building their own cocoon of heat in the cool night air.

"Best we go indoors now, Lily," Albie said with a grin. "I've got far too many clothes on for what I got in mind."

Lily took one final glance at the fortunately deserted street and led him into her bedroom.

As the small sounds of their love-making seeped through the lavender-sprigged curtains, Maria left the little balcony chair with a glow of satisfaction warming her soul; a moment later she was smoothing the brow of her restless granddaughter, leaving Clara free to feed little Georgie, secure in the knowledge that Mama could deal with Lydia's nightmare.

"Mmm – you smell nice," Albie murmured against Lily's skin, kissing his way from her throat to her breast, lingering there for a while before moving lower. Lily was briefly conscious that her belly was no longer taut, but then she forgot everything and wound her fingers through his dark grey curls as he slid even further down. Once he'd started that, there was no more room for embarrassment and Lily let herself go, arching her back and whimpering with pleasure, then she pulled him back up to enjoy his whole weight pressing her into the bed. With a little push she rolled him onto his back and explored his body, trailing her fingers over the scar tissue on his shoulder and cocking an enquiring eyebrow at him. "War wound," Albie explained, and she kissed the scar all the way across his breast. His low moan of delight gave her the courage to continue down the line of hair to his navel. When his manhood rose in response, she glanced up the length of his body, grinned wickedly into his hopeful eyes and, wondering at her own daring, kissed him there as well.

"God, Lily – that's enough!" Albie groaned after a minute.

She looked up anxiously. "Am I doing it wrong?"

"Not wrong at all, me darling, you do it lovely, but I can't wait no longer," he said and grabbed her shoulders, flipped her onto her back and held himself poised above her. "You ready?"

"Oh yes!" she breathed, wrapping her legs around him while he found the place and eased into her slowly. Lily flushed all over with heat as he filled her up and Albie held still for a moment, savouring the sensation of her tight little body enclosing his. When he began to move she matched his rhythm, watching his face until the rising tide of passion overcame her and her eyes closed. Then there was nothing but feeling and the sound of their breathing. Albie held back until Lily cried out, her violet eyes opened, and she shuddered beneath him, then with her body still pulsing around him, he slid one hand underneath to lift her a fraction closer, thrust deeper and let himself go.

If Lily hadn't been in love already, Albie's shout and the look of triumph on his face would have done the trick. He flopped onto his back, panting and grinning up at her as she leaned on one elbow above him, wiping the sweat from his brow back into his hair.

"Whew!" he exclaimed after a few minutes. "That would've rocked the caravan!"

Lily giggled. "There can't be many secrets in a fairground."

"Ah, you'd be surprised," Albie replied, pulling Lily on top of him. The momentum tipped them both off the bed and onto the floor, where they lay in a tangle of arms and legs, giggling like teenagers. After a minute or two Albie said in surprised tones, "See what you do to me – here we go again!" and Lily's eyes widened as his big hands gripped her hips to lower her onto him. She shifted slightly to get more comfortable and Albie smiled. "That's right, me darling, you're in charge this time," so Lily gripped him with her knees like a bareback rider and rode them both to a second climax.

Afterwards, Lily simply lay along him, her legs still straddling his hips and her face buried in his chest-hair, listening to the steady beat of his heart, while Albie stroked the satiny skin of her back and marvelled at his good fortune. They were almost asleep when Albie stirred and said, "That's me done for, Lily – why don't we finish that bottle?" so Lily slipped back into the bathwater, amazed that it still retained some warmth after all that had happened, and returned five minutes later to the living-room to see Albie silhouetted by moonlight, sitting bare-chested on the balcony.

*That's my reputation in shreds*, she thought, mildly shocked by how little she cared. She went out in her dressing gown to join him, and they finished the wine in companionable silence, gazing out to sea.

"I been thinking, Lily," Albie said eventually, "I could go back to the garage if Harry'll take me." He kept his eyes on the dark horizon while he waited for her to answer.

Lily put her glass down on the little table with exaggerated care. "You mean you'd give up the fair for me?"

Albie's hand closed on her wrist. "Get wed too, if you want. All I ask is we live in me cottage, not here – couldn't abide living permanent in a flat."

Lily leaned over to cup his chin in her hand and turn his face so that she could look directly into his eyes. "The fair is your life, Albert, and I'll make it mine too if you'll let me." The expression of relief that swept over Albie's face proved how much of a sacrifice he had offered to make, and she was moved almost to tears. She cleared her throat and released her emotion with a laugh. "I have just one condition, Albert, which is that we procure a larger caravan."

"I ain't got the money for that, Lily, nor for the car to pull one, neither."

"You needn't concern yourself about that, Albert – I have money." She stopped his protest with her fingers. "Gerald left me comfortably provided for, and it would give me enormous pleasure to spend his money on running away with you."

"No wedding?" asked Albie.

"Oh, I don't think that will be necessary, Albert – after all, our surnames are so similar it hardly seems worth the trouble."

***

The next morning they traded in Albie's Austin and Lily's small car for a Commer van with a tow-bar, and on Wednesday they bought a larger caravan. During the week Lily arranged with the bank manager for utility bills to be paid in her absence, and ensured that she would be able to cash cheques wherever she went. She also paid a visit to her solicitor, to lodge vital papers in a deed box, leaving strict instructions that only in the event of her death were William or John to be permitted access. Finally, with advice from Tammy's mother, she went ruthlessly through her wardrobe, selecting only those garments she could wash by hand and wear without ironing.

Early on Sunday morning, when Babcock Fair pulled out of Thambay to move along the coast to its next scheduled stop, Terry Jenkins, the caretaker at Sea View flats, carried her two suitcases down to the waiting caravan. Lily gave him two letters – one resigning her leadership of the WI, and the other addressed to William. "My son will no doubt collect it in due course," she told Terry. "Please don't go to the trouble of delivering it."

"Wouldn't dream of it, Mrs Smythe," said Terry, who knew everything that went on in Thambay, and Sea View in particular. He put the letter into his pocket together with Lily's generous tip. "Don't you worry, Missus – I'll wait till he comes round." By his reckoning, that could be at least another two weeks – William Smythe neglected his mum shamefully.

"And under no circumstances let him have my keys."

"He won't even know I've got 'em," Terry assured her gleefully, and stood on the pavement with a broad grin on his face until the lorries, the trailers and the caravans had disappeared into the distance.

## CHAPTER THIRTY – WILLIAM

A few weeks later, after a morning playing golf, William
Smythe drove along the coast road to his mother's flat. Before
entering the building he stood, hands in pockets,
contemplating the block. These places were beginning to be in
demand – a chap at the golf club had been saying in the bar
that they were changing hands for as much as three and a half
thousand pounds, and he had paid less than three. He was
playing with the idea of buying Mother a converted flat in the
terraced row opposite the station and selling this one. She
didn't need two bedrooms, and he'd come out of the deal with
a thousand profit. Or perhaps he would rent out the seafront
flat and ride the property wave.

His mind occupied with these pleasant thoughts, he
mounted the steps and poked his big red face into the porter's
cubby-hole. "Perkins! Ring through to tell Mother I'm here,
there's a good chap."

Terry Jenkins ground his teeth – *that snooty beggar never has
got my name right*. He lowered his newspaper slowly and took
a leisurely drag on his cigarette before dropping it in the dregs
of his tea. *Boy, am I going to enjoy this!* "Your mum ain't here…
Sir."

"Not here? Not here? Where is she then? It's your job to
know."

"Well now, I'm afraid I couldn't rightly say, not being party
to her confidence."

"She must be here – it's not her Bridge morning – where
else could she be?"

Terry decided he didn't actually want Mr Smythe around
any longer than necessary – and besides, the man was a prime
candidate for a stroke. *Spoil my day, that would, having to deal
with an ambulance or worse.* "She left a letter for you – I've got it
here somewhere."

"Why didn't you say so? Come on, man, come on!"

Terry made a show of searching for it, though it had been burning a hole in his pocket for weeks, and William suddenly realised that the wretched man was expecting a tip. He reached into his trouser pocket, but a raised eyebrow warned him a coin wouldn't be enough, so he extracted a ten shilling note from his wallet and threw it onto the stained desk, from where it disappeared in a flash. Terry pulled out a crumpled mauve envelope and handed it to William, who snatched it and pushed it into his coat, turning on his heel to go.

Terry had been counting on several pints on the strength of his description of William Smythe's reaction to that letter. "Handed it to me herself, she did. What's it say?"

William glared. "When did you say my mother gave you this note?" he demanded, and Terry got his revenge. "Weeks back... Sir. The day the fair left town. Right after I carried her cases down to the caravan."

William's face turned red. "Van! What van? Don't talk rubbish, man!"

"Not van – caravan," said Terry with a barely concealed smirk. "Your mum went off in a caravan."

"Why on earth would she do that?" William paced up and down the lobby, filling the small space with his agitation. "I knew the wretched woman was losing her mind and this only goes to prove it!" He slammed his fist down on the desk. "You must have known she was planning this – why the bloody hell didn't you warn me?"

"No need to be offensive, Mister Smythe," said Terry, his own temper rising. "There weren't nothing to tell." He had no intention of telling Mr Smythe how his mother had spent every day at the fair and every night in the arms of her gypsy lover.

"So where's she gone? She must have said something to give you a clue."

"She just said goodbye as polite as ever," Terry said pointedly. "You want to try reading that note instead of

yelling at me – she's probably told you all about it in there."
He still harboured a faint hope that he'd witness the reading,
but when William made no move to open the envelope, Terry
locked his desk drawer – no way he was taking the risk of Mr
Smythe getting hold of the keys – and stood up. "I've got
work to do – you going or staying?" he asked, removed a
broom and dustpan from his cubby-hole, and began
vigorously sweeping the lobby. William hovered uncertainly
for another minute, but he could hardly admonish the man for
doing his job, so he spun on his heel and returned to his car.

The note ticked in William's pocket like a time-bomb, but
before he could open it he needed a drink. He pressed the
starter, planning to go back to the golf club, but then he had
second thoughts. He daren't risk his friends witnessing his
discomfiture – the Royal George was nearer. Turning his car
with a squeal of tyres that brought Terry grinning to the door,
he shot the few hundred yards along Marine Parade and
shouldered past the lunchtime customers in the Royal George.
Ordering a large gin and tonic, he downed it in one gulp
before taking another to a small table by the window and,
with a deep sense of foreboding, opened his mother's letter.

'Dear William,' he read, 'I shall be away for a while and
will probably return to Thambay in the autumn.'

*Autumn? That's months away!*

'You need not concern yourself about me as I shall be quite
content with my friends.'

*What friends? I know all her friends, but none of those would go
off for months in a caravan.* Too agitated to read any further,
William screwed the letter in an angry fist, knocking his glass
off the table in the process. The landlord hurried over holding
a cloth. "No problem, sir – I'll clear it up in a second."

"Clear it up? Clear it up?" William shouted. "No-one can
clear this up!" and he stormed out of the pub, leaving the
landlord and customers staring after him.

"What's got up his nose?" the landlord asked the bar at
large.

Bert Daly buried a smirk in his tankard – it looked like William Smythe had finally found out his mum had run off with Albie.

Bert kept his own counsel, but Terry Jenkins' tale of Mrs Smythe running away with a fairground gypsy was too good to keep to himself, and it was only because William Smythe never talked to the working class of Thambay that the facts remained hidden from him. It took him a week to learn that his mother had traded in her newish Mini car for a second-hand van fitted with a tow-bar, and another two weeks to discover where she had bought the caravan. The trader remembered the odd couple well. "Nice lady, and the bloke with her was a big chap – muscles like a wrestler."

William couldn't understand it – the signature on the sales slip was definitely in his mother's handwriting. "Are you sure we're talking about the same woman?" he asked. "Small, elderly, name of Smythe."

"She wasn't what I'd call elderly," the trader said. "And she said she was Mrs Smith. One thing I do remember, though – they arrived in a bloody great lorry with 'Something Fair' painted on the side."

Once William had recalled the fair opposite Mother's flat, it was simply a matter of putting his secretary to work tracking it down. Unfortunately the wretched girl hadn't learned to keep her mouth shut about his private life, and by the time he went looking for his mother, the whole town knew what had happened.

Lily had been gone for several weeks when William, after an embarrassing round of golf with three so-called friends who ribbed him unmercifully about his mother's outlandish behaviour, downed a couple of large gins and headed inland to bring his mother home. On the way he fumed about her perfidy, his humiliation, and the inexcusable stubbornness of the caretaker at Sea View in refusing him access to the flat to which that fool of a solicitor had advised him he had no legal claim. Unless he could persuade his mother to sign the relevant papers, she owned her flat – she could come and go as she pleased and might even, God forbid, decide to live there with her gypsy lover.

Hours later he saw the tallest ride – the Octopus – moving its arms over the roofs of the Sussex village. He found a parking-space and switched off the engine. There were scores of people streaming onto the green – *should have realised Saturday afternoon would be busy – I'll stick out like a sore thumb. Oh well – can't be helped.* He got out of the car and adjusted the knot of his cravat, braced his shoulders and marched purposefully through the ornate arch declaring 'Babcock Fair'.

The smell of crushed grass mingled with frying onions and the sharp stink of generators halted him in his tracks. For a moment he was a boy again, breathless from running all the way from Cliff Road with his brother to spend his pocket-money on the Twister and a hot dog. He must have been about twelve when he and John challenged a local boy on the Dodgems – *would have beaten him too if the whole of the secondary school hadn't ganged up on us.* The jeers rang again in William's ears and he ground his teeth, shut his mind on the humiliating memory, and strode determinedly on.

Mothers pulled their children out of his path and the crowds parted to gape after the strange figure in loud check plus-fours. At the sight of his angry scowl, stallholders shrank back with their "Try your luck, sir?" dying unsaid. A man he jostled at the shooting-gallery snarled, "Watch it, mate," only to discover that he'd shot a golliwog clean through its striped waistcoat. William trod on toes and got candyfloss on his sleeve, and was so obviously out of place that Davy dropped his weights and followed him, sensing trouble.

William looked round wildly – *can't see a damn thing for all these rides and booths, but then these people wouldn't have the sense to lay them out in straight lines, would they?* He was so disorientated by the music and spinning colours that he wandered between the striped sides of two booths without thinking, and entered a different world.

Enormous trucks and trailers were parked in a protective screen behind the stalls, a generator thumped right beside his ear. Backing away from the awesome power that could drive a dozen fairground rides, he tripped over a thick bundle of cables, flung an arm out to steady himself, and burned his hand on the hot metal. Cursing, he wrapped his oily hand in a spotless handkerchief, and was about to retreat when he caught a glimpse of flapping white cloth and, driven by some instinct, went to investigate.

Beneath the horse chestnut trees of the village green a score of caravans were parked in two neat rows, with tables and chairs set out in front of their open doorways. Lines of washing dried in the sun, light glinted off lace-curtained windows, a baby gurgled on a tartan rug, and a woman stirred a pot over a glowing brazier. It was a pleasant domestic scene, only different in a few details from many a village street, but all William could see was squalor – *These people don't even have proper homes!*

Now he was actually here, William wished he'd come better prepared. He should at least have worked out a speech because, apart from pacing back and forth at home yelling invective at the walls, he had no idea what to say.

He must have been staring at the woman for several minutes before he recognised his mother, and even then he had to blink hard to make certain. Her hair was different, for a start – she'd obviously not been near a salon for weeks, for the perm was growing out into a soft fluff of curls and the colour was fading. Her clothes too – he thought he'd seen that skirt before, but she was wearing a flowery blouse that was much too young for her, and the short sleeves revealed sun-burned arms rather than the pale skin he remembered. Her face too was tanned and bare apart from some lipstick – this on a woman who never left the house without first applying make-up – and the apron she was wearing was excessively frilly

and, frankly, common as muck. All this was bad enough, but
what stopped William in his tracks – what shocked him into
such immobility that Davy edged closer – was that she looked
happy. The woman he had fully expected to discover at best
regretting her impulsive flight, at worst beaten and down-
trodden, was stirring the pot over the fire with a smile on her
lips and every sign that she was thoroughly enjoying the life
she had chosen.

Unable to bear it any longer, William stepped out of the
shade and Lily looked up, startled into dropping her spoon.
"William! How did you find me?"

"With considerable difficulty," he replied in an angrier tone
than he had intended. "You simply vanished off the face of
the earth – you could have been dead for all I knew!"

Lily retrieved the long wooden spoon and began stirring
again – a savoury smell wafted up William's flared nostrils –
and she said with a total absence of guilt, "I left you a note,
William. And I am surprised you noticed my absence – after
all, I hardly ever saw you."

"That's not true!" William blustered. "Besides, you were
always out with your friends."

"Bridge Club and WI meetings hardly qualify as 'always
out', William, yet I imagine those friends missed me before
you did."

William harrumphed crossly – it was undeniably true that
Mother had been gone for some time before he realised – but
then he remembered his grievances. "Your irresponsible
behaviour has embarrassed me beyond belief, I'll have you
know."

"Oh dear, that is a shame," Lily answered with infuriating
complacency. "Never mind, William – it will be a nine days'
wonder, and no doubt you will recover in time."

"But it's the scandal of the year!" William protested. "We're
going to have to think what to tell people – you can hardly
admit you've been living like this." He gestured at the row of

caravans with their openly eaves-dropping occupants, at the
lines of washing and half-naked children, at the entire
incredible notion that his mother could have chosen this
vagabond life rather than her comfortable home, then he
quailed as two very large men began to close in.

"You OK, love?" one of them called.

"Need any help, Ma?" asked the other.

She waved at them. "I can manage, thank you."

William backed off a step and asked nervously, "Who are
these people?"

"You met them a few weeks ago in Thambay, William –
have you forgotten already? This is Albert and his son Davy."
She held out her hand and immediately Albie came to stand
beside her with his arm protectively round her shoulders. Lily
looked up into his face with such naked adoration that
William was stunned – surely at their age they were past all
that? Shock made him careless. "How could you, Mother?
You're far too old to be picking up a bit of rough. Collect your
things and I'll take them to the car."

Albie clenched his fists, but Lily held him back and looked
pityingly at her son. "Don't be silly, William," she said quite
gently, "I'm staying here," and she kissed Albie's cheek.

Shocked by this open display of affection and angry
because she'd made him feel like a little boy again, William
made a fatal mistake. Grabbing her arm, he said, "Don't talk
such nonsense, Mother – you're coming home with me and no
arguments!"

Albie picked William's hand off Lily's arm as if it was
slime, growling through gritted teeth, "Don't you dare speak
to me missus like that!"

William gasped. "Your missus? What are you talking
about, man? She's my mother!"

"That's as maybe," said Albie. "But no boy of mine would
disrespect his ma that way. Anyhow, me and Lily's together
now so you can bugger off."

Seeing the rage building in Albie's face, Davy thought he should intervene before his father launched himself at the equally red-faced William. "Ma's had a shock, Dad – you look after her while I get rid of him," he said and, pinning William's arms behind his back, frog-marched him all the way across the fairground, through the fascinated crowd, to his car.

Albie folded Lily in his arms. "Our Davy's right, love – you're shaking like a leaf. Son or no son, he didn't oughter talk to you like that, it ain't respectful."

She leaned gratefully into his broad chest, breathing in the scent of wind-dried shirt and warm flesh. "I'm just glad it's over, Albert. And I should be used to him by now – his father's behaviour also left a lot to be desired." She giggled. "I've just thought – I wonder how he'll react when his twins want to come for a visit?"

Albie's deep chest vibrated beneath Lily's cheek in the warm chuckle that she loved. "I suppose we'd better buy 'em a tent."


END

Printed in Great Britain
by Amazon